SALVATION IN DARKNESS

by Nicole Edwards

AUSTIN ARROWS

Rush

Kaufman

BRANTLEY WALKER: OFF THE BOOKS

All In

Without A Trace

Hide & Seek

Deadly Coincidence

Alibi

Secrets

Confessions

Bounty

Off Course

Chain Reaction

To Have and To Hold

Missing Pieces

Smoke and Mirrors

CLUB DESTINY

Conviction

Temptation

Addicted

Seduction

Infatuation

Captivated

Devotion

Perception

Entrusted

Adored

Distraction

Forevermore

DEAD HEAT RANCH

Boots Optional

Betting on Grace

Overnight Love

Jared (a crossover novel)

DEVIL'S BEND

Chasing Dreams

Vanishing Dreams

HEROES & HAVOC

Wait for Morning

Beautifully Brutal

Without Regret

Never Say Never

Beautifully Loyal

Without Restraint

Tomorrow's Too Late

MISPLACED HALOS

Protected in Darkness

Salvation in Darkness

Bound in Darkness

OFFICE INTRIGUE

Office Intrigue

Intrigued Out of The Office

Their Rebellious Submissive

Their Famous Dominant

Their Ruthless Sadist

Their Naughty Student

Their Fairy Princess

Owned

PIER 70

Reckless

Fearless

Speechless

Harmless

Clueless

PRIMAL INSTINCTS

Chase (Volume 1-3)

Capture (Volume 4-6)

Claim (Volume 7-9)

THE JAMESONS OF COYOTE RIDGE

Hot Chocolate Wishes

Rough & Dirty

THE WALKERS OF COYOTE RIDGE

Kaleb

Zane

Travis

Holidays with The Walker Brothers

Ethan

Braydon

Sawyer

Brendon

Curtis

Jared

Hard to Hold

Hard to Handle

Beau

Rex

A Coyote Ridge Christmas

Mack

Kaden & Keegan

Trey

Rafe

Violet

STANDALONE NOVELS

Unhinged Trilogy

A Million Tiny Pieces

Inked on Paper

Bad Reputation

Bad Business

Filthy Hot Billionaire

RULE

NAUGHTY HOLIDAY EDITIONS

2015

2016

2021

SALVATION IN DARKNESS

MISPLACED HALOS
BOOK TWO

NICOLE EDWARDS

COVER DETAILS:

Image: © kjpargeter; © winwinartlab | 123RF.com | *Design:* © Nicole Edwards
Limited

INTERIOR DETAILS:

Image: © winwinartlab | *123RF.com*

Formatting: Nicole Edwards Limited

❀ Formatted with Vellum

To my husband.

Thank you for doing what is necessary for me to continue to live out my dream.

PROLOGUE

Monday, August 5, 2019

ORIANNA MCKAY

———

I wasn't big on the social scene. Didn't matter which city I was in, the parties and gatherings were all the same: boring, predictable, and just plain exhausting.

Not to mention, full of horny twentysomethings looking to sate those irritating urges and find their happily ever after in the process. Wasn't any different for the young and hip here in Telluride, Colorado. In one night, I'd witnessed more than enough *Let's get it on* and *God, please spare us* to last a lifetime, thank you very much.

Netflix and chill—by my damn self—was more my jam. Which was exactly what I'd be doing if it weren't for the fact I was on a mission. One that was about to calendar flip into year seven.

Yep, six years of searching, traveling, and questioning every Tyler, Brandon, and Jacob—face it, no one named their kids Tom, Dick, or Harry anymore—with absolutely no luck. Now I was just plain tired. And perhaps a bit downtrodden. After all, the only thing I had to show for my efforts was a resumé that proved I was an utterly uncommitted jack of all trades.

Thank you, Fate. Or Karma. Or whatever mystical power that kept the universe aligned. Oh, and I couldn't forget my sister. Thanks, Amber. For nothing.

Had it not been for my older sister taking off for parts unknown all those years ago, I would've been back home in Texhoma, Oklahoma, vegging on Cheez-Its and Mountain Dew, watching reruns of *America's Next Top Model*. Instead, I was strolling the streets of Bumfuck, Colorado, looking under every rock I could turn over to see if my sister was lurking. Unfortunately, Amber's last known sighting was proving to be another dead end.

But there was one more place I had to look before I could call it a night. A few more minutes and I could get back to my crappy motel and chill. Tomorrow, if I were lucky, I would be making like dust and scattering.

"Well, look who it is," a gruff voice sounded behind me.

I kept walking, peering into storefronts, knowing damn well Amber wasn't hiding out in a dusty old antique shop, but wishing she'd appear, nonetheless.

"Hey, bitch!"

Curious, I cast a quick look over my shoulder, wondering who the asshole was talking to. Whoever it was, I hoped like hell the woman gave him what for. No man would ever talk to me that way. Not if he wanted to keep his twig and berries intact.

"Yeah. I'm talkin' to you. Come back here."

Instinct had my legs slowing, though I probably should've been moving faster. Single woman out late at night wasn't the smartest move, but I had long ago learned my sister was a night owl, and if I was going to track her down, it would likely be when the creeps were trolling.

"Yeah, that's what I thought. Where you been, Amber?"

I came to an abrupt halt, spinning around to study the man who clearly thought I was my sister.

"I been waitin' for you to show your face. You lookin' for Daddy Dearest?"

It wasn't the first time I'd been mistaken for my sister. Since we both had blonde hair and blue eyes, I could see how someone might think I was Amber.

From a distance.

In the dark.

Without their glasses.

Truth was, I looked nothing like my older sister aside from our fair coloring. While Amber was short, I was all leg, clocking in at five foot six. While Amber had a round face and a cute button nose, mine was all angles. Then again, if I wasn't ten pounds underweight, perhaps I'd have full cheeks, too.

Good news was, I seemed to be in the right place. Maybe. I should've known Amber would be hot on Erik's heels. Chasing our deadbeat father to the ends of the earth was Amber's favorite pastime. My older sister had been following his bread-crumbs since she was old enough to drive.

"I was wondering if you'd ever show your face here again. It's been a long time, sweetheart. You find him yet?" the asshat asked.

Assuming he was talking about my father and unsure how to answer, I kept my expression blank, waited for him to get closer. As soon as he did, I realized how foolhardy my curiosity

3

was. Before I could ask him how he knew Amber, the asshole pounced, throwing one skinny arm around my neck and jerking me backward.

I shrieked, attempting to keep my feet beneath me as he cut off my airway in his effort to drag me into a dark alley. My mouth opened, lungs filling as I prepared to scream when he rammed something into my kidney.

"Don't you dare scream, Amber," he hissed, his foul breath wafting into my sinuses. "I'll shoot you where you stand. Dear old Dad won't be too happy about that, will he?"

Nor would I, but that was moot, I figured.

Rather than punch him in the balls and elbow him in the nose, I whimpered, effectively swallowing the scream before it escaped. Clearly this was a case of mistaken identity, but I got the feeling he didn't care if I was Amber or not. As long as I was a McKay, he would likely be happy.

"I figured for sure Daddy would keep a better eye on his little girl, so imagine my surprise when there you were." He dragged me back a few more steps, then shoved me away, snagging my wrist, the momentum sending me spinning around. My back hit the wall, my breath escaping in a whoosh as his hand locked onto my throat. The matte black gun shifted from my midsection to the center of my chest.

Of course the idiot was holding the nine mil like a gangster, all crooked and at the perfect angle for the shell casing to hit him square in the face. Not that it would matter. The bullet would no doubt hit its target—me—from this close.

"Not sure why he never mentioned how pretty you are," he crooned, his calloused thumb grazing my chin.

Okay, so he *didn't* know Amber? If not, why the hell did he think I was her?

What the fuck?

If it hadn't been for the fact he was the only lead I had on

4

my sister, I would've laid waste to the bastard. Instead, I feigned an innocence I'd long since shed.

At twenty-four, it wasn't like I'd lived a long, haggard life, but considering the shit I'd endured, that warped sense of expectancy and faith had long been sucked right out of me, replaced with a heaping helping of pessimism and disappointment.

Keeping with the facade, I let my eyes go wide, ensured there was a slight tremble in my voice when I said, "What do you want?"

"To warn your father," he snarled. "He owes me quite a bit of money, sweetheart. Makes me angry when he tries to hide from me."

His gaze dropped to my chest, and I didn't need to be a mind reader to know what he was thinking. There was evil in his eyes, highlighted by the sneer on his mouth and punctuated by the fowl stench of his breath.

"Though a conversation could cover it, I'm thinking something a bit more ... tangible."

He squeezed my throat and I had to force my arms to remain at my sides. The asshole had no idea how vulnerable he was right then. It would've taken little effort to relieve him of the gun and put him flat on his back, balls lodged somewhere in the vicinity of his sinus cavity. After all, Krav Maga had been the only class I'd paid much attention to in high school.

Except I needed answers, so I would handle this. Easy peasy. After all, I'd found myself in worse situations before.

I added wild-eyed terror to my expression. "I don't know where he is."

"No matter. Once I'm done with you, he'll find me."

I glared at him, two seconds away from putting him out of his misery when his hand shifted from my throat to my jaw. I saw stars momentarily when my not-so-thick skull high-fived the brick at my back. The move rang my bell enough to have me losing my edge, my brain rattling inside my head, white lights flashing behind my eyes.

"Bet you'll be nice and sweet, huh?" He leaned in, sniffed me.

Could he be any more cliché?

"Fuck you," I snapped.

His laugh reminded me of a hyena. "Got some backbone in there, do ya? I look forward to beating it out of you. But first, perhaps we'll have a little fun."

When he shoved his hand between my legs, my muscles tensed, my weight shifting to my heels, arms bracing to send him flying, but before I could, he jerked away, stumbling in his cheap-ass loafers as though pulled by some invisible force.

From deep within the alley, a man appeared, his larger-than-life body stepping into the halo of light cast by the street-lamp. He walked with the grace of a jungle predator and the menace of death. I couldn't see his eyes because they were shielded by dark shades, but I knew he was focused on my attacker.

"You better back off, man," the gun-wielding asshole warned. "I won't hesitate to shoot you in the face."

"Too late." The stranger's deep baritone echoed through the alley. "You already hesitated."

I considered my options. Flee the scene and risk losing the best opportunity I'd had in months of finding my sister or wait it out. I opted for the latter, continuing with the terrified routine even as I admired the beast of a man who had seemingly come to my rescue. He was massive, his shoulders so broad I wasn't sure he was real. But to be fair, I was most impressed by the mohawk. There was something innately sexy about a man who could rock it the way this guy did.

"Last chance," the asshole warned.

My attention was divided between the two men until the midnight-haired stranger's head canted slightly, as though he was looking my way. Something happened in that moment. I felt it deep inside me. A connection, perhaps. I had never seen this man before, but there was something strangely familiar about him. As though I'd met him in a previous life or something.

I flinched when a shot rang out. I was still staring at the newcomer when the bullet slammed into him, the force sending his shoulder lurching back. He staggered but didn't go down, white teeth flashing as he turned his attention to the asshole with the gun. My breath lodged in my throat.

Were those … fangs?

"I warned you," the gun-toter screamed, his voice quivering. "Back off or you'll get another!"

Everything happened so fast after that.

The next thing I knew, the big man was behind my attacker, the asshole's head bobbing before there was a hideous snap and his lifeless limbs were falling to the ground, limp and … dead.

Well, hell.

Later I would be worried that my disappointed sigh likely wasn't the appropriate response to seeing someone killed only a few feet away. For the time being, I would have to deal with the fact I would not be getting answers from this one.

Now that the dead guy was no longer a threat, my full attention went to the man standing just a few feet away. He was even bigger than I'd thought, clocking in a good foot taller than me. Not sure what he wanted from me, I kept with the frightened woman routine, locking my stare on his face. It would've been smart to take off, but my feet were rooted in place, palms flat against the scratchy bricks.

"Are you okay?" I asked, noticing the slight hitch in my

words. Okay, so maybe I wasn't as unaffected as I pretended. But it had nothing to do with the dead asshole and everything to do with the fact this man had been shot, and he was acting as though it wasn't a BFD.

His head lifted, attention on me once again.

I couldn't seem to move, but he wasn't having the same problem. Before I knew it, he was only a breath away, his big body surrounding me. There was a strange detachment, as though I was watching this happen to someone else as he lifted his hand. His fingers were gentle where they swept over my temple, then around to the back of my head. I flinched, pain blooming. When he pulled his fingers away, I realized there was blood. Likely from my little headbutt with the wall.

He hissed softly, the sight of my blood evidently bothering him.

"Go," he growled, his voice a dark rumble. "Run far and fast."

This time my feet got with the program. I palmed the brick, moving sideways along the wall, keeping my eyes on him. Regret shot through me when I peered down at the dead asshole one more time. I'd wanted to question him, but now I needed to get gone or risk the police taking me into custody. Didn't matter that I was a witness, I had no desire to mix it up with the cops.

When I reached the end of the alley, I peered back once more. The enormous man with the sexy mohawk was still standing there, head turned, following my every move.

I could feel his eyes on me even when I finally turned and fled.

I

Two months later...

ECLIPSE

———

"Hey, E-man! We've got incoming," Miklós called out.

I scanned the room. Despite the fact my *lieterra's* announcement would've been more subtle if he'd used a glowing neon billboard, no one else moved. Not a muscle. I wouldn't be surprised if the archangel Michael was peering down from Heaven wondering why the ruckus or God was pausing in his daily ... whatever it was He did ... to see whether He needed to intervene.

Wait for it...

A sequence of vibrations, chimes, rings, and even a rendition of Pat Benatar's "Hit Me with Your Best Shot" sounded through the war room, signaling that a motion sensor on the property had been activated. Yep, and now everyone within twenty miles of the mansion had been notified, which meant the verbal outburst was merely wasted breath.

Yet it never failed. The *fiestreigh* were like human children announcing the arrival of the ice cream truck.

Rather than remind my *lieterra* of that, I strolled through the rows of tables, coming to stand behind Miklós, who was currently staring at his laptop screen, deft fingers flying over the keyboard.

"Put it on the monitor," I instructed.

Every time I caught sight of the six television screens mounted on the wall, I had to wonder where Penelope Calazans was fifteen hundred years ago, back when we'd first tackled the task of protecting the humans from Lucifer's evil bastards. Those fifty-inch monstrosities weren't the only updates to our mission that Obsidian's *ereswa* had added in the past few weeks, either. Ever since she'd mated with my oldest brother, Penelope decided she wasn't going to sit on the sidelines while everyone else spent their nights working. And when the female put her mind to something, we'd learned right quick to step back and let her work her magic.

Not only had she offered us structure by designing a war room that allowed space to work without distraction, she also implemented a schedule, giving the *fiestreigh* some downtime. We'd been at this gig for a millennium and a half, and I couldn't help but wonder if we would've made more progress if she'd been along for the ride since the beginning.

Crossing my arms over my chest, I studied the image when it appeared on the screen. The black Cadillac Escalade was inching up the long drive toward the house, headlights cutting through the darkness, guiding the way. "How many are there?"

Miklós's fingers never stopped typing, even when he said, "From what I can tell, two. One male, one female."

I leaned closer, studied the green-tinged image. Although human technology had improved by leaps and bounds in the past century, it didn't quite match up to angel eyesight. Had I been outside, I would've been able to see clearly without the strange alien glow distorting the features of the two approaching the mansion.

"Anyone know who this is?" I asked, squinting for a better look.

The conversation around the room disappeared instantly as everyone turned their attention to the screen.

"Looks like Kaj," Reidar noted, moving to stand at my side.

Since Reidar was Obsidian's *ladeare*, I figured he would be the first to recognize my brother's best vampire pal. As for why the male was creeping up on the mansion with dawn only an hour and a half away, that was yet to be determined.

"Did we know he was coming?"

The rumbled consensus was no, we hadn't.

I turned to face Reidar. "Where's Obsidian now?"

"Last I saw him, he was heading up to the third floor."

"I'll get him. You take Gryffyth, Kandarie, and Torak to greet our visitors. Do not allow them entry until Obsidian gives the signal."

"Will do," the *ladeare* said, his expression fierce.

While the males gathered to greet our guest, I disappeared. When I resumed my physical form, I was in the living room on the third floor. The Colorado mansion was home to more than seventy souls—angel warriors, soldiers, a handful of Fae, the *heurosp*, even a couple of civilian humans—which was the reason my brothers and I had designated the third floor as our personal space.

It was twenty thousand square feet of only ours, a place we

could find solitude when the weight of the war we waged on demons bore down on us. While most of the space was allocated to our personal quarters, there was enough left over for a huge room for relaxing, a separate meeting space, as well as a recreation room complete with pool table, a kick-ass stereo system, and a well-stocked bar.

Since most of my brothers were out searching for their *amsouelots*, I hadn't expected anyone to be there, and I was right on the money. The living room was empty, large-screen television dark. The polished wood coffee table gleamed in the yellow glow from the sconces on the wall, and there was the faint scent of lemon polish lingering.

A soft snore drew my attention to the floor.

I smiled when Zeus rolled to his back, the canine's paws kicking up into the air as he slept soundly on the fluffy dog bed in the corner. For the hell of it, I cleared my throat, watched Zeus flip over, dark head popping up, keen gaze surveying his surroundings.

"Lazy dog," I muttered.

Clearly Zeus didn't see me as a threat because his tongue lolled out of his mouth, and I was almost positive the canine was smiling at me.

"You seen Obsidian?" I asked Zeus as I started toward the hallway leading to Obsidian's private quarters.

Zeus hopped to all fours and trotted my way.

"Ah. I think he's coming now." I paused when I heard voices, giving Zeus's soft head a scratch while we waited for Obsidian and his *ereswa* to appear.

"Hey," Obsidian greeted, seeming a bit confused to find me loitering in the hallway.

"Perfect timing. You've got a visitor," I informed my brother, offering Penelope a smile and a nod. "Arrived a minute ago."

Obsidian frowned. "What? How's that possible?"

I understood Obsidian's concern because the mansion was supposed to be invisible to everyone except the angels and Fae who resided there. Not only was the place not on a map, not even detectable by the human government, we'd also erected *dhira* in an effort to cloak us in the event the demons were on the hunt. The shroud of pitch-black mist made it impossible for anyone to see, as well as offered disorientation to any visitor who got close to the property, effectively sending them on their way.

"No clue," I answered, "but it looks like Kaj got a lock on our coordinates."

Obsidian's silver eyes flashed with what I could only describe as hope. He probably wouldn't admit it aloud, but we all knew he'd been worried about the vampire.

"Kaj? Your vampire friend?" Penelope asked, her gold eyes darting between the two of us.

"One and the same," Obsidian said, taking her hand and leading her toward the stairs.

I followed close behind, adjusting the Oakleys shielding my eyes.

"Where's Reidar?" Obsidian asked, his voice signaling he was in warrior mode, ready and willing to defend the mansion against anyone who hadn't been invited. Even a friend.

"He's the welcoming committee." I jogged down the steps behind the couple.

When we reached the main floor, several others were marching our way, long legs eating up the distance to the front doors.

"Do you think he's a threat?" I asked, wanting to know what we were walking into.

"Not at all," Obsidian said, his voice reassuring. "But if he arrived without letting me know, I suspect there's a damn good reason."

Three of the fiestreigh—Magnar, Echo, and Cayden—stood in the foyer, armed to the teeth and awaiting their orders.

"Open the door," Obsidian instructed.

Without hesitation, Magnar pulled open the front door, the three males leading the way outside. Obsidian followed, then Penelope, while I pulled up the rear. Once I reached the porch, I subtly moved around in front of Obsidian's *ereswa*, prepared to protect her should it be necessary. In a casual move, I pulled off the shades, folded the arms, and tucked them into the neck of my T-shirt for safekeeping.

Standing at the base of the steps was six feet seven inches of powerful male vampire. Kaj's jet-black hair was a haphazard mess and in desperate need of a trim—perhaps the style—while his jaw sported a week's worth of dark stubble, and the thick muscles of his shoulders were tense, as though he was expecting a threat and not sure he was ready for one. But those keen celadon-green eyes showed no signs of exhaustion.

I had to give the vamp credit, though. While he was the focus of an army of angels loaded for bear, he appeared unfazed, proving he had brass balls. Or a death wish.

Outside of those who resided in the mansion, Kaj, the vampire Obsidian considered his nearest and dearest friend, was likely the closest thing to family we had here on Earth. During the three hundred years Kaj had been hanging around, I'd spent more than one drunken night in the male's company, but I hadn't heard even whispers of what Kaj was up to for the past eighteen months, ever since the vampire left the mansion after six months of recuperation.

Not for lack of trying, of course. The *fiestreigh* had been attempting to get in touch with him to help with the Perfidious situation, to no avail.

"What the hell are you doing here?" Obsidian prompted, his voice stern.

The vampire smirked, light green eyes glittering with amusement. "Good to see you, too, brother."

I kept my eyes on the female currently slipping out of the SUV. She was slight of build, despite her taller-than-average height for a female. Casting aside her posture, which spoke of defeat and despair, I knew we couldn't rule out her abilities. When it came to vampires, it was always best to err on the side of caution.

For several breaths, Obsidian and Kaj squared off with one another until finally, Obsidian laughed, all tension dissipating at the gruff sound. The two males embraced, smacking one another on the back.

While they bro-hugged it out, I slipped into Kaj's mind in an attempt to get the lowdown, but before I could filter through a single memory, the vampire's head turned my way, those celadon peepers igniting with light, effectively breaking the connection.

"Don't do that again," Kaj rumbled. "I assure you, I'm not a threat."

I would be the one to decide that; however, I'd clearly have to take a different approach because Kaj's mind was closed to me, impenetrable. A new development, for sure.

"Seriously, Kaj," Obsidian said, "what brings you here?"

"As much as I'd like to claim it's a social visit, I'd be lying." His eyes trailed over Obsidian, then darted to Penelope as she moved closer to her *reuthet*. "But it looks like the rumors are true. I presume this is your better half?"

I remained at Penelope's side as she moved down the steps to join Obsidian.

"Most definitely." Obsidian's voice rang with pride as he

placed one big arm over her shoulders. "Penelope, meet Kaj Courtenay. Kaj, this is my *ereswa*, Penelope Calazans."

"*Ereswa*? I assume that's a fancy term for life mate," Kaj teased, offering a polite nod to Penelope. "It's an honor to meet you."

The vampire didn't attempt to shake her hand, knowing full well that a mated female angel could not stand the touch of another male. That wasn't only the case with angels, but all supernatural creatures God had created, including vampires. Considering how much infidelity the humans encountered, I often wondered why the Almighty hadn't done the same for that race. At the very least, it would've shortened that list of commandments they lived by.

"Likewise," Penelope replied with a nod, sliding her hand into Obsidian's when he held it out for her.

"Come in," Obsidian urged, turning to head back inside.

Kaj peered over his shoulder briefly, and I followed his gaze.

The female vampire likely thought she was hidden in the shadows of the SUV, but every male there could see her clearly. I sensed her uncertainty and that innate desire to maintain a safe distance. I'd bet dollars to donuts she had an escape route picked out based on the hard glint in her eyes.

Kaj motioned her forward. When she took a step, Obsidian put his body between the newcomer and Penelope while the others took up a defensive stance, Kandarie and Torak shimmering into existence on the other side of the unknown female. I remained on Penelope's right, my hand resting on the hilt of the half-moon blade sheathed on my side.

"Stand down, angels. She's not a threat," Kaj said, his voice low and even. "Bijou, I'd like you to meet Obsidian. Obsidian, meet my daughter, Bijou Courtenay."

I wasn't the only one doing the whole *what the fuck?* Behind his dark lenses, Obsidian's eyes widened, and knowing him, he was racking his brain in an attempt to figure out when Kaj had mentioned he had an offspring.

Obsidian nodded in Bijou's direction, his furrowed brow telling me he was surprised as well. "Pleasure."

She offered a shy smile, eyes lowering respectfully.

"Please, come in," Penelope said, slipping around Obsidian and motioning toward Bijou. "It's cold out here. We're about to sit down to the morning meal. Would you care to join us?"

Kaj met Obsidian's gaze, clearly seeking his permission, and received a nod in return.

I stayed back as the vampires started toward the house. Before Kaj passed, he held out his hand to me.

"Good to see you again." His voice was the equivalent of *no harm, no foul.* Clearly, he forgave me for the mental intrusion earlier.

Relaxing my stance, I took the proffered hand. "Likewise. Been a long time."

"Probably should've called, huh?"

"Always a good idea." I held out my hand for Kaj's keys. "With the sun coming up soon, you'll be staying."

Kaj smirked. "You won't get an argument from me."

I turned to Gryffyth, tossed the vampire's car keys. "Put the vehicle in the garage."

Gryffyth nodded while I led the way into the house.

We'd made it as far as the kitchen before the *heurosp* currently on duty, including Phillip and Jeffrey, nearly plowed Kaj over in their attempt to greet him. Seemed the vampire had made quite the impression on those who maintained the mansion during his previous stay.

"Quite a fan base you've got," I said when I managed to extricate Kaj and lead him into the dining room.

"They're a good crew," Kaj noted, sounding almost like

19

he'd missed them while he was gone. "I see you've upgraded your digs since I was last here."

I followed the male's eyes as they scanned the interior of the new mansion we'd erected to house us all more comfortably. "It works for us." I motioned for Kaj to precede me into the dining room. "Let's eat, shall we?"

Several of the *fiestreigh* were already there, each of them getting to their feet and greeting Kaj with smiles and handshakes. Introductions were made, and before long, everyone currently in residence had joined the party, dragging Kaj into the fray.

Standing just inside the door, I leaned closer to Obsidian. "I take it you didn't know he had a daughter."

"Not a fucking clue."

I studied the pretty female, who was being introduced by Penelope. Now that I really looked at her, I saw the remarkable resemblance to her father. Same onyx hair, same green eyes. I pegged her to be in her mid-twenties, though I could've been way off. Like angels and Fae, vampires didn't physically age past twenty-five. However, there was an innocence about her, one that was usually chipped away by the hardships of life, privations I wasn't sure she'd seen just yet. Considering the vampires had been put on Earth to protect the humans from the supernatural created by Lucifer, they were fighting the same battles the angels were. It was easy to detect those who'd been at it a while from those who were too young to have seen all the horrors.

"If this isn't a social visit, what brings you to my front door?" Obsidian asked, motioning Kaj to a table as everyone split up, positioning themselves at the tables around the room.

I moved with them, remaining on my feet while Obsidian pulled Penelope's chair out. The three of us waited for her to take a seat before taking ours. Although I suspected Kaj intended to occupy it, I snagged the one that would keep my back to the wall, giving me an unobstructed view of the room.

"I heard whispers you'd mated," Kaj explained as he relaxed in the chair, snagging the white linen napkin from the table. "Thought I'd check it out for myself. Congratulate you in person."

Obsidian's face glowed with pride when he said, "I most certainly did."

Kaj nodded at Penelope. "It's a pleasure to meet the female strong enough to keep our boy in line."

A round of laughter sounded from around the room, the peanut gallery clearly listening in.

"She's strong enough to keep us *all* in line," I said, lifting my glass in a mock toast.

Kaj grinned at Obsidian. "Lucky bastard."

Obsidian's eyes locked on something across the room, causing me to glance over to my left.

"She can join us if she'd like," I told Kaj when I noticed Bijou taking a seat at an empty table.

The vampire exhaled heavily. "She's shy. And stubborn." He winked at me. "Kids."

I laughed though I couldn't relate at all. Until recently, I'd had very little interaction with anyone who hadn't hit a century mark or ten.

"I didn't realize you had a child," Obsidian prompted as the *heurosp* made their way through the room, delivering plates of food and glasses of water, juice, and coffee.

"I didn't realize you were *with* child," Kaj countered, his gaze darting to Penelope.

"We are expecting," Obsidian acknowledged with an enormous grin.

Kaj's expression sobered. "Bijou showed up on my doorstep about a year ago. Introduced herself."

"How old is she?" Penelope inquired. "If you don't mind me asking."

"Not at all." Kaj smiled. "Twenty-seven."

"I take it she's a vampire like you."

Kaj's green gaze held hers. "We can reproduce only with our own kind."

Penelope blushed. "Forgive me. It's been all I can do to catch up on angel life."

"Good news, vampires are similar in many ways," Kaj noted.

That was definitely true. At times, I often wondered what Michael had been thinking when he'd created Obsidian, then molded the rest of us after him. Considering Michael's original warrior had technically come before vampires, it could be said that vampires were similar to angels, just without the wings. Chicken, egg, yada, yada.

"Where's Bijou's mother?" Obsidian asked.

"Dead."

"I'm sorry."

Phillip approached the table, carrying a tray with a silver-domed plate on top.

Obsidian glanced over his shoulder. "Thank you, Phillip," he told the *heurosp* as he set Penelope's plate in front of her.

"You're very welcome, sire," the male replied, bowing as he removed the silver dome and carried it away.

"And the rest of your clan?" I prompted, curious as to what really brought the vampire to our doorstep. Congratulations were all good and fine, but I sensed there was another reason.

"Which one? They're all mine now," he muttered, his tone somber as he glanced between me and Obsidian. "I've had to go to ground in recent months. The shadow beasts have been wreaking havoc on my race for going on a year and a half now.

They've taken out a number of our females, including Bijou's mother."

"Shadow beasts?" Penelope's golden eyes were locked on Kaj.

"Essentially a demon, although these are part human, part dog," Kaj answered easily.

Curiosity glittered in Penelope's eyes. "Like a werewolf?"

I glanced at Obsidian, grinned, and earned one in return. Penelope had shocked us all when she'd come to the mansion roughly three months ago. Thanks to the demons seeking the *amsouelots*, Obsidian hadn't had much choice in bringing her here before he'd had a chance to give her the deets on our true identities. Though we'd all expected the then human to freak out being immersed in a world full of what she'd been taught was merely fiction, she'd surprised us all with her acceptance. And become one herself, in fact.

"More apt would be a hellhound," Kaj told her. "Only this species can shift at will, and they can walk in the sun. Thanks, my good man," Kaj told Phillip when he placed a plate before him.

"I don't mean to sound callous, Kaj, but how exactly did you find me?" Obsidian asked.

I offered a thanks to Phillip, but kept my attention on Kaj, eager for the answer.

Kaj smiled. "Remember the last time you offered me refuge?"

"Two years ago." Obsidian looked at Penelope. "He'd sustained a mortal wound, and I brought him here, healed him myself."

Yes, I remembered that. The vampire nearly died, but thanks to Obsidian's quick thinking, not to mention Acadia's blood, he'd bounced back. Had taken six months, but the vampire eventually walked out of the mansion under his own steam.

Kaj nodded. "If it wasn't for you and Acadia, I wouldn't be here today."

"I thought vampires were immortal," Penelope noted.

"Immortal, yes. Not indestructible." Kaj glanced at all the faces staring back at him.

"*That's* how you found us," I said as realization dawned.

"What does that mean?" Penelope asked, clearly wanting all the details.

Kaj smiled. "Because I fed from Acadia, I have a direct link to her." His thick shoulders shrugged. "Granted, this place still wasn't easy to find, but I'm a male on a mission."

Obsidian paused, his fork suspended between his plate and his mouth. "What mission is that?"

Kaj's gaze swung over to Bijou. "I'm seeking refuge for my daughter. I'm not sure whether you've heard or not, but I've taken on the role of Alpha."

So it *was* true. We'd heard rumors that Kaj had been forced to assume the position because their presiding Alpha—his father—had been taken out.

There was a hint of sadness in Kaj's tone when he said, "It wasn't a position I was looking to fill, I assure you."

"I'm sorry," Obsidian said softly. "We heard rumors, but they were unsubstantiated. You're not an easy male to track down." He peered over at Kaj's daughter. "And you'd like us to provide her safe harbor?"

"In exchange for my help, yes."

Obsidian's dark brow rose slowly. "With?"

"I know your brothers are seeking their mates, and I'm willing to offer our help in any way you might need."

That certainly got my attention, but Obsidian waved him off. "Hold that thought until after the meal."

Kaj nodded, lifted his fork, but before the silver tines made it to his mouth, his head swung around.

I followed his line of sight to see Acadia stepping into the room. The dark-haired Fae's head shot up, amethyst eyes meeting Kaj's. Her hand went to her chest as she stood there, staring. Their eyes locked from across the room, held for the longest time.

I could sense the tension in the Fae, but it wasn't from fear. More like recognition and ... longing.

Without thinking, I slipped into the female's mind. It was an invasion of privacy, sure, but I was curious.

Of course, the instant I saw what she was thinking about, I backtracked right out of her head and briefly wondered if brain bleach was even powerful enough to scrub *that* image from my gray matter.

2

KAJ COURTENAY

While I had every intention of cornering Acadia at some point during my visit, I hadn't expected this. After all, timing was everything. Considering how she'd refused all communication with me since my departure, I expected her to keep as far from me as physically possible.

Didn't mean I wasn't pleased by the turn of events.

Every single thing I accomplished in the past eighteen months had been fueled by the need to get back to her, but I wasn't the sort to expect things to be easy. Least of all, my reunion with the female I walked away from all those months ago.

It was thanks to her unselfish offer to heal me back then

that I'd been able to find her. Ever since I fed from the Fae, I had been connected to her on a deeper level. And what do you know: that connection only seemed to strengthen with proximity. Only, she hadn't realized I was there. I knew because I felt the shift in the air the moment the lovely Fae stepped into the room. Not only because my senses were overdeveloped and I could detect the slightest nuance, either.

Oh, no. It certainly wasn't that simple.

Then again, nothing in my life was these days.

For one, it defied the laws of our creation that the female I'd bonded with happened to be a mystical fairy, the very one who'd nursed me back to health, essentially credited with saving my life.

"Would you excuse me?" I asked Obsidian and the others.

Obsidian offered a clipped nod, his gaze bouncing between me and Acadia. "Careful."

Nothing got by that angel.

"Always."

Of course, I barely made it to my feet when Acadia spun around and fled the room. A true gentleman would've considered that and offered to give her the space she sought, but I wasn't a man in any sense of the word, gentle or otherwise, and the absolute last thing Acadia needed more of from me was distance.

My black leather combat boots were loud on the tiled floor as I followed her through the elaborate kitchen, past the formal seating area, down the long corridor that led to the front door. Despite the fact the fairy was making good time, I knew she wasn't putting too much effort into it. If she had, I never would've caught up to her. While I had a significant number of powers and abilities, the Fae had more, most of which no one was even privy to.

"Acadia, stop," I ordered when I managed to reach her on the stairs leading up to the second floor.

Her footfalls were silent when she came to an abrupt halt. I would bet money that beneath the long, flowing skirt on that magnificent off-white dress, Acadia's dainty feet were bare, as was the rest of her. This particular Fae never wore shoes unless it was absolutely necessary and refused undergarments of any kind. One of many of Acadia's idiosyncrasies that I found innately sexy.

In an effort to keep her from disappearing, I slowly ascended, stopping on the step below where the Fae stood. I didn't attempt to crowd or intimidate, merely admired. As always, Acadia looked flawless and delicate, her beauty radiating out of her. Her silky dark hair was piled in an intricate knot on top of her head, a few wisps hanging loose around her heart-shaped face, highlighting her soft ivory complexion.

My eyes drank her in, and once again, I wondered how the hell I'd managed to keep my distance for the last year and a half. I still remember the day I walked out of the mansion, forcing myself not to look back. Duty and obligation drove me away from her the last time, and it was the same that brought me back.

"How have you been?" I asked, keeping my voice evenly pitched, non-threatening.

Those brilliant amethyst eyes dropped low. "I'm well, *dyrlom*."

Ah, so we were back to that. I thought we'd long since left that nonsensical title in the past.

"For accuracy, it would be *phaal*," I corrected. "Now that I've taken the role of Alpha of my race. Or, at the very least, *tresmar*."

Acadia didn't budge, didn't even spare me a glance despite

it being rude not to, considering I was of a higher station than she, based on those asinine formal greetings she preferred.

"Acadia, look at me."

Her gaze rose slowly, met mine, and held on.

Once more, I found myself entranced by her natural, ethereal beauty. Only Acadia's eyes were enhanced with makeup, her long lashes dark, a hint of shimmer on the lids, the rest of her face aglow with what was graced upon her at birth. But it was her lips I was enamored with. I remembered how those lips had felt against my own, caressing every inch of me during those stolen moments we'd shared during my recovery.

Before I could stop myself, I was cupping her face, brushing my thumb over the soft skin of her cheek. I'd missed her so much that, even as I looked at her now, I could still feel the ghost of that ache in my chest. Walking away from her had been the hardest thing I'd ever done.

Those glossy cupid's bow lips parted slightly, her surprise glittering in her eyes. But shock wasn't the only emotion she was feeling.

"I've missed you, *balisra*."

She didn't respond, but the slight flare of her eyes said she hadn't expected me to admit as much. A memory flashed in my mind and I knew she was the one to plant it there. It was the night I'd left her, gone back to the vampire world.

"If I recall," I said softly, "I asked you to go with me."

Acadia didn't respond, her eyes bouncing back and forth over my face as though trying to read my intentions. It was no longer possible. With my position as Alpha, my thoughts were shielded from everyone, including the Fae and the angels.

When Acadia stepped back, I dropped my hand to my side, exhaling heavily. "We need to talk."

"There's nothing to talk about, *tresmar*."

Feeling the overwhelming urge to dominate her, to make

the female submit only to me, I scaled the last step, peering down at her. When she stepped back, I pursued her until her small frame was pressed up against the wall, surrounded by me. I hovered there for long moments as her breaths became more rapid, her heartbeat thrumming loudly in my ears. She was still affected by me the same way I was her.

"Drop the pretenses, female," I said gruffly, forcing my hands to remain at my sides rather than pulling her into my arms, where she belonged.

Once more, she seemed shocked by my actions, but I didn't much care. The truth was, not a single day had passed since I walked away from her that I hadn't thought about returning, spending the rest of my days making it up to her. It had always been my plan to come back, to court her appropriately, to convince her I was the male she belonged with for eternity.

Of course, life had a way of interrupting the best-laid plans, and I was delayed far longer than I anticipated. I couldn't blame her for being upset with me.

Tucking my finger beneath her chin, I urged Acadia's head back, forcing her to look at me. "You can pretend you don't belong to me, *balisra*, but we both know the truth."

"I know nothing of the sort," she countered, a hint of steel in her words.

I smiled. "Then I look forward to getting you up to speed."

"Why are you here?" she asked, her voice a rough whisper.

"Two reasons. First, I'm seeking refuge for my daughter."

Her eyes flashed with not so much surprise but shock and betrayal.

"I only recently learned of her existence," I said defensively. "I would never keep something like that from you. Not ever."

She seemed to consider that before saying, "And the other reason?"

I tilted my head, let my eyes drop to her mouth, but I didn't lean down. "I've come to claim what belongs to me, Acadia. Once and for all."

"Which is?"

"You."

The slight hitch in her breath had my entire body hardening, but I knew better than to pursue her yet.

Before she could come up with a retort, I stood tall.

"I fully intend to accomplish both." I turned away, needing to return to the dining room. "And I have no intention of leaving until the latter is settled once and for all."

As I descended the stairs, I could feel her eyes on me, and that need, the one I'd been fighting for so long, bore down on me hard.

ACADIA

Frustrating, that was what that vampire was.

Infuriating.

Exasperating.

And so obscenely handsome, it felt strangely taboo for me to be staring at him so. I couldn't count the times I'd dreamed about him over the past year and a half, seen those brilliant green eyes or that luxurious black hair, the hard angles of his face, the chiseled line of his jaw. His image was forever burned into my brain, never to be forgotten.

I watched Kaj walk away, my heart in my throat. It wasn't quite as painful as the last time I'd seen him retreat, though. That horrible day was forever imprinted on my mind, a recurring nightmare that often woke me in the day.

I couldn't believe he was here. More importantly, I couldn't believe he'd surprised me. How had I not sensed he was in the mansion?

Not that it mattered now.

His presence was both a blessing and an irritation. I was relieved to know he was alive and well but peeved to learn he was alive and well *and* hadn't bothered to contact me for the past eighteen months. What could he have possibly been doing during that time that kept him from reaching out? Not so much as a text message to say *hi, how are you?* For the longest time, I had worried he'd been killed, and I'd been left to forever nurse a broken heart.

My heart was still broken, of course. Didn't matter if he waltzed right up and said all the right things, made all those promises I'd longed to hear. I wouldn't forgive him that easily. Oh, no. That vampire was going to grovel at my feet. Even then I wasn't sure I could revert to that naive female who'd so easily given him her heart only to have it shattered.

With a huff, I continued up the stairs, dragging the heavy skirts of my dress behind me. I would seek sustenance later, perhaps once everyone had retired for the day.

My feet were quiet on the carpet as I hurried toward my quarters. The sound of clipped voices brought me up short. I paused only feet from Reidar and Winnie's room as I peered around for options. It sounded like they were standing just inside the door, which meant if I walked by, they would see me.

"It's your home, Reidar. Not mine. We've been over this.

You promised me." Winnie's words were fueled by a fury I could feel wafting out of the bedchambers.

"This is where I belong," Reidar countered hotly. "You knew that when I brought you here."

"Clearly I was blinded by my feelings for you. Time changes things, Reidar. I don't feel comfortable here anymore. I want to go back to California, be near my family. If you love me, you'll go with me."

"Winnie..." Reidar sighed heavily. "I need some time."

"Away from me?" she belted.

"Yes, actually. This isn't... It's not working the way I thought it would."

Hearing Reidar's heavy footfalls moving closer to the door, I panicked, scurrying back the way I'd come. When I stopped at the end of the hall, I prayed no one saw me. As it was, I was too flustered to dematerialize, otherwise I would've been back in my room, where I belonged.

When Reidar's voice carried down the hall, I blocked it out, already feeling like an interloper for having heard their heated conversation. My heart ached for the pair of them, but the truth was, I'd been expecting this to come. The day Reidar brought Winnie to the mansion, declaring she was his *amsouelot*, I had known the truth. That was one of the burdens of feeding off of emotion. There were certain nuances I picked up on, and since my blood was in Reidar's veins, I had a connection to the male.

But it wasn't my place to intervene.

As it was, the angels allowed far more liberties than the Fae should've been granted based on the laws that governed our existence. The Fae were a fallen race, doomed to servitude because of the sins of my elders. Throughout my time with Obsidian and his brothers, I had come to see myself as a member of the family when, in truth, I was as disposable as the *heurosp*.

So when it came to interfering with the relationships of those I served, I kept my thoughts to myself. It was inevitable that Reidar would come to the realization that the human wasn't the one he was destined to be with, but I couldn't be the one to relay that information.

Not to mention, I had other things on my mind. Namely, a frustrating vampire.

With a sigh, I leaned back against the wall, breathing a bit easier when Reidar's voice drifted in the opposite direction.

My thoughts shifted back to Kaj.

Despite what he believed, I was not the female he was destined to be with. I couldn't be. The Fae weren't permitted to mate for eternity. It violated our very station in life for the simple fact that we provided nourishment to the angels who resided on Earth. Should I bond with a male, I could no longer perform my duties, and when that happened...

I shook off the thought. I couldn't go there.

Not now. Not ever.

3

ORIANNA

I exhaled heavily, elbows resting on the cluttered counter as I watched two young men waltzing through the convenience store, eyes greedily ogling the shelves. Despite their eyeballing of the candy, I knew they had no intention of purchasing any of the sugar crap. Had it been early morning, perhaps. The fact that it was going on midnight and these two should've been at home asleep because they had school in the a.m. told me they had something more exciting in mind.

I'd been at this long enough to know those underage kids were hoping to snatch up some redneck soda, a.k.a. brewski, or perhaps a pack of cancer sticks, neither of which I had any intention of selling them.

Their ghosting routine had me peering up at the round

mirror mounted in the back corner of the store. The reflective glass showed one of the boys opening a refrigerator case, reaching inside and... Bingo. Looked like Coors Light was the name of the game.

Turning my attention back to Gwen rocking the cover of *Shape*, I pretended to skim, then dutifully flipped the page as the boys started my way. A squeak on the tile announced their approach, not to mention their hesitation.

The least they could do was *pretend* they were old enough. Sheesh.

"What else for you boys?" I asked, standing tall and closing the magazine.

"This is it." The six-pack made an appearance on the counter, and the boy who'd carried it forward suddenly had a nose itch, his eyes hitting the floor, head tucked down as though I couldn't see the sweat dripping down his fuzzy sideburns.

"Cool." I moved toward the register, raised a hand as though I was going to ring it up, and noticed their simultaneous sighs of relief.

Oh, yeah. Definitely underage.

Pausing before my finger pressed the register, I cocked my head to the side and smiled. "Got some ID?"

"Sure 'nuff," the other one said, snatching his wallet from his back pocket and flipping it open like he was presenting a badge. Probably didn't get a lot of dates, that one.

I nodded my chin, motioning for him to bring it closer.

"Darwin Danvers." I scanned the birthdate, the one proclaiming him to be not twenty-one but twenty-three. "Nice photo, Darwin."

When I peered back up, he shot me a wide grin. "Thanks."

"Didn't get that down at the DMV, huh?"

Double D's grin slipped. "What?"

"It's a fake. And a shitty one, at that," I said, peering over at the other guy. "You wanna try?"

I earned a couple of grumbles before they headed to the door empty-handed. Clearly unimpressed, Double D's friend punched him in the shoulder before they strolled out into the night.

"At least they were entertaining," I muttered as I carried the wheat water back to its rightful home.

Truth was, I fucking hated this job, but I needed something to keep food in my belly and shelter over my head. While I'd expected to be back in Oklahoma by now, I found myself stuck here in Nowhere, Colorado, still in hide-and-seek mode. A couple of leads had led me up to Boulder, another right back to this hellhole, and still, no sign of Amber anywhere.

I'd been about to pack it up when I got word there was an underground gambling gig in town. Since I figured that dead asshole from the alley had been attempting to hassle my father for whatever money he probably owed them, I hoped that would lead me where I needed to go. Unfortunately, while my source knew about it, he didn't know where it was going down. According to him, they moved the party every couple of days to stay off the local PD radar. Always just out of reach. Something I was oddly familiar with.

The sound of an engine had me looking up into the two-pump parking lot.

Speak of the devil.

A redneck rig pulled up, parked in front of the doors. A guy sporting Wranglers and boots hopped down from the cab, and I had to wonder what was the point in jacking up a truck that high. Seemed kind of pointless to me. How did you get anything in the bed of the truck when you needed a ladder just to get in the cab?

The door swung open, bells jingled, and Howdy Doody strolled in, offering a wink and a tilt of his hat.

"What's up, Jed?" I greeted, leaning a hip on the counter and crossing my arms over my chest.

The wannabe cowboy smiled, his eyes instantly dropping to the low-cut shirt I wore.

"You find anything out?" I asked, the same as I had the last time I saw him, over at the club.

"I mighta." He winked, then bent down all chill and shit, resting his forearms on the counter. "What's in it for me?"

A punch in the snout, I thought, even as I said, "Depends on how good the intel is."

"Oh, it's good."

I rolled my eyes. "Where's the gig?"

Jed stood tall, crossed his skinny arms over his chest. "Word is they're settin' up in an abandoned warehouse."

"That right?" Did the fool not know there were at least two dozen abandoned warehouses in and around Telluride? "Probably need to be a bit more specific."

"Down off Maple Street." His grin widened, arms lowering as he pressed his palms to the counter.

I offered a smile, playing him up a bit. "And the guy I told you about? You see him around here?"

Jed shook his head. "Ain't seen no guy fittin' that description."

"But you'll keep an eye out, right? Let me know if you do?"

"Course." Jed cocked one dark brow. "So ... 'bout that payment."

"You know the rules," I told him, mirroring his stance. "Once I find the game, you'll get paid."

Jed huffed, dropped his arms. "Fuckin' dick tease."

Yeah, not even close. More like wishful thinking on his part. Jed was about as useful as a lamp on a deserted island.

However, I figured at some point his lead might pan out, and until I'd exhausted all efforts, I was willing to dangle the line in front of his face.

"I'll check it out tomorrow night," I told him. "I'll hit you up if I find it."

I could tell the nonchalant shrug was meant to make him look cool, but the frustration on his face was evident.

I knew the feeling. I'd found myself crushing on some stranger, but I'd yet to find a hint of the ridiculously hot man I'd encountered in the alley back in August. And the good Lord knew I'd been trying to track him down, but, like Amber, no one seemed to know anything about him.

S ix hours later, I stepped into my apartment and locked the door behind me. I flipped the security latch for good measure, then took a quick stroll through the space, ensuring I didn't have any uninvited guests. I'd learned my lesson the hard way back when one of my landlords thought my desire to pay cash meant I was easy prey. The jackass had been waiting for me one night when I came home from work. He'd taken a bullet in the leg for his efforts, and I'd learned to always double-check before I got settled in.

Of course, there wasn't much to peruse here. Five hundred square feet of nothing fancy was all my limited finances could afford me. The upside was the place was furnished, albeit sparsely and with shitty, secondhand furniture, but since beggars couldn't be choosers, I was dealing with it as best I could.

"It's temporary," I reminded myself for the millionth time.

This had been my routine for the past month. Eight hours on the night shift at the Quick-E Mart, come back here, chow down on a package of Cheez-Its, gulp a Mountain Dew, shower, and sleep. At least I didn't feel like a homeless drifter, though I wasn't far from it. The old man who owned the complex agreed to let me pay on a weekly basis, and as long as I paid in cash, he didn't hassle me. Nor did he offer to fix the stopped-up sink, but luckily, I was good with tools. I'd managed that one on my own, even rigged the shower head to do more than trickle and adjusted the refrigerator so it actually cooled.

I tossed my phone on the couch that doubled as a bed, then made a beeline for the bathroom. It took the water a solid fifteen minutes to reach lukewarm, so I made myself useful while I waited. After stripping down to panties and bra, I tossed my clothes in the basket I would cart to the laundromat in town at some point. I snagged the Cheez-Its and a Mountain Dew, kept with the legwork while I had breakfast and planned my next move. I would find that damn gambling ring if it were the last thing I did. And maybe, if there were a God, I'd find my alley savior while I was at it.

Perhaps it made me selfish, but the weight of hope hung heavily on the latter right now. Probably had a lot to do with the fact I'd neglected my future entirely during my hunt for Amber. From time to time, I fantasized that one day, I'd live my life for myself instead of everyone else. Most folks my age were getting fitted with a cap and gown, gearing up to celebrate life after college. Though I'd had big dreams of rooting for OU from the sidelines, proudly sporting my Sooners gear, and locking down the necessary credits for an accounting degree, I had barely made it across the stage for high school graduation. And the only numbers I was kicking it with were those on the odometer of the POS I'd borrowed from my mother to get me from one side of the country to the other. And back.

By the time the water warmed, I had finished my breakfast of champions, shrouded myself in the fog of despair, stripped off my underwear, and stepped into the bathtub. I yanked the clear curtain closed behind me, shut my eyes, and prayed the warmth would eliminate the cold ache that had settled into my bones for the past couple of months. I knew it had nothing to do with the weather because Telluride was proving to be quite comfortable this time of year. I wasn't sure I was looking forward to spending a winter in Colorado, but for now, I had no complaints.

Nope, these cold chills weren't related to the weather.

Initially, I'd thought I had the flu, but I figured a lack of fever ruled that one out. Not to mention, not many illnesses came with a side order of loneliness and a heaping helping of isolation. Yet something was plaguing me. What, I had no idea, but I was hoping it would make itself scarce soon. Battling it was proving to be a distraction I couldn't afford.

I ran through my triple-S routine—shampoo, soap, and shave—then hopped out, dried off with a threadbare towel, tugged the oversized sleep shirt over my head, and headed back into the living room/bedroom. Everything in this place doubled as something else: couch equaled bed, end table was a nightstand, kitchen table also played the part of a desk. The rest was just decor, including the thirty-two-inch television that didn't work.

I grabbed my phone, flopped down on the lumpy cushions, and made my daily call to my mother. Although it was four in the morning here, it was five in Oklahoma, so I knew Elizabeth would answer. She always answered.

"Hey, Mom."

"Orianna?"

My heart ached at the pain I heard in my mother's voice, along with the drugged slur of her words.

"Yep, it's me. How're you feeling?"

"Good, honey. Just watching reruns of *Friends*. You know how much I love that show."

Oh, I knew all right. I had an intimate awareness of Ross and Rachel, although I'd never seen a single episode.

"Have you found Amber?"

"Not yet, Mom, but I'm still looking. I promise, I'll bring her home as soon as I do."

"And your father?"

"Still in the wind." Then again, I wasn't doing much to unearth Erik. Truth was, I didn't give a shit about the old man.

"Are you being careful?"

I smiled. "Of course I am."

After that night in the alley when that asshole held me at gunpoint, I'd been watching my back. I'd gotten lucky when the white knight appeared out of nowhere and leveled the asshole. Ever since then, I had been attempting to find the guy so I could thank him, but luck did not seem to be on my side these days. However, I was dreaming about him, sometimes so vividly I was almost certain he was right there with me. So there was that.

"Orianna?"

"Sorry, Mom. I'm here." Just daydreaming. Again.

"How's the new job?"

"It's great," I lied.

"And your new apartment?"

New was a relative word, of course. "Fantastic. Feels just like home."

"Well, honey, I wish you were home."

"I know." Except I knew my mother didn't want me to come back until I had Amber in tow. It was one of the many reasons I'd spent so many years searching. "You sure you're all right? Don't need anything?"

"I'm good," Elizabeth said. "The nurse came by earlier, helped me with my shower. I'm feeling much better now."

I took *earlier* to mean yesterday. "That's great, Mom. I'm glad she stopped by."

Elizabeth yawned, a sign she was pushing the envelope with her medication.

"Anyway, Mom, I'll call you tomorrow, let you know if I find anything."

"I love you, honey."

"Love you, too."

After I disconnected the call, I fell over on the couch, stared up at the ceiling, and let my phone fall from my fingers. Now that my daily tasks had the appropriate checkmarks, I purposely blocked out everything—my mother, my job, my deadbeat father, missing sister, abandoned warehouses, handsome man from the alley—focusing on the soft rasps of my breaths. It took a good twenty minutes for the meditation to take hold, but finally, my brain blanked, and I managed to relax.

Like it had every night for the past couple of months, my body began to warm the longer I lay there, a sexual longing pulling me under. And no sooner did the heat begin to stir down low than the images of the man from the alley flashed into my brain. No matter how hard I tried to shut him out, there he was, lingering, ratcheting up that desperate need to feel those strong hands on my chilled skin, anything to warm me.

I had no idea what spurred these strange urges because I'd never had a strong sex drive. No, I wasn't some sappy virgin who was waiting for Mr. Right to come along and sweep me off my feet, but I definitely wouldn't mind a guy who knew how to work the tools he'd been given. Unfortunately, I'd yet to find him. But hope bloomed eternal, right?

Tilting my head back, I reached over and pulled open the end table/nightstand drawer, retrieved my trusty vibrator before flipping off the lamp.

Unlike any of my ex-boyfriends, my battery-operated boyfriend had fantastic stamina and damn good aim, and it'd come in handy these past few weeks.

Relaxing into the cushions, I closed my eyes, hoping to find that connection that linked me to the man in the alley. It wasn't that I really thought he was somehow reaching out to me telepathically because that shit didn't happen. However, I did enjoy the fantasy of it all, my imagination having been hijacked by sinful thoughts of the handsome savior.

I allowed one hand to slide over my chest as I lay in the dark, tugging the T-shirt up to reveal my belly. My skin prickled with awareness, nipples hardening into points. My touch wasn't going to ignite the flames, but it was a start.

"Are you there?" I whispered, knowing I sounded like an idiot but too far gone to care.

When no one responded, I conjured images of the handsome man, remembering him exactly as he had been in that alley. Tall, dark, and deliciously dangerous. Though I tried to hang on to the image of his chiseled face, the most I saw these days was a blurred jaw, dark shades, and the sexy mohawk. I remembered the way that bullet had slammed into him, those strong fingers as they'd searched for the cut on the back of my head. God, I would give anything to feel his touch again.

"I wish you were here," I said softly, flipping on the vibrator and trailing it over my hip bone toward my center.

I wish I was there, too.

My eyes flew open as they did every time his voice echoed in my mind, just to ensure no one was in the room because those words sounded as though they'd been spoken directly into my ear. The dark cadence of his voice was so real I should've been able to reach out and touch him.

Content I was still alone, I closed my eyes once again.

"I wish I could feel your hands on me," I said softly. "It's the only thing I can think about anymore."

Let me hear you pleasure yourself, Orianna.

Of course I did his imaginary bidding, sliding the vibrator between my legs, grazing my clit. It was how it always started: me aware of the toy between my legs, my hand guiding it until, at some point, I would drift. Reality was replaced by fantasy, and in my head, I saw vivid images of the man. He was always kneeling between my legs, his tongue working magic against my pussy, making me moan and sigh.

And like usual, I wasn't sure how much time passed as he worked me over, taking me to the peak again and again before finally allowing me to barrel over the edge into the blissful abyss.

Unfortunately, the aftermath was the same as well. I opened my eyes, instantly missing the warmth I'd felt during those few brief moments when I was sure his hands, lips, and wicked tongue had been on my body.

Orianna?

The voice only sounded in my head, but it was so clear I shot up off the couch, snapped on the light, and stared around the tiny apartment. Aside from the bathroom, there was only one room, so I didn't have to look far to know I was alone.

I need you, Orianna. I don't want to go this alone anymore.

I scanned the empty room, wishing like hell he was there.

"I need you, too," I whispered softly, wondering if I'd finally drifted down that slippery slope into insanity.

4

ECLIPSE

———

My heart was racing, my breaths sawing in and out of my lungs as I lay in the dark, a fragile connection still lingering between me and Orianna.

I need you here with me, I relayed, relishing how she responded as though she knew who I was. As though it was possible she didn't think of me as a murderer, a male she should be scared of.

Like usual, the connection faded all too quickly, and I was left alone in my private quarters, wishing Orianna was there with me. Despite the fact I'd come during those brief moments of shared passion, my cock was still hard, still aching. It had been that way since the night I encountered her in that alley. Little had I known at the time, but I'd been face-to-face with my *amsouelot*. The human male had called her Amber, but that had been a case of mistaken identity. The female was none other than Orianna McKay, the elusive Amber's younger sister and my life mate.

No doubt, I hadn't made the best impression as far as first meetings went, what with killing the human and all. Most males probably opted for dinner and a movie as a means of making a first impression. Not me. Nope. I vividly remembered the shock on her face when I'd snapped that fucker's neck, sending him into Lucifer's waiting arms without an ounce of regret.

Well, that wasn't true. There was some regret. If I had it to do all over again, I would've ensured she was far, far away before I offed the bastard who'd threatened her life. But I would do it again, of that I had no doubt.

Sliding down into the bed, I closed my eyes, willing my body to relax long enough to catch a few z's.

L ater that evening, I was sitting in the third-floor living room, staring at the television screen and flipping the remote in my hand, when Aphotic appeared out of thin air. The sight of my brother made me grin, and not only because I was happy to see him.

Oh, no. It was the dusty Wranglers and the snazzy black felt hat on his head that gave me the most amusement.

"What the fuck are you wearing?"

Aphotic smirked and tugged on the brim of the hat. "You like?"

"I'm not sure I'd go that far." I motioned toward the hat. "Perhaps we should start calling you Tex."

"You could try," Aphotic countered, strolling over to peer at the television. "What're you watching?"

I glanced back at the screen and offered a one-shoulder shrug. "*Avengers.*"

"The new one?"

"No idea."

Honestly, I really didn't know because I'd spent more time staring into space than paying attention to what was happening on screen. My thoughts were stuck on the interaction I had with Orianna early this morning, right before I'd fallen asleep for the day.

"You should check it out," Aphotic stated, always ready and armed to recommend the next best television show or movie. It was a wonder he got anything done for all the time he spent in front of the TV.

"Yeah. Maybe." I clicked the remote to shut off the television. "What brings you by?"

"Obsidian summoned us."

Ah. Right. Family meeting to discuss the status of Kaj and his daughter.

"Hey, I've been meaning to ask…" I got to my feet. "How's Taayin doing?"

Aphotic frowned. "No idea. He's not working with me right now."

I stared blankly at my brother. "What? According to the schedule, he is."

"He was. Took off a couple of days ago. Said he was coming back here. He didn't?"

No, he hadn't. But that didn't surprise me. Ever since the shit that went down with Perfidious, the *lieterra* had made himself scarce. Since Asmia was here at the mansion, having moved officially into the role of Penelope's *ritarro*, Taayin was avoiding the place like the plague. I think it was safe to say he blamed the Fae for what went down.

"They'll figure it out," Aphotic said, clearly reading my mind.

"I damn sure hope so."

"Anyone else here yet?"

"Not that I've seen."

"Up for a beer?"

I grinned as I got to my feet. "Always."

We vanished, reforming in the underground bar.

"Shit!" Malak shouted. "Warn a guy, would ya? Scared the hell outta me."

I studied the male for a moment before glancing around. Considering we were all popping in and out at random times, it was rare to find someone who was surprised by the move. Generally, that meant they were trying to hide something.

"What're you doing down here?" I asked, not bothering to hide my curiosity.

Malak's eyes lowered. "Trying to find some peace and quiet."

"And your private quarters won't do the trick why?" Aphotic asked, making his way behind the bar.

When Malak didn't answer, I realized the male wasn't seeking solitude. "Who're you hiding from?"

Uncertain blue eyes shot toward the stairs. "Raksa."

"You're in luck. He's on patrol," I told him. "Won't be back till morning."

"Something going on with you and him?" Aphotic set a beer on the bar, then rested his forearms on the polished wood, giving Malak his undivided attention.

"Nothing like what's going on with your hat," Malak countered, grinning.

I chuckled while Aphotic preened. The male seemed quite fond of the cowboy duds. Made me curious as to what my brother would've morphed into if he'd been in, say, California rather than Texas.

Before we could launch into more digs on his clothes, voices sounded from the stairwell. A second later, Obsidian, Stygian, and Cimmerian appeared. Three sets of eyes instantly surveyed the scene as they approached.

"Glad you're here," Obsidian told Malak. "I need the *lieterras*."

Shadow's *ladeare* nodded, then pulled out his phone as he started toward the far end of the room.

Obsidian marched over to Aphotic, offered the male a back-slapping hug.

"You ever notice how much of a hugger he is?" I teased.

"Hey, I'm glad they're home," Obsidian said defensively, grinning ear to ear.

That was Obsidian for you. Always wanting the family together. Sometimes I figured he was more of a father figure than a brother, but since I hadn't seen my own father since the male turned me out to the warrior camp, perhaps that wasn't a bad thing.

"Where's—"

"I'm here," Shadow announced when he appeared.

"And—"

"Quit nagging," Piceous grumbled, taking form near the bar.

A round of laughter ensued.

"That only leaves the *lieterras*," Obsidian said, taking the beer Aphotic offered.

Once everyone had a drink in hand, we relocated to the seating area. I plopped down on the leather sofa, Cimmerian taking the spot beside me. Stygian planted himself at one of the high-tops, Obsidian pulling out a chair beside him.

Shadow and Piceous opted to stand, and Aphotic perched on the arm of the other sofa.

"So, what's this about?" Stygian prompted, clearly speaking to Obsidian while his attention was on Aphotic. "What the hell are you wearing?"

Aphotic merely laughed this time, tipping his hat in greeting. "Don't be jealous, brother."

"Jealous?" Stygian's smirk grew. "I was just wondering if we needed to man the door for the trick-or-treaters, 'cause that, my brother, is one helluva Halloween costume."

"Remember when he went through that John Travolta phase?" Piceous asked.

"Which one?" Cimmerian glanced at all the faces. "*Saturday Night Fever* or *Grease*? Because he did both."

The laughter ensued.

"What about his Vlad the Impaler era?" Shadow shook his head, grinning wide. "That mustache."

Aphotic was laughing as much as the others, clearly not at all bothered that they teased him. It was true, though, our youngest brother did go through phases.

Unfortunately, the laughter died off when footsteps sounded on the stairs. Taayin, Søren, Miklós, Decebal, Zadok, Theron, and Stian sauntered out of the stairwell, the *lieterras* scanning the room before joining us.

I watched Taayin, noticing the male's eyes traverse the entire space before he took a relieved breath. Probably worried he'd run into Asmia. I had no idea why those two remained on the outs. One would think Taayin would've been content to know the female was safe and not in the clutches of that demon. Instead, he seemed to be all hung up on the fact the female he loved was not his *amsouelot*.

"As you're all aware," Obsidian began, "Kaj showed up last night, looking for refuge for his daughter."

Obsidian went on to explain the high-level details of the vampire war taking place and the loss of their Alpha. No matter how many times I heard it, I couldn't help but think it sucked ass. The mere thought of any race being targeted for elimination was disheartening. Perhaps once we located all the *amsouelots* and ensured God wouldn't smite them down at any moment, we could help Kaj and his people.

"While I gave them permission to stay temporarily, I need everyone's approval to make it long-term."

That was Obsidian for you. We all looked to him as our leader, but he'd never been the kind to make major decisions without our input. Perhaps that was what made him best for the role. He didn't attempt to run things in a vacuum, knowing the best way to tackle the difficult issues was to be a united front.

"Is he planning to stay?" Stygian asked. "Or just his daughter?"

"I haven't had the chance to talk to him at length yet, but unless anyone objects, I'd like to offer refuge to both, regardless of whether he intends to stay."

"I don't see a problem with it," I told them. "He's always been there when we needed him."

Then, of course, there was the fact the male had bonded with one of the Fae. Granted, I wasn't going to give that thought voice because I respected the vampire. When Kaj was ready for us to know, I figured he'd share.

"Agreed," Stygian said.

"Do we know anything about the daughter?" Shadow questioned.

"Only the basics. She's young. Showed up on Kaj's doorstep a year ago when her mother died," Obsidian explained. "Killed by a group of shadow beasts."

"While I sympathize with her situation, I'd like to know more about her," Piceous noted. "We've got two humans in residence right now, plus Penelope's here. If we're lucky, all of our *amsouelots* will be here very soon. Seems we should know what we're getting ourselves into before we invite two vampires to live with us."

I glanced from face to face, listening as the others weighed in. The vote hung precariously at the fifty-fifty mark, those who knew Kaj not batting an eye while the others were a bit more cautious.

"Søren, can you do some digging?" Stygian asked his *lieterra*.

"Of course."

"Keep it on the DL," Obsidian instructed. "I have no idea what you might uncover, if anything, but it's for our eyes only."

Søren nodded. "Understood."

"In the meantime," Stygian continued, "I see no reason they can't stay here." He peered at Obsidian. "I do think we should get Reidar's input since his *amsouelot* is currently residing with us."

Being that Winnie was human and mortal, Reidar would likely be doubly cautious.

Obsidian nodded. "I'll meet with him when we're done here. Now that we've got that figured out, how about an update."

All eyes shifted to me first, and I exhaled heavily. "I've yet to make contact with the female again," I admitted. "However, we do know where she's currently living and working. I've got Magnar keeping an eye on her as we speak."

"Do you have intentions of engaging?"

I glanced at each of my brothers. "It's a bit more complicated than a simple *Hi, how are ya.*"

"Because she witnessed you killing a human?" Stygian said.

I nodded, then cut my gaze to the floor.

And while my brothers went through their updates regarding their endless searches for the females they were destined to be with, I had to wonder if my *amsouelot* wouldn't be better off destined to someone else.

ASMIA

"Is there anything I can get you?" I offered, doing my best to keep from making eye contact with Penelope as I performed my duties as the female's *ritarro*.

"You could sit."

I could, yes. Or I could simply work off the restless energy that coursed through my veins.

Ever since Taayin took off to help in the search for the *amsouelots*, I'd been on edge, wondering if he would ever return to me. And I wasn't referring to the mission, either. From what I gathered from the updates provided to the *fiestreigh*, the males weren't in much danger aside from the expected encounters with demons. According to the meeting minutes, they spent the majority of their time searching amongst the humans, not trading bullets or blades with evil.

No, it wasn't his life I worried about. I feared his heart would be what never returned to me.

Oh, how I missed him. Every now and then, I would swear there was a cold ache in my bones brought on by his absence. But then I would shake it off because Taayin was not my *amsouelot*, so there were no physical aches from the distance between us. It was merely wishful thinking on my part.

However, the sorrow and grief were real, no doubt about it. My heart had been through the blender, and the only thing I wanted was the chance to talk to him, to figure out what I needed to do to fix things between us.

"Please, Asmia, sit. Catch me up on the gossip," Penelope prompted.

I had feared she would say that. However, as Penelope's *ritarro*, I could deny Obsidian's *ereswa* nothing. It was my honor and my duty to tend to Penelope's every need. Not that the female asked for much, which was both a blessing and a curse. Without something to do, I was left with far too much time to think. And since there was only one thing on my mind these days, the less solitary time I had, the better.

Penelope patted the leather cushion beside her. "Come on. You're making me tired with all your pacing."

Reluctantly, I made my way over.

"What's on your mind?" Penelope probed.

I sighed, a dramatic sound I'd been holding in for so long. On its heels, a sob escaped.

"Oh, Asmia," Penelope whispered, leaning over and putting her arm around my shoulders. "It's going to be all right. He'll be back soon."

"He won't," I countered, giving in to the comfort, allowing Penelope to embrace me.

"He will. He just needs some time."

That seemed to be the consensus these days. What I didn't understand was why he needed time away from me. Ever since Perfidious had manipulated my mind, it was as though Taayin didn't want to be near me. It wasn't like I had anything to do with that. I hadn't recognized the demon at the club, hadn't purposely given in to him. Yet I was the one being punished for it.

Sniffling, I forced myself to sit up. I accepted the tissues Penelope held out, taking the box and settling it in my lap. I popped one out. Then another. Two more for good measure.

"I'm fine, really."

"You're not, but you will be."

As was expected of me, I nodded and forced a smile. "If there's nothing else I can get you, I think I'll go down to the kitchen, see if they need any help."

Penelope nodded, her golden eyes full of understanding. It pained me to know I was dragging down the entire house. Their concern, their pity, they were more than I could bear, but I couldn't seem to get away from them.

"How about a movie before bed?" Penelope suggested. "We'll grab Winnie and Acadia."

I nodded. "Of course."

"Asmia, you know you can talk to me about anything, right?"

I knew that. I did. But the thought of burdening anyone with my problems, especially Penelope, made my heart ache. Penelope and Obsidian were happy, their lives together just beginning. Penelope was pregnant, for heaven's sake. The last thing she needed was for me to get all blubbery on her.

"I know. And I appreciate the offer," I said softly.

Penelope's disappointed sigh rang loudly in my ears as I slipped out of the library, making my way toward the stairs.

No sooner had I stepped off the last step than Taayin strolled around the corner. We both came up short, no words spoken between us. Not at first. He seemed as surprised to see me as I was him.

When he began walking again, his steps bringing him closer, my breath lodged in my throat. He was finally here, standing before me. Surely, I should say something. Anything. Except my voice wasn't working.

Taayin offered a nod of his head, then strolled right past me to the stairs. I turned to see him ascending them two at a time. He never looked back, and another piece of my heart splintered, the pain so strong I would've gone to my knees if Obsidian hadn't appeared. Insistent I would not look weak before him, I forced steel into my spine, then lifted my head.

"Good evening," he greeted, his eyes narrowing as they settled over me.

I smiled. "If you're looking for Penelope, she's in the library."

"I'm actually looking for Reidar. Have you seen him?"

"Not since the evening meal."

"Everything all right?"

I held my smile in place by sheer force of will. "Of course."

Clearly, he didn't believe me, but thankfully, Obsidian didn't press.

If he had, I would've crumbled like a house of cards.

OBSIDIAN

H unting down Reidar was quickly turning into a pain-in-the-ass mission. One would imagine the *ladeare* in charge of manning the schedule for the *fiestreigh* would be easily located. So not the case.

I was about to reroute to the library when I heard raised voices coming from the game room. Rather than waltz over, I paused on the far side, staring over the railing to see Reidar and Winnie going nose to nose, their anger and frustration palpable.

I'd heard in recent days that the pair of them were arguing nonstop, enough that others in the mansion were getting concerned. As I watched them, it was hard to believe they'd only been together a few short weeks, and Reidar was convinced she was his *amsouelot*. Not that destined souls wouldn't have normal, everyday problems like all couples, but I found it difficult to believe they couldn't find common ground.

"I need you to make a decision, Reidar. And I need you to do it now."

Reidar thrust his hand through his hair. "I'm not doing this right now. In case you forgot, I've got a job to do."

"Oh, I haven't forgotten," Winnie snarled. "It's all you ever do. I'm starting to think you love your job more than you love me."

It wasn't my place to say anything, nor was it my place to interfere, so I slipped down the hall to the library. I peeked inside to see my *ereswa* curled up on the leather sofa with a book in her hands. It hadn't been all that long ago when she'd first come to this room, and I'd introduced her to some of the *fiestreigh*. Hard to believe only a few months had passed since then, yet so much had changed.

"What's got your attention, *ayreme*?" I asked as I closed the door behind me.

The smile she gifted me with was one I longed to see on her face every day. I'd made it my mission to ensure she had every reason to smile because she completed me in ways I'd never imagined.

"I thought you were meeting with your brothers." Penelope set the book down on the table.

"All taken care of."

"And Kaj and Bijou? They're staying?"

"For now." I eased onto the sofa beside Penelope, then shifted her into my lap without preamble, a move I was sure she was getting used to.

She giggled as she got situated.

"I was hoping to talk to Reidar. That's why I'm up here."

Penelope's eyes shifted to the door. "I think there's trouble in paradise."

"Sounds like it."

My *ereswa* pressed her cheek to my shoulder. "I'm starting to wonder if Reidar moved a little too quickly with her."

I was wondering the same thing.

"I've tried talking to Winnie, but..." Penelope exhaled heavily. "I can tell she's not happy here. I've tried my best to include her, but I think she's homesick."

I rested my hand over the gentle swell of Penelope's belly. I still couldn't believe we were having a baby. That in only a few short months, our little male or little female would be in the world. There was no denying I was also terrified by the prospect of bringing a child into existence. As far as I was aware, a babe hadn't been born to angels on Earth before. And though pregnancies were extremely rare, the survival rate was good. I wasn't worried in that regard. Mostly.

However, we'd yet to figure out the logistics of the birth. Considering there were no healers within the *fiestreigh*, I had some concerns. It seemed logical that we should have someone available to assist if there were issues. I'd yet to discuss those worries with Penelope, though. The last thing I wanted was to cause any unnecessary anxiety.

"What's on your mind?" Penelope's hand rested over mine.

I pressed my lips to her forehead. "Just reminding myself how lucky I am."

"You are that," she teased. "On a serious note, is there anything I should know about vampires now that Bijou is here and possibly staying for a while?"

"Such as?"

"For starters, how do they feed?"

"The same as you and I."

"From the Fae?"

"Technically, they feed from their own kind, but yes, they can utilize the Fae."

"What about humans? Should I be worried about Oliver?"

I chuckled. "I'm not sure anyone should be worried about him. As far as feeding, Bijou would need stronger blood than Oliver's to survive, so no, I don't think you have to worry about that."

"I guess I should make sure there's a male Fae in residence at all times."

"Probably a good idea."

"Speaking of feeding..." Penelope's fingers trailed over my neck.

My cock swelled from the gesture alone. "Are you hungry, *ayreme*?"

"I'm eating for two, remember?" Penelope repositioned so that she was straddling my hips.

I growled softly as I nuzzled her neck. "Then, by all means, you should take what you need from me."

While she proceeded to do just that, I contributed, too, providing the orgasms we both needed.

The rest we could worry about in the coming weeks. Right here, right now, satisfying this female was the only thing that mattered.

5

ORIANNA

As was always the case, life seemed to get in the way of my best-laid plans. Hence the reason it took three days before I could wrangle the time necessary to scout the abandoned warehouse Jed had told me about.

Feeling like an idiot, I leaned to my left and peered through the grimy window, attempting to catch sight of someone inside. What I glimpsed was nothing more than rows of empty metal shelving units, half a dozen wooden pallets, a step ladder, and what appeared to be the corpse of a forklift, its metal guts strewn across the chipped and scarred concrete in front of it.

Fourth building and, unless I counted finding three homeless men asleep in one of the buildings, fourth disappointment.

I was quickly coming to the conclusion that Jed was a dick.

There hadn't been a soul at the warehouse he'd sent me to, nor at any of the others I'd walked by on my way back to the main drag, except for the one providing shelter to the vagabonds. And I didn't simply peeping-Tom it as I passed by. Oh, no. I could add breaking and entering to my list of mad skills. After all, I didn't expect some underground gambling ring to set up shop in plain sight. Nor did they seem to have a preference for cold and dreary, either.

But the Telluride PD would be happy to know there were no illicit games taking place under their noses. At least not out here.

Which meant I was back to square one, a place I seemed to have frequented far too often in the past six years. A place I was quickly growing tired of being.

With a sigh, I continued to make my way back to Colorado Avenue, peeking in more windows, filling with more disappointment. By the time my destination was in sight, I was cold and tired. Not to mention completely disillusioned.

"Well, now, don't you look tasty."

Spinning toward the voice coming from behind me, I dropped my hand to my thigh and the knife I had sheathed beneath my skirt. The instant my eyes landed on the man, fear rippled in my throat. There was something eerie about him, and not merely in the creeper sort of way, either. There was a menace that seemed to surround him like algae, thick and nasty.

It wasn't so much his appearance. Aside from the fact he was wearing all black and his face seemed oddly pale, he looked relatively normal as far as facial features went. Maybe even a bit more attractive than was usual for men. However, that underlying ominousness did nothing for his appeal.

"Sorry, buddy, not interested," I told him, grateful my voice was stronger than my wobbly knees.

Feigning a casualness I didn't feel, I turned around and continued walking. Heavy footsteps sounded behind me, and I knew the man was following. It took everything in me not to take off at a run.

"Where you headin' off to in such a hurry?" he taunted, his voice closer than before.

"To see my boyfriend," I lied. "He's up here waiting for me."

The man chuckled, the sound dripping with contempt. "Sweetness, didn't anyone ever tell you it's not nice to lie?"

Without looking back, I called out over my shoulder, "Didn't anyone ever tell you not to be an asshole?"

"Ah, honey, I'm just trying to be friendly. Don't you want to be friends?"

Hoping he'd leave if I ignored him, I quickened my pace, grateful I'd opted for my leather high-tops tonight.

The main street was only two blocks up. Not that there were many people out yet, considering it was still relatively early for a Friday, but if I were lucky, a car or two would drive by and send this guy elsewhere.

I cleared one entire block, my destination so close I could taste it, when I caught sight of another person stepping out of the shadows. From this distance, I couldn't make them out, but based on their smaller, thinner build, I got the feeling it was a woman who was now heading straight for me.

Shit.

Had I been anyone else, anywhere else, I might've considered this a good thing. However, luck had never been on my side. Not once in all the time I'd been alive, so why in the world would it be now?

"You did well, Harlan," the woman crooned, her face cast in the shadow from the streetlamp behind her. "She's certainly lovely. I can see why they're looking for her."

They? What the hell was she talking about?

I stopped on the sidewalk, considered my options. Directly in front of me was the woman, behind me the man. To my right, an abandoned warehouse, its identical twin across the street on my left. I had nowhere to go unless I went around or through one of the two people getting closer by the second. My odds of laying them both out at once were slim to none, but taking one out wasn't out of the realm of possibility.

"Look how pretty she is," the woman said as she approached.

Doing my best to keep my distance but hoping to get a glimpse of the woman, I sidestepped, moving into the street. She turned with me, stopping as though gauging my next move. The man, on the other hand, was still advancing, only a few yards separating us.

"I don't have any money," I told them, attempting to move toward the main street and keep a safe distance between me and these assholes.

"We don't want your money, honey," the man said, his voice ringing with amusement.

Of course he would get off on intimidating a woman, wouldn't he?

"We just want to talk," the woman said.

"About what? The weather?" I snapped, feeling a rush of adrenaline now that I was gaining ground on the main road.

"Funny," the woman retorted.

"I wasn't going for funny," I bit out.

I turned to run, but before I could get my feet to meld with the pavement, the man was in front of me.

Like *directly* in front of me. Without passing by me.

Frowning, I peered over my shoulder. What the fuck?

My feet faltered, causing me to stumble as I tried to put space between me and Harry Houdini here. And if that hadn't been weird enough, I blinked and the woman was standing beside me. As though she'd abracadabra'd to my side.

"We won't hurt you, pretty girl," the woman said, her voice oddly seductive.

"Then what do you want?" I insisted. "And don't tell me it's to talk."

The woman lifted her head, her black eyes glittering with evil. I knew I needed to run, but my legs wouldn't get with the program, as though I'd been submerged in quicksand.

"You're looking for your sister, aren't you?" The woman's pale face tilted to the side, sinister eyes studying me.

Suddenly, I stopped fighting. "How do you know that?"

"Amber, is it?" the man taunted.

I tried to keep my eyes on both of them, but it wasn't working. They were moving around me, circling and assessing.

"Tell you what," the woman prompted, "meet me at this party, and I'll tell you exactly where you can find your dear sister, Amber."

"What party?"

The woman conjured a small card, passed it over.

I snatched it, making sure there was no skin-to-skin contact. I glanced at the address jotted in small block letters.

"Do you know her?" I demanded. "My sister."

"I'll tell you everything you need to know when I see you. Party starts in half an hour. Don't be late."

Before I could launch another question, they both vanished into thin air. I spun around, peering into the shadows, trying to see which way they'd gone.

Because there was no way in hell I would believe they simply went up in smoke.

Nope.

No way.

ECLIPSE

After chowing down at the evening meal, then checking in with the *fiestreigh* in the war room, I met up with Magnar to get an update on Orianna.

Looking not at all happy about being pulled in from the field, the male relayed what I'd come to expect: Orianna was working at night, sleeping during the day, and for the past few days, she'd done nothing else, her little Subaru POS still parked in the same spot it had been in for the past three weeks because she preferred to walk to her destinations.

I already knew all of that without ever leaving the mansion.

Granted, that didn't mean I should be sitting on my thumbs. I knew I needed to be out there, spending some time following Orianna, instigating our formal introduction, but as had been the case for the past few weeks, I couldn't bring myself to do it.

Not because I didn't want to engage with her. I wanted that more than my next breath, and I'd proven as much with our early-morning telepathic interactions. It was a risk to slip into her mind, but I'd taken it time and time again. The other morning, I'd even gone so far as to tell her I couldn't keep going on like this. A moment of weakness on my part, but that didn't make it any less true.

The problem was, I had killed a man in front of Orianna, and I seriously doubted the female had any desire to mix it up with the likes of me. Just because she thought about the male who saved her in that alley did not mean she wanted to spend time with me. On the other hand, our interactions were heating up, and she seemed to be reaching out to me more, sparking more hope than I had any right to have.

So, once again, I had Magnar out monitoring Orianna's movements while I sat around on my ass, pretending to chill. Never mind the fact that chilling would require my brain to stop racing a million miles a minute, something it showed no signs of doing anytime soon.

Movement in my peripheral vision had me glancing over from my spot on the sofa in the sunroom.

"Where're you headed off to?" I asked Kaj when the vampire strolled by.

Kaj stopped, turned, stared up at me as though assessing. Always assessing, that one. Or maybe it was a trait all vampires possessed because I'd yet to meet one who didn't do it.

He must have come to a decision, because Kaj slowly ascended the steps, paused at the top.

"I need to check in." Kaj's eyes briefly darted to the television before landing on me again. "Maybe you want to go with me."

"Where?"

"Telluride. Vampire club."

I grinned as I sat up straight. "Vampire club? In Telluride? Right."

"Don't believe me, angel?"

Maybe I did, maybe I didn't. With Kaj, I never knew what was real and what was fiction. I'd heard stories from the vampire that I knew were a load of horse shit, others morbidly real. Either way... "What's the name of the place?"

"The Dungeon."

Okay, quick with the answer. Likely truth.

"Don't worry your pretty little head, angel. We keep all our clubs on the QT."

Seriously doubtful. Humans were a nosy bunch, and try as we might, no amount of sticking to the shadows had ever kept us completely anonymous. The rule was angels and vampires were to coexist with humans; however, we were to maintain our anonymity at all costs. For the most part, my brothers and I had managed, though not even angels were perfect. As for vampires ... yeah, they'd overstepped that boundary centuries ago.

I got to my feet. "You're telling me there are no humans at this club?"

"Never said that, but I assure you, they leave happy come morning, only good memories escorting them out."

While I wanted to believe all vampires used their whole mind-scrub thing to keep the humans oblivious to the fact they walked amongst them, I had to wonder how many humans were intimately aware of the marks they wore on their necks for days after a trip to a fang-banger club. Considering their numbers, it was no longer feasible for vampires to exist without being embedded in human society. Lucky for them, they were relatively good at blending. More so than angels, anyway.

"Sure, I'll go with you," I said, curious to see this Dungeon for myself. "Bijou coming with?"

Kaj shook his head. "Safer for her here."

"Want to take my ride?" I offered.

A wicked grin revealed the vampire's sharp fangs. "You gonna talk my ear off?"

"That was the plan." I conjured the keys, then dangled them in front of Kaj. "But I'll let you drive."

"In that case..." Kaj snagged the keys from my hand and disappeared.

I followed, materializing in the twelve-bay garage between my Bugatti Chiron Sport and Aphotic's Lamborghini Aventador SVJ. A second later, I was in the passenger seat, Kaj behind the wheel.

"Man, I've missed these toys." Kaj stroked the steering wheel like it was a woman. "Anything I should know about her?"

"Treat her like a whore, not your girlfriend."

"Ride her hard." The vampire grinned. "Got it."

The male was cautious as he backed my baby out of the garage. However, that was about as far as the prudence went. A quick flash of fangs was all I saw before Kaj slammed pedal to metal, the car shooting off like a missile.

"Vamps can't see through *dhira*," I noted.

"Not with my eyes, no."

Ah. So Kaj was using his ears to compensate for his lack of sight. Made sense considering the acuity of their hearing. While angels could hear far beyond the realm of humans, vampires' auditory perception bordered on supersonic.

"All right. Now that you got me, what do you want to know?" Kaj prompted as he steered into a winding turn, the car handling it with ease.

"For starters, how long are you planning to stay?"

"As long as you'll have me." Kaj's tone lost all amusement.

"I thought you were seeking refuge for Bijou."

"She's my main priority, yes. And if that's all you and your brothers have to offer, I'll be outta your hair ASAP."

"And if we let you stay?"

"Then you'll have the full support of my resources for whatever your endeavors."

I considered that for a moment. We'd been attempting to

get the vampires to assist in locating the *amsouelots* but hadn't gotten much in the way of help lately. A few tips here and there, but nothing substantial. Definitely not anything that had helped to locate the remaining five.

"What'll your clans think about you shacking up with angels?" I asked.

"They'll think I'm doing what's necessary for the survival of my species." Kaj cut his eyes over briefly. "When I said our numbers are dwindling, it wasn't an exaggeration. I've lost upwards of ten thousand females in the past three months."

"Fuck," I hissed. "Man, I'm sorry."

"Yeah, me, too. They're targeting our females, eliminating our ability to procreate."

By *they*, I assumed Kaj was referring to the shadow beasts. Word on the Misplaced Halos board was that their numbers were growing rapidly, and Kaj had confirmed that.

"And what are you doing about it? To ensure the survival of your race, that is."

A disappointed sigh drifted my way before Kaj said, "Unlike your kind, we can't breed with humans."

I chuckled. "And you think we can?"

"I think you've got the ability to turn them."

Yeah. We did have that, though it wasn't as easy as the vampire probably believed. The only humans we were permitted to turn were *amsouelots*. And that required the human to die and be resurrected. I still wondered how Obsidian made it through. Just thinking about taking Orianna's life made my chest burn.

"But you can mate with Fae." I watched Kaj to gauge his reaction. I remembered the male's response to Acadia, had seen with my own eyes the longing on both their faces.

"Or so legend goes," Kaj quipped, "but you know those rumors are mostly bullshit."

True. Though human myths claimed vampires could turn humans into the undead, that wasn't even remotely accurate. While we were all God's children, the man upstairs was the one and only Creator, the only one capable of giving life. Not to mention, vampires were alive and breathing, the same as everyone else. Though it would've been a nifty parlor trick, I couldn't imagine a world where the bite of a vampire could create more. They had to go through the process like everyone else, and mating was restricted to within each race.

"Are you and Acadia a thing?"

Once more, Kaj cut a look my way. "Let's just say, if she'll have me, I'm hers."

The admission raised a dozen questions, most pertaining to Acadia's status within the *fiestreigh*. Like my brothers, I had come to care for the Fae within our ranks. Not only because they ensured our survival but because they'd become family.

"Just out of curiosity, are any of our males at risk? You know we have to feed from the Fae."

"I've got more willpower than most," Kaj stated. "But it won't hold out forever, no."

Great. Probably needed to get a warning to the males at the mansion.

"If you don't mind me asking," I continued, "what happened to the previous Alpha?"

Kaj's gaze shifted back to the road. "They resided at a camp in Seattle. During my last couple of days here, I got word they were under attack. I wasn't there to witness it, but the story is, Kardobahn killed forty beasts on his own before he succumbed to his injuries. The male had watched those fuckers tear his mate's throat out, as well as that of his two youngest sons. One of them was only six months old."

"Fuck." That sucked.

"Wiped out the whole clan before I could get there. The

Zenith and I were attacked shortly thereafter, my warriors slaughtered."

I knew the Zenith were the vampire's answer to the strongest males of their kind. The warriors who were tasked with protecting the Alpha.

"Who's at the helm? Who's leading the shadow beasts, that is?"

"My guess is the *trielair*. But I've yet to encounter any of them."

I couldn't remember the last time we'd come up against the *trielair*. I hoped they were all in Hell, bowing before their leader, not trolling the Earth for their next kill. However, it did make sense that they'd be leading the efforts to eliminate the vampires. Eevuhl, Mizuhree, and Aguhnee were the most vile, vicious creatures to have ever emerged from Hell. More so than Lucifer, even.

"We'll help you," I offered, unable to sit back, knowing the male's entire race was at risk, those he cared about being slaughtered.

Those celadon-green eyes shifted my way, a grateful smile reaching all the way to his eyes.

"So," I said, turning my attention to the windshield. "You going to drive this thing? Or just Miss Daisy it?"

A deep, rumbling laugh escaped the vampire before the car lurched forward on the dark, winding road.

"Better?"

I chuckled. "It'll do."

Ten minutes later, the car slowed as Kaj steered up a paved driveway. "One of the best-kept secrets in Telluride."

"This is a vampire club?" I asked. "I figured there'd be more gargoyles. And coffins."

Another chuckle from the vampire. "Owned and operated

by Darko and his mate, Talia. He's a first lieutenant, keeps track of the clans in this region."

"Looks like he does more than that," I noted as I climbed out of the car and studied the structure before me.

"Vampires like to have a good time, too." Kaj chuckled. "Come on. I'll show you."

As I followed the male up to the front doors, I let my senses scan the grounds. Though they were hidden relatively well, I was aware of six males guarding the perimeter, two more standing sentry near the house. All vampires, all armed to the teeth.

"We've had to ramp up our protection details for our mated females," Kaj explained as though reading my mind.

Kaj opened the front door, allowed me to step inside before him. I scanned the horde of bodies gyrating close together throughout the open area. While the outside resembled a residence, the interior lost the illusion. There were no separate rooms, no delineation within. There was a bar lining one entire wall, somewhere between seventy and eighty feet long, highlighted by neon green lights running the length of the shelves of bottles and manned by three males.

I caught the scent of both humans and vampires, the coppery stench of human blood combined with the familiar aroma of sex.

"Remember what I told you, angel. The humans are safe here. No need for you to protect them."

Giving Kaj the benefit of the doubt, I followed him through the throng, then up a short staircase to a second level. Before the vampire made it across the room, bodies began to rise, eyes lowering respectfully as Kaj led the way toward the back. I gauged their reactions, noting how those same vampires showing respect to the Alpha were casting looks at one another as well as the male who got to his feet.

Something was definitely off about this whole thing.

A larger male appeared, his wide grin splitting his eerily handsome face, fangs flashing. He moved right up to Kaj and bowed quickly before the two embraced in a brother-like hug. Again, there was something off in the male's movements. As though someone or something had disrupted his plans for the evening.

"Darko, I'd like to introduce you to Eclipse. Eclipse, meet Darko."

Unlike humans, vampires and angels didn't use the customary handshake for greeting. Instead, we both nodded our heads, eyes locked.

"Angel," Darko acknowledged, his voice deep and rich, eyes assessing—yeah, definitely a vampire thing.

So I was the disruption. Evidently, the male hadn't anticipated Kaj bringing an angel to their barbecue.

"Vampire." I glanced back at Kaj. "Mind if I check out the place?"

When the male nodded, I made my exit, leaving the vampires to their business while I did a little reconnaissance of my own.

6

KAJ

It had been years since I'd stopped by this particular establishment. Still looked and smelled the same, as did the male who owned it. The difference was the number of bodies seated around Darko, the males armed with blades and bullets, decked out in leather and looking like they had some training. Not enough based on the fact the two males at the end were leaning over the rail in their attempt to snag the attention of a female.

"Is something wrong?" I asked Darko, noting something off about the male.

Darko's smile remained intact. "You didn't mention you were bringing a plus one."

"Problem with that?"

"You brought an angel." Darko all but spat the word out.

"I did." Since I had no intentions of explaining myself to the male, I peered over at his mate. "You're looking lovely as always, Talia."

As was custom, the female curtsied before me.

Unlike Kardobahn, I wasn't all that keen on the formal customs; however, I'd long ago listened to the wisdom of my elders. If and when the time came for me to rule his race, shucking custom was the equivalent of making all males believe they were equal, when in truth, the race wouldn't survive if that were the case.

I was learning quickly, having been thrust into the role after my father's demise. Needless to say, these past few months had required patience as I dealt with not only the slaughter of my people but their underhandedness as well.

"How's Bijou?" Darko asked, motioning me toward seating in the back.

"As well as can be expected," I answered, taking a seat and ensuring my back was to the wall. "I think she still hates me for forcing her to leave Georgia."

"I can imagine. But she's safer here. I assume she's close by."

The comment seemed out of character for Darko, but I chalked it up to concern. We were all dealing with a wealth of devastation. It made sense they were looking out for one another.

"She's safe," I said, watching Darko until the male met my stare. "It's my understanding you've got some rogues in the area."

His wide shoulders squared, a defensive move that gave me the answer I was looking for.

"We've gotten word of a few, yes. However, they're being taken care of."

"In what manner?" I glanced around the club, my senses scanning vampire and human alike.

"As of right now, they're being held on charges of treason."

My eyes narrowed, once again settling on the vampire. "Held where?"

"There's a reason this place was dubbed the Dungeon. We've got a handful of cells belowground."

Which explained the additional sounds I wasn't able to place.

"And who's seeing to them in the meantime?"

"I've got males rotating in and out, twenty-four-seven. I assure you, they're safer here than out there."

"How do you figure?"

"You're not the only one who takes offense to traitors, *phaal.*"

I would hope not.

"But I hope you aren't here only on business," Darko continued. "Be a waste to ignore the pleasures laid out before you."

There was only one pleasure I had any interest in. For the past eighteen months, I'd refrained from taking a female— human or vampire. Of course, feeding was a different sort of beast. It wasn't like I could ignore the biological function that kept me alive.

"Perhaps I could find someone who pleases you," Darko offered, motioning a human female over.

I shook my head. "Absolutely not." I pinned the male with a stare. "If you knew anything about me, you'd know I don't partake of humans."

"My apologies," the male said quickly. And while his words were apologetic, the gleam in his eye was not.

Not that I was surprised by the blatant disrespect. I'd

encountered plenty from the males of my race in recent months. As with any aristocracy, there were those who resented the families who'd held power through the centuries. Being that I was Kardobahn's oldest son, I was the heir to the throne, so to speak. And now that I was stepping into my role as Alpha, there were plenty who would prefer to see me in the ground like my father.

Fortunately for them all, I had no intention of being overtaken anytime soon. Not by death and certainly not by some misguided vampire.

ORIANNA

Because it went along with the whole social thing, I had never been big on parties.

Too many people, too much noise, everyone pretending to be someone they weren't, all in an effort to get their fix, whatever that might be. Drugs, booze, sex. They were all vices, and parties were where everyone congregated to sate theirs.

It looked like tonight's event was not the exception.

After finding those abandoned warehouses really abandoned, I figured for sure I would go back to my apartment empty-handed. Of course, the weirdos I'd encountered had once again given me the gift of hope. And while I seriously doubted the woman was trustworthy, I didn't have the option of being choosy these days. I'd been down this road a hundred times over in my search for answers. It hadn't taken long to realize I could leave no stone unturned. Even then, I always seemed to be one step behind my sister.

One day, I thought. One day this pursuit would lead me right where I was meant to be. I only hoped that wasn't a nursing home.

It all started when my mother was brutally attacked, left for dead in an alleyway not too far from the hospital where she'd worked as a triage nurse in our hometown of Oklahoma City. Kinda ironic that Elizabeth McKay had spent all her time saving people's lives only to find herself barely clinging to her own with no one around to help her. The incident was chalked up to a tragic case of wrong place, wrong time, a tragedy that left my mother confined to a wheelchair, the lower half of her body paralyzed and useless.

Random, they'd said.

Pure and utter bullshit.

According to the worthless detectives who'd closed the case with minimal effort, my mother had been an arbitrary victim in a personal attack gone horribly wrong.

First of all, what attack went right? It was an attack. That bitter, nasty word did not roll off the tongue easily. Secondly, how many muggers skipped over the pocketbook full of cash, hands glittered with expensive jewelry in lieu of beating a defenseless woman to a pulp? None? Yeah. That was my thought, too.

Of course, that was only the first of many unfortunate incidents to trickle through my family. Over the years, my father had endured countless injuries at the hands of those *random* attackers. Or so he claimed. I had stopped believing in coincidence after the third time. By the tenth, I knew there was a reason.

And those events had ignited the tragedy that was my life.

In an effort to shield his children—or so he claimed—Erik McKay had convinced my grandmother to spring for boarding school. With our education dealt with, he packed my sister and me up, shipped us off, and officially washed his hands of us. Someone probably should've told him safe was a relative term because uprooting our lives and forcing us to leave our mother had resulted in something else entirely. While Erik had resumed his day-to-day as a licensed plumber and his nightly rounds with booze and cards, Amber and I were left to fend for ourselves.

Those two kids who'd suffered unnecessarily had done what any tragedy-stricken adolescent would do. We went off the rails, seeking solace in booze and sex, looking for anyone to bestow even a smidgeon of acceptance upon us and failing miserably.

Never one to rock the boat, I didn't put up a fight. At twelve, I hadn't had much of a say in anything I did, so I went along with the plan. As for sticking to the straight and narrow … yeah, that was a no-go. Unfortunately, Amber—fifteen when this all went down—was the one who veered too far off the path to find her way back. By the time I was old enough to help my sister, it was too late. Amber had disappeared.

In pursuit of my troubled sibling, I'd traipsed across the US and back, through big cities and small towns, following one failed lead after another. And here I was, the cataclysmic result of human incompetence, the only one sound enough to make the effort. My mother was barely coherent, still suffering thanks to injuries from the accident, along with her addiction to prescription meds. The gifts from that random attacker just seemed to keep on coming.

Of course, my father was likely the biggest fuckup of us all. Erik had disappeared off the grid completely four years ago, abandoning his job and his wife in lieu of running from the mob his gambling addiction had gotten him indebted to. As for Amber ... well, I had no clue what she was up to because my sister was MIA, likely taken by those same goons out to make an example of our father.

The fate of my family had structured my destiny, sent me on this never-ending search. Every day when I woke tired and lonely, I vowed I would continue my pursuit until I found Amber—dead or alive. Once I did that, I would go after the assholes responsible for destroying my entire world and put them in the ground, where they belonged.

Was Amber here like that woman claimed? I seriously doubted it. Luck wasn't something I relied on because it had failed me time and time again. The most I could hope for was that these people might shed some light on the situation, tell me where to look next so I could one day drag my sister back to our mother and give her what-for.

I paused as the sidewalk gave way to fancy pavers, painstakingly laid by hand, herringbone style, to form the long driveway—a mere introduction to the monstrous estate that sat grandly before me, designed to both intimidate and beguile. With night in full bloom, the lights were on, strategically placed to highlight and accent. I was impressed, no reason to deny it. Perhaps envious.

While I stood there, admiring the splendor derived from more money than sense, I thought about the woman who told me to come here. There was something off about her, but I couldn't quite put my finger on what it was. Aside from the David Copperfield routine, that was.

Perhaps by coming here, I was proving the one thing I'd denied all along. Maybe I was an idiot after all.

But I was a persistent idiot, if anything.

Figuring what the hell, I pushed forward. There was a fifty-

fifty chance whoever resided within these walls knew where my sister was.

As I strolled up to the front doors of the two-story mansion with its modern charm and lush landscape, I couldn't help but wonder why random strangers would be invited to parties like this. Based on the volume of high-end vehicles angled in the designated spaces on the circular drive, this was a shindig for the rich and famous. Considering there was no one lingering outside, I assumed it was well underway, which worked to my benefit.

As I made my way toward the wide front steps, I didn't encounter a soul, which was as much a relief as it was a surprise. No one to question why I was there, no one to scrutinize my attire. I doubted my casual ensemble was appropriate for a gala, but it would have to do for tonight. I didn't have the time nor the inclination to backtrack in an effort to blend. In my defense, the woman hadn't mentioned a dress code.

Before I reached the front steps, I paused, sensing someone out there, staring back at me. Figuring there were security guards monitoring the grounds, I glanced around but saw no one.

A flash of yellow caught my attention. I squinted in the dark, attempting to make out what it was.

"Oh, God," I whispered, my breath catching in my throat.

Eyes. Those were glowing eyes peering back at me. While I couldn't make out the details, I sensed it was human. Too tall to be an animal.

I found myself trapped, held there momentarily by some invisible force. My heart pounded in my chest, anxiety replacing determination as fear blossomed hot inside me.

And just like that, the feeling disappeared as though released like air from a balloon.

Exhaling heavily, I shook off the weirdness. Likely some

drunk guest using the foliage as the facilities, and here I was thinking it was something ominous.

The distinct thump of bass startled me, drawing my attention to the front doors.

It was now or never.

I was standing on the bottom step when one of the two doors flew open, and a large guy stumbled out, laughing uproariously. His bloodshot eyes briefly met mine before another snort of laughter escaped.

Quick reflexes were the only thing to keep me from being trampled as he marched down the stairs at an angle. I turned to watch only to see him trip over one of the stone pavers surrounding the bushes. He nearly went ass over teakettle, saved when his palms crashed into the concrete.

Which seemed to amuse him all the more.

"It's time to get you home, you jackass," a man said, appearing at the door a second later. He smiled down at me, too. "Have fun in there. One hell of a party."

Yeah, it looked like it.

"Come on, you lightweight," the man said to the other. "Upsy daisy."

While the two rambled incessantly on their way down the path, I scaled the steps to the open door.

Once I cleared the threshold, I closed the door behind me and turned to survey the scene. The house looked nothing like I expected based on the exterior. There were stained concrete floors, huge stone pillars holding up the ceiling two stories above. Oddly enough, there were no windows, only solid stone walls, which meant the exterior was merely a shell, a facade to hide the depravity that took place within.

The music blared, seeming to come from all directions, and there were people everywhere. Some lingered against the walls, engaged in God only knew what, while others swayed and gyrated on what I assumed was a dance floor.

Good news was, my attire wouldn't be an issue.

My attention was drawn to the second level, only a few steps higher than the main floor. It spanned the space, offering the occupants a higher vantage point to watch the debauchery. And that was the only way to describe the chaos. This was a den of seduction and sin, and those in residence were completely oblivious to everything except each other.

It felt like another dimension, and I wondered how my sister had found this place. *If*, in fact, she was there.

Something told me the woman who'd given me the tip didn't have a clue who Amber McKay was, but as I'd told my mother I would do, I had no choice but to follow up.

After all, it seemed to be my destiny.

No matter how much it truly sucked.

7

ECLIPSE

As I stood near the back wall, surveying the humans and vampires, the hair on the back of my neck stood up, my skin tingling with warning. As usual, I expanded my senses, allowing them to spread out over the twenty thousand square feet before me. I picked through the noises and smells until I located the anomaly. The instant I made the connection, my heart kicked in my chest.

I felt more than saw the female descend onto the club floor, smiling as though she belonged. She raptly held my attention as she moved with purpose toward the bar, flagged down a bartender, and ordered a gin and tonic.

She didn't look like a gin girl. No. More like ... hmm. I would've pegged her for one who liked a good, stout lager like I did. But, as they said, opposites did attract, right?

As I remained on the perimeter of the space, I wondered what the odds were that I would've stumbled upon her tonight. Here, of all places. Hell, it wasn't until a month ago that we'd managed to nail down an address for the elusive Orianna McKay. Then again, technically, Orianna hadn't had one until she moved into the five-hundred-square-foot furnished apartment in the heart of Telluride after taking a job at a local convenience store.

Now she was lingering in a vampire club.

Question was, how the hell had she found the place? More importantly, what were her intentions now that she was there? Clearly she didn't realize what she'd stumbled upon; otherwise, she would've run for her life.

With drink in hand, Orianna strolled through the mass of bodies, heads beginning to turn, nostrils flaring in anticipation. After all, vampires had a keen sense of smell to go along with their other heightened senses, and this female was fresh blood. My fangs tingled with the urge to feed, something I'd put off for far too long. Considering I couldn't stand the touch of another female, I didn't have much of a choice, now did I?

As the female weaved through the masses, I admired her pouty lips, long lashes, a nose slightly tipped upward. Dressed more like a teenager than a grown woman in her short, pleated black skirt and skintight, long-sleeve, red T-shirt, she made my mouth water. I even found the black leather tennis shoes an odd yet appealing accessory. She certainly wasn't like the other females here, dressed in barely there dresses and four-inch heels. No, Orianna was far more alluring as she was.

I had to give her credit. She was quite adept at pretending to blend when she most definitely did not. Even her casual brush-offs seemed kind, though she couldn't possibly know the male she just waved off wanted to sink his fangs into her neck.

Then again, it was good for all of them that she wasn't cozying up to this crowd. Due to the fact I'd already bonded with her during our encounter in the alley two and a half months ago, I couldn't promise I wouldn't bring the place down in a crumble of rock and dust if I caught sight of a male getting handsy.

"Looks like you've found something interesting."

I only spared Kaj a brief glimpse as the vampire approached.

"Aw, hell," the male drawled. "She's the one, huh?"

She most definitely was.

"So tell me, what are the odds she'd show up here tonight?" Kaj mused.

"No fucking clue."

"You do realize this is probably the worst place for her to be, don't you?"

Oh, yeah. I knew.

"May I offer my vein," a human female suggested, stopping directly in my path.

I didn't look her way.

"Why don't I show you someone who'll take you up on that," Kaj told her. "You good here?"

Though I nodded, I wasn't sure how much truth there was in that answer. I was in caveman mode at the moment. The only thing I wanted to do was throw Orianna over my shoulder and whisk her off anywhere but here. The primal male inside me was eager to get her alone, strip her down, and feel those long legs wrapped securely around my hips. As far as I was concerned, that was the only way to sate these intense urges, to relieve the pent-up frustration.

"I'll check back in a little while. Stay outta trouble," the vampire said as he motioned the human blood bank in the opposite direction.

Moving toward my *amsouelot*, I inched past a male sinking his fangs into the neck of a female. Curious, I reached into the male's mind. I found the vampire was directing thoughts of euphoria into the female's frontal lobe, rewiring her brain to believe their intimate interaction was about sex, not feeding. I didn't approve of compelling humans to do our bidding, but as long as the vampire wasn't dropping bodies in his wake, I figured it really wasn't my place to intervene. After all, vampires weren't in the business of drawing attention to themselves any more than angels were.

"No, thanks," the soft voice sounded, drawing Eclipse's attention. "I'm actually looking for someone."

"How do you know you haven't found him, baby?" a male remarked.

Remember whose house you're in, angel.

My gaze shot over to Darko, who was standing at the railing on the second level. The male was watching me intently, clearly reading my body language.

Stay out of my head, vampire.

A devilish smirk was the vampire's response.

It took effort, but I gave a curt nod, assuring the vampire I wouldn't cause trouble. Provided this asshole understood Orianna was not on the dessert menu tonight. Not for him, at least.

Figuring now was the perfect time for my path to cross with the oblivious female, I purposely moved to intercept and stopped as Orianna did her best to shrug off the irritant hoping to latch on to her vein.

"Leave," I ordered the vampire.

The male turned to face me, likely gauging his chances of taking me down. He must've realized they were slim to none because he offered a hiss but backed away, nonetheless.

Light blue eyes lifted slowly, perusing my six-foot-six-inch frame before coming to a stop on my face. I waited patiently for recognition to dawn, preparing myself for the repercussions. This was the first time we'd come face-to-face since the incident in the alley, the time when I had killed the human male who'd been threatening her.

Her pretty face remained expressionless, though I saw the curiosity there. Orianna knew who I was, but there was no fear, no desire to flee.

A smile would've revealed my fangs, so I held off, content merely to observe the heat I recognized in her eyes. It was what was known as *amnigh*, a phenomenon that affected *amsouelots* —souls destined to be together, their divine decree sealed by the Fates. Ever since our initial meeting, our souls had begun the dance, attempting to pull the two of us back together. Because so much time had passed, I knew it would increase tenfold before the night was over.

"Looking for someone?" I prompted, studying her lovely face, memorizing every soft, alluring angle.

Orianna took a sip of her drink, her smile sweet yet blasé, as though my mere presence wasn't affecting her. "As a matter of fact, I am."

"Who?"

"What business is it of yours?"

For the past few weeks, I'd been fearing our next encounter. After I'd killed the male in the alley and she'd run for her life, I had expected Orianna to scream bloody murder when I formally introduced myself. Instead, she was considering me with skeptical yet inquisitive eyes.

Two could play that game.

"I figure you've got two options, *sezari*. Either you're forthcoming with some information or I'll simply compel it out of you."

"Compel?" She snorted, a sound that was oddly endearing. "Is that code for something? Torture, perhaps?"

My lip curled in a smirk I couldn't help while my gaze dropped to the pulse in her neck. "Though tempting, not necessary."

"You won't hurt me," she said.

My eyes snapped back to hers. "And how do you know that?"

She turned to face me more fully, both hands holding her glass. "I remember you from the alley. If you wanted to do me harm, you would've done it then, when you killed that asshole."

Her comment caught me off guard. She didn't seem at all bothered by the fact I'd taken a life.

Since I couldn't lie to her, I figured there was no reason to pretend otherwise. "You're right, I won't hurt you." However, she was the only one who was safe from me.

"How's the shoulder, by the way?"

I frowned, confused. "Shoulder?"

"You were shot that night."

I glanced down at my shoulder, remembered the blazing pain I'd felt when that bullet had struck me. The worst had been Obsidian removing it, knowing my pain was transferred to Penelope in the process.

"It's fine," I told her, meeting her gaze.

"I'm glad to hear it."

Despite her bravado, when I took one step toward her, Orianna moved back. I continued my pursuit until she was backed against the iron bars of a cage currently imprisoning two human males, who were making out like it was their last night on Earth.

"I didn't catch your name," she said softly, the words coming out as a rasp. "I'm Orianna McKay."

I could smell her. Not fear. Intrigue. She was a risk taker, and she was turned on by my nearness. Oddly, it stirred something deep inside me.

"And you are?" she repeated.

"Eclipse."

The female stared at me for the longest time before surprising me yet again.

"What's with the sunglasses?"

"Light sensitivity," I said easily.

"Yeah. Okay."

"Why're you here?"

"I'm looking for my sister."

"Amber?"

Her eyes narrowed. "How did you know that?"

"The asshole in the alley. He called you Amber."

She nodded, clearly accepting my answer.

"Why would your sister be here?"

"Someone told me she would."

"Who?"

She shrugged, then casually glanced around. "A woman I ran into. Told me she knew her. Gave me this address."

Ah, hell. She'd been lured here. Likely by a vampire who caught her scent and hoped to sample a taste before the night was over. Or worse. Now that we knew there was a faction of vampires who'd stepped over to the dark side, it was possible she was drawn here to be handed off to Lucifer's demons.

"Someone was fucking with you."

Orianna frowned. "Why would they do that?"

I stepped to the side, motioned toward the room. "Perhaps they wanted to ravish you in the melee?"

Her gaze swung from me to a female currently aligning her fangs with a male's carotid. She huffed a laugh. "Like I'd willingly participate in—"

From our position, there was no disguising what the vampire was doing.

When Orianna stepped closer to me, as though I would protect her from someone doing the same to her, a surge of adrenaline flooded my veins.

"What the hell is going on?" she whispered, turning her head to stare up at me.

"It's a vampire club," I told her, again aiming for transparency.

Those pretty eyes narrowed in disbelief. "Vampires? Seriously?"

I offered a slight shrug. "Look around, *sezari*. How else do you explain it?"

"Vampires don't exist," she argued, although she did turn her attention to the other patrons.

I allowed her a moment to take it all in, to witness first-hand the male currently feeding from a female, another with his hand thrust between a female's thighs, her eyes closed, mouth open as she rode the waves of orgasm. But it seemed to be the two females in the corner who caught Orianna's attention. Both were latched on to a male's neck while he writhed and squirmed beneath their onslaught.

"Still think they don't exist?" I asked, keeping my voice low.

"No," she said, spinning to face me. "They do not."

I shrugged again. "If you say so."

"If you're so damned convinced, prove it," she insisted, taking a step closer.

Yep, danger was her middle name.

I studied my *amsouelot*, admiring the steel in her spine. Despite the fact she was a foot shorter than me, as well as at least a hundred and twenty pounds or so lighter, the female didn't seem the least bit intimidated.

Figuring what the hell, I snagged the glass from her hand, set it on the table beside us. I took her hand and led her to the dance floor.

"How is this proving it?" she asked, staring up at me.

The music was loud, but the industrial screech and thump had nothing on the rapid beat of her heart pounding in my ears.

"Patience," I muttered before taking her hand and tugging her close.

When her arms wreathed my neck, we both inhaled sharply. The way her body fit against mine was ... well, it was fucking perfection, as though she'd been created only for me.

Then again, she had, hadn't she?

We remained like that for the longest time, moving to the music, my body aligning with hers until we were both breathing heavily, her eyes glazed. The fact that she didn't move away wasn't lost on me. It was as though she was eager to have me touching her. If she was like me, it was a relief to have that cold ache gone, even if it was only temporary.

And oh, how I wanted to touch her. Every-fucking-where.

When the song changed, morphing into a dark, thumping number, I slid one hand up her arm, gripping her wrist and unlocking her arms from around my neck. I then turned her so she was facing away from me, pulling her back so her luscious ass was intimately pressed against my thighs. Sliding my arm over her shoulder, I planted my hand on her belly and nuzzled her neck, inhaling that sweet lavender scent I remembered from the alley.

I'd spent weeks thinking about her, interacting with her on a telepathic level, but nothing compared to having her in my arms.

"What are you doing?" she rasped, tilting her head to give me better access to her pounding pulse.

"Proving it."

Her soft hand slid over my arm, holding me close, not pushing me away. "How?"

"Keep watching," I urged, hoping to pay attention long enough to prove anything other than the fact I wanted her with a passion that defied logic.

ORIANNA

Easier said than done, I thought as Eclipse's big body pressed against me.

From the moment I noticed him watching me from across the room, I knew our paths would cross. Or at least I'd hoped they would. I'd recognized him instantly, remembering our interaction in the alley as well as the strange visions since that night, and had hoped that luck was finally on my side. What were the chances I'd run into him after countless weeks of attempting to find him?

Good, it seemed, because this was definitely the white knight I'd encountered. Only, I wasn't quite sure he was as noble as I'd made him out to be in my head. I didn't need to know anything about him to know he was dangerous. More so to my sanity than anything, but for some stupid reason, I'd allowed him to lead me out here to prove a claim that was, at its core, preposterous.

Vampires.

As if.

Of course, I would've likely followed him anywhere, which was almost as ludicrous as the whole vampire thing. Yet I couldn't fight the overwhelming attraction or the desperate ache that had taken up residence between my thighs. I hungered for him in a way that defied logic, unlike anything I'd ever felt.

Funny, my mother always told me when I found my soul mate, I would know. I couldn't help but wonder if there was some truth to that. Granted, I wasn't crazy enough to believe in soul mates. No more than I believed in vampires. But I could not deny the attraction.

"Don't look away." The deep baritone rumbled through me, heating my blood and causing a familiar warmth to pool between my legs.

I was vividly aware of the big hand that spanned my belly, gently holding me in place. When his other cupped my neck, gently urging me back against him, a lightning bolt of desire slammed into me. The possessive gesture should've made me panic, only he wasn't hurting me. He wasn't even applying pressure. The move was meant more to keep me from turning my head, but I felt the brush of his hand on my throat all the way to my core.

"Watch how he tilts her head just so." Eclipse's voice was a steady whisper in my ear, his warm breath sending a tingle down my spine.

I inhaled sharply as Eclipse mirrored the man's movements, slightly tilting my head. I kept my eyes straight ahead, watching the man's lips graze the woman's slender neck. Warmth trickled through my sex when Eclipse did the same to me, his smooth lips brushing my oversensitive skin.

"He's kissing her," I said, my voice wrecked by the lust coursing through me.

"He's not kissing her."

I swallowed hard when Eclipse's tongue grazed my neck, even as the man pulled the woman's long hair back over her shoulder and leaned down once more.

"He's preparing for his next meal."

I knew I should've been terrified—likely Eclipse's intent with this stupid show—but I was too turned on to be scared. Part of it was due to watching such an intimate act between two people, but more so because my mystery savior was touching me. Everywhere.

The man lifted his head and met my eyes briefly before his upper lip curled back and revealed...

"Oh, God." A trickle of fear bloomed in my bloodstream as the man leaned forward and pierced the woman's flesh with those wicked sharp canines.

Eclipse's hands tightened on my neck and my belly, holding me against him. "Believe me now, *sezari*?"

I would've sworn my eyes were playing tricks on me if it weren't for the fact my body was aflame with sensations. No way was I dreaming. Not even those strange fantasies I'd had for the past few weeks could measure up to what I was feeling now.

The woman moaned softly, closing her eyes as she gave herself to the man ... vampire ... *whatever* he was.

Could this be real? Or was it some elaborate hoax? Maybe cosplay. People did that, right? Didn't have to be Halloween for people to dress up and pretend to be something they weren't.

Of course, that didn't explain the weirdness I'd witnessed tonight when the woman and man from the warehouses had disappeared in thin air.

A memory assaulted me. The night in the alley when

Eclipse had killed the man who'd mistaken me for Amber. I remembered the moment he'd looked at me. I'd seen...

I spun around in his arms, staring up into his face. I cupped his cheeks roughly and used my thumbs to shift his upper lip back.

His canines were strangely sharp, but not nearly as long as I'd— Holy shit. Right before my eyes, those fangs descended from his upper jaw, growing longer.

"You're one of them," I accused, even though it sounded ridiculous. Vampires didn't exist.

Did they?

"I assure you, *sezari*, I'm not a vampire."

Before I could call him a liar, a body slammed into me from behind, forcing me to fall against Eclipse. My natural reaction was to tear into the rude asshole, so I pivoted around to do just that and found myself face-to-face with the woman who'd told me about the place.

For a second, I was stunned into silence, but my brain finally kicked back online.

"Where's my sister?" I demanded, stepping forward into the woman's personal space.

The woman responded with a flutter of thick, black lashes, a slight tilt of her lips. "Oh, sweetheart, I have no idea."

Aware that several people had turned to watch us, I wasn't about to back down. "Then why'd you tell me she was here?"

A smile pulled the woman's ruby-red lips back. "Why else?" She took a step closer, then lifted her gaze above Orianna's head. "I'm sorry, lover. But she's here for me tonight."

"Actually, she's not," Eclipse said, his voice a deep, dark rumble.

The woman evidently took that as a dare because she countered with, "Don't worry. I'm more than happy to share."

Share? What the hell was she talking about?

"I don't share," Eclipse stated, his big hands resting on my shoulders as he pressed against me once more. Even though I couldn't see him behind me, I knew Eclipse had lost his playful air. There was no seduction in his tone or his tense body. He was in warrior mode, and this woman was his target.

Stuck between the two warring ... creatures, I couldn't seem to move. I was already pressed against Eclipse while the woman with the evil eyes closed in on me.

Screw this. I was not about to be some toy for them to fight over.

"You lied to me," I snarled.

"I like to refer to it as using information to my advantage."

"How did you know about my sister?"

The woman smiled devilishly, then tapped a long black nail against my temple. "Hard to miss when she's a constant thought in your head."

Frowning, I let the words come together, tried to make sense of them.

"So, what? You were reading my mind?" The woman's expression appeared pleased. Clearly she'd wanted me to come to that conclusion. "You bitch."

"No need to get testy, honey." The woman laughed softly. "By morning, none of this will even matter."

"What the hell does that mean?"

As though in a trance, I could do nothing when the woman lifted her hand, skinny fingers tipped with long, coffin-shaped black nails reaching out and teasing my hair. It was the same feeling I'd had outside, as though someone was controlling my movements, rearranging my thoughts. But rather than fear, this time, I was overwhelmed with desire.

An animalistic growl sounded from behind me. "Last warning, vampire. Back. Off."

The woman wasn't at all intimidated by Eclipse, her black eyes shooting to his face once more. "Or what?"

The next thing I knew, the woman was gripping her head, crying out as though in pain as she stumbled backward. The move drew the attention of everyone near us, a round of hisses sounding as the partygoers turned rabid.

"Fucking angel!" someone shouted, the words inciting more hisses, the gyrating bodies separating as they began circling us.

I was seconds away from full-blown panic when suddenly everyone froze where they were.

Well, everyone except for Eclipse, who began maneuvering me out of the fray.

"Can't take you anywhere, can I?" an enormous man asked, strolling toward us as he gestured in the direction of the exit. "I think it's time we call it a night."

"Agree," Eclipse rumbled, taking my hand and pulling me alongside him.

I sidestepped the immobile bodies, wondering what the hell kind of game these people were playing. No one was moving, as though they were trapped inside their skin. I stared in disbelief as we weaved between flesh-and-blood statues.

"What'd you do to them?" I asked.

"Don't worry," the stranger said. "I'll release them once we're outside."

Release them? He was doing this?

Okay, so much for this *not* being a dream. Had to be. This was far too creepy.

Time to wake up.

Pinching myself, I inhaled sharply when pain shot up my arm.

"You're not dreaming, *sezari*."

The hell I wasn't.

109

The man who'd joined us opened the front doors and gestured for me to step outside. I glared at him as I passed, waiting for my alarm to go off and wake me up.

Cool air caressed my overheated skin when I stepped outside. Everything was exactly as it had been when I arrived a short time ago. The house was cloaked in darkness, all those fancy cars still parked in front. No one was out there to intervene, which meant...

"Where're we going?" I demanded when Eclipse nudged me down the stairs toward the cars.

"Party's over for us," the stranger told me.

"Who're you?"

He smiled, and once again, I got a flash of fangs. "Name's Kaj."

"What the hell is going on?" I snapped, jerking out of Eclipse's hold and dividing my attention between the two men. "Who are you? Better yet, *what* are you?"

Kaj was the one to answer. "Well, I'm a vampire, and my buddy here ... he's an angel."

God, he said it like I should've suspected as much.

Wait. He said...

I snapped my attention to Eclipse. "An angel?" I laughed, though I didn't find this the least bit amusing. "An angel with fangs. Right."

"Looks like you've got some explaining to do," Kaj told Eclipse. "Why don't you take the car, and I'll meet you at the mansion."

Mansion?

Before I could launch another question, the man just disappeared. *Poof!* He was gone.

"I have got to wake up," I muttered as Eclipse guided me down the line of vehicles.

"You're not asleep, Orianna."

When he stopped in front of a fancy foreign sports car, I laughed. "Yeah. Right."

The next thing I knew, I was buckled into the passenger seat, Eclipse behind the wheel. He steered the car out of the lot and down the winding path while I tried to wrap my head around everything. Not only had I been immersed with vampires—and angels, if Kaj was to be believed—now I was riding in a car that cost upwards of three million. I only knew this because I'd been fascinated with sports cars since I was little. It was one of the few things I'd ever had in common with my father.

When we finally hit the main road, I turned my attention to Eclipse. Part of me wondered if this was some elaborate scheme to kidnap me. Would I wind up in some dark dungeon, that evil woman waiting for me?

"You're safe," Eclipse said, his voice firm.

"Are you reading my mind?"

"Not intentionally."

I stared at him, jaw unhinged. No way was this really happening. Vampires didn't exist. Nor did angels. Although I would believe the angel thing was probably more likely.

No.

They didn't exist.

"What the hell is going on?"

Eclipse exhaled slowly. "Do you seriously need a recap? Or is that rhetorical?"

I frowned, then stared out the windshield. "I'm gonna wake up."

I would. Any second now, I would open my eyes and see my shitty apartment.

One...

Two...

"You're not asleep," Eclipse said softly, his hand sliding over mine.

I watched as he linked our fingers, felt the warmth of his skin. Oddly, the gesture soothed me, and I got the strange sense that I could take him at his word. He wouldn't hurt me.

Or was he making me feel that way? Could he project the way the vampire did?

I shook my head, not giving those absurd thoughts a chance to take root. This was not real.

"I have to be asleep," I mused, unable to look away from his big hand. "I've dreamed about you enough these past few weeks. Plus, I'm under a lot of stress. So it makes sense I'd have some fucked-up nightmare about fanged creatures. Definitely stress."

"Those weren't dreams, *sezari*."

My gaze darted to his face. "What does that even mean? That word? *Sezari*."

"It's lost in translation," he said simply.

"Translation? So what? It's Spanish or something?"

He chuckled. "Or something."

Yeah, okay.

It really was time for me to wake up.

8

REIDAR

When Winnie told me she was going to hang with Penelope, Asmia, and Acadia for movie night, I decided it was time to hit the streets.

Truth was, I was feeling a bit claustrophobic these days. Ever since I brought Winnie back to the mansion, everyone was treating me as though I was made of glass. Sure, I knew they were simply trying to keep me with my *amsouelot* rather than out fighting demons, but I could only handle so much. Not only was I feeling like two thousand pounds were riding shotgun on my chest, I needed some time away, a few minutes of fresh air to clear my head.

Whatever was going on with Winnie ... with both of us, actually ... well, it was more than I could take. Not for the first time, I wondered if I'd jumped the gun in assuming Winnie was my *amsouelot*. Something was seriously off between us, and I couldn't imagine two souls destined to be together could end up with a disconnect the size of Texas.

So here I was, out of the mansion, breathing in the fresh mountain air and looking for a fight. Exactly what I needed to clear my head.

"Not sure how I drew the short stick," Rinc grumbled as we strolled through the empty downtown area. "What exactly are you hoping to find out here?"

I had no idea how to answer that, honestly. For the past few weeks, the *fiestreigh* had been patrolling the streets of Darkness and the surrounding small towns, looking for any signs of Perfidious, only to come up with nothing. The *mesonneir* had gone to ground, likely biding his time after he'd pulled that stunt with Asmia. As for what he was waiting for ... well, that was the million-dollar question. Now that Penelope's soul was safely ensconced in Heaven alongside Obsidian's, she couldn't be their target.

"I was thinking the same thing," Zadok huffed, the *lieterra's* attention scanning the group of people who sauntered down the empty street, seeming to have ventured too far off the beaten path.

Being that it was a couple hours after the rowdy Friday night crowd had called it a night, I didn't expect to encounter any humans. This tiny town was locked up tight. The only humans out were usually of the adolescent variety, attempting to wreak a little havoc.

"Is it just me, or does something feel off? By this point in a night," Rinc stated, "we would've encountered a couple dozen *impietans* already. Where the hell are they?"

"This isn't the big city," I told the male. "Be grateful for the reprieve."

"Reprieve? I'm starting to think Perfidious and his band of merry assholes are on vacation," Zadok uttered.

"Maybe." I wished we could get that lucky, but I doubted the demon was off on some island, sipping margaritas and enjoying the atmosphere.

A shrill sound from behind me had me pausing, allowing my senses to sweep out over the area.

"Demon." *Finally!*

"Three of them," Zadok corrected.

Rinc grinned, obviously pleased by the news. "One for each of us."

Working as a cohesive unit, we reversed our path, heading down the darkened street that ran parallel to the main thoroughfare through town, leading deeper into what passed for an industrial section.

"Make that four," I noted as we turned the corner to see a cluster of demons making a beeline to the humans on the next block.

Great.

"These aren't *impietans*." Rinc's frown denoted his confusion.

"*Neillohs*?" Zadok asked, referring to demons sent to Earth from Hell rather than humans who were turned.

"Definitely not," I answered. The question was, who the fuck were they? It had been eons since we'd encountered any without the IQ of a bag of rocks.

Rinc went to the right, Zadok to the left, allowing us to surround the demons and hopefully get the humans to safety.

"Look at this one," one of the female demons said as she surveyed a human male. "So handsome. The attractive ones always taste better."

"Taste?" The male laughed, then peered over at his buddy with a grin. "Honey, I'll give you something to taste."

Fucking lovely. The idiot was taunting the thing.

This was going to be fun.

The problem with demons was that they didn't care to fight. Though they were a worthy opponent when engaged, it wasn't easy to redirect their attention once they'd set their sights on their goal. And this female was already in pursuit of the human male who had no fucking clue what she was.

"Don't mean to crash the party," Rinc announced, "but we'd like to have a word."

Several high-pitched growls sounded as the demons spun to face the oncoming threat. All except the female. She was taking full advantage of the distraction.

"What the fuck?" one of the humans shouted. "Come on, Joe. Let's get outta here."

"Yeah, Joe," I muttered under my breath. "Listen to your buddy."

Unfortunately, Joe didn't listen, but his friends had the sense to scatter. While Rinc and Zadok distracted the other three demons, I chased after the female. Tossing up a barrier to keep her and the human from straying further, I snagged one of my trusty push-daggers from its holster.

"He's not much of a challenge," I told the female.

She offered a momentary glance in my direction. Enough time for me to shift the barrier between it and the human. I sent the command for the male to run. A second later, Joe's Nikes were getting acquainted with the pavement, carrying his ass far, far away.

There was something off about this one. I had encountered thousands of demons in my time, but this one wasn't the average, everyday demon. Not an *impietan*, no. Something else.

"Well, I guess you'll have to do," the demon hissed, black eyes locking on me.

Finally, a worthy opponent.

"Sorry, I'm already taken."

Though demons generally only wore the skin of a human, this one seemed to have a human form. Sure, I could see beneath to the hideous creature slithering inside that epidermis, vile and evil and reeking of death, but it seemed more animal than demon. Again, this one was unlike any I'd ever seen before.

When it lunged toward me, I pivoted, drawing it closer.

A growl erupted from the thing.

"Here, Fido," I taunted. "What're you waiting for?"

A snarl was the response, followed by a flash as the thing shifted into...

"Fucking hell," I grumbled.

Before I could lunge at the beast, it returned to its human form, moving closer.

Never one to back down from a fight, I headed right for it. Rather than collide, the instant it was within arm's reach, I shot my fist forward, right into the chest, impaling it with the dagger I clenched in my fist. I waited for the flash, the tar-like sludge, the stench, but it never came.

Instead of blue light, the demon offered a sinister grin and a snarl.

"Uh, Reidar, my man, I think we've got a problem."

No sooner were the words out of Zadok's mouth than I understood what he meant.

Rather than turn into sludge, the demon spawned another, the new one forming directly beside it, identical in appearance.

Son of a bitch.

I risked looking over to see the three demons Rinc and Zadok had set out to eliminate had pulled that multiplying shit. Now there were six swiftly circling the males. I locked my sights on the two females, my brain skimming through history to come up with a plan to defeat these assholes.

"Fucking hell!" Zadok shouted. "They're multiplying again."

Of course it was never easy. Lucifer was always coming up with new ways to fuck us over, and it appeared the devil got the credit for creativity this go-round.

"How the fuck do we kill them?" Rinc shouted.

"Trial and error," I told them, conjuring one weapon after another in an attempt to waylay the demons, who were multiplying rapidly.

Didn't seem to matter the weapon or the delivery, every attempt we made created a new one until we were surrounded.

"Now what?" Zadok asked, shifting so his back was to me and Rinc.

"Fuck if I know," Rinc muttered.

Clueless as to how to get our asses out of this fire, I shot a telepathic message to Obsidian: *Now might be a good time for you to lend a hand. And I mean* right now.

A second later, the warrior appeared at my side.

"What the fuck?" Obsidian's head swiveled as he took in the scene.

"Exactly," Zadok quipped.

It only took a few words for me to relay the situation and how we'd gotten ourselves into it.

"I want you three to leave," Obsidian ordered.

"Leave? What? So you can get your ass kicked?" I snorted. "Not a chance."

"I said leave," Obsidian growled.

I was gearing up for an argument when Stygian appeared.

"Go," the male ordered.

I got with the program, dematerializing out of the circle of demons and reforming on the other side. Rinc and Zadok did the same.

From his new vantage point, I watched as Obsidian and

Stygian held the demons' attention. Their enormous wings appeared—one black, one white—stretching out as far as they could go, creating a feathered barrier while the warriors' faces lifted skyward, arms outstretched, palms up. They were summoning energy from the universe, I realized. Their combined powers drew the demons and their duplicates into a mishmash of limbs. The hissing and screeching increased as the things were overwhelmed by pain.

"Now!" Obsidian ordered.

The wind picked up, the powerful force sending me back a couple of steps. A bolt of blue lightning struck down from the sky, silencing the demons, their ashes scattering on the wind.

"What the fuck was that?" Stygian asked, his eyes scanning the shadows for more.

Right before my eyes, Obsidian stumbled, his knees buckling, wings retracting.

"You two have to get back," I shouted, knowing that the weaker they got, the less of a chance they'd be able to. "Now!"

Stygian nodded, then vanished, Obsidian not far behind him. I followed their lead, reforming on the front steps of the mansion.

Holy fuck.

The two warriors were laid out on the gray stone, flat on their backs, their bodies temporarily taxed from using so much power. After all, summoning lightning from the sky wasn't something that could be done easily.

I threw a palm up on the reader, waited for the door to unlock. When it did, I swung it inward and shouted for some assistance.

"What's going on?" Basker—one of the male Fae who'd been summoned back to the mansion—came running, stopping at the sight of the two warriors chilling on the cold gray stone. The instant he realized Obsidian was laid out flat, he dropped to his knees beside him. "We need to get him to Penelope."

Yes, that was probably wise. The warrior would mend faster with the blood of his mate.

"What the hell happened?" Kaj asked, appearing in the mix.

"We've got a serious problem," I told them as the group gathered.

"What he said," Obsidian muttered, eyes still closed.

Kaj stared down at the warriors in concern.

"Shadow beasts." Stygian groaned as he attempted to sit up.

Shadow beasts? Seriously? That explained why I didn't recognize what they were. I'd never had the pleasure, and now I wasn't sure I wanted to again.

"Aw, hell," Kaj rumbled.

"We have to help them," Basker stated, his tone cool and collected, eager to do his duty.

"They'll be fine," Zadok assured the Fae. "When they combine their powers, it drains them. They'll need about twenty-four hours to recover. Then good as new."

"What can we do for them?" Basker asked.

"For starters, we can get them in the house. Preferably upstairs," Kaj said, his tone full of authority. He turned his attention to me. "You need to get the word out to the others."

"Will do." I glanced down at Obsidian. "You good, boss?"

Obsidian nodded, though even that looked like it required too much energy.

PERFIDIOUS

I lifted my glass to my mouth, took a long swallow. I stared out the grimy window into the night and did my best to ignore the noises coming from Seraphina as she slurped and sucked Sirius in the far corner. Never before had their lack of discretion bothered me, but it looked like I'd finally had my fill.

"Rumor has it the vampires are pledging their loyalty to the angels," I said absently.

Sirius grimaced. "That's absurd."

As far as I was concerned, it was a smart move. With the vampire numbers dwindling thanks to Lucifer's unleashing of the shadow beasts, it benefited both parties to team up. Not that it would do them any good in the long run, but it would definitely extend the war. Luckily for us, there were always those who weren't quite sure where to pledge their loyalties. Those traitors were now in the employ of demons, doing some of the dirty work and getting none of the credit.

"Yet it's true." I cleared my throat. "Would you get him off already?"

Sirius grunted and groaned, mumbling obscenities at the bitch kneeling before him.

I was two seconds from disappearing them elsewhere when Sirius howled his release before shoving Seraphina off of him.

Exhaling heavily to ensure they understood my frustration, I got to my feet and strolled across the room, turning my attention to Seraphina. "Do you have an updated count on the dead vampires?"

She shrugged as she wiped her fire-engine-red lips with the back of her hand. "Last I checked, they weren't my problem."

I was tempted to set her ablaze, send the vicious bitch back to Hell. In the past couple of weeks, I'd grown tired of her. Then again, I'd grown tired of everything. Ever since I lost my connection with Asmia ... nothing seemed to matter anymore. Well, nothing except finding her.

"Then what exactly *is* your problem?" I snapped at the demon, reminding myself I did have a job to do.

Seraphina had the audacity to glare at me. "Cleaning up your mess seems to be my main focus."

My mess?

"You did blow off your orders to eliminate the human," Sirius remarked. "Seems you're both showing your incompetence."

I would show the little shit incompetence.

"It's true," Seraphina said, purring as she scanned Sirius from head to toe. "He's too focused on other things to care that the female's now immortal."

"Doesn't mean she can't be killed," the distorted rumble of a demonic voice said.

Spinning around, I found myself nearly toe to toe with Eevuhl. Instinct had me taking a single step back. It wouldn't behoove me to show fear, but when it came to this particular demon, it was a natural response. The only thing more deadly than the males of the *trielair* was Lucifer himself.

It took effort not to cringe or, hell, to run from the fucking room. "What the fuck are you doing here?"

Eevuhl stood before us in the human form he'd obviously acquired recently. From what I could tell, he'd picked up the husk somewhere in Texas, complete with cowboy hat and belt buckle. He looked like a dumb ass.

The demon's gaze cascaded over me, critically judging before he smirked, his black eyes glittering with menace. "Good to see you, too, underling."

Taking another step back, I managed to keep a decent distance between me and the evilest creation to have ever traversed the human realm. Aside from Eevuhl's brothers, Aguhnee and Mizuhree, that was. The *trielair* was Lucifer's top-level, the demons responsible for eliminating entire civilizations since the dawn of time.

"Nice ... jeans," Seraphina purred, her eyes raking over Eevuhl's form.

The demon's gaze shifted to her. "The best I could come up with on short notice."

"I have a fondness for cowboys," she told him. "It's been a while since I've saddled up. Let me know if you'd like a ride."

The thought of anyone being defiled by that demon had me shuddering.

"Why are you here?" I demanded, reaching for the tequila Sirius had brought as a gift from the last soul he'd stolen. It took effort, but I managed to hide the slight tremble in my hand.

"I thought you'd be happy to see me, Perf," Eevuhl said with a demented grin. "After all, someone's got to clean up the mess you've made."

For fuck's sake. Why did everyone keep bringing that shit up?

"There's no mess," I declared.

"No?"

A loud ruckus sounded from the other room. I peered around Eevuhl to see what it was. There, in the middle of the abandoned warehouse, were two dozen demons, none having yet acquired a human form. The creatures reminded me of gnomes. If gnomes were horribly disfigured with arms too long for their short bodies and heads too large. There were also the red scales that covered them, glistening with the oily red puss that oozed out of their pores.

"Why are they here?"

"Like I said," Eevuhl sneered. "Someone's got to clean up your mess. I brought them along to assist."

Though I hadn't seen any of the *trielair* in nearly two centuries, Eevuhl hadn't changed a bit. Not counting the human form, anyhow. There was still the stench of death and destruction that lingered, the slick layer of evil that coated his black soul like a plague.

"As for why I've invaded your residence, that's simple," Eevuhl supplied. "The sun's about to come up. You're going to provide me shelter."

"Why in hell would I do that?"

Eevuhl took a step toward me. "Should you refuse, I'll send you home. Let Lucifer take care of you. He's not happy, Perfidious. You've gone off task."

It wasn't that I feared Hell, but the thought of dealing with Lucifer at the moment didn't sit well. I still had things I needed to take care of before I ventured below. Namely, claiming the blond Fae as my own. Screw Obsidian and his female. I couldn't give a shit less that they'd sealed the bond, their souls now residing safely in Heaven.

"I don't need your help," I told Eevuhl. "I've got the situation under control."

The demon cackled, an evil sound that slithered in the stale air like an oily film. "You are aware they've mated, are you not?"

"Of course I am. I'm not an idiot."

The look Eevuhl gave me said he believed otherwise. "Lucifer's deemed your scheme to steal the Fae a fool's errand."

Well, hell. So much for keeping my plans on the DL.

"The Fae?" Seraphina's glittering blue eyes pinned me in place. "What is he talking about?"

"Oh, you haven't told her? Informed your lackey that you've become fascinated by a fucking fairy? Tell me this, Perf. What'll you do with her when you acquire her?"

Keep her. That was what I intended to do. I would make her my queen, have her at my side for eternity.

Strong hands gripped my head. Before I could duck out of Eevuhl's grip, pain shot through my skull.

"Ah, yes," the demon quipped. "You've fantasized about mating her, making little demon spawn. How romantic." His nostrils flared with distaste.

"Who is he talking about?" Seraphina asked, her pissed-off gaze still locked on me.

"Asmia," Eevuhl said, shoving me away. "The Fae belonging to those fucking angels."

As though betrayed by the revelation, Seraphina moved toward Eevuhl.

"You do not want to do that," I warned her, though I didn't give a fuck if the demon ripped her to shreds or not. She had no loyalty to anyone but herself, proving so when she ran one long nail down Eevuhl's chest.

"Oh, I think I do," she crooned. "Perhaps, finally, a male who can handle me."

Eevuhl stared back at her, black eyes glittering.

"You're as good as dead," I mumbled, draining my drink.

"He's right," Eevuhl growled, his gaze raking over her. "But I'd love to feel those sweet lips wrapped around me. After, I'll give you to my males." He jabbed a thumb in the direction of the warehouse. "They need something to play with. Or better yet, maybe I'll feed you to my shadow beasts. They do enjoy a juicy treat."

Seraphina stumbled back, evidently heeding the warning when it came from the demon's mouth.

"However, it'll have to wait until I've secured shelter for the day."

"Fine," I hissed. "You can stay here. But you can make your own hole in the ground."

Eevuhl smirked. "I've got some who'll gladly help me." His eyes shot to Seraphina. "Especially if I reward them for their efforts."

"Then what?"

The demon's head cocked to one side. "I don't know yet. Lucifer sent me here to lead the charge for the *amsouelots*. One might've slipped through our fingers, but there's still six to go." He peered around. "Only, now I'm quite curious about this Fae. Perhaps I should introduce myself. See if she's an appropriate mate for you."

"You will not," I snarled. "You stay away from her."

Eevuhl cackled again. "Not a chance, Perf. She's as good as dead."

I didn't doubt Eevuhl's intentions. The demon followed Lucifer's commands to the letter, even managed to handle his tasks from Hell. In the past year, Eevuhl had increased the number of shadow beasts roaming Earth, his mission to make the vampires extinct, eliminate the natural protectors of humans so the damned could take the realm as their own.

Bartering with the demon was my only option, considering it was imperative I maintain my position. If Eevuhl sent me back to Hell before I secured the Fae, it would've all been for naught. And I wasn't one to admit defeat.

"What if we make a deal?" I offered.

Eevuhl's dark brows rose, disappearing beneath the brim of that stupid fucking hat. "What did you have in mind?"

"I get the Fae, and you can have *her*." I nodded toward Seraphina.

"Perfidious!" Seraphina screeched. "What are you doing?"

I kept my eyes locked with Eevuhl's. "She'll prove entertaining enough. For a while."

The demon's black eyes trailed over Seraphina before his two-pronged tongue slithered over his lips.

"Once I have the Fae," I told him, "I'll help you with the *amsouelots*."

Eevuhl shook his head. "Once you have the Fae, you'll lead the shadow beasts."

I narrowed my eyes. "Why would I do that?"

The demon smirked. "Because if you don't, I'll eliminate that little fairy before you ever get a taste of her."

Eevuhl did not make empty threats, I knew. Now that the demon had seen inside my head, Eevuhl knew who she was, and there was no doubt he'd eliminate her just to punish me.

"Fine. I'll leave the *amsouelots* to you, and I'll lead the shadow beasts. But you have to tell Lucifer you've reassigned me."

Once more Eevuhl's black eyes shot to Seraphina. "Deal. But the demon is mine to do with as I wish."

I smiled.

Killing two birds with one stone.

Nice.

9

OBSIDIAN

I managed to get to the third floor with the help of Rinc and Zadok. As soon as we made it through the door, I nodded toward the living room sofa, needing a minute before I made the trek down the hall. If it weren't for the fact I'd pulled a lightning bolt out of the heavens, I probably would've felt like a pussy. Then again, I wanted to see them pull that shit off.

Footsteps sounded on the stairs, and I felt the presence of my *ereswa* before she appeared. Simply knowing she'd felt my need for her warmed me immensely.

"What happened?" Penelope came to an abrupt halt when she stepped around the corner.

"Damned if I know," I grumbled, exhaustion pulling at me from all directions. Summoning a lightning bolt wasn't as easy as it appeared, likely the reason I hadn't resorted to doing it in over two hundred years or so.

Clearly in tune with my physical state, Penelope hurried over. "Are you hurt?"

I shook my head, met her worried gaze to assure her. "Just physically drained. It'll pass."

"Kaj is requesting to come up," Reidar announced from where he stood near the door.

"It's fine. But I want you three to stay," I told Rinc, Zadok, and Reidar. "Get Malak and Magnar. And the *lieterras* who're here. We need to talk."

"Will do," Reidar said before disappearing.

I turned my attention to Penelope. "Come here, *ayreme*."

She settled at my side without hesitation, her hands moving over my chest, my neck in her attempt to find out for herself if I was injured. The heat of her body worked wonders to replenish my strength.

"I'm fine. I promise."

Her golden eyes caressed my face. "You need to feed."

"I will. In a few minutes."

She didn't seem happy that I was putting it off, but I knew she understood.

I peered over at Stygian. "You good?"

The male chuckled. "Been better, but I'll live, sure."

When Reidar returned, Malak, Magnar, Søren, and Miklós were with him, all with mirroring expressions of concern.

"Tell us what happened before you summoned me," I instructed as I put my arm over Penelope's shoulders, pulling her against my side.

"Weirdest damn thing," Zadok said, perching on the arm of the sofa Stygian had fallen onto. "Found four demons cornering some humans. Rinc and I corralled three of them.

Reidar went after the one who trapped one of the males. Seemed good and fine."

"Right up until they multiplied," Rinc added, eyes wide. "No bullshit. Dagger pierced its chest cavity, and the bastard doubled. No matter what we hit them with or where, they kept coming, one after another."

"Rather than die, they doubled," Reidar explained. "Which was when I called you. You know the rest."

Kaj appeared, strolling through the door to join us. "You got a firsthand glimpse at their newest trick, huh? We've been having this issue with shadow beasts for the past few months."

"Those were shadow beasts?" Rinc muttered. "Fucking hell."

I sighed. I hadn't encountered a shadow beast in a decade or so. Last I heard, they'd been sent back to Hell. I'd only heard of their return from Kaj, and unfortunately, now I'd seen it for myself.

"I assume they just keep multiplying?" Stygian asked, his voice guttural, as though it struggled to pass his vocal cords.

Kaj nodded. "It's why we've had to go into hiding."

"Because you can't fight them," Zadok mused.

"Exactly." Kaj peered at all the faces staring back at him. "We don't have the same abilities you do. They're slaughtering my people because they can. We're no match when they multiply. At first, they caught us by surprise, wiped out two entire clans in the northeast, including the females and their young. They're responsible for taking down Kardobahn, as well."

"The previous vampire Alpha," I explained when half a dozen eyebrows rose in curiosity.

"Our numbers are dwindling," Kaj continued. "Which is the reason I've been seeking shelter for the single females. Though not ideal, they're pretty inconspicuous amongst humans, so I've called in a few favors."

The vampires were restricted to living in the shadows as the angels were. However, unlike them, the vampires had long ago ignored that rule and immersed themselves in the fold. In their defense, the majority had managed to keep their existence a secret, pretending to be human as much as possible.

"How the fuck do we kill them if they keep coming?" Rinc asked, though I didn't think he was expecting an answer.

"Never seen anything like it," Zadok added.

"So you haven't had any success at all?" I asked Kaj.

"The only thing we've found that'll take them out is fire."

"And lightning," Reidar stated.

Kaj met Obsidian's gaze, held it. "Too bad no one else knows that trick."

"Did you warn the others?" Rinc asked Reidar.

"Sent the word out to the *fiestreigh* and on the message boards for anyone monitoring it."

"Is that why you brought Bijou here?" Penelope asked Kaj.

"She's my only child," he said softly. "And I know she'll be safe here, should you agree to house her."

"What do we get in return?" I asked because we'd yet to address this.

"Assistance from my clans," the vampire said simply.

"But you admitted they're nearing extinction," Stygian countered.

Kaj chuckled. "Never did I say that. While we're dwindling in numbers, I still command far more than you have at your back."

"How many are we talking?" I inquired.

"Across the globe? Several hundred thousand. Most are civilians implanted in human societies, but I've still got armies. I just need some time to get them realigned. And I'm offering them to you in return for protection for my daughter."

"And the Zenith?"

Shadows passed through Kaj's green gaze. "They were killed during our last mission to save Kardobahn."

"What's a Zenith?" Penelope inquired.

"Vampire warriors," I answered, my eyes still on Kaj. "You mentioned you had information on Perfidious."

"I do." His keen eyes skimmed the males in the room.

"And that would be?" Stygian's tone reflected his frustration.

"Once I receive your declaration of protection, I'll tell you everything I know, as well as give you access to my resources."

"I've got conditions," I stated, glancing at Stygian and receiving a nod. "I've talked to my brothers, and we're willing to give you and Bijou refuge. However, we're digging into Bijou's past."

Kaj nodded. "I would expect no less. You'll find nothing of concern, I assure you."

"Maybe not, but it's still necessary. I also need you to know that my brothers are seeking their *amsouelots*. That's their top priority, so the mansion's a bit understaffed."

"Which makes this mutually beneficial," Kaj said. "If you'll allow me to assist in the endeavor, I will gladly do so. In return, you'll help us fight the shadow beasts. This is not a problem that's going to go away."

"Why's that?" Stygian asked, his shoulders squaring as though readying for a fight.

I doubted my brother could stand, but I admired his good intentions.

"Because Eevuhl, Mizuhree, and Aguhnee are topside."

Son of a bitch.

"Who are they?" Penelope inquired.

"The *trielair*," Reidar explained. "The top level of Lucifer's army."

"There's only three of them?" Penelope asked.

"Thank God for that," Stygian grumbled.

They didn't need more than that, I knew. Those fuckers were ridiculously powerful.

I fought to sit up straight, my body still far too weak, which meant it was time to feed.

"How long have they been here? The *trielair*?" The words came out strained as I shifted.

Kaj shrugged. "I suspect it's been recent. No more than three months."

"Since Michael paid us a visit," Stygian noted, sitting up as well.

I explained to Kaj how Michael had visited to relay the leak of the *amsouelot* names.

"Timing's about right. It's also when we started to encounter the double-down demons. My guess is with the *trielair* topside, the shadow beasts have become more powerful."

We needed to devise a plan, and I had to be at full strength to do that. "Let me feed." I managed to get to my feet. "Reidar, send Soraya up for Stygian. And Kaj, I'll meet up with you in a little while."

It took tremendous effort, but with Penelope's help, I succeeded in getting down the hall to our private quarters. I didn't have enough strength to will the door open. Luckily, my *ereswa* was catching on to her newfound powers quite well.

"Sit," she urged, directing me toward the sofa.

With zero finesse whatsoever, I flopped onto the sofa. I heard a crack and worried that I'd busted the damn thing, but I was too exhausted to care.

As was the case anytime she was close, I felt stronger the instant my female straddled my lap. I planted my hands on her hips, squeezed gently. I remembered the days when we'd been joined intimately for hours on end. Thankfully, the *amnigh* had dissipated, but that didn't mean my desire for her had lessened. I still wanted her with every breath I took, even when I knew my body wasn't capable of sating either one of us.

"Take what you need from me, *reuthet*," she whispered softly, sliding her hair over her shoulder and baring her neck for me.

I spared no words as I leaned in, my fangs descending seconds before I latched on to her vein. Instantly, the power in her blood strengthened me, and I knew it wouldn't be long before I would be at full strength.

Definitely a good thing, considering what we found ourselves up against.

KAJ

"Any sign of Eclipse?" I asked when I walked into the kitchen to find Miklós sitting at the counter, his laptop in front of him.

With dawn upon us, I felt it was my responsibility to ensure the male had made it back home. Not that Eclipse couldn't handle himself, but the last thing I wanted was to endure the wrath of the angels if, God forbid, something happened to him.

"I'm tracking his car," Miklós said, eyes never shifting from the screen. "Not sure where he's going, but it looks like he might be making his way here."

Good to know.

"Will you be joining the others for the morning meal, sire?" Jeffrey asked from where he stood, prepping at the granite counter.

I nodded, figuring that was the answer the male was hoping for. The smile I received in return confirmed my suspicion. Although I once had a loyal staff, as had my family, I'd never seen anything quite like the *heurosp* who worked for the angels. Those males and females took tremendous pride in their work, and they took great satisfaction in pleasing their masters, as they referred to the angels.

"Have you seen my daughter?" I asked, the question not directed at anyone in particular.

"I believe she's in her private quarters, sire."

Nodding my thanks to Jeffrey, I strolled toward the back stairs. I passed the small office, the main-floor laundry suite, another closed and locked door. The narrow stairway led both up and down. I opted to go up to the second floor, wanting to check in with Bijou before I ventured down to the war room and attempted to find a way to help the angels in whatever mission they deemed priority.

As I strolled onto the second floor, I had to admit this was the first time I'd relaxed in months. I couldn't remember the last time I walked down a hallway and didn't anticipate a threat of some kind. Ever since the raids that took down Kardobahn, I'd been looking over my shoulder, expecting someone or something to appear with the intention of taking me out, too. And every time I looked back, I was reminded that I was on my own, no one to watch my back or fend off an attack. A wash of sorrow covered me as I remembered all I'd lost in those attacks. Not only my father but the Zenith, the males I'd fought alongside for as long as I could remember. They were all gone, eliminated by those fucking beasts.

I exhaled heavily. Sometimes I wasn't sure what was worse, the shadow beasts whose goal was to eliminate us in our entirety or the fucking traitors who wanted nothing more than to step over my body in their efforts to rise to power.

Both were part of the reason I'd sought out Obsidian. Not only because I needed to ensure my daughter's safety but also because I needed a place to regroup. A safe place. Where I could breathe without worrying about a knife lodging into my lung from behind. Until I figured out what my next steps were, which included gaining solid ground on my reign, I feared I was doomed to my fate, constantly expecting my own demise.

I paused outside the door of the room they'd offered Bijou. I was about to rap my knuckles on the wood and request entry when a sharp pain hit me square in the chest. It was so powerful I stumbled, gripping the doorjamb to keep myself upright. The pain was intense enough to have me thinking I might need medical attention or a defibrillator at the very least, but I knew it wasn't some internal failure of my body. No, this was something far worse than a heart attack.

Forcing myself to stand tall, I strolled farther down the hall, pausing outside the library doors. They were partially open, giving me an unobstructed view of the interior. My gaze swept over one entire wall of literature, past a cold fireplace, beyond the empty furniture that sat stoically in the center of the space, past the windows and drapes.

Then I saw her.

My female.

Only Acadia wasn't alone.

I watched, the ache in my chest intensifying, as one of the males in the house drank from her vein. Probably a good thing the fucker was taking from her wrist rather than her neck;

otherwise, I wasn't sure I would've been able to refrain from slaughtering him.

As it was, that pain radiating through me was a direct result of my female feeding another. With her blood in my veins, I had a direct link to her. For the past eighteen months, I'd gotten familiar with the discomfort. But it wasn't until my return to the angels' residence that it had grown to epic proportions, the potency threatening to take me out at the knees.

I focused on Acadia, the way her eyes were cast downward, her back ramrod straight. She didn't seem engaged with the feeding whatsoever, but there was no reluctance on her part, either. She was performing her duties as they were outlined. As I'd learned during my time with her, the Fae were there to feed the *fiestreigh* as well as the warriors slated to protect humans. The mystical fairies were little more than servants in this vast world, even if no one within this residence treated them as such.

While I had no right to intervene, I wasn't sure how long I would be able to sit back and watch this, literally or figuratively. At least distance had provided some relief. But seeing her, witnessing it with my own two eyes ... that was more than I'd bargained for.

It took effort, but I managed to force my feet to move, my legs carrying me back to Bijou's room. I shoved that image of Acadia to the back of my mind as I lifted my hand and knocked.

Bijou's soft voice called out a hasty, "Come in."

I opened the door and the smile I had forced morphed into the real thing when I saw her sitting primly in one of the upholstered chairs near the fireplace. As had been the case every single day since Bijou had appeared in my life, I felt a sense of peace. For whatever reason, seeing my daughter was a comfort I never even realized I was missing. How could I have known, though? Until a year ago, I hadn't even known I had a child. I'd missed out on so much, and I didn't even know who was to blame. Me? Bijou's mother? Fate? Karma? Someone had caused the rift that made me unaware of my own blood walking upon this Earth, but I didn't know who.

"Just thought I'd check in," I said softly, closing the door behind me.

Bijou's bright green eyes lifted to my face. For a second, she seemed pleased to see me, but that drifted off quickly. "Are you all right?"

Figuring I probably looked as bad as I felt, I fought back the discomfort that churned in my chest. I'd gotten so used to it that I hadn't considered what it looked like from the outside.

"Just tired," I said because it was partially true. I was exhausted. "And you?"

Bijou glanced around the room before meeting my gaze. "Not sure I've ever been anywhere as lavish as this. Fresh flowers, sheets ... it's a bit surreal."

"I know it's not what you want, but for the time being, this is the safest place for you."

Bijou nodded, always acquiescent. Sometimes more than was appropriate.

"Will you be remaining here?" she asked.

"For the moment, yes." At least until she was settled in. Once that happened, I wasn't sure what I was going to do, but I figured I had a few days to figure that out.

We stared at one another for long moments before Bijou finally spoke.

"I'm not sure what I'm supposed to do about ... feeding."

This wasn't the first time we'd come up against this issue. The two of us had been battling that biological demon for quite some time.

Though it was rare, a mother or father could and did feed

their children once the child reached the age at which he or she required blood. Once a vampire reached puberty, their world changed intimately, including their need for blood to survive, which for some families became an issue. Most families outsourced their blood needs to someone not related since their blood proved to be stronger. As for me and Bijou, it probably wouldn't have been an issue if we'd known one another better. However, in the beginning, neither had thought it appropriate considering the level of intimacy feeding entailed.

And now, as the Alpha, I was unable to feed another unless it was my own mate.

"Angels feed from Fae," I explained. "And there are many within the mansion. That's their ultimate duty. I'll talk to Penelope, see if she can get one lined up for you."

Bijou nodded. "Thanks."

"Anything else?"

"I met Acadia," she said, surprising me.

Considering she'd met quite a few angels and Fae within the mansion, I knew Bijou brought this up for a reason. I waited patiently to hear what that was.

"I can smell you on her." There was a hint of sadness in her eyes.

Not sure what to say to that, I nodded.

"Does she know you've bonded with her?"

As though on cue, the tightness in my chest released, the pain drifting away, which I knew meant Acadia had finished providing blood to the male.

"She knows," I admitted.

Not that it mattered. Yet.

IO

ECLIPSE

After leaving the Dungeon, I drove through the streets of Telluride, ensuring we didn't have a tail, while Orianna sat quietly in the passenger seat.

I could tell she was still trying to wrap her head around all that had happened, and she wasn't getting anywhere in her attempts. There was a distinct smell to her confusion, one that had a sweetness to it. But it was her lack of fear that kept me calm, had me trying to come up with a plan to get her to safety.

My first thought was to get her to the mansion, to hide her away from the evils out to get her. However appealing the idea of kidnapping her was, I knew I had to handle this better. What I did now would lay the groundwork for our future. I didn't think making her my prisoner was going to win me any awards. So, I'd nixed the idea.

For now.

Once I was convinced no one was following us, I took a left, aiming the car back to the main drag. Although it gave away far more than I wanted to this early in our relationship, I didn't bother to ask Orianna for her address as I steered the car in that direction. Considering all she'd witnessed tonight, appearing as a stalker was likely the least of my worries.

"What really happened back there?" she asked, glaring at me from the passenger seat.

"You'll need to be a bit more specific."

"That whole mind-meld thing you did to that woman? Or the freeze-frame your buddy pulled?"

"She's a vampire, not a woman. And I merely gave her a warning, so she'd understand I was serious," I explained. "And Kaj ... well, he's a vampire. I can't speak to his talents."

"You're still on that, huh?"

I glanced her way. "On what?"

"That whole vampires-are-real thing."

"They're real."

Orianna snorted, then turned her attention to the front window. "Where are you— How do you know where I live?"

"I know a lot of things about you," I admitted.

"Like?"

"Where would you like me to begin?"

"Do you do that on purpose?"

I stopped the car in front of her building, then glanced over. I raised my eyebrows, waited for her to elaborate.

"Deflecting. You do it so easily."

I could've made light of the situation, come up with a dozen redirects, but I knew it would only delay the inevitable.

"There're some things you need to know about me," I told her.

"Oh, good. Since you seem to know *everything* about me."

146

She smacked her hands against her legs. "But what's to know? I've already learned you're an angel who likes to hang out in vampire bars. What else is there?"

Before I could launch into the basics, the hair on the back of my neck stood up. Reaching out with all my senses, I scanned the surrounding area, locking on the vampires approaching from the east. So much for being in the clear. There were three of them, two males and the female from the bar, and they were teleporting rapidly and closing in fast.

"Hold on."

Orianna let out a muted squeal when I put my foot to the floor. The tires skidded on loose gravel but got purchase as I steered out of the lot and back onto the street. Rather than go away from the threat, I headed toward the vampires, the Bugatti taking off at warp speed.

"What are you doing?"

"Outrunning a vampire," I told her, hands on the wheel, eyes on the road.

"Are you serious?" Her head turned as though she was attempting to peer behind us. "She's on foot."

As though I'd summoned her with my thoughts, the female appeared directly in front of us.

Orianna shrieked at the same time I muttered, "Shit."

A quick change of plans had us barreling into a corner. Thankfully, the car was made for speed, which I figured was the biggest advantage I had over the vampire. Only her ability to dematerialize could allow her to stay close on our tail and even then, she wouldn't be able to keep up.

"Is that the woman from the club?"

Despite the fear I detected in Orianna's voice, I kept my eyes on the road. "Like I said, she's no woman."

Another hairpin curve appeared up ahead, and I turned into it with ease. When we hit the straightaway, I put the pedal to the floor, sending Orianna back into her seat from the G-force.

"What does she ... it ... whatever." Orianna huffed her frustration. "What does she want?"

"You."

Another quick turn had us heading northwest, in the direction of the mansion. I hated the idea of luring the vampire there, but once we hit the *dhira*, she'd get turned around. At this point, I was out of options, and keeping Orianna safe was my only objective.

"I don't understand. Why did she say she knew my sister?"

"She probably read your thoughts. Figured it was an easy lure."

"For what? So she could get me to the club and feed on me? Seems a bit over the top, don't you think?"

Yes, in fact, I did. I made a mental note to talk to Kaj, to see if we could get a bead on the rogue vampires. From what I could tell, they were much closer to home than I would've liked.

"What the hell?" Orianna leaned forward, tried to see in front of us. "What's going on? Why can't I see anything?"

"It's called *dhira*." I reached over, pressed two fingers to her temple. "It's a darkness cloak that we erected to shield ourselves."

Orianna's eyes widened, likely surprised that she could see through the darkness with no problem. When I removed my fingers, she sat back, expression one of disbelief.

"Who could you possibly need to hide from?"

"Lucifer."

Her head snapped my way once more. "You're not joking, are you?"

"Not even a little."

Orianna sighed. "Where are you taking me?"

"To my house. You'll be safe there."

"Safe from the vampires?"

"Safe from everything," I muttered.

Except me.

T en minutes later, I pulled the Bugatti into the garage, the big door closing silently behind us.

By the time I was out of the car, Orianna was slack-jawed once again, eyes wide as saucers as she gave the cars a good once-over.

"Is that a Lambo?"

I smiled. "It is."

She turned and surveyed the rest of the vehicles in the garage. Aside from the fact we parked our vehicles there and kept a vast array of tools in monstrous metal boxes, it wasn't much of a garage. The *heurosp* maintained the space as though it was the main living area. There were no grease stains, no dirt, only shiny surfaces, and sparkling clean cars, trucks, and SUVs.

"That's a ... a Koenigsegg CCXR Trevita?" Her mouth fell open. "I heard they'd planned to make three of these but only ended up making two."

I nodded at the car. "I won't tell if you won't. You definitely know your cars."

Orianna smiled. "You could say I've got a fascination with them." Her hand went to her chest. "And that's a LaFerrari. Holy shit."

For whatever reason, it pleased me she was impressed, more so that she was so well-versed in high-performance vehicles. I found it interesting she noted all the sports cars, not paying much attention to the Range Rover or the GMC truck. Seemed she had a preference.

Taking her hand, I led the way into the house, down the wide corridor.

"You live here?"

"Along with my brothers," I confirmed. "As well as the *fiestreigh*."

"*Fiestreigh?*"

"Soldiers."

She stopped suddenly, peered up at me. "Soldiers?"

Seemed we were getting nowhere with the explanations.

"I really need you to talk to me," she implored, eyes cautious.

"I will, *sezari*. I promise."

I saw the way her throat worked when she swallowed, felt the slight tremble in her fingers. The adrenaline was waning, and fear was taking over.

Unable to help myself, I cupped her face. "You can trust me, Orianna. You're safe with me."

"Why is it so easy for me to believe you?" she whispered. "Everything inside me tells me to run, but I can't seem to."

Because she was meant for me, but I kept that tidbit to myself for now.

"Come on. Let's find somewhere quiet to talk."

She swallowed hard but finally nodded.

In an effort to assure her she was safe, I led her through the main part of the house, introduced her to Phillip and Jeffrey, the *heurosp* currently preparing the morning meal. Both males seemed overly pleased that they had another *amsouelot* in residence, their shoulders firming as they watched her, gearing up to fulfill her every wish.

After we'd completed our pleasantries, I led Orianna up the steps into the sunroom, then out onto the back patio before I realized the *dhira* made it impossible for her to see anything.

"So can you see through this ... what did you call it?"

"*Dhira*. And yes." But she couldn't because she was making a beeline for the pool.

Tugging on her hand, I redirected her back into the house, where it was safe.

"So a no on outside," Orianna muttered.

"We'll try downstairs," I told her as I made my way to the stairs leading belowground.

The good news was, she wasn't attempting to run out of the house; however, she was scanning every inch as though taking stock of the exits should they be necessary.

"Eclipse."

The voice came from behind me, so I paused on the stairs, peered up. Reidar was standing at the top, watching me closely.

"Give me a minute," I told the *ladeare*.

Reidar nodded.

When I made my way into the bar room, I found Malak and Raksa standing in the far corner. Based on their rushed whispers, they were arguing.

"I need the room," I informed them.

Malak's blue eyes hardened before he offered an understanding nod. Without a word, the two males marched for the stairs leading up to the main house.

"Who are all those people?" Orianna asked when we were alone. "Soldiers?"

"Yes, but they're also my family," I said because it was the easiest explanation. "Have a seat."

As though considering her options, Orianna peered around the room before moving toward the bar. She perched on the stool I'd motioned her to while I headed around behind the bar.

"Want a drink?"

"I don't suppose you have Mountain Dew," she said with the first smile I'd seen since we left the Dungeon.

I bent down and opened the mini fridge we kept stocked with everything from water to beer. The thing was full of Coke, 7-Up, and A&W, but it was the work of a blink for the Mountain Dew to appear. I grabbed a can, stood tall, and took one of the crystal glasses from the rack. I added a couple of ice cubes, poured half the soda into the glass before passing it over to her.

Orianna was staring at me, her brow furrowed.

"What's on your mind?"

"Why do you really wear the sunglasses?"

Not only could I not lie to her because she was my *amsouelot*, I didn't want to. As far as I was concerned, there was no reason to sidestep the truth. Considering all she'd witnessed—me killing the human, the vampires at the club—I felt as though she could handle the truth.

With a sigh, I removed the glasses and held her gaze.

Orianna's pretty blue eyes widened. "Your eyes ... they're glowing."

Yep. They were.

"Why?"

I chuckled. "Why not?"

She offered that look, the one that said *don't play dumb*, which only made me laugh again.

"You've got fangs," she noted. "Your eyes are silver, and they glow. I'm almost positive you gave that woman a brain aneurysm back at the bar."

"Vampire," I corrected. "The female was a vampire."

She huffed a laugh. "*That's* the part you want to correct me on?"

"The rest is accurate."

"Your buddy said you're an angel."

I held her stare, nodded.

Her gaze dropped to the glass. "I know this has to be a dream. What I don't understand is why I haven't woken up yet."

Walking around the bar, I came to stand behind her. I turned the stool so that she was facing me, removing the glass from her hand and setting it on the wooden counter.

"This is not a dream," I told her, keeping my voice gentle. "You're not asleep, and yes, those were vampires. I am an angel; my eyes do glow, and I killed that male in the alley without hesitation."

"Why?"

I frowned, studied her face. "Because he was going to hurt you."

She swallowed hard but maintained eye contact. "So you did it to protect me?"

I noticed the soft rasp to her voice. "I'd do anything to protect you, Orianna. Anything at all."

That admission seemed to shock and confuse her.

"Why me?"

Well, hell. That was harder to answer than telling her vampires existed. I wasn't sure she would understand that her soul was destined for mine, that we'd been aligned long ago, back before she was even born.

Rather than having to go into detail, I offered a small smile. "Why not you?"

Her eyes bounced over my face as though looking for the truth.

I realized I was waiting for her to fall apart, to freak out, panic. Orianna did none of those things, accepting everything at face value. It wasn't a normal reaction for a human.

But right now, none of that mattered. Not the fact I'd killed for her, not the past couple of hours. The only thing I cared about was that she was there with me, safe.

"I know it's a lot to take in, Orianna."

"Understatement of the century."

I smiled, grateful she could still tease me.

Because I wanted to touch her, I cupped her face, brushing my thumb over the smooth, warm skin of her cheek. My gaze dropped to her soft pink lips.

"You're going to kiss me, aren't you?"

I grinned. "I'm thinking about it."

In fact, I'd thought of little else since I first laid eyes on her tonight.

"What are you waiting for?"

I met her stare. "I'm worried once I start, I won't be able to stop."

"No one's asking you to."

Maybe we were both dreaming because I could not wrap my head around how easily she was accepting me.

When her hand lifted to my face, I didn't flinch, only drew oxygen deep into my lungs. The air seemed to crackle between us, my body flooding with heat.

"How about this?" she prompted. "You kiss me, and I'll let you know if I want you to stop."

A rough rumble sounded in my chest as I cleared the distance between our mouths. I hovered there momentarily, the two of us sharing air before I pressed my lips to hers. The soft sigh she released hardened my entire body, and when she nipped my lower lip, teasing me, I slid my hand behind her head, held her there as I licked my way into her mouth.

Her soft moans vibrated through me, had me leaning closer. And when her arms circled my neck, every ounce of decorum escaped me. With my mouth fused to hers, the only thing I could think about was sliding into the heat of her, penetrating her slickness with the aching erection pressed intimately against my zipper. All those nights I spent invading her mind were nothing compared to the feel of her against me.

Realizing I was damn close to losing my fragile grip on my control, I pulled back.

"Don't you dare stop now," she muttered, jerking me back to her.

This time, I kissed her with the passion that had been bottled up inside me for centuries. I stepped closer, her knees widening to give room for my hips as I tilted her head back, fusing our lips. The speed at which we ascended into dangerous territory rivaled that of my Bugatti.

Soft fingers curled around my neck as she held me in place, as though she thought I would release her before she was ready. The only reason I stopped was so we could catch our breaths.

"This is so much better than those dreams," she whispered, her breath fluttering against my face. "But I knew it would be."

I pulled back enough to meet her eyes. "How's that?"

"I know things. I've seen them."

I added more space between us, wanting her to elaborate.

"In all fairness, I don't know if it's future or past, but this is déjà vu for me. I've been here. With you."

Because I knew she couldn't lie to me, I had no choice but to believe her even if I didn't fully understand.

"My mother calls it second sight," Orianna continued. "I often get these visions."

"Are you awake or asleep when it happens?"

"Both. But I can never tell if it's future or past, and I can never see myself."

"But you've seen me."

"Not until recently, but yes. I have."

"You've seen me kissing you?"

She smiled, a hint of color coming into her cheeks. "No." She motioned around the room. "But I've seen this space before. The jukebox, the pianos. It's all familiar, like I've been here."

"What happens in this vision?"

"We're together," she said softly. "As in comfortable, like we've been together for a long time."

This tidbit of information was interesting, and I had to wonder if there was a reason the *amsouelots* seemed to have certain psychic abilities. For instance, Penelope had the skill of detecting others' emotions. Or she did before she'd taken the leap from human to angel. And now Orianna was telling me she had precognitive talents.

Orianna was staring up at me, her eyes locked on mine. "You don't believe me?"

"I do," I assured her.

"Good." She chuckled. "Because it's not nearly as farfetched as vampires and angels."

True.

Her pretty blue eyes remained locked on my face, shifting around as though she was memorizing me. I could sense her curiosity, knew if I slipped into her mind, she would still be running through the dozens of questions she had for me.

I brushed her hair back from her face, then cupped her cheek once more. "I need you to stay here with me, *sezari*."

Her gaze bounced over my face. "Need, not want?"

"Oh, I want you here with me, too."

"Why?"

"To keep you safe."

"Is that all?"

I couldn't help but smile. "Not even close."

"Then tell me. Why do you want or need me to stay here?"

"Because you belong to me, Orianna. You're my *amsouelot*.

My soul mate," I clarified. "I've been waiting for you my entire life. Now that you're here, I don't ever want to let you go."

I could sense her skepticism, but there was something else, too. Hope, maybe?

"You say that like you've been alive for a long time." Her eyes narrowed. "How old are you?"

"One thousand, six hundred and ninety-seven."

Those blue orbs went from squints to saucers. "Seriously?"

I nodded.

Sure, it was probably far too much to reveal this early on, but I felt better having said it. Orianna needed to know who I was, that there was something bigger than the two of us, something more powerful than the desire we had for one another. Even without destiny flexing its powerful muscles, I would've wanted this female.

"Say you'll stay with me," I urged.

I wanted to kiss her again, but I refrained. Barely. She was considering my request, and I wasn't about to interrupt.

"Okay."

Yeah, that came a little too easily. "But...?"

Her smile was both mischievous and wicked. "You have to help me."

"With...?"

Orianna's expression turned serious. "I want you to help me find my sister."

Little did she know, but I would help her no matter her request. I was devoted to her, would walk through the fires in Hell for her. But there was one major problem.

"I'm sorry, Orianna. That's not possible."

She looked as though I'd struck her, her body jerking backward. "So, what? You just intended to fuck me, then send me on my way?"

When she tried to get down from the stool, I gripped her

wrists, held them firm against my chest to keep her from running. I leaned forward, staring down at her until she met my gaze. I could see the anger churning in her eyes, could feel it surrounding her like an aura. My female fed off that anger, had allowed it to fuel her for so long.

Keeping my voice low, I leaned closer to her ear. "I fully intend to be inside you in the very near future, *sezari*. And as often as you'll let me after that."

"Fuck you," she hissed, her eyes glossing over with unshed tears.

"As for sending you on your way ... that's certainly not my intention."

She fought my grip on her wrists, then planted her hands on my chest. Her insistent shove didn't move me, so I helped her out, stepping back to give her space.

"I'm good enough to be your whore, but not good enough for you to help me find my sister?"

Christ Almighty. How had we gone from making out to her attempting to reduce me to ash with a glare?

I took another step back. "I wish I could, Orianna. I really do."

"I thought you said you were an angel?"

The word *angel* came out with the same emphasis she would've put on something she detested.

"Aren't angels supposed to be good?"

In myths, sure. Sometimes I wondered if there'd ever been any good in me. But I didn't reveal as much to Orianna. I figured she had enough to deal with at the moment.

"I think it's time for me to go," she said, hopping down from the barstool. "Thanks for the drink and the entertainment."

I didn't move, didn't speak. I couldn't.

"I guess I'll just see myself out, then."

"Don't go," I said softly, needing her to stay with me. Not only because the past few weeks had been hell or because I couldn't stand the thought of her being out there alone. Now that I'd touched her, kissed her, our souls were entwined. Any distance between us was going to be brutal.

There was a hint of regret in her eyes when she said, "I don't want to leave, but if you won't help me..."

"I told you, I can't."

Orianna's voice was raised when she asked, "Why the hell not?"

I turned away, unable to look her in the eye when I said, "Because your sister's dead, Orianna."

Her sharp inhale was like a blade through my heart.

II

ORIANNA

———

Dead?

Nope. No way. I wasn't buying it.

Amber was not dead.

She couldn't be.

"You're lying," I snapped.

"I'm not." There was so much sympathy in his voice it was hard not to believe him.

But why should I? I didn't know him. Not really. A couple of interactions didn't count.

Plus, this was likely some carefully crafted ruse. Like angels or vampires were even real. This was all some elaborate hoax designed to... I had no idea what his goal was, but I wasn't falling for it.

With a huff, I strolled toward the stairs. I was so out of there.

"Orianna, please wait."

"Fuck you," I bit out, not bothering to look back at him. "You can go to hell for all I care."

"Actually, I can't," he muttered.

The flippant comment only pissed me off more, had me pivoting around and marching right up to him. He was tall, I'd give him that, which made my attempt to go nose to nose with him impossible.

"Who the hell do you think you are?" I ground out, nailing him in the chest with my finger. "You seduce me, then bring me here for what? You think I'll just fall into your arms? Maybe break down into tears because you say vampires are after me and my sister's dead? I'm not that girl, Eclipse. I don't need or want your protection."

He didn't move, just stared back at me, those iridescent silver eyes so...

"I'm not that girl," I repeated. "I'm not going to fall apart." Even as the words slid past the lump in my throat, I couldn't stop the tears that formed. "Why would you say that? That my sister's dead?"

Damn it.

His silver swirling eyes remained on me, and I could see his sympathy, knew somewhere deep down that he wasn't lying.

Truth was, I had suspected something had happened to Amber. I used to see visions of my sister all the time, but those had dried up sometime in the past two years. Every day I waited anxiously for another to appear, feeling defeated when it didn't. But that didn't mean I would give up. Not until I knew for certain.

"I'll help you any way I can," Eclipse whispered.

"You can still help me find her. Even if she's ... dead," I forced out of my constricted throat.

Eclipse put his hands on my shoulders before pulling me into him.

Instinct made me want to pull away, but I couldn't, my body drawn to him like a magnet, his warmth something I needed.

It felt strange to be held by anyone. I honestly didn't expect it, but now that I was in his arms, I found it was the only place I wanted to be. No, it didn't make any sense at all. I'd long ago stopped relying on people to provide comfort or safety. I'd spent far too much time alone in the world for that. But I wasn't alone here, now, with him. Eclipse was ... he was a comfort I longed for and never expected to find.

"I've got you, *sezari*." His arms tightened around me.

It was then I realized my knees had weakened, the weight of the world I'd been carrying for so long finally too heavy. How long had it been since anyone had hugged me? Held me? Wanted to make me feel safe?

Forever and a day, I realized.

Was it such a bad thing to want someone to lean on? To know there was a safe place to fall when I couldn't keep going? It was such a pleasant thought, I wanted desperately for it to be real. Him, anyway. As for Amber...

"I know you think I'm in denial," I said, my cheek pressed to his chest. "But until I see her for myself..."

Eclipse brushed his hand over my hair. "I know." His lips touched my forehead. "Stay with me, *sezari*. Don't go."

I nodded, more to give myself permission than to tell him I would. The mere thought of going back to my cold, lonely apartment made my chest ache. Then, of course, there were the... God, was it true? Vampires were real? And now they were out to get me?

"Come on, *sezari*. I'll take you upstairs and get you something to eat."

My legs felt strangely numb, but I managed to walk as he steered me up the stairs into the main part of the house. Like before, there were people everywhere. Several like Jeffrey and Phillip, who I assumed were staff who took care of the house, all dressed in black and white, working diligently in the kitchen that seemed to be the heart of this home.

"Good, you're here." An enormous man wearing sunglasses identical to Eclipse's marched toward us, his attention on his cell phone.

My heart stopped beating for a second as he approached, my legs automatically shifting back until I banged into Eclipse. A strange tingle of awareness hummed beneath my skin. I'd met this man before. No. I didn't meet him. I'd seen him. In a vision.

When he looked up, I saw his expression change as though he was surprised to see me. I did my best to hide the slight tremor of fear that trickled down my spine. I had no idea what it was about him that stirred the trepidation.

"Obsidian, I'd like you to meet my *amsouelot*, Orianna McKay. Orianna, this is my brother Obsidian."

"You recently mated with Penelope," I said, surprised as the words tumbled out of my mouth.

Obsidian's shoulders squared as he went on the defensive. "How do you know that?"

Damn good question. "I ... I don't know."

He regarded me for a moment, kept me locked in place. I couldn't see his eyes, but I got the feeling there was a lot of glaring going on behind those dark lenses.

"I'm sorry," I said quickly. "I didn't mean... I don't mean any disrespect."

"She has visions," Eclipse said, as though that would explain it all away.

"Is this true?"

I nodded.

That seemed to settle him somewhat. As though knowing I'd glimpsed the future or past made it all better.

"Penelope will be down in a moment," Obsidian stated, his attention shifting to Eclipse. "Would you care to join us for the morning meal?"

"We're actually going to have something brought up," Eclipse said. "Everything all right?"

"Not even remotely, but we can discuss it tonight. Will you be around?"

Eclipse's silence was telling. I wanted to know what his brother was referring to, but he didn't want me to hear it.

I peered up at Eclipse over my shoulder. "If you'll just point me in the right direction…"

"I'll take you up," he said, then lifted his gaze to Obsidian's. "And I'll come back down to talk."

Obsidian offered a nod, then I was being ushered forward, through the kitchen, past a fancy living room, down a wide hallway to a set of stairs. The house was extraordinary. All dark wood and medieval charm. What one might expect a castle to look like. I was entranced by every detail: the rich wood floors, the iron accents, the torch lamps on the walls. If it weren't for the waning adrenaline, I would've asked for a tour. Instead, I simply allowed Eclipse to direct me where he wanted me to go.

We made it up one flight of stairs only to curve around to another.

"How many floors are there?" I prayed not too many more.

"Three."

"Plus a basement?" Rather impressive, considering every floor seemed to branch out, perhaps going on forever.

NICOLE EDWARDS

Once we made it to the third floor, Eclipse used his palm to unlock a door before leading the way inside. I found myself in what appeared to be an entertainment space complete with a large television, two black leather sofas, a square coffee table. The burgundy rug beneath the furniture was the only pop of color in the otherwise monochromatic theme. Tucked neatly into a corner were two black and white beds.

"Do you have pets?" I asked.

"Canines. Zeus and Aphrodite. They're around here somewhere."

I hoped they were the friendly kind. Last thing I wanted was to unexpectedly run into Cujo.

"They won't harm you."

Yep, mind reading again. I would have to remember that.

"Do you have any other brothers and sisters?" I asked as he steered me down a wide corridor. "Besides Obsidian?"

"Total of six brothers. No sisters."

"Big family. Are they angels, too?"

Eclipse stopped and peered down at me, his hand on the doorknob.

"What? Your vampire buddy said you were an angel. You confirmed."

"But you don't believe me?"

Oh, I believed, although I wasn't sure I should. "If you say it's true, then I believe you."

As far as wrapping my head around it, that would come with time and a whole lot of explanation.

When Eclipse opened the door, I stepped into what was by far the most opulent bedroom I'd ever seen. The room had to be close to two thousand square feet. The enormous bed—definitely bigger than a standard king—was the main attraction, complete with thick black posts that shot eight or so feet up into the air, held together by an ornate iron bar running

166

through each post. The comforter was a rich red, the throw pillows satin black. There was a small area that appeared to be for lounging, complete with a black leather chaise, matching black armchair, and a big-screen television mounted on the wall over a fireplace, which was currently crackling, the flames giving the room light.

"This is your room?"

"My private quarters, yes."

Ah. Even a fancy description for it.

I peered up. The ceiling seemed so far away. Fifteen, maybe twenty feet high. Even the decorative molding matched the bed. Interesting.

I headed for the window. Pulling back the heavy black drapes, I found myself up against some sort of thick, matte black metal covering. I peered over my shoulder at Eclipse. "What are these?"

"Shutters. They automatically close half an hour before dawn and rise half an hour after dusk."

After letting the drapes fall back in place, I turned toward Eclipse. "The house seals up tight during the day ... because you can't be in sunlight, either?"

"Correct."

"But you're an angel?"

"Same as with vampires." There was a smirk at the corner of his lips.

"So you sleep during the day then?"

"Yes. But there's always someone up. The *heurosp* are on rotations, so if you ever need anything, they're there."

I wasn't sure what I might possibly need, but that was good to know.

"Bathroom's through there," he said, motioning to a set of doors with opaque glass framed by black lacquer.

"Would you mind?" I asked.

"Not at all. If it's all right, I'm going to step out and talk to Obsidian. I'll be back soon."

I nodded, feeling a bit awkward knowing I would be alone in his private space but appreciating a moment to myself, nonetheless.

He waited for me to go into the bathroom before Eclipse turned and left the room. I closed the pocket doors behind me, then stared at the ridiculous space Eclipse called a bathroom.

"More like a bath*house*," I muttered, taking stock of all the white and gray marble laid out before me.

There were two sinks set in floating black lacquer cabinets, separated by a huge vanity. The entire wall was one enormous mirror, which made the space appear even bigger than it was. There was a step-up, circular tub in the center of the room, framed by the same posts that were on the bed. Hidden in the ceiling were red lights that gave a sexy vibe.

But the shower was what impressed me most.

I walked around a marble wall that provided privacy for the numerous rain shower heads and body jets mounted in the walls and ceiling. I walked through it and out the other side, smiling to myself.

"Impressive. But does it have a toilet?"

Indeed, it did. Enclosed in its own room was a fancy toilet complete with heated seat and bidet.

Once I'd used the facilities and washed my hands, I headed back to the bedroom. I considered snooping but thought better of it, choosing to take a seat in the leather armchair as I stared at the black screen on the wall.

The instant my butt hit the soft cushion, my entire body felt as though it was weighed down by an invisible force.

"Dead," I said softly, feeling my chest tighten.

How could Amber be dead? How could I not have known? And if that was the case, why was there always another thread to pull, another lead to follow? Everything I'd done over the past six years had led me back here for what? To find out Amber was no longer on this Earth?

What was I supposed to tell my mother? How could I tell Elizabeth McKay that her oldest daughter was gone forever? I was almost certain Amber was the only reason my mother had clung to this life in the first place. As long as I was searching, there'd been hope in my mother's voice. What would happen now?

So much for denial, I thought as a sob ripped from my chest.

12

ECLIPSE

It only took a few minutes to get the scoop from Obsidian. In fact, I got the gist in six words: multiplying demons, shadow beasts, lightning bolts.

For fuck's sake. If it wasn't one thing, it was another.

"How is she?" Obsidian asked, his concerned gaze shooting skyward before settling on my face once more.

I paced away. "I'd like to say she's taking all this rather well."

"Which part?" Obsidian chuckled. "You being an angel? You killing a human? You being her destiny?"

"All of the above."

"But?"

I turned to face my brother. "But she's taking all this *too* well."

I went on to tell Obsidian about the vampires at the club, the pursuit once we'd left.

"Well, Penelope didn't seem surprised by the news when I told her what I was. Maybe we're just not as inconspicuous as we've tried to be. Does she know who you are? To her, I mean?"

"That I'm the male she's destined to be with?" My attempt at a chuckle was a bit more strangled than I intended. "I might've mentioned it, but I'm sure it was overshadowed by the news that I'm also the male who can't help her find her sister because she's dead."

Obsidian winced. "Man, I'm sorry."

Yeah, I was, too.

"She has visions?" Obsidian asked.

"From what I gather, yeah. But she hasn't relayed any of them to me. Well, nothing other than she saw herself here. With me. We'd been together a while."

"Well, that's good news."

I hoped so.

"Although I'd like nothing more than to grill you for more details, I know you need to get back to her." Obsidian planted a firm hand on my shoulder. "If you need anything at all, we're here for you."

"I know." I turned and left, eager to get back upstairs.

After stopping in the kitchen to give a food order, I dematerialized, taking form outside my private quarters. I took a deep breath and opened the door, coming to a halt when I saw Orianna sitting in the leather armchair, her knees pulled up to her chest. I could hear her sobbing, and I didn't need the ability to read minds to know what was causing her pain.

Man, I was a real jackass. I didn't want to tell her the news about her sister, but I had no choice. Lying to her wasn't an option, and the last thing I wanted was to lead her on a fool's errand. Didn't mean I couldn't have found a better way to relay it, but I'd never been the suave type.

Not that I wouldn't help her find Amber's body. I was hoping to call in a few favors from the boys upstairs.

Purposely making a bit more noise than necessary, I closed the door behind me.

Orianna's head flew up, eyes darting over to me. She wiped her cheeks as she dropped her feet to the floor.

"I'm having food brought up," I told her as I carefully moved closer.

"Is everything okay with your brother?" She sniffled, wiped her eyes again.

"It's complicated," I admitted.

She studied me for a moment. "Everything seems to be these days."

I honestly couldn't imagine all she'd been through in her search for her sister. Though she was the most beautiful female to have ever crossed my path, I could see the wariness on her face. There were shadows both in her eyes and below them, proving she'd had a go of it, making her look far older than her twenty-four years. I wanted nothing more than to shield her from the pain, protect her from it, to give her the life she'd deserved all along. Hell, I wished I could take it all away, let her start anew with me.

"There's one thing that's not complicated," I told her, holding out my hand and urging her to come to me.

To my relief, she didn't hesitate, getting to her feet and walking over. When she was near enough, I took her hand and pulled her into me. Despite the strength I glimpsed within her, she seemed out of sorts. Not fragile or broken but in need of something. Comfort, perhaps? It brought me tremendous plea-sure to hold her, shield her from the dangers of the world, to offer her a safe haven. In fact, I was content to do nothing more than that for as long as she needed it.

Something told me she didn't need it as much as I thought.

When Orianna tipped her head back, those cornflower-blue eyes searched my face, but I wasn't quite sure what she was looking for. I initially intended to spend the day comforting her, but that went out the window when I saw the flash of heat in her gaze. All hints of propriety disappeared when she reached up and removed my sunglasses.

"I like to see your eyes," she said softly, setting the sunglasses on the dresser behind me.

"Why aren't you scared of me?" I asked, not sure why I chose now to broach the subject.

"Why should I be?"

"I killed a male," I said.

"It was self-defense," she countered. "He shot you, Eclipse. And threatened me."

Reasonable, fine.

"The fact that I'm an angel," I noted.

Orianna exhaled heavily. "Believe it or not, I've met all types. Never an angel or a vampire, mind you. I guess I just haven't seen anything that scares me yet."

And I prayed she never did.

"Enough talking, Eclipse."

When Orianna closed the distance between us, I dropped all pretenses, cupping her face and leaning down until my mouth met hers.

For whatever reason, I had always thought of human females as fragile. That so wasn't the case with Orianna. There was a steely strength within her that made me believe she was strong enough to withstand anything.

The soft moan that escaped her spurred me, had me sliding my hands down to her ass, lifting her with ease. Her legs wrapped around my waist, her arms around my neck, and I felt complete for the first time in nearly seventeen hundred years of existence.

Without releasing her, I put one knee on the bed and eased her down beneath me, lips fused, tongues searching. When I lifted my head to look into her eyes, there were so many things I wanted to say, but Orianna cut me off with a finger pressed to my lips.

"No talking," she whispered. "Just make me feel, Eclipse. That's all I need right now."

That was all I needed, as well.

And as I did as she asked, all thoughts of food were forgotten.

Long minutes passed as we worked to remove the clothing that kept our bodies separated. First my shirt, then hers. I grazed the smooth mounds of her breasts as I reached beneath her and released the catch on her bra. Orianna wasn't shy, removing the black lace and tossing it over her head. As I stared down at her dusky-pink nipples, my cock twitched behind my zipper, the damn thing eager to be inside her. I, of course, ignored it because there was far more I wanted to explore before then.

Cutting my gaze to her face, I took one hardened tip in my mouth, sucked gently. When her hands curled around my head, urging for more, I gave her every ounce of my attention. I sucked and licked until she was writhing beneath me, her fingers locked in my hair, tugging roughly. I moved lower, sliding my tongue over her flat stomach, pausing to dip into her navel before continuing my trek.

I could feel her eyes on me as I unhooked her skirt, lowered the zipper on her hip, and tugged the black fabric down. It joined the pile of clothes on the floor as I admired her smooth, pale skin against the red of my comforter. Her blond hair was spread out around her, her eyes flashing with heat, all that smooth ivory flesh available to me. With my feet on the floor, I bent at the waist as I trailed my finger up the inside of her thigh, pausing at the apex.

"Touch me," she urged, her eyes never leaving my face.

I slipped my finger into her panties and tugged them to the side, revealing the glistening pink folds of her sex. A rough growl escaped me as I dipped my head low, grazing her slick heat with my tongue.

Orianna moaned, her legs falling open as I lapped at her sweetness. She tasted exactly as I imagined, the perfect blend of sex and sin. It went right to my head, made that fragile grip on my control slip. Using my fangs, I ripped the delicate lace of her panties before tossing them aside and burying my face between her thighs. I plunged my tongue into her, her sexy moans and urgent pleas the music to which I feasted.

I only stopped so I could suckle her clit, flicking the tiny bundle of nerves with my tongue until she was whimpering, her fingers once again tugging at my hair.

I felt her pulse against my tongue seconds before she cried out my name, her body thrashing as she came apart at the seams.

And fuck, if that didn't make me feel invincible.

"Please ... Eclipse..." Orianna jerked my hair, attempting to move me.

I chuckled as I lifted my head and brushed my lips up her belly, gliding through the valley between her breasts. I joined her on the bed once more, holding myself over her as I licked my way into her mouth, letting her taste herself on my tongue.

"My turn," she said, pushing at my shoulders.

Since I could deny her nothing, I fell to my side, allowed her to force me to my back. I admired the lean lines of her body as she got to her knees, jerking at the button on my jeans. I chuckled when she sighed, finally content once she'd freed my erection.

That raspy laugh died in my throat, drowned by a rough growl when she wrapped her lips around me and drew me deep into her mouth.

I wasn't sure what I expected from Orianna when it came to sex, but her aggressive need to sate both of us surprised me. I admired her willingness to take what she wanted, to bestow an immeasurable pleasure in her quest. It seemed we were extremely compatible in that regard.

My hips shot up off the bed, my hands fisting in the comforter to keep from reaching for her. I didn't trust myself right now. The pleasure she wrought robbed me of my senses.

Orianna wasn't a sweet, innocent lover. However, I wasn't interested in either of those. Oh, no, I wanted this female exactly as she was. Strong, independent, earnest, and determined. As she worked my dick with her mouth and hand, I held on, refusing to come until I was seated deep inside her. Granted, holding off was easier said than done. When I was seconds from detonating, I reached for her, pulling her onto me before rolling, her body once again beneath mine.

"This is where I need you," I rumbled as my lips trailed along her jaw. "Beneath me."

It was the work of a moment to get my jeans down my thighs, but I didn't bother kicking my legs free. I couldn't wait that long, nor could she, because Orianna's fist wrapped around me, guiding me between her legs. As I plunged into her welcoming heat, she gasped, her hands gripping my hips, holding firm to keep me from going deeper.

Pausing, I stared down at her. "Did I hurt you?"

She surprised me with a smile. "Slow. I just ... need you to go slow."

Fusing my mouth back to hers, I began rocking my hips,

her slick heat enveloping me inch by inch. She was so tight, her body clenching around me like a velvet vise. The deeper I went, the more she relaxed, her body acclimating to take all of me.

When I was buried to the hilt, I lifted my head once more. "Still want slow?"

Orianna grinned, shaking her head. "Definitely not."

I eased out until only the head of my cock was inside her, then pushed in deep as I watched her face. Her mouth opened on a beautiful moan as I began to slide out and in, pushing as deep as I could go.

"More. Eclipse ... I need more."

Bracing my upper body on my elbows, I pumped my hips forward and back, driving into her harder, deeper, faster until I was drilling her. Her body stretched tight as she tilted her head back. My gaze dropped to her neck, my fangs punching out, throbbing with the need for her blood. I ignored the desire as I drove us both closer to orgasm, loving how vocal she was, how her hands moved over my arms, clutching me as though she never wanted to let go.

When she peered back up at me, I knew what she saw. My eyes were glowing brightly, the emotion she invoked drawing to the surface. While the pleasure was intense, there was something else at play here. Never in my life had I been with a female who touched the deepest parts of me. Orianna was my one and only, the love of my life, my *amsouelot*. And this feeling, I prayed it wasn't too good to be true.

She reached up, her hand gliding over my cheek, then sliding behind my neck.

I didn't resist as she urged my head down, our eyes locked. But when she turned her head, baring her neck for me, I growled low in my throat.

"Please..." she whispered, tugging my head down with a firm grip. "Don't fight this."

My breath locked in my chest when my lips slid over the sensitive skin of her neck. I could hear her heart beating, the rapid thrum of her blood moving through her veins.

How I resisted, I wasn't sure, but I continued to stroke her flesh with my own, desperate to come deep inside her, to mark her as mine for eternity.

"Take from me," she demanded, tugging my head again.

Something inside me snapped. Her demand triggered a desperate hunger that only she could sate, an urge so strong it overwhelmed me. The next thing I knew, my fangs were piercing her vein, her warm blood filling my mouth, sending immense power to every limb. My heart pounded in my chest, my cock swelling. Her taste was like the sweetest ambrosia, an aphrodisiac unlike any other. Never had I tasted anything as good.

Orianna held my head in place, her body going rigid beneath me as she cried out my name, her sex milking me as she came.

Somehow, I managed to pull my fangs free, closing the wounds with two swipes of my tongue. No sooner had I pushed up onto my hands than my head fell back on my shoulders, and a deep rumble roared up my throat, my body jerking and twitching as I came inside the warm, wet depths of her body.

KAJ

I was walking down the corridor to the guest room Obsidian had so kindly offered when I heard the animalistic rumble. Following on the heels of the sound was a surge of energy that nearly knocked me off my feet.

Planting my palm flat on the wall, I barely avoided knocking one of those ancient framed paintings to the floor. Granted, it would probably look better there, but I wasn't all that into art.

More sounds ricocheted through the mansion, piercing my sensitive ears. Soft moans and urgent growls drifted in the air, but there was only one that truly caught my attention. I could hear her breaths and the thrum of her blood across the distance.

"Acadia," I moaned, her name falling from my lips as my body hardened.

Ah, fuck. What the hell was going on here?

It took three tries, but I managed to stumble the few steps to the door of my room. I had no clue where I was going, but I knew I needed to be somewhere private because whatever this was ... my cock was raging and in desperate need of release. It throbbed to the point of pain, the scrape of denim against my flesh nearly unbearable.

"Kaj..."

Pivoting, I saw Acadia walking into my room, her head held high, amethyst eyes glowing brightly.

So I wasn't the only one affected. Good to know.

"What *is* that?" I asked.

"It's what's known as *gathenya*."

Yeah, that was completely lost on me. I'd heard Obsidian speak in his native angel tongue before, but I'd never bothered to learn myself. However, I wasn't an idiot, and I didn't need a translator to know that what it boiled down to was some sort of sexual vibration that stimulated the need for sex.

"How long does it last?"

Those beautiful eyes dropped to my fly. "Until you've sated the urge."

"Not helping," I grumbled, turning away. "Close the door."

When she remained on the same side as me, I knew the reason she'd come to me. It wasn't out of concern for my well-being or to give me a quick lesson in what to expect around here. She needed me the same as I needed her.

Desperate to sate the ache, I ripped my T-shirt over my head and tossed it onto a chair before reaching for the button on my jeans. I managed to remain upright, turning to see Acadia's eyes wandering over my naked chest, and if I wasn't mistaken, the lust I saw there was spurred by more than just the strange energy pulsing through the mansion.

"Strip, Acadia."

Her eyes danced over me as I forcefully yanked the laces on my boots loose enough to toe them off, then shucked the denim shackling my legs.

A moan escaped me when I wrapped my fist around my rigid cock, stroking roughly.

"Now," I commanded, remembering how this female had always enjoyed my dominating nature.

"As long as you understand this is a one-time thing."

"Sure." She could believe whatever she wanted.

Those amethyst eyes began to brighten more as she worked that complicated contraption she called a dress. Seconds felt like years as she loosened the strings and removed one layer after another until, *finally*, she was gloriously naked. I sucked air in through my nose as my fangs shot down from my jaw, the need to feed as powerful as the urge to fuck.

There were no more words spoken as I picked her up and carried her to the nearest flat surface, which happened to be the frilly couch. But rather than toss her onto it, I set her on her feet and turned her away from me. Unable to resist, I curled my hand around her jaw, pulled her lips to mine. Her kiss was just as I remembered, achingly tender yet fueled by an unmistakable passion.

"Kaj ... please."

I managed to release my hold, urging her to bend over the back of the sofa.

I growled low in my throat as I nudged her legs apart with my feet. I was desperate to be inside her, to feel the smooth walls of her sex clutching me. By the time I aligned my cock with the slick entrance to her body, I was gasping for air, the need overtaking me.

Acadia cried out as I thrust in deep, the sound so familiar, one I'd missed for so fucking long. I never admitted it aloud, but I ached for her. Not only this, either. More. Just being in the same room with her ... it settled the beast within me. I knew deep in my marrow that she belonged to me, but I'd purposely ignored it because I'd had more important things to take care of.

But right this instant, as I filled her body, I knew there was never anything as important as her.

Bracing my hands on the back of the sofa, I plunged into Acadia as she wound her arms around me. When her soft hands rested atop mine, I spread my fingers wide, allowing her to twine our fingers. I knew what she needed from me. The emotional energy she would draw from this encounter alone would sustain her for days, and I was more than willing to give.

"I'm going to bite you," I warned, my mouth hovering over her shoulder.

I took her soft moan as encouragement. As I drove my hips forward, retreated, and plunged in again, I raked my fangs over her smooth flesh. Acadia angled her head, giving me direct access to the vein I sought. I held myself there as I took from her body, giving all of myself in return. And when I couldn't hold out any longer, I stabbed my fangs into her neck, taking deep pulls in an attempt to satisfy the bloodlust.

"Kaj..." Acadia's fingers tightened on me, her sex clutching me as she shuddered in my arms.

I didn't stop feeding or fucking, taking all she was willing to offer.

Mine.

I shot the single word into her mind, needing her to know this was where she belonged. With me. Always.

Even as I drove us both to an earth-shattering climax, I knew walking away from her again was not an option. And I hoped like hell she didn't expect it to be.

13

ACADIA

S urrounded by Kaj's massive body, I gave in to the overwhelming desire. No male had ever been able to quench my needs the way he could. The energy I took from him was more powerful than any I'd ever siphoned. And the way he took me felt more like a claiming than a means of sating our baser urges.

As soon as I felt the powerful spasms deep within me, I knew this was a mistake. Rather than seek him out, I should've fled. It had been my intention from the instant I'd stepped foot inside the room. And while I'd been eager to sate the urge from the *gathenya*, I'd promised myself I wouldn't allow those long-buried feelings to arise.

Oh, who was I kidding? Nothing had been buried, certainly not my feelings for the male. Regardless, I'd failed.

"Stay," Kaj urged as he slipped from my body.

"I can't." I couldn't. Seriously.

"You can," he insisted, lifting me off my feet as though I weighed absolutely nothing.

To balance, I threw my arms around his neck, held on tightly. Kaj bypassed the bed, moving into the adjoining bath. A dozen memories flooded me as he flipped on the shower, then urged me to join him by lowering my feet to the floor. As though he feared I would run, he took my hand and brought it to his lips.

We'd spent so much time doing exactly this. Back when he was recovering from his injuries. It was during those months that I'd fallen in love with the male, only to have my heart shattered into a million pieces when he walked away from me. A year and a half should've been plenty of time to heal that wound, but the moment I glimpsed him in the dining room, I knew I would never be completely healed.

"Look at me, *balisra*."

Forcing my eyes to his face, I tried to ignore the way my heart fluttered, the warmth that consumed me simply from looking into those intelligent green eyes. Kaj's other hand caressed my cheek as he watched me, seemingly peering into my soul. It unnerved me, but as had been the case before, I couldn't seem to turn away from him.

"How I've missed you," he whispered, pulling me in close, his thick arms wrapping tightly around me.

I fought the sigh that threatened to escape as his warmth seeped into me. I attempted to tap into his emotions, to steal a little more to keep me going, but he'd somehow closed himself off to me.

Pulling back, I peered up into his handsome face. The dark stubble on his jaw and the shaggy black hair a stark contrast to the celadon-green eyes that seemed to glow. Never in my life had I seen a male who was so intriguing. But never had I met a more infuriating one, either.

Though I attempted to keep my distance, I caved for a moment, savoring the feel of his skin, the warmth of his embrace. I had missed him so much while he had been away, but I had to remember he was the one who left.

Kaj shifted, his hands cupping both sides of my face as he forced me to look at him. I attempted to shield my emotions, but I knew he would see them anyway. He'd always been able to detect what I was feeling, even when I didn't want him to.

His eyes danced over my face briefly before he released me. I half expected him to usher me out, but instead, Kaj reached for the body wash on the shelf. I didn't move, even when he soaped his hands and began sliding them over my shoulders, down my arms. A soft hum escaped as he continued his trek, massaging and kneading as he took great care to wash me. His hands were reverent, his fingers teasing when they plucked my nipples and later dipped between my thighs.

Only sex.

That was all this was.

He wasn't caring for me; he was reigniting the flames, attempting to stoke the conflagration that would no doubt roar to life the longer we were in here.

Only. Sex.

As long as I could keep that in mind, I would be fine. At least that was what I wanted to believe, anyhow.

I remained motionless as he washed me from neck to toe. By the time he was finished, I was trembling, but I figured that was his intention.

"I'm going to kiss you now," he whispered, cupping my cheek and leaning down, his lips hovering over mine.

It would've been wise to push him away, but as his breath fanned my lips, I found I couldn't bring myself to do it. Not yet.

And when his lips fused to mine, a flood of emotions surged through me, threatening to drain my supply quickly. I loved how dominant he was, so subtle yet insistent. He knew exactly what to do to turn me on, exactly how to kiss me, to make me burn and ache.

Kaj took my wrists, planting my palms flat on his chest. "Take more from me, *balisra*."

I felt him open himself up to me again, the surge of power flooding me as I feasted on his energy with my hands. The next thing I knew, I was backed against the tiled wall, and with a quick flex of his muscles, Kaj lifted me off my feet and held me suspended, back to the wall. His green eyes settled on my face as I felt the thick head of his erection pressing insistently against my sex. The power that moved through him astonished me, the way he could so easily maneuver me as he pushed deep inside. I cried out as pleasure assaulted me once more, my body giving in because there was no denying that yearning I had for him.

When I tried to pull back, both emotionally and physically, Kaj stopped moving, his erection buried deep inside me. I could feel him pulsing, his sexual energy coming off him in waves.

"Tell me you want this," he urged, tilting my head and forcing me to look at him.

I couldn't tell him. I wouldn't. Maybe it was true, but I wasn't willing to risk having my heart ripped from my chest again.

I saw the disappointment on his face as I felt his body tense. And when he retreated, I almost cried out from the loss as he withdrew from within me. I managed to remain quiet, to keep my disappointment to myself. His warmth disappeared as he set me on my feet once more.

My heart squeezed in my chest, the ache I'd lived with for

so long returning with a vengeance. I loved Kaj; there was no denying it. Even now, after all this time.

But I had my pride. Not to mention, I knew the repercussions. If I were to love him unconditionally, my existence would no longer be necessary. It would defeat the very purpose of my presence here on Earth.

"When you're ready," Kaj whispered, "I'll be here, *balisra*. I'm not going anywhere. Never again."

My breath hitched, but before I could reveal too much, I reached for a towel and fled the room. I had enough sense to grab my dress before evanescing my physical form and returning to the safety of my room.

MICHAEL

T wo down, I thought as I stared at the list of *amsouelots* the warriors were searching for.

The papyrus paper with its now broken seal was the original document that had been maintained in the vaults by the Fates since the beginning of time. It had once sat alongside countless other scrolls, all depicting the alignments of souls. Once the souls were united, their destinies officially sealed by the Fates, the scrolls were then burned, the ashes scattered over the blessing fountains so the angels within the heavens could continue to watch over them.

Hard to believe someone had bypassed all the safeguards and exposed the names of those belonging to my warriors. I still had no idea who had uncovered them or even how they'd been able to. But what bothered me more than the fact someone had done it was *why* they'd opted for those names specifically. Those vaults contained millions of names of destined souls, but they'd purposely targeted the seven who were closest to me.

Why?

Oh, I had my suspicions, of course.

Everyone knew there was no love lost between me and Lucifer. No matter how I dissected this, I knew my brother was the only one who stood to gain anything. Obsidian, Stygian, Cimmerian, Eclipse, Piceous, Shadow, and Aphotic could've continued on as they'd been doing without knowing who their *amsouelots* were. At least not until the time was right.

As for when that might've been, I didn't know.

But Lucifer had never been a patient male. Didn't surprise me that he had created his own timeline, positioning the humans like chess pieces, all in an effort to take what didn't belong to him: my warriors.

Back when I dispatched Obsidian and his brothers to Earth, I honestly hadn't expected them to be needed for this long. Fifteen hundred years was a long time, and from my vantage point, another fifteen hundred was likely in the cards because the humans were having enough problems on their own. They could hardly manage to keep the fragile threads of their existence from unraveling, thanks to their own greed and lust. No way could they sufficiently protect themselves against the evil that walked amongst them without intervention.

Which was the very reason Obsidian was brought into existence in the first place. I had always been a forward thinker, and Obsidian was my answer to saving the humans from themselves. The others were an afterthought, but a good one, I would admit. The seven of them were a force to be reckoned with. Not exactly invincible, but damn close.

But that was the problem, wasn't it?

Lucifer wanted them for his own armies. The most powerful beings to have ever graced Earth were vulnerable now, probably Lucifer's plan all along.

Or perhaps Lucifer was playing me. With the warriors distracted by their new mission, Lucifer was gaining a stronghold on the humans, and he was getting damned creative in his efforts. The longer he held it, the more of a mess we'd be cleaning up once the warriors were refocused on the real mission. Especially if Lucifer succeeded in eliminating the vampire race. I had never cared much for the fanged species my father created using the mold I developed for Obsidian. However, there was no denying the vampires were my warriors' best option in shoring up our reserves. We would need the numbers in order to defeat what was coming.

Sure, it was still imperative that the warriors locate their destinies, protect them, but I wasn't sure that was the top priority right now.

While I thought linking the warriors with their *amsouelots* would solve the issue, keep my warriors out of the hands of the enemy, there was a new problem on the horizon, one I hadn't anticipated. The risk of what was to come was high, but the more I contemplated what it meant, the more I realized ... it was time.

14

ORIANNA

———

I wasn't sure how long we'd been asleep when I woke, this time to a darkened room.

I managed to extricate myself from Eclipse's grip and make a quick trip to the bathroom. Once I relieved myself and washed my hands, I took a moment to look at the woman in the mirror. My attention was drawn to the puncture wounds on my neck as I reached up and brushed my fingers over them. I remembered the instant when Eclipse had sunk those razor-sharp teeth into my flesh. A heat so powerful had surged through my entire body, along with a liquid ecstasy that had sent me free-falling. Not even the best orgasm had ever compared to that one overwhelming moment.

Odd how I could reflect on it now and not be scared. I

should've been, I figured. The man I'd shared a bed with, the one who'd been inside me, had fed from my vein. It should've had me panicking; instead, I was wondering when he would do it again.

Perhaps I was in shock.

Yes, that made perfect sense. I was in shock. I had learned some very disturbing news last night, and the only way for my brain to process was to pretend it was all okay. Not only had I learned my sister was dead, but I also discovered some disturbing news about the world in general. According to what I'd seen with my own two eyes, vampires did exist. And if Eclipse was telling the truth, so did angels. Since I had no reason to doubt his word, I was forced to view everything differently.

Running my hand over my hair to tame the mess, I gave those bite marks one last look before heading back into the bedroom.

My original intention was to get dressed and slip out, but as I stood there staring at the sleeping ... angel, there was a strange pull deep inside that told me leaving was not the best thing right now. Never having been the sort to ignore my gut instinct, I decided now was not the time to start.

So rather than fumble for my clothes, I returned to the bed, slipping beneath the thick down comforter and back into Eclipse's arms.

"You stayed," he said softly, his hand sliding down my spine to cup my ass.

His skin was so warm and smooth, I let my hands do the walking, gliding across the thick contours of his shoulder, over his biceps, down his ropy forearm, and back up, shifting closer.

"I stayed," I agreed, urging him onto his back.

As for why I was still there, why I didn't want to leave him,

I didn't know. But I would have plenty of time to ponder that later. Right now, the only thing I wanted was to feel him inside me again. To have those big, strong hands running over every inch of me, to taste his kiss. More importantly, I wanted Eclipse to remind me I was alive. I'd felt like nothing more than a shell of myself for so long, but last night, he'd reminded me I was still here, and I could still feel.

Straddling his thighs, I continued to peer down at him when his eyes opened, the molten silver cutting through the darkness. I'd never seen anything quite so intriguing as the way his eyes shimmied and swirled, as though lit from within. It was another thing that should've scared me, but when it came to Eclipse, there was no fear. Only intrigue and a blossoming warmth that I wanted to explore further.

As I sat astride him, I dragged my fingertips over the smooth flesh covering rock-hard muscle, outlining the planes and angles, working my way lower as his eyes remained locked on my face. Almost as though he didn't want to look away. I knew the feeling. There was an undeniable connection between us.

Running my fingers over the rigid contours of his abdomen, I stopped when I reached the thick shaft resting against his belly. The memory of him pushing inside me had a chill teasing my skin. He'd been bigger than I expected, thicker than my body could easily handle, yet I had acclimated after a moment, taking him fully. I was eager to feel him inside me once more.

I stroked him firmly as I straightened my spine, using the glow of his eyes to see his reaction. The light disappeared momentarily when he closed them, his back arching, hips thrusting upward, driving that steely length into my hand.

In a daring act, I slid my other hand between my legs, teasing my sensitive flesh. When Eclipse turned his attention

to the movements, I heard the rasp of his breath, felt the anticipation in his body.

"Keep doing that," he uttered hoarsely.

"What?" I teased my flesh, ensuring he could see my movements. "This?"

"Yes. Touch yourself."

I immediately thought about those fantasies I'd had,
hearing him say that same thing before, only he hadn't been
there with me at the time.

But I was.

The words sounded in my mind, my eyes locking on his. He
was inside my head. I could feel him there.

"How?" I asked, stroking us both in tandem, ensuring the
pleasure didn't fade.

"Telepathy," he replied, his big hands sliding over my
thighs. "It was the only way I could be with you."

"I tried to find you," I admitted. "After the night in the alley."

Something passed over his face. Regret? Fear?

"I was worried you'd be scared of me."

Because he'd killed that man.

I shook my head. "It takes more than that to scare me."

Are you scared of me now?

"Not at all." His erection flexed in my hand. "Those nights
when you came to me like that ... it felt amazingly real."

"Better than this?" he asked, his hand sliding over mine,
his thumb pressing that sensitive nub between my thighs.

"No. Not better than this." I moaned, letting my hand fall
away as he took over teasing my flesh.

It took only a few minutes before I was worked up to the
point of panting. I could feel him flexing in my hand, knew he
was seeking the same thing I was.

I lifted my hips, leaning forward as I guided the thick crest through my slick folds before sinking down on him. Slow and steady, allowing my body to once more get accustomed to the exquisite intrusion.

Eclipse's head tipped back. "Orianna ... *sezari*. Fuck, you feel good."

I didn't know why, but I loved that word, especially when he said it that way, almost reverently. Didn't matter that he followed it with crude curses, that only proved how intense the moment was.

His hands slid up my thighs, squeezing gently as I rocked my hips forward and back, taking more of him inside me. He never rushed me, offering himself up for my pleasure, urging me to continue with the deep rumbles that escaped him. It was almost as though he was purring, and I took it as encouragement, giving me permission to let myself go.

When his hands lifted, his fingers brushing over my nipples, I leaned into them, sighing as he kneaded the sensitive flesh. I began rocking faster, chasing the orgasm that seemed to stay just out of reach, pleasure crashing like waves against the rocky shoreline.

Take what you need, sezari.

I locked eyes with Eclipse, held on as I willed him to continue.

I was with you then, like I'm with you now. Always. Forever.

A lightning bolt of lust slammed into me as his voice sounded in my mind.

"More," I whispered as I toppled forward. "I need more."

Eclipse's big hand curled behind my head as he guided my mouth to his. Our tongues twined and danced as he took control, pumping his hips up, driving into me. I held myself still, loving the way he filled me completely. The urgent shift of his hips told me he was close.

Suddenly he pulled his mouth from mine and growled. "Come for me, Orianna. Let me feel you."

The desperate plea was what set me off, my body shattering into brilliant fragments of light and energy. My fingertips tingled as the orgasm consumed me.

A disappointed sigh escaped when Eclipse pulled out. But it didn't last long because he flipped me onto my stomach before sliding into me from behind, driving deeper than he'd been before. I gripped the sheets in my fist as he filled me to overflowing. When I felt his breath on my shoulder, I tilted my head, wanting to feel his lips on my neck, his fangs in my flesh.

His soft rumble said he knew what I was thinking.

"Please," I whimpered, pushing back against every delicious thrust, attempting to increase the friction.

Those soft lips grazed my skin seconds before he pierced me. Once more I was flying, and the sensation was mind-blowing. Not only was I aware of him moving inside me, it felt as though we were connected on a much deeper level. Then, an odd thought flitted through my mind. *What does his blood taste like?*

Eclipse growled roughly before he released my neck. His tongue swiped over me once, twice, and then his weight lifted off me as he began plowing into me from behind. I cried out as unimaginable pleasure consumed me.

I'd hoped it would never end when another orgasm barreled down on me, ignited by one final thrust of Eclipse's hips and that deep rumble that reverberated in his chest.

I relaxed into the mattress, then didn't move a muscle. I couldn't. Sleep pulled me under even as he remained deep inside me.

OLIVER

Although I originally rejected nearly every invite to join the others for both the evening and morning meal, I woke tonight feeling a bit different. Maybe optimistic, even.

I wasn't sure what it was or why I was compelled to get into the thick of things, but I couldn't shake it. Even the twenty-minute shower hadn't returned my shit-on-the-world attitude, and quite frankly, it was starting to bug me.

And okay, fine, maybe these people didn't deserve my fuck-the-world bullshit. They had, after all, given me the opportunity to fit in here. Now that I wasn't being held against my will, I could admit I didn't mind the angels so much. Mostly. Not that I stayed because of them. Nope. I owed that to Penelope, though I wouldn't be the one to tell her as much.

I knew I was hard on my sister, more so than she deserved, but I had my reasons. More accurately, I carried the secrets of my mother and father, the ones they pleaded with me not to tell Penelope. Despite my anger and hatred for dear old Mom and Dad, I had managed to keep them to myself all these years. And I fully intended to keep right on doing so, provided one of those sneaky angels didn't slip off into my head and uncover the cold, hard truths. By keeping my distance, I ensured they didn't have the opportunity.

"Good evening, sire," Phillip greeted when I joined the man in the kitchen.

"Evening, Phillip," I said kindly.

For some strange reason, I liked Phillip and Jeffrey and the two dozen or so others who worked within the mansion. As a matter of fact, I liked all the staff in the angels' employ, which was another thing that baffled me. From the moment of my arrival here, even during those days when I was forced to stay, they'd all been gracious and kind. I'd yet to find a reason to send a scathing remark their way.

Perhaps I was evolving.

"The evening meal shall be served momentarily, sire. May I get you anything while you wait?"

"I'm good. Thanks," I called out as I strolled through the open doors to the dining room, expecting the place to be empty.

My breath caught in my throat when I saw her sitting in the far corner. The most beautiful woman I'd ever laid eyes on was making herself comfortable at a table near the shuttered window, her attention on an electronic tablet in front of her. I didn't recognize her, but that wasn't surprising. These days, more and more of the angels and Fae were traipsing in and out of the house. Now that Penelope had helped them devise a schedule to allow some to come home while others went out, there was always a new face here at Angel Central.

But none of them held a candle to this particular face.

God, she was lovely. The silky shine of her midnight hair, the smoothness of her fair complexion, long, dark lashes that shielded what I could only assume were beautiful eyes...

As though she heard my thoughts, the woman's head lifted, eyes landing on me.

Holy mother of God, those eyes were so much more than

202

beautiful ... a pure crystal green that shimmered and glowed. And those soft pink lips...

I stood there, completely lost in her beauty while she studied me, a quiet inspection from head to toe before a small smile pulled at her succulent mouth.

"Good evening," she said kindly, her voice as lovely as her face.

"Hi ... uh ... good ... hi." Yep, that was me, unable to string together a sentence.

Like the others I'd encountered here—aside from the staff —she didn't conform to social niceties. She didn't avert her eyes, merely stared as though she expected a third eyeball to sprout on my forehead, or maybe another nose.

"Would you care to join me?" she offered.

"Yes." Though the word came out, my feet didn't move.

She motioned to the chair beside her. "Perhaps you'd like to have a seat."

A seat. Yes, I would like to have one. Now.

Why wouldn't my feet move?

The sound of laughter rumbling behind me got my legs with the program. I moved toward her, intent on utilizing that chair beside her before someone else did the honor.

As I neared, an odd feeling overcame me, one I wasn't sure I'd ever experienced before. In that brief moment in time, I got the strangest sensation I was in an alternate reality, one where only the two of us existed. Gone was the hatred and anger I'd been filled with for years, in its place, a sense of ... well, I'd go so far as to say it was peace, but it was so foreign, I wasn't sure I could accurately name it.

Somehow, I managed to pull out the chair, to drop my ass into the seat, all while never looking away from her.

The woman held out her hand, and I lost all sense of decorum, staring at it unexpectedly, as though I had no idea what to do with it. Or maybe I was scared to touch her. Fearful that if I did, I would never want to let go.

"My name is Bijou," she said kindly. "My father is Kaj."

"Kaj?" I tried to place the name, couldn't. "Bijou."

She smiled, and I nearly fell out of my chair. "You must be Penelope's brother. Oliver, is it?"

I nodded, dumbfounded.

Before she could lower her hand, mine shot out, clasping hers as though it were a lifeline that would pull me out of the treacherous water and right to the shore.

Delicate fingers curled around mine, shaking gently but firmly. "It's a pleasure to meet you."

"Yes," I rasped, unable to look away.

Someone cleared their throat from across the room, startling me from my stupor. When I looked up, I noticed a big male staring back at us. His icy green eyes were similar to Bijou's. He had the same onyx hair, the same fair coloring...

Shit. Her father.

I instantly dropped her hand, then peered over when Bijou chuckled softly.

"Doesn't take much to intimidate you, does it?"

"Are you an angel?" I asked, though even as the words came out, I realized they sounded like a cheesy pickup line.

When she smiled, I was awestruck, my eyes fixated on the pointed canines the move revealed.

"Vampire."

"Vampire?" Confused, I waited for the punchline. When one never came, I cleared my throat. "You're serious."

"Very. Why? What are you?"

"Human." Though I appeared to be in the minority here in this mansion.

"It's a pleasure to meet you, Oliver, the human," she said kindly, laying her soft fingers on top of my hand.

There was an immense pressure somewhere in the center of my chest. It was difficult to breathe, though air seemed to be filtering in and out of my lungs just fine.

"Are you staying here? With the angels?" I asked, glancing up when one of the servers came over, carrying ceramic pots of coffee and a tray full of mugs.

"My father's seeking refuge for me here," she said, her gaze still moving over my face as though she was as surprised to see me as I was her.

"Refuge? Are you in danger?"

"Only from the demons hell-bent on eliminating the vampire race."

I let the words penetrate my gray matter. I tossed them around, but no matter how hard I tried, they didn't make sense. Vampires?

"And you? Are you staying here?" Bijou asked.

I nodded.

"Because you're in danger?"

"You could say that... I mean, no. Not anymore. I was. From my girlfriend. I mean, ex-girlfriend. She was a demon. Is. She *is* a demon. Or maybe she's dead. I don't know."

Her soft laugh settled over me like an ocean breeze.

I realized I sounded like an idiot, but no amount of acknowledgment was making my tongue work any better. I was completely awestruck by this ... vampire. Bijou. She was lovely in a way I'd never seen before.

When Bijou ducked her head, I realized I was still staring.

"I apologize," I said softly.

"Don't," she said, her hand resting on mine once more. "I like the way you look at me."

My gaze flipped back to her face. "You do?"

She nodded, and I detected an innocence about her, one I didn't expect to encounter in this day and age.

I was captivated by the shiny black hair that slipped over her shoulder when she moved, the way her light green eyes surveyed the room constantly, as though seeking danger.

"How long have you been here?" she prompted after I passed her a cup of coffee.

"Almost three months, I think. Time seems irrelevant these days. One minute bleeds into the next." I smiled as I reached for the small pot of cream.

"But you like it?"

I found myself nodding, though I was surprised by my admission. "And you? How long do you plan to stay?"

"Indefinitely, I guess."

"You don't sound pleased by that."

"My father ... he can be a bit ... what's the word?"

"Asshole?"

Another soft laugh came from her, this one making my entire body harden.

"Not exactly what you'd call the king of the vampires. Not if you want to keep your head, anyway."

My eyes rounded like saucers as I glanced over at the big vampire who was now sitting with Obsidian and Penelope. "King?"

"Technically, Alpha."

"Wow. Is that an elected position?"

Bijou shook her head. "His father was the Alpha. When he died, the position passed down to my father."

"And that makes you what? Vampire royalty?"

She chuckled, then ducked her head. "Actually, I'm a bastard. My mother and father weren't mated when I was conceived."

"And here I thought vampires were myths."

She smiled sweetly. "We thought the same about humans at one time."

I laughed, couldn't help it.

"You have a very nice smile," Bijou said softly.

I could've said the same about her, but at that moment in time, I couldn't find my voice. I felt a shift inside me, like puzzle pieces were being clicked into place or the final touches were being put on a painting. I felt whole for the first time in my life, complete in a way that confused the hell out of me.

And I had the distinct feeling Bijou was the final piece.

15

ECLIPSE

I woke to the sound of movement. First the shutters lifting, then bare feet pattering around the room. I knew where I was, even knew who was making the noise, but I kept my eyes closed.

"Crap," Orianna muttered.

"Problem?"

I heard her sharp inhale of breath and smiled as I rolled to my back. Evidently, she thought I was still asleep.

"I didn't mean to wake you."

Easing into a sitting position, I pulled the sheet over my lap to cover the erection her nearness inspired, my attention turning to the female snatching up clothing and tugging it on piece by piece.

"Going somewhere?"

She turned to look at me. "I have a life to get back to. If I'm not at work in twenty minutes, I'll be fired."

Part of me wanted to throw out a barrier, keep her from leaving the room. I wasn't too proud to admit I wanted her to stay forever. And not only because that cold loneliness would consume me once she was out of sight. No, I wanted her to stay because … well, because I wanted to get to know her. More than just how perfect she felt against me, how easily she soothed every part of my soul. Although a few more hours of that wouldn't bother me in the least.

"Have you seen my panties?"

I noticed the blush that suffused her cheeks as her eyes scanned the floor.

"Please don't go," I said softly.

Those cornflower-blue eyes darted to me, but they didn't linger. "Like I said, I've got a life to get back to."

So that was the way she was going to play it?

"Orianna…"

The smile that formed on her face was forced, her eyes never meeting mine. "Look, Eclipse. About last night … or today. Whatever. That was fun and all, but…"

"Fun?" I snorted. "That's not quite the word that comes to mind. Maybe mind-blowing. Or earth-shattering. Cataclysmic, even."

She rolled her eyes, but her smile was softer, a bit more relaxed.

I doubted she wanted me to wait her out, but I was curious as to what excuse she would come up with, so I remained where I was, watching her.

Finally, she spun around to pace to the far side of the room, turned back. "I don't know what's going on here." She motioned toward the bed as she neared. "This … whatever all that was…" She exhaled heavily, then sat on the edge of the bed at my feet. "I haven't quite wrapped my head around any of this yet."

"Any of what?"

"You. Me. This." She glanced over her shoulder. "Vampires and angels. Was any of that real? Or was I dreaming?"

"It's real."

"Which means nothing is as it seems, and my sister really is dead."

I felt the pain as it washed over her. "I'm sorry, *sezari*, but yes."

Another exhale, this one rich with exhaustion. "I was worried you would say that."

"Call in to work," I found myself saying at the same time I was thinking *or quit altogether*. I preferred she do the latter.

"I just started there. If I do, they'll fire me."

I smiled because there was absolutely no conviction in her words. "Good. Let them. We'll spend the night together."

As she peered back, I saw her smile in profile. "Didn't we already do that?"

"If you're talking about what went on here"—I patted the mattress—"that was how we passed the daylight hours. It's night. Time for us to get up."

"So you're a night owl, too, huh?"

"I ... uh ... can't go out in the sun," I reminded her, watching for her reaction.

"Oh, right." Her eyes darted to the windows. "Like vampires."

I smiled. "We share a few characteristics."

Orianna turned, resting her knee on the mattress. "Just out of curiosity, what exactly do you have that they don't?"

"A way with the ladies, for one."

She barked a laugh that eased some of the tension inside me. "Yeah?"

"I don't hear you complaining."

"I'd probably give you an A for effort."

Fucking hell, I loved when she teased me like that. I'd never encountered a female who was so straightforward, so easy to talk to. And despite the hardships she'd experienced, Orianna didn't seem jaded.

She smiled. "What else?"

I forgot what we were talking about, too caught up in staring at her, the way her blond hair hung over her shoulders, just barely hiding the fang marks I'd left on her neck. "Else?"

"Characteristics? What makes you different from vampires?" Her smile was radiant.

"Most noticeably? Probably the wings."

All signs of amusement faded from Orianna's expression, her eyes widening. "Wings?"

Figuring this was a conversation that required sensitivity, I decided to put it on the back burner for the moment.

"The evening meal's being served," I informed her. "Since neither of us ate this morning, perhaps we should go down, get some grub, then we'll figure out what to do for the rest of the night."

"What do you usually do at night?" she prompted, still watching me intently.

"Fight."

Her eyebrows rose. "Who do you fight?"

"Demons?"

The laugh that came from her was part disbelief, part hysteria. "You fight demons? Oh, my God."

Since it was clear she wasn't going to make a decision on whether to depart, eat, or something else altogether, I swung my legs over the edge of the bed and got to my feet. I padded to the bathroom, relieved myself, washed my hands and face, then returned to snag my jeans from the floor. Orianna was still sitting on the bed, same position as when I left. Obviously, she was trying to wrap her mind around the information I'd given her. Didn't surprise me that she couldn't. Most humans went to church to interact with God and His children. She was getting to know an angel on an entirely different level.

I bent down, grabbed my discarded T-shirt. As I stood to pull it on, soft fingers fluttered over my back. "Are these the wings you were referring to? It's a nice tattoo."

I held myself still, enjoying her touch. "There's no ink in my skin."

I felt her breath, and I assumed she had moved closer to inspect.

"So ... how?"

"Wings, *sezari*. When they're necessary, they'll emerge."

After tugging my shirt on, I turned to face her.

"Will you help me find my sister?"

The words were spoken so softly and with a desperation that made my chest ache. "Of course I will, *sezari*. Whatever it takes. But right now, let's go downstairs." I reached for her hand. "I'll introduce you to some of the others. We'll share a meal, then make a plan to get this search underway."

To my surprise, she nodded, taking my hand and allowing me to lead the way out of my private quarters.

When we reached the dining room, I was glad to see it was full. Orianna, on the other hand, seemed a bit hesitant, her hand tightening around mine as I led the way inside.

Penelope was the first to get to her feet. She gave Obsidian's shoulder a gentle squeeze before she made her way over, her *reuthet* following close behind.

I greeted her with a smile. "Orianna, I'd like you to meet Penelope Calazans, Obsidian's mate. Penelope, this is Orianna McKay."

213

"It's so nice to meet you," Penelope greeted, offering Orianna a hug that seemed to surprise my *amsouelot*.

Orianna pulled back, nodded to them both.

"Would you like me to introduce you to the others?" Penelope offered, her gaze briefly cutting to me.

I nodded my approval, then watched as Penelope led Orianna from one table to another, introducing her by name. I noticed she didn't make a reference to Orianna being my *amsouelot*, and I figured that was wise since I'd yet to give Orianna the lowdown on what it all meant, aside from destined to be together, yada yada.

"Things better this evening?" Obsidian asked, standing shoulder to shoulder with me.

"She's still here. I consider that a good thing."

"Good point." Obsidian turned to face me. "I hate to have to tell you this, but Michael wants a meeting."

I studied my brother, trying to read between the lines. "With me? Or all of us?"

"All of us."

That relieved me somewhat. While I wasn't intimidated by the archangel, the last thing I wanted was a tête-à-tête with the male. The last one we had was more than a century ago, and I still remember how well that had gone.

Turning back to look at Orianna, relief washed over me as she strolled in my direction.

Unfortunately, that was short-lived when her eyes rolled back in her head and she swayed on her feet.

BIJOU

I couldn't deny there were plenty of things to keep me distracted from my frustrations. I'd probably go so far as to call it drama. What with all the angels and Fae fluttering around in an attempt to figure out what turned that human's knees to Jell-O and all.

I'd witnessed it as it went down. One second, the pretty young human was offering a timid smile, the next, she was passing out, barely kept from crashing to the floor when Eclipse appeared at her side, preventing her impact with the floor.

A quick glance at my companion told me Oliver was distracted by the show. He was no longer staring at me as though I was from another planet. That was good, I figured.

Not that I minded the human's attention. Oddly, I was a bit flattered. Not since I'd been revealed to be Kaj's daughter had a single male given me so much as the time of day. Even the male who was courting me at the time had eased off, treating me like a leper, as though I was tainted simply because my father was the race's Alpha.

It made sense that it wouldn't matter to Oliver. And he didn't seem fazed by the way Kaj had stared at him across the room during the evening meal, his eyes all but shooting daggers at the male who had the audacity to speak with me. Either Oliver was incredibly brave or ridiculously stupid, but I was going to assume the former.

A scurry ensued as Eclipse lifted the female, easily carrying her out of the dining room while the others remained where they were, staring after the pair. Well, everyone except Penelope. She was right on their heels, eager to assist. Not surprising. Since the minute I arrived here at the angels' residence, Penelope had been more than welcoming. At first, it was frustrating because I wanted the angels to be assholes—to use Oliver's word—but instead, they seemed rather pleasant. Which made it difficult for me to keep my mad on.

"Have you been to the theater yet?" Oliver asked when the ruckus died down.

I peered over at my new friend. He was a handsome male, I'd give him that. Not quite what I was used to. By nature, vampires were more... well, *attractive* came to mind, but I wasn't sure that was the correct term because I'd met plenty of attractive humans. But there was something about Oliver. Beneath the nice packaging, I sensed an anger that bubbled down deep. There was something else, too, but I couldn't quite put my finger on it. Almost as though whatever it was had been shielded from everyone.

"There's a theater?" I stared into his pretty brown eyes. "Here?"

He nodded, then got to his feet. "I'll show you."

Since there was nothing I could do to assist the human and no one else seemed interested in what I was doing, I found no reason to decline, so I pushed back my chair and got to my feet. I peeked into the sunroom as we passed on our way to the back stairs. More angels and a few Fae had appeared, circling the human and her mate, their eyes reflecting their concern. Perhaps I should've stayed so I gave the impression I was concerned, as well. It would've been the politically correct thing to do, but at the moment, I wasn't feeling all that PC. In fact, I was tired of putting on a front. It was all I'd been doing for the past year, ever since I introduced myself to my father.

Being the perfect daughter to a male I hardly knew was far more difficult than it sounded.

My attention shifted to Oliver. I admired his profile, noting the stubble along his jaw, the sharp angle of his nose, the flecks of gold in his hair. Based on the small pinhole scar on his ear, I had to assume he'd had a piercing there at one time.

"Is it true you and Penelope are twins?" I asked.

His eyes cut over to me. "Yes."

I memorized his features, taking a snapshot in my mind. I pulled up one of Penelope and compared the two as I continued to follow Oliver up the stairs to the second floor. Odd how they had absolutely no similarities aside from the coloring of their hair and eyes. In fact, as I mentally compared them, I wondered how they could even be related. Usually, siblings had some distinct similarities, be it the structure of their bones, eyebrows, shape of their eyes, nose, even lips. I was surprised they shared even a little of the same DNA at all.

As for why I was so curious, I didn't know. I figured it was due to that hole I sensed inside Oliver, that piece of him that was being shielded from others. Had the angels picked up on that? Surely they had. From what I'd seen, they weren't the type to simply allow anyone to invade their ranks. They were doing a background check on me, after all.

"If it's not intrusive, might I ask how old you are?" I prompted as we started down the hallway on the second floor.

"Twenty-eight. You?"

"Twenty-seven."

"Not to sound like an idiot, but is that the same in human years?" he asked. "I mean, I assume you're immortal and all that."

I smiled over at him. "As far as physical maturity, we're the same. We reach puberty at the same time as humans. But when it comes to how I'm viewed, I'm still considered a child in the eyes of my elders."

"Interesting."

"Annoying, really," I admitted.

"At what age are you considered ... an adult?"

I laughed. "At least one hundred."

His eyes widened as he stopped. "Wow. That's..."

"Old?"

Oliver chuckled, the sound like the rough scrape of gravel. As though he didn't do it often.

"How old is your father?"

"Five hundred and twenty," she said easily.

"So, no time limit on the ability to reproduce?"

"No, though females are only fertile once every few years." I figured that was God's way of keeping a handle on the reproduction of the species.

"Here we are." Oliver opened the door to reveal an enormous theater room.

I preceded him inside, my eyes wandering the space. There were several rows of plush leather recliners, all with consoles between them, facing a white screen that was the full width and height of the wall, a good thirty feet across, maybe twenty feet tall. The walls on each side were covered in thick black drapes that hung from ceiling to floor, a few well-placed sconces providing light.

"Something specific you'd like to watch?" he asked, heading over to what appeared to be a laptop positioned on a table at the back, right next to what looked to be a fully stocked concession stand complete with a popcorn and soda machine. "Thanks to Apple, we've got anything and everything you could want."

I couldn't even remember the last time I watched a movie. "What sounds good to you?"

"I'm more of an action guy myself."

I found that sweet. Having experienced plenty of action in my lifetime thanks to the war between vampires and shadow beasts, I wasn't sure our definition of action was the same.

"How about *Hobbs and Shaw*?" he suggested.

I'd never heard of it, but I found myself nodding, figuring it would be nice to hang out with someone my own age for a change. I liked the idea of making a friend here at the mansion, especially if I was going to be here for a while.

After he hit a few buttons on the laptop, Oliver joined me, then motioned me down a few steps. I followed his lead, moving to the second row of seats before easing down into the luxurious recliner.

"There's a blanket and pillow in the console." He lifted the edge to prove it. "And if you want popcorn, simply push that button." He pointed to a silver button on the top of the console. "A *heurosp* will deliver it."

I grinned, getting comfortable as he punched another button on the console, dimming the lights as the movie began playing on the screen.

As I relaxed, I focused on the movie, forcing everything else from my mind, but it wasn't easy. Thoughts of Reve drifted in, reminding me of the male I missed with all my heart. The male who'd vowed to love me for eternity only to disappear as soon as he learned who my father was.

Oliver chuckled at something on the screen, and I peeked over at him. I studied him in profile momentarily before glancing back at the screen.

Perhaps Oliver would be a good distraction from the heartbreak I'd endured. It would be nice to have someone to confide in, someone who would share their own personal experiences. That was something I'd never had with Reve. As much as I'd wanted us to be together, he had never really been the sort to open up.

And maybe, if Oliver was open to the idea, we could do a little digging into that dark spot I sensed within him. Perhaps we could reveal that part of himself he probably didn't even know he was hiding.

16

ORIANNA

I had no idea what had happened, but when I came to, I was sitting on a buttery-soft leather sofa, half a dozen men and a few women standing around. Their expressions reflected the same thing: concern mixed with more than a little confusion.

"There you are," Eclipse whispered, brushing my hair back from my face.

Feeling like a spectacle, I dropped my feet to the floor and sat up quickly. The move had my head spinning, but I ignored it. Or tried to. For a second, the room went topsy-turvy, my stomach lurching with the sensation. I inhaled deeply through my nose, out through my mouth. A repeat of that a few times and the vertigo lessened.

"Are you all right?" Penelope asked from my other side.

I managed a nod. "Yes. I'm sorry about that. I just..."

I closed my eyes as the vision overtook me once more. I was standing over the body of a man. No, not a man. Obsidian. His eyes were closed, and Penelope was kneeling beside him, cradling his head as she rocked, tears flooding down her face.

"Oh, God."

"Bring her some water," Penelope insisted.

"Perhaps we should give her some air," someone suggested before the bodies began to scatter.

"Talk to me," Eclipse urged, one long finger curling under my chin to turn my head toward him.

His eyes moved over my face as though assessing to ensure I wasn't going to topple over again.

"I..." I swallowed hard. "I saw something."

His beautiful face contorted into a frown. "What?"

I looked up, my gaze searching until I found the male in my vision. "I saw you," I told Obsidian. "I don't know what it means. I just..."

"What did you see?" Penelope's voice was soft, her hand gentle as it settled on my arm.

Dropping my gaze to my hands, I inhaled, then released it slowly. "I saw Obsidian lying on the ground. You were holding his head and crying."

Penelope's sharp gasp tore at my heart. It was the one thing I'd always hated about revealing my visions. Most people thought I was crazy, and I couldn't necessarily blame them. It was always worse when the visions weren't necessarily pleasant.

"You were in a bright white room, no color whatsoever. I have no idea what it means, or if it's past or present..."

I breathed in through my nose, out through my mouth.

"Have they always come to fruition?" Obsidian asked. "Your visions?"

Without looking up at him, I nodded. It pained me to admit that because most of the time, I had no idea what the visions meant. "But they aren't always cut-and-dry. It's often open to interpretation."

"What else did you see?" Eclipse asked, his voice calm and comforting.

"That's all." I cut my eyes to Penelope. "Except ... I don't mean to be intrusive, but ... are you pregnant? Or were you?"

Penelope nodded. "I am, yes."

"How far along?"

Penelope's hand instantly went to her belly. I got the sense she was protecting what was most precious to her. "Nine weeks."

I exhaled heavily. "Then I think it's far in the future. In my vision, you're quite pregnant."

A rough growl had my head snapping up to Obsidian.

"What?"

Eclipse was the one to speak. "Angel pregnancies aren't the same as humans'."

"How so?"

"Where human female pregnancies last forty weeks, angels are on a much faster timeline. More like twenty weeks."

"Seventeen," Penelope said. "On average."

"Oh." Well, that certainly changed things.

"In your vision, could you see what was wrong with Obsidian?"

I closed my eyes and let the images replay in my head. "I don't see any blood, no visible wounds. But his eyes are closed, and ... I'm not sure he's breathing."

The couch cushion shifted, and when I opened my eyes, Penelope was standing next to Obsidian, her arms around him. It was then I noticed the extreme difference in their sizes. The man was enormous, like a mountain, and she was a much smaller ... hill.

"How often do you have these visions?" Eclipse asked.

"I haven't had many lately," I admitted. "But I used to have them all the time. Mostly about my ... family."

I tensed when I remembered the first time I'd had one. I was ten years old, and the image I saw was of my mother lying cold and unmoving in an alley. At the time, I thought it was a nightmare, and I'd kept it to myself. Nearly two years to the day later, it had come to fruition. Had I revealed it to my parents, perhaps my mother never would've been hurt.

Eclipse's hand moved over mine, and I realized I was trembling.

"It's all right, *sezari*," he whispered. "Let me take you upstairs."

Unable to find a reason to argue, I nodded. I allowed him to tug me to my feet, then followed as he walked down the steps and through the kitchen.

By the time we reached Eclipse's bedroom, my legs were weak. No, my entire body was weak. As though my muscles were finally taking a vacation, giving in because someone else was strong enough to carry my burden for a while.

"Eclipse!" I squealed in surprise.

The next thing I knew, I was in Eclipse's arms, my face tucked against his neck. I breathed him in and relaxed.

"What are you doing?" I mumbled when he set me on my feet in the bathroom.

"Bathing you," he said softly before proceeding to undress us both.

I hadn't even noticed he'd turned on the water in the tub, but I was grateful when he lifted me once more and carried me up the steps, then settled us both in the warm water. I didn't pull away from him, simply wrapped my arms around his neck and held on for dear life.

God, I was tired. Exhausted really. I hadn't even realized how much until now. It was as though the past six years had taken their toll on me, draining all my energy reserves. Probably didn't help that I hadn't eaten in... I couldn't recall the last real meal I had. Cheez-Its and Mountain Dew had become my only source of nourishment for so long.

"I've got you, *sezari.*" Eclipse pressed his lips to the top of my head.

"I believe you," I whispered, pressing my lips to his neck. "I don't know why, but I do."

His big hand cupped the back of my head as I kissed my way up to his jaw. We remained like that for long minutes, making out in the tub, neither moving to explore further, simply settling on the tongue-to-tongue action. It was nice, but of course, the heat it inspired in me was far too powerful to ignore forever.

Without thinking, I repositioned so I was straddling Eclipse's thighs. He clearly knew what I needed because he took over, redistributing my weight as though I was little more than a feather. His hand slid under my thigh, angling the hard ridge of his erection to my core. With a sigh, I sank down on him slowly, allowing the blessed friction to send chills over my skin.

"You feel so good," I whispered, resting my cheek against his as he maneuvered once again, his hips angling so he slid deeper inside me.

I moaned softly, then buried my face in his neck as he rocked his hips forward and back. The pleasure was intense as he moved, the friction making my skin tingle, my nipples pebble. It was utter perfection, and I held on to the feeling for long minutes.

"Eclipse..." I nuzzled his neck, my tongue licking over his skin.

Suddenly another vision appeared, this one robbing the air from my lungs. I saw myself lying in a room, my body unmoving as Eclipse leaned over me. I knew I was dead, but oddly, that didn't scare me. But there was pain, only I didn't think it came from my body. It was an emotional turmoil. Seeing Eclipse hurting was something I couldn't fathom, the thought of him being in pain...

"Come back to me," Eclipse rumbled in my ear.

I jolted out of the vision, my lips seeking his. And when he kissed me, a warmth filled my entire being. It was so much more than mere lust. In fact, it wasn't a chemical reaction at all. No, this was more. Deeper.

I was falling in love with this ... angel.

And I was falling fast.

ECLIPSE

I knew I was invading Orianna's privacy as I slipped into her mind. I felt her acceptance even as an image of the mating chamber played in her head. I sensed her peace, her acceptance of me taking her life. I saw myself leaning over her, guarding her body until she returned to me. But what surprised me most was the fact there was no fear on her part.

Not for herself, anyway. Her concern was only for me and the pain I endured because ... yes, I felt her love for me.

It was a humbling moment, one I wanted to last forever. Not only because I was buried in her tight sheath, her arms wreathing my neck as our tongues mated the same as our bodies. This was the perfect moment, the one I'd waited a life-time for. Having her here with me, even after such a short period of time, had changed my perspective on everything. Well, mostly everything. There was still no way in hell I could fathom taking her life in order to merge our souls. That was pure and utter bullshit as far as I was concerned, but—

Suddenly, Orianna pulled back, her pretty blue eyes meeting mine seconds before her head fell back on her shoulders, and she cried out my name. I stared at her, my cock pulsing. She was so beautiful like that, all soft, smooth skin, the lines of her body mesmerizing me. I watched as her nipples pebbled tightly, her body vibrating as I pushed in deeper. Gripping her hips firmly, I rocked her on me, savoring that moment when we were one, nothing separating us. Orianna's breath hitched, her nails digging into my shoulders as I pulled her hips toward me, burying myself as deep as I could go.

"Eclipse..." Orianna's eyes opened as she leaned forward, pressing her forehead to mine. "I want to feel you come inside me."

Her words, whispered in that sexy rasp, had my cock twitching, that familiar electricity tingling at the base of my spine.

"Now," she urged, her inner muscles squeezing me.

I held on for as long as I could, relishing the feeling of her surrender. And when I came, it was with her name falling from my lips.

This time when Orianna relaxed against me, I eased deeper

into the water, holding her tight as I shifted her so she was settled on my lap once more.

"I need to know everything about you," she said, her voice weak with exhaustion.

I grinned. "What do you want to know?"

"I don't know. Have you always been here? I mean, I don't even know if Heaven's real or not."

"It's real," I assured her. "We've been here for fifteen hundred years now."

"We?"

"My brothers and I."

"Are your parents still alive?"

"They are," I confirmed. "Both of them. They reside in Heaven."

"Do you have a relationship with them?"

"No. Not since they sent me to Michael."

"I'm sorry."

"Don't be." I felt nothing for the archsire and archdam who had created me. Perhaps I had back in the beginning, but it didn't take long for me to realize they were merely the vessels that had given me life. Matthias and Teodara created me, raised me, even, but they'd long since passed me off like they had every male offspring they birthed.

"Who's Michael?"

"An archangel. He sent us to Earth to protect humans."

"I should be surprised," Orianna said, still relaxed against me. "And I'm sure I will be. Later."

"Why later?" I asked.

"Because right now, I'm simply too ... content."

Of all the emotions she could've felt, I was surprised by that one. "May I ask why?"

I felt her cheeks pull up in a smile. "Because I'm here with you. Just like this."

I pressed a kiss to her forehead.

"I'm so tired," she said softly.

"Sleep, *sezari*." I knew she needed it. I hadn't even considered how taking her vein would drain her, but I suspected that was the reason for her exhaustion. Her body hadn't yet recovered, and it didn't help that she hadn't eaten anything in a while.

"Not like that," she whispered. "It's more than physical."

I remained silent, hoping she would continue.

"I've spent so long looking for Amber. I've traipsed across the country and back. I won't give up. Not until I see her for myself. But this is the first time I've stopped to take a breath in a long time. It feels good."

Since the only thing I wanted was to make my female happy, it helped to hear her admit that.

"I've got you," I said softly. "And I always will."

"That's what scares me," she said, her words slurring.

"It can't be changed, *sezari*. You might as well accept it."

She chuckled softly. "Easier said than done."

Maybe.

17

REIDAR

"How's she doing?" I asked Eclipse when the male joined us in the war room shortly after the sun went down and the evening meal was consumed.

"Better."

The sigh of relief that followed spoke to the degree of concern Eclipse had been carrying around for the past four days, ever since Orianna collapsed during the evening meal. The past few days were chaotic to say the least, everyone moving about in hopes of helping in any way they could, wanting to ensure Eclipse's *amsouelot* had everything she needed.

"She seems to be settling in well," I added, hoping to encourage the male to talk.

Eclipse nodded, smiled. "I'm not sure she's got much of a choice. Penelope and Acadia are doting on her like she's royalty. Not to mention, I think Jeffrey's her self-proclaimed biggest fan."

I chuckled. "She does have a way with the *heurosp*, doesn't she?"

For the past few days, ever since Orianna's vision of Obsidian, the entire mansion had been keeping a close eye on the female. Partly because they were curious as to her visions, but more so because it was becoming clear that Orianna's health had become Eclipse's primary concern. Since we were all there to support the warrior, we were offering the same to his *amsouelot*. And while the *heurosp* hadn't shucked their duties that supported the rest of us, it was clear Orianna had become their number two concern, right after the pregnant Penelope.

"Well, I'm glad to hear she's getting better."

"Which is what brings me down here," Eclipse said, his gaze scanning the various computer equipment in the room.

"What do you need?"

"For starters, my *lieterra*."

I glanced around. "Miklós is currently on patrol, but I can get him back here if you need him immediately."

Eclipse shook his head. "No. But I want him off rotation for a while."

"Of course." I stepped up to one of the laptops, keyed in a few commands to pull up the week's schedule. I made a couple of adjustments, then turned to Eclipse. "Done. Next?"

Eclipse's attention shifted to the computers. "I want a laptop delivered to the third-floor conference room. Whatever Orianna might need to do some internet searches."

"I can have it delivered within the hour. Any specific access you want her to have?"

Eclipse's eyes narrowed, his voice lowering. "I want to find her sister."

I nodded. "I'm sure we can do that. We can track her movements, see—"

"Her sister's dead," Eclipse said softly. "So it's more of a recovery mission."

Oh, damn. That fucking sucked.

"Which is why I want Miklós to help her," Eclipse continued. "I'm hoping they can utilize the Misplaced Halos boards and see if they can trace her last whereabouts. We need to know what happened to her. If at all possible, we need to recover her body, have her put to rest appropriately."

"Of course. I'll—"

"I need to talk to you."

The shrill sound came from behind Eclipse, the voice drawing every conversation in the room to a halt. When Eclipse turned, I noticed Winnie standing in the doorway, hands on her hips, eyes narrowed on me.

Perfect. Just what I didn't need right now.

"I need a minute," I told her.

"No. Now."

Luckily, Eclipse appeared understanding because he offered my shoulder a sympathetic squeeze before he vanished.

As I stared at my female, I wished I could do the same. The vanishing part. The past few days had been … well, they'd been hell if I was being honest. Had it not been my night off, I would've been out with the others, tracking down these damn shadow beasts. As much as I didn't look forward to tangling with them again, it sure as shit beat the alternative, which these days was arguing with Winnie.

"Søren, can you cover for me? I'll be back in a few."

Stygian's *lieterra* nodded, the sympathy in his eyes something I was getting used to seeing. Seemed everyone in the mansion had caught on to the nonstop bickering that was going on. No matter how much I tried to placate Winnie, she found something else to bitch about.

"Let's go upstairs," I urged Winnie, directing her back into the hallway.

We strolled up the stairs, through the kitchen, an icy chill coming off Winnie as we passed Penelope, Acadia, and Orianna. The three females were sitting at the island, Penelope and Acadia ensuring Orianna downed every last bite of the turkey sandwich in front of her.

Although Penelope offered her best friend a quick wave, Winnie ignored it, marching forward as though no one else was in the mansion.

I gave Penelope an apologetic shrug, following Winnie. God forbid I stop to chat with someone. I did that yesterday, and Winnie launched into a tirade about how everyone else was more important than she was.

Truth was, I had no idea what was going on with her or why she was so hell-bent on going back to California, but it was a rant that was becoming all too familiar.

When we finally reached my room on the second floor, Winnie slammed through the door, her anger palpable.

I closed the door, the soft *click* sounding overly loud in the room.

As though that was the trigger, Winnie spun around, hands going to her hips. "When are we leaving?"

"I'm sorry. What?"

"Back to California, Reidar. Don't play dumb with me."

"Who's playing, Winnie?" I snapped. "I have no idea what you're talking about."

She huffed, hands flying. "I told you, I want to go home. You said you'd go with me."

"No," I drawled slowly, then shook my head. "That's not what I said."

I didn't want to accept the fact that Winnie wasn't my *amsouelot*, but it wasn't the first time I'd thought as much. Long before today. I hated to think I'd jumped the gun, ultimately altering Winnie's life indefinitely, but I was slowly coming to terms with it. Key word being *slowly*. And for whatever reason, Winnie thought I was simply blowing her off.

That so wasn't the case.

"It's not as easy as it sounds," I said with a long exhale. "Winnie, we can't simply go to California."

Her eyes narrowed. "You keep saying that! But you won't tell me what that means."

It meant we'd be starting over. As in our lives. For one, I would be rendered *fallen*, sent into the human world to live out my mortal life. If I didn't have doubts about us, I would've been content to commit to Winnie for another fifty or sixty years. A few weeks ago ... sure, I would've walked away from this world and followed her anywhere.

But as difficult as it was to admit, I didn't think I was the male Winnie was meant to spend her eternity with.

"Can you tell me why you want to go so badly?" I asked, giving the female my full attention.

As was the case anytime I asked that question, Winnie turned away from me. "I just do."

"Is it your family?"

"Of course it is."

Lie. I could detect it, and that wasn't the first one she told me. In fact, Winnie had been lying to me for a solid month now, which was the first clue I had that she wasn't my *amsouelot*. She was keeping something from me, but I didn't know what it was. Out of respect for her, I refused to slip into her mind and find the truth. I owed her more than that.

"I need to get back to work," I told her.

"Oh, trust me, I know I play second fiddle to your job, Reidar. You care about it more than you care about me."

Arguing was a waste of time. No matter how many times I told her otherwise, Winnie kept with the same tune.

"We'll talk in the morning," I told her.

"If I'm still here."

Moving toward her, I said softly, "Winnie, I'm really sorry. Whatever I did, whatever's given you the idea you don't matter..."

Winnie spun around. "You, Reidar. You've given me the idea. It's a wonder you sleep in the same bed with me."

"I'm trying, Win. I'm really trying."

I could feel the anger coming from her. Had I detected even a hint of hurt, I probably would've dropped to my knees and begged her forgiveness despite the fact I didn't know what I'd done. However, I got the feeling this didn't have anything to do with me at all. Something was luring Winnie back to California while she was insisting someone was pushing her away.

I reached up to cup her face, but before I could make contact, she jerked away.

"Just go back to work. If I'm here when you're done, we'll talk."

With that, I walked away, wondering if this would be the last time. She made the threat so often I figured at some point she would make good on it.

ORIANNA

"I know I keep saying this, but you look so much better."

I smiled at Penelope. "I feel better."

Honestly, I hadn't realized how exhausted I was until the other day when I collapsed under the weight of that last vision. Since then, Eclipse had all but confined me to bed rest. At the beginning, I argued, insisting I was fine.

I so hadn't been fine. Not only had my body been screaming for some R and R, my emotional well-being had taken a hit as well. Not easy to spend so long chasing one goal only to hit a wall. Finding out my sister was dead was the equivalent of a concrete barrier getting intimate with a semi going sixty miles per hour. The crash was inevitable, and it took Eclipse pointing it out for me to see it.

Insert bed rest and some quiet, and I was as good as new.

Over the past few days, I'd learned quite a bit about myself, though. One, I didn't so much mind someone taking care of me from time to time. No, I didn't intend to put my feet up for the rest of my life, but a few days had reset all my levers, and I felt more like myself than I had in the past ... forever.

The downside? Well, that would be the fact the only outfit I brought with me was getting a bit snug. Luckily, I spent most of my time in Eclipse's room, either naked or wearing one of his super-comfy T-shirts. But if they kept shoveling food down me, I would easily put back on those ten pounds I'd inadvertently lost. Which was all good and fine, but my wardrobe would have to be updated if that happened.

If I didn't know better, I would think that was Eclipse's goal.

"I hoped to find you here."

That familiar voice triggered an immediate smile response as I turned to see Eclipse coming toward me from the front of the mansion.

"I thought you went to the war room." I lifted my head to meet his kiss.

"I got chased out of there. Went upstairs to take care of something."

I figured Winnie was the one to chase him off. Based on the way the woman had stormed through the kitchen a little while ago, no one would want to be in her direct path.

According to Penelope, Winnie was going through a rough time right now, and the best thing we could do was give her space. I had to take her word for it because I hadn't spent much time with Penelope's best friend from high school. Aside from a brief introduction and a couple of words in passing, we hadn't talked.

"Mind if I steal her for a little while?" Eclipse asked, his question directed at Penelope and Acadia.

"Of course not." Penelope grinned. "Remember, you still owe me a movie."

I got to my feet. "That I do. How about Friday?"

"It's a date."

Eclipse was shaking his head.

"What?"

"I don't understand how women can spend five minutes together and become best friends."

"It's been more than five minutes," Acadia said with a smirk. "At least six."

I laughed. "Definitely six."

Admittedly, it was a bit odd for me to have forged a bond so quickly, but I enjoyed Penelope's and Acadia's company. The two women were persistent, something I wasn't used to. In fact, aside from Amber, I had never really had any close friends. It was rather nice.

"Well, she's mine for the time being," Eclipse told them, linking his fingers with mine.

"See you at morning meal." Penelope nodded, as though that was a definitive, not a question.

"Yes, you will. I promise."

I allowed Eclipse to lead me out of the kitchen, then down the hallway to the elevator to the third floor.

"I can walk up the stairs," I assured him.

"Not necessary. That's what the elevator's for."

Funny he should say that. For the first full day I was down, Eclipse insisted on carrying me up and down the stairs. At least he now allowed me to walk on my own.

When we stepped out of the elevator onto the third floor, Zeus was snoozing on the sofa. As soon as he heard us, his head popped up, and his tongue lolled out of his mouth.

"Hey, buddy." I went straight for him, perching on the cushion beside him so I could give him some love. It was the least I could do, considering he'd been keeping me company while Eclipse was working.

"This way," Eclipse said. "He can come with you."

I smiled at the dog. "You hear that? We get to hang out some more."

When I got to my feet, Zeus did the same, falling into step with me.

"Where're we going?"

"Conference room."

Turned out the conference room was down the hall to the left, beyond a couple of doors and what appeared to be a laundry facility. From what I'd seen, the mansion was more the size of a resort hotel than a residence. Based on what Penelope told me, it housed seventy people and employed another couple of dozen. Made sense they'd have laundry rooms on every floor.

Eclipse led the way into a large room complete with a conference table that seated ten people. On one wall was a projection screen, and on the table, there was a triangular telephone.

"It's just decor," Eclipse said, nodding at the phone. "Cimmerian said it made us official. Apparently, humans prefer those things."

I smiled. "Telephones?"

"That fancy conference shit."

Chuckling, I skimmed the rest of the room, a little surprised there weren't motivational posters on the wall. Not that I'd ever visited a conference room before, but I watched plenty of television. I knew the drill.

At the far end of the table, there was a laptop.

"Are you putting me to work?" I teased.

"Actually ... I'm bringing someone in for you to put to work."

No sooner did I get "Who?" out of my mouth than Miklós stepped into the room.

"Hey," Eclipse's right-hand guy said with a smile.

As usual, Miklós was impeccably dressed with his fancy silk button-down—this one almost the same royal blue as his eyes—stretched across his enormous chest and his fancy gray slacks with their perfect crease. The cuffs sat atop a pair of black Ferragamo loafers polished to a shine, not a scuff mark in sight.

In direct contradiction to his perfectly pulled-together wardrobe, Miklós's sandy-blond hair was pulled back into a man bun, a few wisps blown back from his face. His beard and mustache—both of which were more blond than brown—

were perfectly trimmed, as though they weren't about to let down the rest of him the way his hair did.

I had the chance to talk to Miklós a few times over the past couple of days when he stopped in the kitchen to chat while Penelope and Acadia were force-feeding me protein and carbs. And when I wasn't talking to him, I was getting the scoop on how things worked within the structure of these soldiers and the warriors—how they referred to Eclipse and his brothers. According to the intel I received, Miklós was Eclipse's right-hand man, otherwise known as a *lieterra*. Of all those who worked for Eclipse, he was closest to Miklós, having spent the past four hundred fifty years working side by side, ever since Miklós was assigned to him.

"What exactly is it we'll be doing here?" I asked Eclipse.

He leaned in and pressed a quick kiss to my lips. "Miklós is here to help you find your sister."

My heart kicked in my chest a couple of times, but the pain was a bit duller than it had been a few days ago.

"And believe it or not," Miklós said, "we've got quite a few things we can do without ever leaving the mansion."

That would certainly be nice. Heaven knew I'd had no luck pounding pavement for six years, so I wasn't sure I believed perusing the internet was going to do much good, but at this point, I was willing to give it a shot.

"While you two get that underway, I need to step out for a bit."

That got my attention.

"Just to help Kaj." His voice was softer; clearly he'd detected my concern. "I promise to check in."

Unable to resist, I put my hand on his cheek and kissed him, letting it linger. It was strange that in just a few days, I'd come to worry about him. Especially when he went out to fight, as they all referred to it.

"Be careful."

"Always, *sezari*."

Another quick peck and he was strolling out the door, leaving me alone with Miklós.

"He's always careful," the angel said.

"Are you reading my mind?"

He chuckled. "Don't need to. You care for him. That's evident. And if I can give you any reassurance whatsoever, I'm happy to."

"So, if you're his right-hand man, why aren't you working with him?"

"I'm more of his assistant, you could say. Magnar's his *ladeare*. He's the one Eclipse leans on out in the field."

"Do you fight?" I figured he must, considering the way he was built.

"When it's necessary, sure."

It would take some time to understand all the logistics.

"So, where do we start?" I asked, taking a seat in front of the laptop Eclipse had acquired forme.

"First off, let's get you up and running on the Misplaced Halos boards."

I peered over at the angel. "The what now?"

"That's the term used to refer to angels and vampires."

"Misplaced Halos?" I couldn't help it, I smiled. "Sounds like a rock band."

"We're far more badass."

For the next couple of hours, Miklós proved how true that statement was.

18

ECLIPSE

"Still no bead on those vampires?" I asked, falling into step with Kaj as we made a pass through one of the empty downtown streets.

"No." The male peered over at me. "And not for lack of trying. Fuckers all but disappeared."

I had a difficult time believing that. Kaj might've lost the majority of his high-level ranks, but there were still plenty of boots on the ground. And vampires were a tight-knit group. It was the main reason my brothers and I utilized the Misplaced Halos boards. Most of those were maintained by the vampires keeping tabs on one another. Someone knew where these traitors were; it was just a matter of unearthing them.

"So why are we out here?" I asked.

"Because someone knows something."

That was generally the case, sure. But for the past three hours, we'd yet to encounter anyone who knew the female responsible for luring Orianna to the Dungeon or the vampires she was with.

"Any news from Darko?"

A soft growl was Kaj's response.

"Do you trust the male?"

"No reason not to."

"Doesn't answer my question."

Kaj peered over, his green eyes narrowed. "Right now, I don't know who to trust."

"Me," I said with a smirk. "You can trust me."

"Can I?"

My smirk pulled into a full-fledged grin. "Have I ever given you a reason not to?"

"Not yet."

"You're a glass-half-empty kinda guy, huh?"

Kaj grinned, the first one tonight.

"How's Acadia?"

Another soft growl.

I was coming to learn that meant the vampire had no comment on the subject. Made hunting with him rather dull.

"Since we're not gonna chat about feelings, why don't you tell me what your plans are."

"What plans?" Kaj muttered.

"For starters, how long you planning to shack up with us?"

The male laughed. He actually fucking laughed. "Not like you don't have enough room."

"True." We had more room than we knew what to do with. Granted, most of the rooms were taken, and with Penelope and Obsidian expecting, I heard they were looking to do some construction. Something about adding a nursery or some shit.

"Plus, I think Jeffr—" Kaj came to a halt, holding up his hand.

I allowed my senses to span across the area, taking stock of what and who was nearby. Two humans ducking behind a Dumpster, one male, one female. The smell of chemicals and burning plastic left me to believe they were sharing a crack pipe. In one of the abandoned warehouses, I detected three bodies, all tucked in for the night beneath a pile of rags and newspapers.

It was during the sweep inward that I picked up on what Kaj had. Three males—not human, angel, or vampire—strolling down the alley running parallel to us.

Shadow beasts? I projected into Kaj's mind.

Based on their scent, yeah.

Hmm.

We'd yet to encounter any since Obsidian's run-in with them a few days ago.

Because I knew it would require more than just me and the head vampire, I sent out a request to Magnar, asking my *ladeare* to home in on my position and make an appearance. With backup.

Less than a minute later, Magnar appeared with Echo, Cayden, and Ajax at his side. A minute after that, Reidar and Raksa joined the party.

Kaj shot off some hand signals, motioning for four to go one way and three to follow him. I opted to go in the opposite direction of Kaj. Considering we were the strongest as far as powers went, I figured it might work in our favor to get these bastards corralled between us.

Taking off at a jog, I led Echo, Magnar, and Ajax back the way we'd come. We slipped between two abandoned buildings and came out on the other side. The three males I'd detected were sniffing the air, likely having caught our scent.

"Strategy?" Magnar asked, voice low.

Damn good question. If these were shadow beasts, blades and bullets weren't going to cut it.

"See if we can maneuver them toward Kaj," I said.

Magnar, Echo, and Ajax spread out behind me, the three males forming a wall of muscle while I tossed up a barrier that would help direct the demons backward. It worked, though we garnered the full attention of the beasts. A couple of snarls sounded, proof they'd picked up on my little trick.

At the far end of the alley, Kaj appeared, Reidar, Raksa, and Cayden behind him. All dressed in black, they blended with the night. With the exception of the light glinting off the steel blades they handled and the green glow igniting in Kaj's eyes.

Although I would've been thrilled to go hand-to-hand with these assholes, we'd already learned our usual methods of elimination weren't going to do the trick. So, rather than drag shit out, I focused on Kaj.

You said fire works, right?

Kaj nodded from his end of the alley.

Think you can give them a shove my way?

Of course. Just say the word.

I stopped, spreading my legs wide as I summoned the energy from the universe. Not quite the same amount required to draw a lightning bolt from the sky, but it was a bit more than I was used to handling, which meant I would be drained when this was all over. Because I trusted my males to get me to safety afterward, I closed my eyes, drew in more energy as I lifted my hands, palms up. Sparks ignited between my fingertips, then ignited into a full-blown flame.

On three, I told Kaj.

One...

Two...

Three!

I opened my eyes to see Kaj pull his hands back, then shove them forward, the move forcing a wave that displaced the energy between us. The shadow beasts were caught directly in between. With that wave pushing them toward me, I did the same maneuver, launching the flames out from the palms of my hands, essentially turning my arms into flamethrowers. I nailed two of the demons on the first shot, singeing them to ash. Before Kaj and I could gear up for the next round, the third beast shot twenty feet into the sky, landing on the rooftop to the north.

"He's mine!" Kaj yelled before he vanished.

Because I knew the male couldn't eliminate the damn thing without some help, I sent Magnar and Ajax after the vampire even as I dropped to my knees.

"Mansion," Reidar barked. "Now."

I nodded, but I'd already wasted too much effort. I couldn't disappear myself, no matter how hard I tried.

Didn't matter. Even as I let gravity take me to my ass, Reidar was already on the phone making calls. Someone would come for me. Of that I was certain. And the four males now surrounding me would ensure nothing happened to me in the meantime.

ORIANNA

"We've got incoming."

I finished typing the message I was working on. Miklós and I had been working nonstop for the past few hours, perusing the Misplaced Halos boards, dropping a few messages in the hopes of finding someone who had seen Amber.

When I looked up, I noticed Miklós's perfectly groomed eyebrows were cast in a deep-set V, eyes narrowed.

I sat up straight, stretched out my arms. "What's wrong?"

Miklós held up a finger for me to wait as he spoke directly into his phone. "I need a sitrep."

He was quiet for a moment, likely while someone was rambling on the other end, but I could see the concern in his deep blue eyes. When he thrust a hand through his hair, tugging the shoulder-length strands out of their neat little bun, I got the feeling the news was bad.

"What is it?" I asked, my voice soft but stern when he set his phone down and shot to his feet.

"It's Eclipse."

Like a jack-in-the-box, I was vertical. "What's wrong?"

"Nothing." There was an oddly reassuring note in his tone. "However, he is going to need to feed."

"What does that even mean?"

His eyes dropped to the fang marks on my neck.

"No." I grinned. "I know what it means. But why? Why does he need to feed?"

"I'll let him tell you himself."

When he started moving, I followed, marching out of the conference room, down the wide hallway. Zeus trotted alongside me. Every so often he would nudge my hand, a silent reassurance he was there with me. Evidently, he was the only one who seemed to sense my panic.

"At least tell me if he's injured."

Miklós peered over. "No, of course not. I would tell you if he was."

I wasn't sure I believed him, but considering I had no recourse, I merely followed him down the stairs to the main floor, onward until we reached the garage. Obsidian had already arrived, clearly having received the news.

"The only reason we brought him in," Obsidian explained, "is because he wasn't strong enough to dematerialize. He's not injured, but he is drained and will need to feed."

I nodded.

"On blood."

I smiled and tilted my head to the side. "I'm rather familiar with that part."

Although, I wasn't sure I'd actually fed Eclipse yet. Every time he was at my vein, it seemed more like an intimacy than a necessity.

The instant the exterior door began to rise, my gaze swung over. I watched impatiently as the blacked-out SUV pulled in and the door closed behind it, but not before the cold gusts of air ripped through the warmth. I wasn't sure what I expected, but it wasn't to see Eclipse get out on his own or walk over to me. He didn't look any worse for wear, merely exhausted.

Unable to resist, I walked right into his arms when he held them open. My face pressed to his chest as I let his warmth seep into me, another reassurance that he was all right. I had no idea how long I stood there, my arms around him, his hand gently sliding over my hair, but it wasn't until someone cleared their throat that I pulled back.

"Any word from Kaj?" Eclipse asked Obsidian.

"Not yet, but the sun's coming up soon. He'll be back."

That seemed to placate Eclipse because he took my hand, linked our fingers. "I'm gonna call it a day."

Obsidian nodded. "I'll have Jeffrey bring food up."

"Tell him to wait a couple of hours," Eclipse added.

"Will do."

As expected, Eclipse led the way to the elevator, only this one was in a panel in the garage, blending perfectly, as though it didn't exist.

"How many of these things are there?" I asked, an attempt to make conversation.

"Three." His arm went around my shoulder, and he pulled me into him, as though he needed me to be there.

The trip up took only a minute, the door making no noise when it opened on the third floor.

Planting my hand on his hard stomach, I leaned into him as we walked down the hallway. We'd come from the opposite direction than usual, so the distance to Eclipse's private quarters wasn't nearly as far.

"Miklós and Obsidian said you need to feed," I told him when he made a beeline for the bed.

He nodded. "I do. But it can wait."

"No, it can't."

Evidently my tone was stronger than Eclipse expected because his eyes shot to my face.

I smiled, pleased I could get this strong, powerful angel's attention. "Look, you took care of me. Now it's my turn to take care of you."

He shook his head. "Not the same thing, *sezari*."

"How do you figure?"

Eclipse removed the dark shades that covered his eyes. Those molten silver irises were churning.

"For starters, caring for you doesn't require my blood."

"So?"

"So?" Eclipse's shoulders tensed. "You've just regained your strength, Orianna. I'm not about to deplete it again."

"What's the alternative?" I asked, but as soon as the words were out of my mouth, I wasn't sure I wanted to know the answer. I'd already heard how the Fae were there to fuel the angels. My thoughts instantly drifted to Acadia, the stunningly flawless fairy I spent quite a bit of time with these past few days. The thought of Eclipse at her neck ... yeah, no way. Even thinking about it made my vision go red.

"It's not like that, *sezari*."

The laugh that bubbled out of me rang with fear, not amusement. "No, Eclipse. I ... I can't handle that."

"Okay, but we'll wait. At least until you've eaten."

I noticed the gaunt look on his face, could see the exhaustion in the lines forming around his mouth.

"I am perfectly fine," I insisted, eliminating the distance between us. "Now, where are we going to do this?"

Eclipse seemed surprised by my demanding tone, but if that was what it took to get this angel to understand I was serious, then so be it.

I stopped directly in front of him, staring up into those mesmerizing eyes, my hands resting on his chest. I felt the muscles flex beneath my palms, realized his entire body was harder than it had been when we were in the elevator.

"I want to take care of you," I said softly, ensuring he heard both my sincerity and my insistence.

"The Fae are here to—"

I narrowed my eyes. "Do you want to be with me, Eclipse?"

He frowned. "Of course I do."

"Then you won't bring that up ever again."

"But it's true."

"Perhaps. But if you put your mouth on another woman—fairy, angel, vampire, whatever—you will never put your mouth on me again."

Based on the way his eyes widened, I'd shocked him. Good. I wanted him to know I had no intentions of sharing him. Not with anyone.

"Now, where are we going to do this?" I repeated.

The next thing I knew, Eclipse's hand was fisted in my hair and his mouth was fused to mine. I could taste his passion, his need. He wanted what I could offer him, but he didn't want to hurt me.

"I'm stronger than you give me credit for," I mumbled against his lips.

He growled, then his hands were cupping my ass, lifting me off my feet. I didn't have time to shriek before I was on my back on the bed, his enormous body moving over me. Rather than bring his mouth to mine once again, Eclipse straddled my legs as he stripped his T-shirt off, tossing it to the floor. My eyes trailed down the sinewy lines of his torso as he dragged my T-shirt up and over my head. I silently pleaded for him to be careful because the clothes I wore were borrowed, but the words never came out.

Turned out, I liked him like this. All aggression and power, taking what he wanted, while underneath all that passion, I saw the ease with which he treated me. By the time we were both naked, I was panting, desperate to feel him.

As he held himself over me, I propped up on my elbows, pressing my lips to the strong column of his neck. He tilted his head, giving me better access as I licked his skin. He smelled so good, a natural scent unique to him.

When his big hand cupped the back of my head, the move holding me at his neck, I sucked his skin into my mouth, latching on firmly. He groaned, a dark rumble vibrating through his chest. I kissed and licked, working my way up to his ear.

"I want to feed you, Eclipse." I nipped his earlobe. "I want to heal you. Only me."

Another dark rumble escaped seconds before he crushed his mouth to mine once more.

19

ECLIPSE

I had never felt a hunger this great. And I knew there was only one capable of quenching it, sating me, healing me. Her words, her touch ... they triggered the animal within. It took every ounce of my remaining strength to keep from tearing the flesh at her neck in my efforts to take what she so willingly offered.

"*Sezari...*"

"Take from me, Eclipse," she whispered, tilting her head to the side.

My eyes locked on the pulse in her neck, all that soft flesh. Brushing her hair back, I leaned in and inhaled her sweet lavender scent. How she still smelled the same, I wasn't sure. For the past few days, she'd showered with my soap, yet Orianna still smelled sweet.

Her hand curled behind my head, urging me closer.

"I need to be inside you, *sezari*."

She relaxed beneath me, her legs spreading, giving my hips the room they needed as I moved over her. My cock pulsed when I felt the silky heat of her core. Her soft moans brought me back from the brink, reminded me her pleasure was far more important than my own needs. I doubted she realized the magnitude of what she was offering. Sure, I'd taken her vein a few times, but I'd yet to truly feed from her.

Soft fingers curled around my shaft, stroking me, making my entire body tremble with anticipation. And when Orianna guided me into the blissful heat of her body, I felt some of my strength return. She did that to me. As though my entire existence was now fueled by this one female.

"Feed," she demanded, her fingers clutching the back of my head.

"I don't want to hurt you." The words rasped out of my mouth as immense pleasure overcame me. The smooth walls of her pussy clutched me as I sank in deeper.

"You won't."

How she could be so certain, I didn't know. But her trust in me was humbling.

I shifted my hips, retreating slowly, then sinking inside her as I rested my upper body on my forearms.

"You have to be still for me," I whispered, licking her neck. "Don't move."

"I'll do my best," she said with a soft chuckle.

I focused on the flex of my hips as I rocked in and out of her, her body stretching around me, the friction igniting the flames within me. My fangs elongated, preparing for her offering.

"Be still," I said once more as I dragged the sharp tips across her flesh.

Orianna's hands clutched my back, her thighs tight to my hips.

I closed my eyes, inhaled deeply, then pierced her flesh. The soft growl that escaped was in response to her hiss of pain. I hated the idea of hurting her, but I knew it would dissolve quickly. By the time she was moaning softly, her blood had filled my mouth.

It only took a few seconds before she came, her pussy fluttering around me. I sealed my mouth to her flesh as I took long, deep pulls from her vein. At the same time, I continued to slide in and out of her body, her slick heat and her thick, sweet blood drawing my orgasm closer and closer.

While I took from her, I gave as much as I could in return. I punched my hips forward, driving deep, careful not to tear her flesh with my fangs in the process. Long minutes passed, but I was keeping track. There was only so much of her blood she could part with. As it was, she would require a much longer recovery than I would have if I hadn't fed.

When her fingers slid down my back, I sealed the wounds on her neck, licked my lips, and lifted my head. I met her glassy gaze, realizing I'd taken more than I should have.

"Hold on to me, *sezari*."

Her smile was so fucking sweet as her arms wreathed my neck.

I shifted my hand around her thigh, changing the angle as I thrust inside her again and again. I let her body consume me, giving her all that I was as I breathed her in. I was surrounded by her in every way. I could hear the rapid thump of her heart, smell her sweet scent, still taste her blood on my tongue, feel her smooth, warm flesh against my own. If my eyes had been open, I would've seen her beautiful face as I pulled another orgasm from her supple body.

"Come for me again, *sezari*."

261

Orianna whimpered, her body clutching me both inside and out. I growled, let the pleasure-pain overwhelm me. The need to come was intense, but I held back for as long as I could, wanting to give rather than take.

And when the sensations bore down with an intensity I'd come to expect, I plunged into her harder, deeper, faster, squeezing her thigh and pressing my face into her neck as I claimed her as mine. My hips jerked, my cock pulsed as I filled her.

Mine.

The instant the word came to mind, I projected it into Orianna's brain, ensuring she understood this street ran both ways.

Orianna cried out once more, her muscles locking down on me, another orgasm driving up through my shaft, surprising me with the power behind it.

When my body stilled, I didn't pull out of her. I was still hard, still aching. Instead, I rolled, taking her with me. When she was draped over me, I palmed her perfect little ass as I pumped my hips, her silky sheath reigniting the heat in my veins. We remained like that for long minutes, her body limp even as she moaned and begged me to make her come, all while her blood mixed with mine, refueling my cells, giving me strength unlike anything I'd ever felt before. Not even the Fae could provide this sort of overwhelming power.

"Kiss me, *sezari*," I whispered.

Orianna turned her head, her mouth meeting mine. I held her firmly, one hand on her ass, the other on her head as I took us higher and higher. I didn't let up until she shattered around me. Only then did I let myself go once more, driving as deep as I could, filling her with my seed. In that moment, I had my first thought of my female carrying my child.

I would later realize that was the first of many. Despite

my many fears, I knew our destiny was sealed, our lives mapped out. And while I wanted nothing more than to spend an eternity with her, I couldn't help but wonder whether I would ever be strong enough to do what had to be done. I wasn't sure I had the ability to bring her harm in any way.

Not even the thought of tying her to me for eternity was enough to calm that fear.

KAJ

For fuck's sake!

These angels and this goddamn motherfucking mating heat...

I wasn't sure how the hell they survived in this place. Didn't matter that I had no desire to get myself off, my cock had a mind of its own. Damn thing was throbbing, and the urge to come hovered within reach without so much as a breath in the damn thing's direction.

Of course, I knew that ignoring it wouldn't work. Nor would a hand job. The latter would curb the pain but not quell it completely.

Still, I remained where I was on the leather sofa in the underground bar, the lights off. I was alone. The angels had scattered as soon as that damn energy flooded the mansion.

Not me. Nope, my date was a bottle of JD. Every so often, I would French-kiss the damn thing, not bothering with a glass.

The night had gone to shit after that fucking shadow beast escaped, leaving me chasing the darkness. That itch for a real fight didn't ease up one bit. In fact, it was spurred on by the thoughts of traitors in my midst. The idea of vampires turning on their own ... it made me feral.

"Kaj?"

The softly spoken word had my eyes darting upward, locking on the sinfully beautiful Fae taking the final steps into the room.

"Acadia?" My throat went dry as I stared at her. Tonight, she wore an exquisite purple gown that hugged her every curve. The triangle opening at her chest gave me the slightest glimpse of her ivory skin, the delicate swell of her breasts.

She'd come to me, I realized. Though I'd thought about summoning her, knowing she would ease me because she felt it her duty, I had refrained. I told her I would wait for her, and I meant it. Even if I suffered nightly in my quest to show her I was the male for her.

"I need you," she whispered.

I sensed the heat in her veins, saw the glitter in her amethyst eyes.

"I'm here, *balisra*. Whatever you need."

Even from across the room, I could smell her arousal, see the hunger in her eyes, but her hesitation was the most telling.

"What do you want, Acadia?"

The long, smooth column of her neck flexed as she swallowed.

"Tell me." I leaned over the arm of the couch, set the half-empty bottle of whiskey on the floor.

"You," Acadia said, the word so low I wasn't even sure she'd spoken it aloud.

"Come to me, *balisra*."

She stumbled once on her way over, but Acadia finally came to me. She even held out her hand when I reached for her.

My heart ached for her, and though these were the only moments I had with her—when the mating heat was unbearable for all within the walls of the mansion—I considered it a blessing to some degree. Despite the fact she was holding herself back from me, I would never refuse her. For as long as she would have me, I would be there.

"You are weak," she said.

Some males might've taken that as an insult, but I knew she was referring to my strength. I hadn't fed in some time, and it was beginning to weigh me down. However, now that I was residing in the same house as her, I refused to feed from any female who was not Acadia. Unfortunately, my pride kept me from seeking her out.

A softness overcame her face, as though she worried for me. I knew deep down she did, but it would take time before she trusted me the way she had before.

"How do you want me?" I offered, leaving the next move to her.

That seemed to trip her up, because her eyes fluttered, disappointment replacing her concern. It pained me to put that expression on her face, but again, pride was a powerful emotion, and I refused to grovel.

"Tell me," I insisted, my voice deeper than before, my need building to astronomical proportions. The mating heat wasn't the only thing fueling me, though. There was a desperate hunger I harbored only for her, and it was growing stronger with every passing second since the last time I had her.

"I want you to take me," she said on a soft moan.

"Gladly, *balisra*."

Without another second of hesitation, I drew her to me, meeting her halfway as I got to my feet. I crushed my mouth to hers even as I began tugging at that beautiful dress that covered her even more beautiful body. It occurred to me that we weren't in a private space, but I didn't care. My need for her overwhelmed my common sense.

The dance ensued as clothes began falling to the floor. Her dress, my shirt. It helped that she wore nothing beneath that glittery fabric, and the instant she was naked, I could no longer hold back. With my arm curled around her back, I eased her onto the leather sofa, my knee settling between her thighs.

I ripped at my leather pants, shoving them down my hips even as I feasted on her mouth, inhaling her soft moans as her fingers ran over my flesh. She was coming apart beneath me, and I hadn't even penetrated her yet.

"I need you," I warned. "More than is safe right now."

"Take me, Kaj."

God, she didn't realize what she was offering, but damn it if I wasn't going to take everything she was willing to give.

Confined by the leather on my thighs, I positioned myself over her, relied on her to guide me home. I inhaled sharply, pulling my head back as my cock slid into the tight sheath of her body. A deep growl barreled through my chest, her tight cunt milking me as her hands drew me closer. She was all I could see, all I could feel. Everything about this female over-loaded my circuits, sharpened my hunger.

I met her eyes as my fangs shot down from my jaw. "I fear I'll hurt you."

"You won't."

Acadia was stronger than she looked, I knew. She proved it by pulling my head down to her neck. I fought her only for a moment before giving in. Without preamble, I bit her, tearing through her flesh as I sought the ambrosia that fueled me. Her sharp inhale told me I was too rough, but it didn't slow me. I couldn't hold back as I drew her blood into me at the same time I pushed myself deep inside her.

Time stood still as our bodies remained locked, my cock tunneling in her warmth, her blood sliding down my throat. Within minutes I was reenergized, the power from her blood making me feel invincible, as though I could conquer the world as long as she was at my side.

Problem was, she wasn't at my side. Acadia wasn't mine to have. Not yet, perhaps not ever. That pain was what had me disconnecting emotionally, pushing back from the brink as I focused on her.

From beneath me, Acadia remained silent, the complete opposite of our times together back before I'd walked away. I wanted that female under me, the one who cried out my name with so much passion just the sound could make my cock explode.

Didn't mean she wasn't taking what she needed. Though she remained silent, save for her soft moans, Acadia's body rocked against me, her knees locking onto my hips as I flexed and shifted, impaling her as we both chased that elusive climax.

It took effort, but I managed to release her flesh from my mouth, my fangs retracting as I licked her, healing the wounds on her lovely skin. Only then did I launch an all-out assault with my body, driving us both to the precipice. I kept us suspended in the ether for long seconds, groaning as my body fought to unleash my seed, the need to mark her overwhelming.

"Kaj!"

It was my name on her lips that shot me over the edge. I pinned her to the leather cushion with my full strength as I pumped myself deep within her. She cried out once more, her body shuddering around me as she came.

Rather than curl up beside her, which was the only thing I wanted to do, I took my cues from her. The moment her hands fell from my shoulders, her body went lax beneath me. She was disconnecting, not only physically but emotionally. Pushing me away.

Because she'd come to me, I gave her the space she sought. I got to my feet, adjusted my pants, tucking my still-hard cock away and pretending it didn't matter that she used me. As much as I wanted to believe I could wait an eternity for her to forgive me, I knew that wasn't the case.

As I trudged up the stairs, my destination the cold, lonely bed I slept in every night, I figured there was one positive thing in all this: at least she'd come to me rather than go to another male in the house.

For now, it was something.

20

ORIANNA

After having spent a total of three weeks at the mansion, I was used to using the shutters' nightly ascent as an alarm clock. However, I was awake this time, staring up at the darkened ceiling as Eclipse slept soundly beside me. My brain wouldn't slow down, making it impossible to sleep. Today I was meeting with Barin, my guardian angel.

The thought made me smile.

Guardian angel.

I'd always thought that was something made up by people who needed someone to give credit to for their good fortune. According to Eclipse and backed up by Penelope, guardian angels were real. Every human had one, though apparently, those particular angels were a bit overworked, overseeing roughly fifty souls each. Luckily for me, Amber and I shared the same one, and the angel had agreed to meet with me at Eclipse's request.

Not that I knew what I was supposed to ask him. From what I gathered, he was the one who determined Amber was in fact deceased because he lost his connection with her, something that only occurred when a human died.

Though the idea of Amber being gone from this world forever still caused an unbearable ache in my chest, I needed to know for sure. And the only way that would happen would be if I saw Amber's remains for myself. Until that time, this was merely a rumor, and I refused to pass along information to my mother based on secondhand information.

Plus, if Amber was gone, my sister needed a proper burial, an eternal resting place. How I would afford that, I wasn't sure, but like everything else, I would figure it out. Perhaps this guardian angel could point me in the right direction.

Eclipse grumbled beside me, his arm shifting over me as he pulled me close. I smiled as I settled into his warmth. This was what he did nearly every evening. Rather than hop out of bed, eager to get the night underway, he would cuddle up with me beneath the thick blankets. My gaze swung to the fireplace as I waited for him to become alert enough to reignite the flames with his mind. I knew that had to take place before he would even consider getting vertical.

Right before my eyes, the flames roared to life in the fireplace, crackling as the warmth began trickling through the enormous room. Despite the fact the heater worked, Eclipse preferred to use natural warmth. He also claimed body heat was the most efficient way to keep warm, hence the reason we slept naked. As for whether I believed him or not, it didn't matter. It didn't take much for him to talk me out of my clothes.

"How long have you been awake?" he mumbled against my neck.

"A few minutes."

"You do that every night, and you might give a male a complex."

I chuckled. "Why's that?"

"If I recall correctly, I wore us both out early this morning."

That he had. For the past couple of weeks, he'd been treating me with kid gloves. Ever since he fed from me the day he was injured, Eclipse was catering to my every whim despite the fact I was fine after the incident. And every single time since. A little weak, maybe, but a full meal always solved the problem. And yes, in a matter of thirteen days, I was pretty sure I gained at least five pounds. If I kept this up, I wouldn't be able to borrow any clothes much longer.

Speaking of clothes...

"I was thinking maybe I should go back to my apartment."

Eclipse grumbled the same as he did whenever I brought that up. I'd been at the mansion for three weeks, alternating between wearing the outfit I came here in, Eclipse's too-large T-shirts and his sweatpants, and a couple of outfits Asmia had offered me. It wasn't that I owned a lot to begin with, but I would've felt better if I had a few of my things.

"I was thinking maybe we should bring your apartment here," Eclipse whispered, his lips sliding over the curve of my shoulder.

A sweet shiver danced down my spine. "Here? As in ... you want me to move in with you?"

Evidently, he heard the confusion in my voice because Eclipse propped himself up on an elbow and nudged me onto my back.

"Is that a problem for you?"

"Maybe." I honestly wasn't sure what to think. "Why would you want me here?"

"Because this is where you belong," he said simply, his silver stare sliding over my face. "With me."

My first instinct was to argue. Only the words didn't come out. The old me would've told him it was time for me to go, that I belonged in my shitty little apartment, all alone, continuing my search for my sister. But I couldn't form the words. The need to argue was impulsive, but my desire to stay here with him outweighed it.

Of course, that made me feel like a pussy. I had never relied on anyone to take care of me. Not since ... well, not since before my mother's attack. It wasn't like I ever had family to rely on. My father's only concern was himself, and then my mother couldn't take care of herself, much less anyone else. Boarding school was the same. I was forced to grow up then, and over time, I learned the only person I could depend on was myself.

Two weeks ago, I probably would've been able to make a convincing argument. But these past few days had been enlightening. Not only did I realize there were people willing to care for me, but I learned I could care for them as well. I'd developed friendships with Penelope, Acadia, even Miklós. And I harbored a deep fondness for Phillip and Jeffrey, though I knew they were merely doing their jobs. The thought of leaving any of them indefinitely didn't sit well.

But the idea of waking up alone without Eclipse ... that was unbearable.

"Only if you want." Eclipse's lips brushed my cheek. "I won't force you to do anything, Orianna."

"I know." My eyes met his, and I smiled. "I don't want to leave, either."

His relief was written across his face as he exhaled heavily. It warmed me to know he'd hoped I would stay.

I reached up and cupped his cheek. "I'll stay, but that doesn't mean we can spend all our time in bed."

"A majority of it?"

I chuckled, then moaned when his hand snuck beneath the blankets and curled around my breast.

"We're meeting with Barin," I reminded him.

"The male can wait."

"For?"

Eclipse slid down the bed, his head and the rest of him disappearing beneath the blankets.

"Oh, God," I groaned as his mouth settled between my thighs.

Yeah. He could wait.

Hell, everything could wait.

ECLIPSE

B y the time I made it down to the war room, the nightly patrol had already left. I probably would've joined them, but I wanted to be there when Orianna met with Barin. The male had agreed—under duress, mind you—to have a sit-down with my *amsouelot*. It wasn't standard protocol for guardian angels to meet with those they were sworn to watch over, but in this case, I figured Orianna deserved to hear it for herself.

"What time's Barin showing up?" Miklós asked, getting to his feet and tucking his laptop under his arm.

"He didn't tell me. Why?"

Miklós met my eyes. "I've got a lead on one of the sister's previous residences."

I raised one eyebrow, urging him to continue.

"I thought maybe you'd want to take a field trip."

"She won't let me go without her," I informed my *lieterra*. And the thought of her out there while those traitorous vampires still walked the streets did not sit well with me.

"I'll come with you," Miklós offered.

"Where?"

"About a forty-five-minute drive from here. I dug up some information on an apartment her father had leased. He abandoned the place, and they've yet to clean it out. Word is there was a young female staying there with him. Description matches Amber."

"Have you told Orianna?"

"Not yet."

I considered it. If I didn't relay this information to my *amsouelot*, I feared she would hate me for it. And since I had no reason not to, aside from the fact I feared for her safety, I knew I couldn't hold back.

"Fine. I'll let her know, but I want Magnar along for the ride."

Miklós nodded. "I'll gas up the Range Rover, meet you in the garage. Say half an hour."

I offered my *lieterra* a quick nod, then vanished, reforming just outside the third-floor conference room, where Orianna was still working on finding her sister. When I strolled in, her eyes lifted, and a smile formed.

"Hey. I thought you'd be out tonight."

"I was going to, but something came up."

Orianna leaned back in her chair and regarded me. "Something that involves me?"

The heat I saw in her eyes was tempting, but I managed to refrain. Sexing her up right now was the best idea I'd ever had, but as was always the case, we were battling daylight, which meant we had to get out there and back before we risked being trapped by the sun's deadly rays.

"Miklós found a lead on one of Amber's last known addresses. Thought we'd head up there, check it out."

She shot to her feet. "We?"

"You, me, Miklós, and Magnar."

As she approached, I realized there were tears in her eyes. Instinct had me reaching for her, cupping her cheek.

"What's wrong, *sezari*?"

"Nothing. It's just … it's been a long time since I've had a legitimate lead."

"Don't get your hopes up yet. We're just going to check it out."

She nodded. "When do we leave?"

"Now."

As I led her to our private quarters so I could weapon up and get her into something warmer, I relayed the information as I'd heard it from Miklós.

"What about Barin?" she asked, referring to the guardian angel.

"He didn't give me a time frame, but I'll make sure he doesn't leave until you've had a chance to talk to him."

She smiled. "You're gonna hold a guardian angel hostage?"

"If that's what it takes, yeah."

Twenty minutes later, we were pulling out of the garage, Miklós behind the wheel, Magnar riding shotgun, and Orianna and I in the back seat. The conversation shifted from the mission to the weather, with Miklós easily carrying on with Orianna as though they were best friends.

I watched my *lieterra*, noticing the way Miklós continuously peered back at her in the rearview as he spoke. For some reason, that made me smile. Knowing the most important male in my life was close to Orianna made me relax a bit. I knew Miklós would ensure she was protected in the event something happened. I knew the same was the case with Magnar, but the *ladeare* was tasked with watching my back at all times, which meant Orianna wouldn't be his main priority, no matter what I instructed.

"When we get there, Magnar and I will go in to check it out. Once I give the signal, you can bring her in," I told Miklós.

"Of course."

"If you sense anyone approaching, I want her back here immediately." It wasn't my first preference, but the Range Rover was moveable as well as bulletproof; therefore, it was our best option.

Miklós met my eyes in the rearview mirror and nodded.

The sound of a magazine being ejected and reinserted was the only sound as we pulled into the parking lot. Magnar always gave his weapon a once-over, even though he'd probably done the same back in the garage.

"Apartment two-A," Miklós instructed as he pulled into a parking space.

I leaned over and pressed my lips to Orianna's. "You stay with him at all times. Understand?"

"Yes."

Without looking back, I climbed out of the SUV at the same time Magnar did. The two of us blended into the night, slipping around the building toward the rust-colored stairs I'd noted when we pulled in. The place wasn't so much a complex as it was a couple of ratty buildings dissected into four units in each. The stench of garbage from the Dumpster wafted over as we headed up the stairs, Magnar watching my six while I kept my hand on my Glock, keeping it lowered so as not to draw attention.

A curtain pulled back on the window of the first apartment we came to. A set of eyes peered out but then disappeared, scanning right through us as I shielded us from view.

When we reached the second-floor landing, I nodded to Magnar.

The door lock was a joke, the thing slipping free with minimal effort of the mind. Once inside, Magnar went toward the single bedroom at the back while I detoured through the kitchen. A quick scan of all hiding spots resulted in nothing, which was exactly what I'd hoped for.

Clear, I told Miklós.

"Keep the lights off," I instructed Magnar when the male joined me in the living room.

"Copy that."

Two minutes later, Miklós followed Orianna into the space, the male holding his weapon at his side as he locked the door behind them.

I removed my shades, my eyes providing plenty of light to see by.

"They haven't cleaned out the place," Orianna noted.

"No. From what I can tell, he abandoned it not too long ago," Miklós explained. "Whatever's here, he left behind."

"A month ago? Was Amber with him then?"

Miklós shook his head. "No. But they said she stayed here at one point, left, came back. Word is he left for a while, too, but came back, rented the place again, but only stayed for a couple of weeks that time."

Orianna nodded, heading for a pile of mail sitting on the scarred laminate counter. She skimmed briefly, tossed it aside, and moved into the kitchen. I watched her, hating the disappointment that replaced her hope. There was nothing here that would tell us anything about Amber's most recent whereabouts or what she'd been up to on her journey, but I got the feeling it was the closest she'd been to her sister in a while.

By the time Orianna finished checking every nook and cranny, half an hour had passed. While that wasn't a long time, in my book, it was an eternity. We had no idea where those vampires were or their motivations. It was very likely they were keeping an eye on the outskirts of Darkness, waiting for us to emerge. To hope they'd given up was too much to ask considering the demons were intent on eliminating the *amsouelots,* and the bounty was probably high. A traitorous vampire would likely have plenty of patience.

"We ready to head out?" Miklós asked Orianna.

She nodded, her eyes scanning the floor as though hoping something would be there.

"You two clear the way," I instructed the two males. "I'll bring her down when you give the all-clear."

Miklós nodded, then led the way out the door. The lock engaged upon their exit.

"I'm sorry there's not more here," I told Orianna, pulling her into my arms, wishing like hell I could eliminate the pain she was feeling.

"I didn't think there would be," she said softly. "But hope's all I've had for so long. Never any luck, though."

"We'll find her, I promise."

"If we can't? At what point do I give up?"

I hugged her. The question was rhetorical, I knew. Orianna wasn't the sort to give up. Closure was what she needed. Something to confirm the search for Amber was no longer necessary. I understood that need. Through the centuries, I moved forward with only one purpose. I knew I would one day find the love who would complete me. Never had I questioned how long the mission would take because it didn't matter. The only thing that did was getting to that moment when my *amsouelot* would be with me. When Michael revealed the danger that had come to the females slated as ours, that mission changed altogether. Even now that Orianna was with me, I knew she wasn't completely safe. Wouldn't be until I made the ultimate sacrifice.

But until the time came when I could wrap my head around that, I vowed to protect her and to make her happy, regardless of the mission. She was my end goal, always had been, always would be.

All clear, Miklós's voice sounded in my head.

"Let's get back to the mansion so we can meet with Barin. Maybe he'll have some better news."

Orianna wiped her eyes as she pulled away.

"We won't give up," I promised her.

This was only the beginning of our journey together. I had no intention of letting her down. Not now, not ever.

21

ORIANNA

There was no denying I was disappointed.

Unfortunately, it was a feeling I was all too familiar with.

However, it helped that I wasn't the only one feeling the letdown. Though they kept their expressions blank, I could tell Miklós and Eclipse had both hoped we would find something. I hadn't had that before. No one to go with me to even look, so that was one positive to come out of this. Meeting Eclipse had changed everything. Since our paths crossed, I'd stopped being alone.

Granted, at the moment, I sort of wished I was. Not completely alone, but some privacy with Eclipse would work. As we rode in the back seat of the Range Rover, my body was warming, and it had nothing to do with the heat from the vents blowing back on us. Nope, this was a sensual heat that stirred in my womb and radiated outward. It wasn't unfamiliar because I'd felt it numerous times since I met Eclipse, but from time to time, it would creep up on me. Even now, at the most inopportune time.

As though I'd summoned him with my thoughts, Eclipse's head turned toward me. Those dark glasses shielded his eyes, but I knew he was peering into my mind.

A soft groan was his response as his hand rested on my thigh, squeezing gently. It was his reassurance that he was feeling the same thing I was.

Twenty minutes.

I smiled as his voice sounded in my head. Twenty minutes seemed like an eternity. Every rotation of the tires had heat blooming hotter, deeper. I kept my gaze trained out the window, watching the night pass in a blur. It did little to stave off the building desire, even as I tried to understand why now. Why here? We weren't alone, and I'd just wandered through an apartment that once belonged to my father and possibly my sister. Nothing about this situation should've had me wanting Eclipse, yet there was no denying it.

By the time the world disappeared into an endless blackness, I was gritting my teeth and trying not to rub my thighs together. Another few minutes and we were pulling into the garage. I was trying to figure out how I would make it up to Eclipse's room when he barked out a clipped command for Miklós and Magnar to leave us.

As soon as the front doors shut, Eclipse had me in his arms. He pulled me across the seat, positioning me so I could straddle his thighs in the cramped back seat. I crushed my mouth to his as his big hands snaked beneath my sweater, palming my breasts roughly. I whimpered and moaned, grinding my hips down to increase the friction where I needed it.

"Not enough room," I complained.

He released one of my breasts, the door opened, and then he was lifting me out, his hand palming my ass as he held me to him. I clung to him as he headed for the elevator. The thought of those torturous few minutes it would take to get upstairs had me whimpering again.

"Here," I insisted.

Eclipse growled softly, a sexy sound that had my core clenching, the emptiness inside me desperate for him.

My backside met the hard surface of one of the work benches, but it didn't last long. Some twisting and maneuvering ensued as Eclipse yanked my leggings down. Trapped in my own clothing, I laughed, then proceeded to free one of my legs even as I tugged at Eclipse's shirt with the other, not allowing him to get too far away. When our bodies came together the next time, heat exploded within me. During the melee, he'd freed his erection and wasted no time pushing inside me.

I grunted as the penetration stole my breath, a scorching heat following close behind as I orgasmed from the exquisite contact.

"Fuck," Eclipse groaned before crushing his mouth to mine.

The kiss was punishing, but the way he filled me was perfection. I clung to him as he took me right there in the garage. There was no finesse as I raced headlong into another orgasm. Each one dragged a ragged, desperate groan from Eclipse, had him thrusting harder, deeper, faster, as though my release was his only objective. One after another, my climaxes ignited the flames between us until we were consumed by the obliterating inevitability.

"Eclipse!" My head fell back as a mind-numbing release slammed into me, an explosion rocked me to my core, decimating my atomic makeup and pulling me back together at the same time.

The sound that escaped Eclipse could've been my name or a series of curse words. Not that it mattered because his hips drove forward one final time, his fingers digging into my flesh as he jerked me toward him. That sensation of him spilling deep inside me triggered another quake, leaving me trembling in his arms, attempting to catch my breath.

Thankfully, he took over from there.

"Bed, now," he mumbled against my ear.

"You won't hear me complaining," I slurred, resting my head on his shoulder as the elevator door sealed us into the small space.

ECLIPSE

Two hours later, after Orianna and I made our way back down to the kitchen and indulged in ham and provolone sandwiches, my *amsouelot* hinted that she wanted to take a nap. Figuring the emotional drain was taking its toll, I sent her back up to our room and went in search of Obsidian. I found my brother in the war room, along with Miklós, Søren, and Zadok, who was still at the mansion while Taayin filled in for him, covering Cimmerian's ass.

"Looks like trouble," I teased when I joined the males. "What's going on here?"

"We just got word Perfidious is out and about."

Well, didn't that just put a damper on my good mood.

The demon had gone to ground for weeks, so it was surprising, not to mention disappointing, to hear he was making an appearance. Of course, I had to wonder about the timing, considering we'd slipped Orianna out of the mansion only a few hours ago, and this was the first sighting in quite some time. Coincidence? Doubtful.

"Where's he at?"

"That's the bad—"

"Remember the female at the club?" Kaj asked, his voice coming from behind me.

The interruption had me turning in time to see the vampire approaching, eyes hard.

"I remember."

"She's been working with Sirius."

A burning anger ripped through my veins at the news. "So you do have traitors in your ranks?"

"Trust me," Kaj said, his voice a low growl, "my ranks are secure. It's the civilians who are working with the demons."

I wasn't so sure that was the case, but I held my tongue.

"What's being done about it?" Obsidian asked, getting to his feet and coming to join us.

"Darko's got quite the collection," the vampire said. "They're being kept in the dungeon."

"At a club where you bring humans?" I snapped. My anger needed an outlet, and this male was the three-prong equivalent that would get the brunt of it.

Kaj shook his head. "Beneath the club. An actual dungeon."

"And you're telling me you didn't know they were there?" I found that difficult to believe.

"I had no idea." The acknowledgment seemed to bother Kaj as much as the idea bothered me. "Now, I've got to decide what to do about them."

I stared at the vampire. "Seems pretty simple to me."

Green eyes narrowed to slits. "You're saying I should condemn them to die?"

"How else do you stop the bleeding?" Seemed pretty fucking rational to me. "You let them live, what's to stop the others from doing it?"

"Loyalty," Kaj said, glaring back at me.

I snorted. "Seems to be lacking for you right now."

"Enough," Obsidian bit out.

I spun to face my brother. "This female he's referring to ... she lured my *amsouelot* to the club."

Concern replaced Obsidian's frustrated expression. "That changes things."

"I'd say it does." I turned back to Kaj. "I'd bet money she lured Orianna in order to pass her off to Sirius."

"He's not our only problem," Søren stated. "Word's going around that Eevuhl's here. In Darkness."

"Fucking hell," I growled.

"You and Orianna are grounded for the time being," Obsidian commanded.

There was no reason for me to argue. The mansion was the safest place for Orianna right now. The demons would not get to her as long as she was within the walls. Of course, keeping me in was an argument for a later time. No way would I sit back when there was a chance I could take the demons down once and for all. And a member of the *trielair* ... no way would I let that opportunity pass me by.

"Her things should be here within the hour," Miklós informed him.

"What're you talking about?" Obsidian asked.

"I'm moving her into the mansion," I explained, taking a deep breath as we shifted to a less heated topic. "And yes, before you ask, she agreed."

Obsidian nodded as though that made perfect sense. "Who'd you send?"

"Echo volunteered," Miklós answered. "And Asmia asked to go with him."

Eclipse's head snapped over to his *lieterra*. "Asmia? She's with him?"

Miklós nodded, his brows lowering. "Yes. Is that a problem?"

"Fucking hell," Obsidian growled. "You"—his finger shot toward Zadok—"get Magnar up to speed. I want eyes on her ASAP. And tell him not to leave her side until she's back here."

"What's going on?" Kaj asked, his confusion as potent as Miklós's.

"Perfidious has a hard-on for Asmia," I explained. "If he picks up her scent..." Yeah, there was no need to go any further than that.

"Oh, shit." Miklós shot to his feet. "I'll go with them."

I shook my head. "No. I need you here."

"But—"

I could see the male's concern, felt it even. However, as my *lieterra*, we couldn't risk Miklós or Zadok being intercepted by Perfidious or, worse, Eevuhl. The males knew too much, and the last thing we needed was an all-knowing angel in the hands of the *trielair*.

"I'll keep you updated after I talk to Magnar," Zadok told Miklós before he vanished.

"I didn't think it would be a problem," Miklós said, his eyes imploring Obsidian.

"It doesn't matter now."

Obsidian was right. Unfortunately, Asmia's fate had already been decided. One way or another.

ASMIA

"Were you down for the evening meal?" I asked Echo as I exited the truck we borrowed to carry Orianna's things back to the mansion.

"I was, yeah."

"What happened? Clearly, I missed the action," I told him, leading the way down a dark, dingy corridor to apartment 1-E.

"Winnie tore Reidar a new one."

"That sucks." I stood to the side while Echo willed the door unlocked with his mind.

"Worse is it's getting ridiculous. Can't sleep with those two bitching at each other nonstop. Something's going down with that human."

"Is she okay?"

When the male stepped back, I led the way inside, coming up short when I got a good look at Orianna's digs. For whatever reason, I expected ... something else. Based on the smell, the carpet hadn't been cleaned since it was laid down, likely two decades ago. The paint on the wall was probably at one point white but, over time, had turned a dull yellow and had the faint scent of ... cigarettes.

"She's fine, but I can't say the same for Reidar," Echo said, dumping the small stack of boxes onto the counter. "Why don't you take the bedroom. I'll get what's in here."

I slowly spun around the space. "I don't think there's a bedroom."

"Okay, the bathroom then."

I nodded. After I formed the box and taped the bottom, I carried it with me to the bathroom. As I moved through Orianna's private space, I glanced around, attempted to picture the female living here. It wasn't easy.

Granted, I didn't know her well. We talked on occasion, but I was the one keeping my distance. Not because I didn't like the human. She seemed nice enough. But as had been the case for weeks, I wasn't feeling much like entertaining.

I perched the box on the closed lid of the toilet, then began filling it with the few things I found in the medicine cabinet. Next came toothbrush and toothpaste, followed by shower essentials. By the time I was done, the bottom of the box wasn't even covered.

Girl lived simply, that was for sure.

I returned to the living room—or was it a bedroom?—and headed for the drawers in the table. When I uncovered Orianna's personal toy, I wrapped it in one of the threadbare towels and discreetly tucked it into the box. Next to join the personal items were the few outfits I uncovered in the one and only closet in the space.

"She travels light," I said as I pulled out two pairs of shoes, three pairs of socks, a couple of skirts, three T-shirts, and two pairs of jeans, which seemed to be the extent of Orianna's wardrobe. Not even a coat.

Once the closet was empty, I lifted her box and got to my feet. I closed the closet door and turned to check on Echo.

"Where'd you go?" I called out, clearing the few feet to the small galley kitchen, expecting to see him kneeling to empty the cabinets.

Nope. Not there.

Seeing that the bathroom door was open, I headed that way, intending to tell him I was done. Before I got there, a ruckus sounded out in the corridor.

"Echo?"

As I headed for the open front door, I wished I had a weapon of some sort. Probably would've made sense to come armed, considering all that was going on these days. We weren't safe outside the mansion, certainly not with the demons circling Darkness. Yet I'd been so eager to get out of there I didn't think about bringing anything with me.

With an odd sense of trepidation, I stuck my head out into the hallway. I glanced left, then right, but saw no one.

Relieved that no humans were being attacked in the hall-way, I spun around to grab the box, intending to give Echo shit for abandoning me. He could've at least told me he was leav—

"The lovely Asmia graces me with her presence."

The voice drew me up short, had fear replacing the air in my lungs. With dread washing over me, I slowly pivoted, my brain working overtime to identify something I could use as a weapon. Considering the closest thing was the vibrator at the bottom of the box, it wasn't looking good for me.

A dark-haired male with bright blue eyes was standing in the doorway, blocking the exit. I didn't recognize him, but I sensed the evil within. Definitely not human despite the meat suit he wore.

"Do I know you?"

"You've no idea who I am, do you?"

Hearing the menace in his words, I swallowed hard, then willed myself out of there.

Nothing happened.

I tried again, desperate to dematerialize. The only thing that happened was my panic ratcheted up a notch or ten.

"Sorry, gorgeous. It won't work."

The male stepped closer, his eyes locked with mine. It was then I saw past the facade, beyond the glittering, clear blue eyes, and into the soul of the demon.

"Perfidious."

He smirked. "In the flesh." He chuckled, tugging at the lapels of his fancy suit. "Well, technically, not my own, but it works nicely, don't you think? I've upgraded since last I saw you."

I tried to back away, but my feet wouldn't move. He was holding me there with the power of his mind.

"What do you want from me?" I hissed.

Another smirk. "Not *from* you, gorgeous. It's *you* I want."

I frowned, attempting to process his words.

"Asmia!"

I heard Echo's voice coming from outside, the shout bouncing off the concrete.

"Go, Echo! Run!"

Of course the male wasn't going to listen. He was a soldier, not a pansy.

Echo's response was a grunt.

It was Perfidious's demonic laugh that amped up my fear.

"What did you do to him?"

"Don't worry. As long as you do what I say, he'll be fine."

"Let him go," I insisted.

Perfidious stepped out of the apartment, turned, looking

down the hall as he lifted his hand. Suddenly, Echo was standing before him, Perfidious's hand buried deep in the male's chest.

No! God, no! I sucked in air, tried to scream, but nothing came out.

The demon's gaze returned to me. "I'll make this simple, sweetheart. You have two choices. You take a little trip with me, and the male walks away unscathed. Or..."

Echo groaned, eyes squeezing shut as agony ripped through him.

Perfidious chuckled. "Or I rip his heart out of his chest, and you can mourn his dead corpse. Your choice."

"Let him go," I insisted. The rage built inside me, but I was unable to move, frozen from Perfidious's control.

"Asmia, no," Echo hissed. "Don't you dare go with him."

Unable to look anywhere except into Perfidious's eyes, I saw his intentions as clear as day. He gave me a glimpse into the future. Echo lying on the ground, his heart cast aside, lifeless eyes staring up and seeing nothing.

I would not be the reason for his death.

"I'll go with you," I ground out. "But you have to swear to leave him alone."

Perfidious's hand retreated from Echo's chest, the male falling to the ground in a heap. The demon held it up to show he wasn't holding Echo's heart.

"It's time we made our exit," Perfidious stated, holding out his hand for me.

This time, when I tried to move, my legs worked. Knowing Echo's life was at stake, I didn't attempt to escape, rather walked up to Perfidious and placed my hand in his. I shivered when he touched me, hatred boiling deep in my gut.

"Care to say goodbye?" Perfidious taunted as we stepped over Echo's body.

"We will find you," Echo declared, his voice so low I could hardly hear him. "I promise you, Asmia. We will find you."

I nodded, holding the male's gaze. I could see the pain there, and it made my chest ache. He felt responsible, though he shouldn't. This was clearly my destiny, likely long ago etched in stone.

"It's okay, Echo. I'll be fine," I said, oddly thinking that was the first and only time I'd ever lied to him.

22

ECLIPSE

———

"Where is she?" I asked when I joined the others in the war room, having been summoned by Obsidian with news on Asmia.

I hoped that meant they'd found her because the males we sent to retrieve her hadn't been gone long. Not even long enough for me to make my way back to my room to check on Orianna or to fill her in on what was going on.

Obsidian nodded to Echo, sitting in a leather chair, head hanging down, looking defeated. It wasn't a look he usually sported. Echo had been with the *fiestreigh* for going on five centuries now, and for the past few months, he'd been allocated to me. Like the others, my brothers and I had come to trust Echo with our lives. The male had proven his worth time and again, always forging headlong into battle and never—not one fucking time—leaving anyone behind.

From Echo's expression, that wasn't the case this time.

"Perfidious took her," Obsidian said softly, motioning me to the other side of the room. "Threatened to kill Echo if she didn't go with him."

Of course she went with him. Asmia would do whatever it took to protect those she cared about.

"Son of a bitch," I growled, following my brother. My shoulders were tense, worry flooding me as I thought about the Fae and what that fucking demon was doing with her. "What are we going to do? Have you notified the others?"

"Not yet."

"You should."

Obsidian nodded. "I agree."

While it wasn't ideal to bring our brothers in and pause the search for the *amsouelots*, Asmia was a member of our family. Finding her and bringing her home needed to be our top priority. No doubt our brothers would feel the same way.

"Have you told Taayin?"

Obsidian removed his dark glasses and rubbed the bridge of his nose, a sure sign he was at a loss. There was pain in his eyes, warring with concern. "I don't know how to tell him."

Didn't matter how they relayed the information, Taayin was going to lose his shit. Not that I would blame the male if he did. God knew I would've gone ballistic if those fucking vampires had managed to get their hands on Orianna.

"Does Penelope know?"

Obsidian shook his head. "I'm not sure she can handle the stress. What with the baby and all."

Made sense on some level. Penelope was in week eleven of her pregnancy. With nine weeks at best—more like six in actuality—left, they were keeping a close eye on her. In the last few days, Obsidian's tension had skyrocketed, his concern for her evident, and this couldn't be helping.

"She's going to find out." If she hadn't already.

"I know."

"You have to tell her before that happens, Obsidian. Why don't you take care of that? Perhaps you and Penelope can relay the news to Taayin. I'll take care of rounding everyone up and getting them back to the mansion."

Clearly Obsidian needed that subtle push because he didn't bother walking out; he vanished, something he was not apt to do most of the time.

Turning to Reidar, I asked, "Where's Miklós?"

The male shrugged. "He was here when Echo showed up, but then he disappeared."

Son of a bitch.

Just what we didn't need today, two males carrying the weight of this on their shoulders. If I had to guess, like Echo, Miklós was likely bearing the brunt of the blame. But we didn't have time for the who-done-it game. The ideal thing to do would be to hit the streets, find Asmia, and bring her home. Sooner rather than later.

"All right. Here's what I need you to do..." I barked orders, delegating to the others so I could follow up with Miklós and find Orianna. I assigned every soldier a task, not stopping until the war room cleared out, with the exception of Reidar.

"I want you to get the message boards updated. Put up a reward for any information leading to her safe return."

Reidar nodded. "Good idea."

I doubted it would help, but at this point, I was willing to try anything.

"And check with Oliver. See if he wants in on this mission. We could use all hands on deck right now."

"I'll hit him up and give him something to do."

When I was satisfied we covered all our bases, I headed up to the main house, glancing from room to room in search of my *lieterra*. When I reached the third floor, I made a detour to my private quarters but stopped in the living room when I saw Orianna kneeling on the floor, petting Zeus while Aphrodite fought for her affections.

I took a moment to drink her in, grateful that she was there with me, safe in the mansion. I didn't want to think about the horror show Asmia was privy to now that Perfidious had her in his grimy paws.

Orianna looked up at me with a smile so bright I was grateful I had on my shades.

"I was about to come down and find you," she said. "Then I found these two, and we got a little sidetracked." Her eyes landed on my face. "Uh-oh. Is something wrong?"

I went on to explain the incidents with Asmia and Perfidious—both past and present.

"Oh, my God. She was kidnapped by a demon?"

I nodded, watching her face. Orianna seemed to sort through the information before narrowing her eyes on me. "What can I do to help?"

Honestly, I expected a few more questions. Such as, *Since when are demons real?* Or *How on earth did angels get mixed up with Fae?* Then again, this was Orianna. My female seemed to take things at face value, even if they defied everything she'd ever been taught. Perhaps one of these days, she'd pelt me with all those inquiries, but for now, I would gladly take her up on her offer to assist.

"I've got all available *fiestreigh* out looking for her. I'm waiting for my brothers and the rest of the *fiestreigh* to get back to the mansion. Once they're here, we can double our efforts to locate her. In the meantime, we need to man the message boards."

Orianna gave Zeus and Aphrodite one last pat on the head before coming to stand in front of me. "I can definitely help with that. But I've got another idea. I mean, it's not foolproof, but from time to time, I can get a vision of a specific person if I can touch an object they've touched. Preferably something they use often. A hairbrush, razor, that sort of thing."

"It's worth a shot," I told her. "I'll show you to Asmia's room."

As I led Orianna down the stairs to the second floor, I couldn't hide the pride I felt. Without question, my female was willing to help save someone important to me.

If I didn't already love her, no doubt I would have after that.

ORIANNA

I followed Eclipse down the stairs to the second floor. We traversed a carpeted hall, lined on one side by doors, the other a wrought iron railing that safeguarded from the long fall to the main floor below. I could hear people moving around, and from the sounds, more than a handful were occupying the space. Rather than quell my curiosity and peek, I opted to focus on the task at hand: help find the Fae and bring her home safely.

It felt strange to be offering to help do anything other than locate Amber. But the instant I saw the concern etched on Eclipse's handsome face, I knew it was the only thing I could do. Whether or not it worked, I had to at least try. I, of all people, knew what it was like not to know where your loved one was, and I would've given anything to have an army of people helping me back when I first started looking for my sister. Perhaps if I had—

"This is her room." Eclipse exhaled slowly, then turned the knob and opened the door.

We paused when we noticed Miklós sitting in one of the upholstered chairs near the bed. He had his head in his hands, elbows on his knees. I glanced up at Eclipse, curious as to what was wrong.

The concern on Eclipse's face told me everything I needed to know. For some unknown reason, Miklós felt responsible. Perhaps I would get the information later. Right now, I didn't want to waste any time.

Eclipse cleared his throat, drawing Miklós's attention up.

The angel got to his feet, shoulders slumped. "Sorry. I'll leave you be."

I wanted to tell him to stay, but the truth was, this would work better if I had no distractions.

"Would it be possible to be alone for a few minutes?" I asked Eclipse when Miklós slipped out between us.

"Of course. I'll come back and check on you shortly."

I stepped into the space. I couldn't help but smile at the girly decor surrounding me. It was a bedroom made for a princess, decked out in several shades of purple and interspersed with silver and white. The king-size bed was made, pillows situated with precision, as though whoever had done it was allergic to chaos.

I ran my hand over the silky comforter as I moved across the room. The antique furniture was polished, the light wood gleaming, the intricate knobs and pulls shiny despite their age. On top of the nine-drawer dresser were several silver frames, all showcasing pictures of Asmia and a man in various poses. I picked up one, stared at the two beautiful people. Like *really* beautiful, the sort of magnificence that defied logic and reason. They looked happy together, both smiling as the man hugged Asmia to him, his arm securely around her shoulders.

Setting the frame down, I inhaled deeply. There was a light, fresh scent that lingered in the air, and I wondered if that was Asmia's perfume. It was uniquely female and vaguely familiar, as though I'd smelled it somewhere in the mansion before.

I made my way across the room, past the thick shag rug— also purple—that fanned out from beneath the bed, through the double doors leading to the en suite bath. It was much like the bedroom, the walls and tile a brilliant white, accented with various shades of grape and chrome, from the towels hanging on the bar, to the rugs in front of the sink and the shower. Even the toothbrush was purple.

I stepped over to the vanity and opened the wide drawer. Inside was a hairbrush and a thick-bristled comb, along with an array of makeup. I took the hairbrush out, closed the drawer, and returned to the bedroom, taking a seat on the velvet bench at the foot of the bed. With the brush held firmly in my hands, I stared at the pictures of Asmia before closing my eyes and focusing on breathing. In, out. Slow and steady.

Forcing a vision was never something I was good at, but I knew from experience it was a possibility. My only concern was that I wanted this too much. Because of my anxiety, I feared I would fail.

From somewhere beyond the door, I could hear voices, deep male baritones drifting up from the open floor below. I squeezed my eyes closed and fought to focus. They needed to be quiet or—

"You're safe now, gorgeous. Right where you belong."

Holy shit. This had to be who Asmia was with. Didn't look much like a demon with the fancy suit and shiny shoes.

"You won't keep me here, Perfidious. They'll come for me."

"Perhaps they'll try." The man snickered. *"But trust me, we won't be here long. And we'll keep moving to ensure your safety."*

I studied the man with his dark hair and clear blue eyes, wanting to be able to give an apt description of him. I shifted my focus to the room they were in. It looked like a warehouse or maybe a dungeon. Dark and dingy, similar to the abandoned warehouses I visited when I was looking for Amber.

"Why are you doing this?" Asmia asked.

"Because you're my mate, gorgeous. Even if you don't realize it yet."

"Never," Asmia snapped. *"I belong to no one."*

"Oh, but you do. And it won't take much effort to manipulate the Fates, have them realigning your destiny, if it's the last thing I do."

I groaned when the vision faded, slipping away on a whisper of breath. I kept my eyes closed for a second, allowed the snapshot image to remain in my mind so I could relay everything to Eclipse. Whether it would help, I didn't know, but I would do my best to—

The image flashed brilliantly in my mind once more, the man moving toward Asmia.

"Oh, God," I cried out when the image flashed. The dark hair and chiseled jaw gave way to... "He's the devil."

The face was grotesque, the skin pulled too tightly over the features, complete with beady eyes and a distorted nose. There were bumps on his head. No, scratch that. Those were horns. Short, stubby protrusions with sharp points.

I inhaled sharply when the image warped, returning that of the human man, who looked normal in comparison.

The sound of the doorknob turning had my eyes shooting open. The hand holding the brush was over my heart as though I needed to assure the organ I was safe and sound, no devils here. Eclipse stepped inside, Obsidian and Penelope right behind him.

Who knew what I looked like, but based on the way their eyes widened, it couldn't have been good.

"*Sezari?*"

"I'm okay." I wasn't sure if I was assuring him or myself.

"Anything?" There was so much hope on Penelope's pretty face.

"I saw her." I glanced between all three faces. "Looks like he's taken her to an abandoned warehouse. I don't know where. Couldn't see out any of the windows." I exhaled heavily. "He was telling her he's going to realign their destinies. I don't know what that means. Something about manipulating the Fates so she belonged to him."

Eclipse glanced over at Obsidian briefly.

"But it gets worse," I admitted, drawing their attention back to me. "That *thing* she's with..." I inhaled deeply, the image flashing in my brain once more. "He's a devil. Like, literally. Horns and all."

When they didn't appear surprised by that, I frowned.

"He's a demon," Eclipse explained. "Did you see him in his natural form?"

"The vision flashed between the two. He looked like a man, then..." More breaths in, more out. Slow and steady. "I can try again if you'd like," I offered when no one spoke. "I'm not sure what good it'll do."

"We appreciate your efforts," Penelope said, her voice edged with pain, her eyes ringed in red. Clearly she'd been crying.

I held up the hairbrush. "I'd like to keep this for a bit. I'll hold on to it. Maybe another vision will come."

Obsidian nodded before leading Penelope from the room.

Eclipse offered his hand, and I accepted it, allowing him to pull me to my feet.

"Thank you for doing this."

"I wish someone had offered the same when Amber took off." Once again thinking that she might be alive if they had. "I'm not sure what good it'll do, but I can give a decent description."

He pressed a kiss to my forehead as he pulled me into him. "Thank you for this. Asmia's family," he said softly. "She's only been here for a century or so, but she's..."

"You don't have to explain," I said when his words drifted off. "I get it. Family's family. And we won't stop looking until we find her."

Eclipse pulled back and peered down at me. His hands cupped my face, and I saw something glittering in his eyes. Not heat. No, not like we'd experienced before. This was more than that. Something powerful, all-consuming.

"Come on," he finally said, breaking the eye contact. "Let's go downstairs. My brothers are arriving, and I'd like to see where we're at."

Without argument, I headed for the door, allowing him to steer me with a hand on my lower back. The first thing I noticed was the sounds had amplified in the house, more conversations, more movement. Definitely more people.

As we headed down the stairs, we passed several men and women—or were they angels?—coming out of rooms or going in. On the main floor, we had to weave through bodies. Dozens of people were scattered about, some sitting, others standing. I took stock. Some I recognized, many I didn't. Based on the way they greeted Eclipse with warm smiles, I had to assume they were all family. I couldn't help but wonder what it would feel like to have a family like this. One that was there for one another—in good times and bad.

Speaking of family, I needed to call my mother, let her know I was all right. I'd been dutiful in my conversations, but admittedly, I'd missed a few here and there. Every time I did, guilt racked me.

"Orianna, I'd like to introduce you to Stygian and Aphotic. Two more of my brothers."

Pulling myself from my thoughts, I smiled and held out my hand as was an appropriate greeting. "It's nice to meet you."

Stygian smiled, his gaze dropping to my hand. "Forgive us if it seems rude, but trust me, you do not want us touching you."

Feeling shunned, I dropped my hand.

Eclipse chuckled and pulled me against his side, hugging me tightly. "The touch of another male will cause you pain, *sezari.*"

"Pain?" I peered up into his face. "Seriously? Is that an angel bonding thing or something?"

He chuckled. "Or something."

Well, that certainly explained a lot. And made me feel a little less like a leper.

"What about you? Will you feel pain if a woman touches you?" I asked, figuring it was only fair.

"Yes. The touch of a female would be unbearable."

I patted his chest and pulled out of his arms. "Good."

Aphotic chuckled. "She suits you, brother."

"That she does," Eclipse agreed. "More than you'll ever know."

"Have you seen Shadow or Piceous?" Stygian asked, his gaze locked on Eclipse's face.

"Not yet, but I'm sure they'll be here shortly."

"Good. Because we need to get a plan underway. And fast."

Hoping I could contribute to helping to bring their family member home, I clutched Asmia's brush tightly in my hand and remained on the periphery. These people knew Asmia best, knew what we were up against. If I wanted to help, I had to take direction from them. Something I wasn't familiar with but was relieved to have. When it came to my search for Amber, I'd been on my own the entire time.

23

OBSIDIAN

———

The shouts sounded from the entry, drawing my attention and that of everyone currently in residence. We'd gathered in the sunroom to discuss preliminary plans, but before we could get underway, the ruckus redirected our efforts.

Leading the pack, I came to a stop in the hallway at the front of the house, my brain processing what I was seeing.

"What did you do to him?" Rinc seethed, going chest to chest with Valterri, the two enormous males glaring daggers at one another.

Beside them on the floor was Taayin. The male's eyes were closed, his jaw slack. He was out like a light.

"He's not dead," Valterri growled. "Merely incapacitated."

"You fucker. I'll rip your head from your goddamn—"

"Enough," I snarled as I marched down the hallway.

I took in the scene, scanning the space before diving into Valterri's mind to get a personal account of what happened.

From the *ladeare's* memories, I gathered that Taayin overheard the conversation between Valterri and Cimmerian. Not surprisingly, Taayin went apeshit when he learned Asmia had been taken. To keep him from doing harm to himself or others, Cimmerian had knocked him out with a touch to his head, then had Valterri bring him to the mansion.

Which explained why Cimmerian was late.

"Get Taayin to his quarters," I commanded Valterri. "Stay with him. Let me know when he's awake, but don't let him out of that room."

Valterri nodded, hefting Taayin's lifeless body—which required some serious leg muscles and a grunt—over his shoulder and carrying him up the stairs.

Penelope appeared as the scene settled, her eyes wide with concern. "Was that Taayin?"

"Yes." The pain on my *ereswa's* face damn near broke my heart. Since I told her about Asmia, Penelope had been crying, her sorrow so strong I could feel it in my own body.

"He didn't take it well," she said softly, no surprise in her tone.

Malak, Shadow's *ladeare*, turned to me. "I know this is going to sound entirely shallow, but tell me she's not his *amsouelot*."

I shook my head.

Taayin had wanted her to be. And while Malak was right, it was entirely inappropriate to think, it was the only saving grace at the moment. If they'd been destined by the Fates, Taayin was as good as dead. An angel would not survive without his mate.

"Get out of my fucking way!"

"Son of a bitch," Eclipse grumbled, turning to race up the stairs to the second floor.

I was right behind him, hoping to intervene before Taayin caused too much damage.

Right before my eyes, Taayin's arm shot out, his fingers wrapping around Eclipse's throat as he lifted him off the floor and threw him over the railing. A round of shouts sounded even as Eclipse vanished, taking form with both feet planted firmly on the main floor, saving himself. Before I could reach Taayin, Valterri dropped to his knees, hands around his throat, gasping for air.

Though I understood his pain, I cut off Taayin's power by using my own. Valterri fell over as he fought to fill his lungs.

"Where is she?" Taayin demanded, appearing only a foot from me, his blue eyes lighting up the entire room. "Where the fuck is she, Obsidian?"

"I don't know. But we'll find her."

The deep growl that sounded from Taayin was nothing short of a wounded animal and had every male in the room standing tall.

"I'll kill every single one of you," Taayin declared, his eyes scanning the space.

"Relax, Taayin," Stygian said softly, attempting to ease the beast.

"Every. Single. One." Taayin's gaze went to me, then over to—

The instant the male's eyes locked on Penelope, I lost my shit. My arm extended, a bolt of energy exploding outward, rendering Taayin motionless. The male was trapped in his own body, but his rage was so intense I wasn't sure that would hold him for long.

Stepping closer to the *lieterra*, I lowered my voice. "I feel your pain, but you even *think* about harming my *ereswa*, we'll have serious problems. Understood?"

Some of the heat seemed to dissipate from Taayin's eyes, replaced by unshed tears, and what I prayed was regret.

"Obsidian." Penelope gripped my arm. "Let him go. It's okay. He won't hurt me."

I had to weigh my options. Like Taayin, we were all frustrated and angry. Asmia was family, but no one ... absolutely no *fucking* one would threaten my mate. Not and live to remember it.

I hated to do it, but I knew Taayin needed the reprieve. Pressing the palm of my hand to his forehead, I sent him into a deep sleep. One he wouldn't come out of until I was ready for him to.

"Why'd you do that?" Penelope shouted, starting toward Taayin.

I stopped her with a firm hand on her arm. "Don't touch him, *ayreme*," I snarled. "If you do, I'll kill him where he lies."

She jerked back, clearly surprised by the rage in my voice. Hell, I surprised myself.

"Okay, why don't we all take a second to breathe?" Stygian suggested, planting a firm hand on my shoulder. "We need to think rationally so we can get Asmia back. We all expected Taayin to take the news hard, and this could've been handled better. But for now, he's right where he needs to be." Stygian turned to Valterri. "Let's get him to his room and I'll throw up a barrier to keep him there in the event he manages to wake up again."

The male nodded, then hefted Taayin's lifeless body over his shoulder once more.

"Just out of curiosity, how exactly did he do that?" Stygian asked, motioning toward Eclipse as our brother appeared at the top of the stairs.

"Never underestimate the power of fear." Especially when it came to a female. "I want everyone to meet in the bar. It should hold all of us. I want to know what the plan is to find Asmia. The minute the sun goes down, I want boots on the ground. Understood?"

A rumble of agreement sounded as everyone turned to head down to the main floor.

When Penelope was the only one remaining, I moved toward her. She stared up at me, eyes wide, and I felt like a complete ass for my reaction. I was out of line, but the truth was, it was a natural response.

"I'm sorry, *ayreme*. I shouldn't have reacted that way."

"We all want to find her," she said, gripping my forearms.

"And we will," I assured her.

"What about Taayin? You can't just lock him up."

"I can and I will. He's no good to anyone right now. Least of all Asmia. Until he can calm down, he's safer where he is."

I could see she didn't believe me.

I could feel her need to help find Asmia, her concern for the female. Every single soul in the mansion felt the same way. With the sun about to come over the horizon, we were trapped for the time being. But as soon as the sun went down tonight, I would have every able-bodied soul on the streets.

And we wouldn't stop searching until we brought her home.

MICHAEL

I hated to break up the party, but...

Okay, I didn't so much hate it. And I knew it wasn't a party. More like a wake based on all the frowns.

I could've told them all was not lost. Not completely. Yet.

Maybe tomorrow.

Fine. I wasn't a pit of fucking sunshine. Never had been, never would be.

Though it wasn't appropriate for the humans to see me, I made the trek through the main floor in my corporeal form while I peeked in the various rooms, looking for Obsidian and his boys. While the *heurosp* weren't technically human anymore—it was a long story, really—I did my best not to interact, ignoring the deep bows and greetings.

Why couldn't Obsidian simply tell me where he was going to be? That would make it significantly easier. On everyone.

Thankfully, with unparalleled hearing, I pinpointed their location relatively quickly. It wasn't a picnic getting my wings down those damn stairs, though, but the fault was on me. I opted to walk a few steps in their shoes, and by the time I reached the bottom, I was deeply regretting the mood I was in.

"Fucking hell," I grumbled, stumbling out of the stairwell as I flapped one wing to bring it back to its uncrimped glory.

"Oh, my God," a female voice squeaked.

"Not Him, sorry," I rumbled, taking stock of all the souls in the room.

Looked like everyone had shown up for the festivities. Close to a hundred angels and Fae crowded into one space, a few humans sprinkled about.

"Michael," Obsidian greeted, that stern, not-at-all pleased expression firmly in place.

The male's acknowledgment had the same effect it always did. Pride and something akin to love filled me as I peered over at my greatest creation.

"Obsidian," I returned, waving a hand. "Someone care to offer me a drink?"

Unlike in Heaven, there was no one rushing around to do my bidding. Also unlike in Heaven, there was quite a bit of animosity being launched in my direction. Damn warrior angels. Didn't they know it wasn't healthy to hold a grudge?

"Why are you here?" Stygian questioned.

At least he was relatively cool. I knew Hell would freeze over before Shadow or Piceous would direct a question my way. Without being prompted, anyway. Those two had been harboring deep-seated anger for centuries, and based on their dagger glares, I didn't think they intended to turn those frowns upside down anytime soon.

"No refreshments?" I rolled my eyes and moved deeper into the room. "Fine."

It wasn't like I could imbibe in their earthly victuals and libations anyway. But would it kill a guy to offer?

In an effort to keep my restlessness at bay, I wandered through the open space, eyeing the *fiestreigh* interspersed throughout.

"Nice jacket. Looks good on you," I told Raksa. "Brings out your eyes."

The male's gaze swung over to Malak briefly before lowering.

So he was feeling some heat for a co-worker. Good for him. I always wanted them to find happiness. God knew they deserved it, considering they'd devoted their entire existence to keeping my father's creations safe from the evils of the world. A Band-Aid fix, my ass. Fifteen hundred years in, I would have to say my father had been wrong about one thing. Those angels knew how to get shit done.

Someone cleared their throat. Likely Obsidian. Probably attempting to get me to pick up the pace.

Fine.

Turning toward the male I created with my own two hands, I nodded.

"What the fuck?" Obsidian grumbled when we took form in their third-floor... whatever this room was.

"We need to chat. Privately," I said by way of explanation.

"The proper way is to say so," Obsidian countered. "Give a male a chance to tie up his previous engagements."

"Yeah, well. No time for pleasantries," I told him.

"So what's the rush?"

"We've got a situation." I picked up the eight ball sitting on the red felt, studied it. I never understood the allure of this game, but my warriors seemed enraptured by it. Had to be since they had two of these tables in their residence.

"We do," Obsidian confirmed. "And if you'd let me get back to it, we could address bringing Asmia home."

I set the ball down and made a trip around the table. "It's not about bringing her home, per se."

Oh, I understood their desire to. I would've had to be an idiot not to feel the eager anticipation lingering thick and frothy in that lower-level room.

I was a lot of things, but an idiot I was not.

Obsidian's silver glare was pinned right on me. "Then what's it about?"

"Well..."

24

OLIVER

I wasn't too proud to admit I almost shit my pants when that fucking angel appeared, all winged and tatted like some holy badass.

"You okay?"

The words were spoken softly from my right and it took a second to register Bijou's voice.

"No," I said at the same time I nodded an affirmative.

A fucking angel.

With wings.

Seriously.

"I take it you've never seen one in their feathered form?" Bijou teased.

"No." I peered over, aware my eyes were like saucers.

Her smile was so damn sweet, it was almost enough to put a kibosh on the weirdness factor. But not quite.

"You know your sister has them, too, right?"

My gaze shot across the room to land on Penelope. "Wings?"

Bijou giggled. "So that's a no."

What the fuck?

"Hey, man. You think you could give us a hand?" Reidar asked, stepping right in front of me.

Peering up at the angel, I cocked an eyebrow. "With?"

Reidar nodded in the direction of the war room. "You've got some mad skills, and I was hoping you could see if you could hack some traffic cams."

"Why can't Miklós do it?" It wasn't that I was opposed to helping out, but I usually took a back seat to the experts. "Or Søren?"

"Miklós is ... he's out of commission at the moment. And Søren's taking care of something else. If you can't, it's no big."

"I'll do it," I announced.

Reidar had been cool with me, after all. Well, after our trip to the mansion, anyway. I couldn't say the guy was my favorite, considering he hog-tied me in the back seat of his Camaro and hauled my ass all this way without so much as an introduction. But considering he'd plucked me straight out of what I didn't realize was a fucking nightmare, I felt a tad indebted to him.

"Cool." Reidar led the way to the war room.

"Do all of you have wings?" I blurted, the words tumbling right out of my mouth.

Reidar peered over at me, smirked. "Yeah."

Leaning back, I gave the guy's enormous back a quick scan. No way was he hiding that shit under that tight T-shirt.

"If we flaunted them, wouldn't do much for keeping on the DL, now would it?"

"Guess not."

"Here we are." Reidar motioned toward a fancy setup on one of the back tables.

"What's this?"

"Your new workstation. Like?"

My head snapped over to the angel. "Mine?"

Reidar nodded, his gaze scanning all the fancy shit laid out before us.

I checked it out, eyes greedily raking over the cool new toys. Looked like an Apple store had hacked out a hairball of amazing right there.

"Figured you'd need a place of your own."

"For?"

"Helping out." Reidar frowned as I turned toward him. "Considering all you've done, I just thought..."

I waited.

"Thought we'd bring you on full-time. That is if you're looking for employment."

"Is it a paid position?"

"Of course." Reidar grinned. "I mean, you've got some cool digs to chill in, but the rest ... we don't expect you to hide out here forever. Just try to keep a low profile for a while longer."

A month ago, I would've still been on the kiss-my-ass bus, but after watching them work for the past few weeks, it became clear they weren't simply blowing smoke up my ass about being in danger. Hell, Søren went so far as to pull up an image of Seraphina in all her natural glory. To think I'd dipped my wick in that... A chill raced down my spine.

"You cool?"

Pulling myself out of the gutter thoughts, I nodded. "I'm cool. Traffic cams."

"Yep." Reidar tapped a bright yellow Post-it stuck to the top of the table. "This is Orianna's address. The last place Asmia was seen. Since she wouldn't have gone willingly, Perfidious couldn't rely on her to vapor-it to his hideout, so we're hoping the cams got a glimpse of them. According to Orianna's vision, they're holed up in a warehouse. Don't have a clue where."

"But if I can tie in their movements..." I dropped into the chair, pulled the keyboard toward me.

I couldn't stop the smile that formed. Back before I was dragged kicking and screaming to Angel Central, I dreamed of a setup like this. Now ... now I was getting into the thick of it. Being useful for the first time in a long damn time.

"I'll be back to check in," Reidar called out. "I need to follow up with Obsidian. See what Michael wanted."

I nodded, not even sure what the angel said. I was too busy getting acquainted with my new baby.

ΛCADIA

I could feel Kaj's eyes on me, knew he was tracking me as I moved across the room. I did my best to ignore him, but it wasn't easy.

It dawned on me that he might be thinking about the last time we were together in this room. On that particular sofa, in fact. He had been on top of me, his big, strong body pushing deep in—

"Hey, you got a minute?"

As I came to a complete stop, my gaze collided with Eclipse. It took a moment to eject that erotic image from my head as I focused on the male's face.

"Acadia?"

Yep. That was my name.

I gave my noggin a mental shake to free myself from my thoughts, then focused on Eclipse. "Something wrong?"

"Maybe." He canted his head toward the far side of the room, started walking.

Hoping I could prove useful in the efforts to find Asmia, I followed the male.

"I need you to do something for me," Eclipse said softly as he tucked into an empty corner.

"Anything, sire."

For a moment, Eclipse's attention drifted over my head, locking on something behind me. When he glanced back, I could see the concern in his eyes.

"It's not my place to pry, but..." He exhaled heavily. "Look, I had a chat with Kaj, and he told me flat out that you're his mate."

I narrowed my eyes, gearing up to tell him that was nonsense, but Eclipse stopped me when he held up his palm.

"Like I said, not my place to pry, but for the sake of ... safety ... I was thinking it would be best if you refrain from your duties for a little while."

By duties, I knew he meant feeding the males. Angels required the blood of a Fae to survive unless, of course, they could feed from their *amsouelot*. Since most of the males in the mansion weren't mated, I was a necessity. I wasn't even sure he realized the repercussions if I did agree to bow out. If he knew my entire existence was on the line, surely he wouldn't be making such a suggestion.

"Thank you for your concern," I said softly, holding his gaze, "but Kaj is not my mate. I have no loyalty to him, and if the males need me, I've a duty to support them."

Eclipse leaned in, careful not to come in contact with me. "Acadia, the last thing we need right now is for a vampire to go apeshit with everyone in residence. I get that they don't bond with their females the way we do, but ... have you ever met a mated vampire?"

Having been sheltered within the *fiestreigh* for most of my existence, I hadn't interacted much with other races or species. However, I was all too aware of what it meant to bond with a vampire. It was all I could do to ignore the twenty-four-seven need I'd been plagued with for the past year and a half. Never mind the fact it had intensified tenfold since Kaj returned to the mansion. I blamed that overwhelming heat for surrendering to him the last time. Right here in this very room.

"I know how to be discreet," I assured Eclipse. "My duty is to the *fiestreigh*, not to Kaj. They need me, especially now."

I knew he couldn't argue with me there. Despite the fact the other Fae had returned to the mansion, we were still thirty-nine to eighteen, which was roughly two to one, in favor of the angels as far as body counts went. And while Fae could replenish with the energy cast off by the angels without the need to feed for weeks at a time, there was still only so much blood the Fae could spare. With the angels needing their strength for the fight ahead, I wasn't willing to hide in the shadow of Kaj's misplaced affections. Perhaps I wasn't up to speed on the bonding rituals of all species, but I knew more about vampires than I was willing to let on. And there were a few key characteristics Kaj hadn't displayed, which made me question his intentions.

Eclipse exhaled heavily. "Then I ask that you proceed with caution. Safety's paramount. For all of us right now."

I nodded my agreement. I had no desire to push Kaj's buttons.

Lifting my skirt to keep it from dragging the floor, I curtsied respectfully to the male, then turned and headed toward the stairs leading up to the main house. I'd promised to meet Torak, and the last thing I needed was for the male to think I wasn't available. It wouldn't take much for rumors to spread, and having everyone to believe I was off-limits because of Kaj was not on my list of things to do.

A sharp squeak rattled out of my throat when the Alpha vampire appeared not two feet in front of me on my ascension into the house. The already cramped stairwell felt even more minuscule with him in it.

My hand instantly went to my chest, as though my heart needed the pressure to remain in place.

As usual, I bowed appropriately. "Good evening, *tresmar*."

My heart hopped right past my hand and into my throat when Kaj stepped in close, effectively blocking my path and sandwiching me between his big body and the stone wall.

"Good evening, *balisra*."

I couldn't quite prepare myself for his touch, so the instant he brushed a stray curl away from my face, a traitorous shiver ran down my spine, warming me from the inside out.

Kaj's green eyes brightened, as did the sinful smirk on his mouth.

"Despite your denial," he said, his voice little more than a gruff whisper, "it is true, Acadia. I have bonded with you. The only reason I have yet to make it official is for your benefit, not mine."

I narrowed my eyes. "If you would excuse me, I have an appointment."

Kaj's thumb brushed over my cheek. "Don't think I'm not aware of where you're off to. Or the fact that you're feeding the angels, allowing them to sink their fangs into your vein. I feel it, *balisra*. There's a dark echo in my soul every time I share a part of you with one of them. Pain, unlike anything I've ever known, blooms within me, rocking me to my core. Yet I've endured in an effort to keep you safe."

I stared up at him, shocked by his admission.

"And while I'm stepping aside for the time being, that doesn't mean I can hold back forever. Eclipse is correct, a bonded vampire is a dangerous beast. At some point, I will require your ultimate surrender, and when that day comes, I assure you, all those characteristics you believe are absent will be front and center, making me a danger to every male in this household, be it angel, human, Fae, or vampire."

Kaj's lips were a mere breath away from my own, and it was all I could do not to lean forward just to get a brush of their warmth.

"Kaj ... please." I didn't know if I was asking him to kiss me or pleading for him to step away.

He clearly believed it was the latter because the male took a single step back, his touch falling away.

Rather than give in to my traitorous desires, I latched onto the pain my heart endured when he walked away the last time.

Without so much as a goodbye, I drifted off, reforming on the second floor. But rather than meet Torak in the library as I promised, I avoided everyone by racing to my own room, closing the door behind me.

If only I could shut out my feelings as easily as I could the souls.

25

Asmia

———

Cold and dark...

Funny how my surroundings were now reflective of what I was harboring in my heart for these past couple of months. All stemming from the same creature, too: Perfidious. The demon who turned my world upside down, then threw a loopty-loop in for good measure.

But even as I sat on the hard dirt floor, surrounded by titanium bars, more earth, and a solid wall of rock, I felt no more alone now than I had when Taayin turned his back on me, walked away without giving me a chance to apologize. Maybe this was my punishment for betraying him the way he believed I had.

Or perhaps this was the damnation I'd always heard about, the one strictly reserved for Fae, God's cast-outs.

It wasn't enough that I was enslaved to the angels, handed to them on a silver platter to maintain their existence, keep them strong? That was God's punishment, right? His means of exacting vengeance for the sins of my ancestors? Well, it hadn't worked out too well for Him. Somewhere along the way, I found pleasure in that subjugation, a place I belonged, a family who cared.

Maybe God didn't approve of that. Not enough pain to be considered penance. Better to be enslaved to the damned. After all, my life was to be one of servitude, wasn't it? Only now, I would be chained to a demon for the rest of my existence.

From outside the cell, I could hear voices, though I had no idea who they belonged to. Well, other than Perfidious, that was. His dark tenor was unmistakable. When I first arrived— hours, days, however long ago that was—I'd heard a shrieking female, but thankfully, that one had exited the building. Whether she was pissed to leave or upset I was there, I didn't know. Nor did I care.

Truth was, I didn't care about much of anything. When I closed my eyes, I still saw Echo's pained face, and I could only imagine the agony he was enduring, believing he was responsible for my being taken. He was a good male, he didn't deserve to bear the brunt of that. Thankfully, time would ease his torment, give him new memories to crowd out the pain of the past.

I briefly wondered what Taayin thought. Had they told him? Did he even care? More than the others, that was. I knew he cared. He was a noble male, one who did not shirk his duty. Because I was a member of the *fiestreigh*, he would be searching for me if they asked him to. But aside from that duty, was he concerned? Did he miss me?

Because I missed him. More than I wanted to admit.

I expected tears to fall, but they never came. Perhaps I'd

simply cried too much lately. Not once since Perfidious had walked me out of that apartment had I felt the urge to spill tears. Granted, the anger was building, and God forbid that demon stroll in here with his arrogant ass. I was saving every last ounce of my strength so I could take it out on his hide. If Perfidious thought I was a helpless female, he had another thing coming.

And if he thought keeping me naked down here was going to intimidate me ... well, he could get fucked, as Eclipse would say. Thinking of the male made me smile sadly. I hoped things were going well for him and Orianna. I'd sensed how good they were together, how much they cared for each other even in the short time since they'd met. Then again, it wasn't time that made the heart grow fonder. No, that was absence, or so I'd heard. At some point, I figured I'd look back on the family I left behind with fondness, remembering the good times without the sorrow equated with not having had the opportunity to say goodbye.

Footsteps sounded on the hard-packed earth, and I knew who was coming before Perfidious made an appearance. That haughty air of his was stifling, circling him, choking out all the air in the room. He believed he'd won even though no one else had been playing the game.

"How fare thee, gorgeous?"

I didn't bother looking up. I wouldn't give him the satisfaction. Instead, I sat on the ground, legs crisscrossed. I was naked, and this position gave him a glimpse of all my private parts, but it didn't matter. He thought he'd beaten me by stealing my clothes. Truth was, I didn't care. Not if he looked, not even if he touched. This was merely a vessel I was encapsulated in. My soul was elsewhere, my heart safeguarded because it belonged to another. He could physically hurt me, he could force me to touch him, but he could never take what was most precious to me.

I'd been a victim of his mind control before, and I knew it was only a matter of time before he trapped me within the confines of it again. Before long, I would be his slave in every sense of the word. I had no illusions that I was getting out of here anytime soon. This was my own fault, so I was going to get used to it. And when he forced me into his bed or wherever a creature like him laid his head, I knew I would have no say in the matter. But I refused to let him win.

Before he could begin to break me with his magic, I would lock up all those memories, those good feelings, and tuck them deep within my heart, hidden from him. Even if I remained in his clutches for the rest of my immortal life, he would never take those from me.

"Stand up and greet me appropriately," Perfidious ordered, the door swinging open.

I bided my time, remained where I was, head down, fingers clasped in front of me.

"Did you hear me?"

Oh, I heard him. Unfortunately.

A firm hand curled under my chin. I took a deep breath, then another as Perfidious slowly lifted my head so I was forced to meet his eyes.

I gave him what he wanted. My lips curled up in a smile, and the instant I saw approval in his eyes...

I lashed out, dragging all of my nails down both sides of his face, scoring his flesh, his precious blood seeping out of the wounds, essentially ruining the human suit he was wearing.

That would teach him.

ECLIPSE

"I don't know about you guys, but I'm thinking we should hit the hay, regroup at sundown, and..."

The rest of Aphotic's words were drowned out by the roaring that suddenly filled my head. It was compounded by the blistering heat that pummeled me from all angles.

"I... Oh, fuck..." I didn't bother with an explanation as I disappeared myself, resuming form in my private quarters.

There, reclining on the leather chaise lounger, was the most luscious female I'd ever had the pleasure of seeing. Her eyes were wide, her body writhing as though trying to scratch an itch but not quite making contact.

"Eclipse ... what is going on?"

I could feel the heat pulsing through her, knew her body was aching for mine, so I didn't waste time with the whole undressing ordeal. Instead, I willed both of our clothes off as I moved toward Orianna, then used the power of my mind to ignite the flames in the fireplace. Partly for warmth, more so for ambience, because on some level, I was still trying to impress the girl. Granted, I wasn't sure Orianna noticed anything as she writhed and moaned, her hands sliding over her bare skin, which, heaven help me, was almost too much.

"Come here, *sezari*," I crooned as I joined her, lying on the chaise lounge and sliding my hand behind her head, pulling her mouth to mine.

Instantly, Orianna's tongue sought entrance as her fingers slid into my hair. Shards of pain morphed into a delicious pleasure as she jerked me closer, her breaths rasping against my mouth as her lips mated with mine. She was liquid fire in my arms, rubbing herself against me in the most delicious ways.

Filling my hand with the smooth warmth of her breast, I pressed up against her. The flash boil that had been my hormones dropped to simmer in an instant, offering a modicum of relief and an opportunity for us to explore. Not that it lasted long. The moment Orianna's hands began to slide over my shoulders, down my chest, wandering and teasing, the flames licked at me once more, but this I could handle. This I knew what to do with.

"I don't know what that was," Orianna moaned, tilting her head to the side as I dragged my lips along the smooth column of her neck. "I felt like... It just hit me all of a sudden. I needed you. Desperately." She cupped my head, holding my mouth to her neck. "And then there you were."

I groaned low in my throat when those deft fingers on her other hand curled around my shaft, stroking me firmly.

"Careful," I warned, sliding my lips along her jaw. "It'll be over before it gets started."

"I need to feel you," she moaned, trying to get closer. "Inside me. It's... There's an emptiness..."

"We'll get there," I assured her.

Orianna pulled back, glared at me. "Now, Eclipse. Right now."

I laughed when she attempted to take over, pushing me to my back as she threw one leg over my hips, positioning herself where we both wanted her to be.

Using the chair's contour to my advantage, I shifted so I

was reclining, able to see every glorious curve of her body, every sinful shift of her as she guided my cock between her thighs. My gaze dropped lower, another rumble sounding in my chest as her slick heat coated the sensitive tip seconds before she angled for penetration.

"Fuck..." I groaned at the same time she whimpered.

The smooth walls of her sex clutched me intimately as she eased over me, a slow, steady blanket of heat coating me, the glorious caress tightening my muscles, pleasure assaulting every nerve ending.

Fucking hell, she felt good like this, owning me as she worked herself down inch by amazing inch. My groin tightened, the intensity of her heat surging through me. It wasn't until I was buried to the hilt that she relaxed somewhat, her movements slowing as her eyes locked with mine.

"This what you need?" I asked, planting my hands firmly on her hips and rocking her gently so as not to let the friction abate.

"God, yes."

I could do nothing more than watch as she took her pleasure from me. Orianna maintained control, swinging her hips forward and back, slow and easy at first, her eyes caressing my chest as she found a rhythm that suited us both. I didn't move to rush her, simply chose to observe and enjoy. It had been a hectic, emotional night, and this ... being with her like this was more than I could've ever hoped for. Which, now that I thought about it, was the same thing I reflected on anytime I was with her. Such a treasure she was, and my life ... I could no longer imagine a world without her in it.

Careful not to affect the rhythmic thrust of her hips, I slid my hands upward, beyond the curve of her waist, pausing to knead her full breasts. Her skin was so warm, so soft, but it was the way she leaned into me, encouraging me to take what she was offering, that stole my breath.

"Yes," she whimpered. "Touch me. Don't stop touching me."

"Never, *sezari*."

I would've been content to do this for a lifetime, watching her ride me, working herself on the thick ridge of my erection, using my body to sate hers. I'd never experienced anything like it before, never felt so fucking complete until she walked into my life. Now that she was with me, I knew there was no going back.

The minutes stretched out as she ground herself on me. No rush, only unadulterated ecstasy warming us both, causing perspiration to dot our skin as the sensations intensified.

When Orianna tipped her head back, her hand sensually sliding up her neck, I was fixated on the movement, the way her fingers gently caressed the puncture marks I left the last time I fed from her. My fangs elongated, my jaw throbbing as hunger took over. It wasn't so much that I needed to feed, but there was a desperation that bordered on bloodlust. What I took from her recently wasn't nearly enough to sate me, and it seemed my brain was kicking over to survival mode.

Dropping my hands to her hips, I focused on guiding her movements while rocking up into her.

"More," I urged. "Take more of me, *sezari*."

She opened her eyes and looked at me. It took tremendous effort and ridiculous strength to hold her stare rather than pull her toward me so I could sink my fangs into her neck.

As though she knew what I needed—and perhaps she did —Orianna slowed the delicious grind as she moved her hair to one side.

"Will you feed from me?" she whispered.

I swallowed hard, my fangs throbbing incessantly.

Her blue eyes were as hot as gas flames, her words a rough rasp against my senses when she said, "I want you to feed, Eclipse. And I want to feel you come inside me when you do."

A desperate growl raced up my throat, but I managed to hold myself back, keeping my hands firmly on her hips, my fingers digging into the soft flesh.

Orianna leaned forward until her breasts were crushed to my chest. She rested against me, her forehead on my shoulder, her hips once again undulating. Her back arching and bowing, a sensual flow as her body glided perfectly along mine. It wasn't until her hand slid behind my head, guiding my lips toward her neck, that I opened my mouth, my fangs descending more as the thrum of her blood in her veins beckoned me.

"Hold still for me," I growled.

Orianna's hands went to my shoulders, her body pressing tightly against me as I wrapped one arm around her back, securing her in place. I inhaled her sweet lavender scent, kissed the soft skin over her pulse, but then my hunger for her took over.

I didn't hold back this time as I pierced her neck. Her blood filled my mouth, warm and rich, intoxicating me as I took what she willingly offered. With my fangs buried in her vein, my cock in her pussy, I gripped her hip with my other hand and began driving up into her. Her soft whimpers and moans spurred me on until I was too far gone to stop.

Her sex clutched me, pulsing as her orgasm crested from the euphoria that came with me feeding from her. I drank her down as I punched my hips upward, driving in deep, retreating slowly. Wanting to make her come a dozen times.

Seconds turned to minutes, but I didn't stop until the hunger abated completely. Only then did I seal the wounds I created before shifting our positions, forcing her backward so she reclined at the opposite end of the chaise, her head hanging down. I took advantage of the new position and the control it offered me. With my feet on the floor, I took control, owning her body as she lay out before me, a sexual offering. I shifted her legs over my thighs, her ankles digging into my lower back as I pumped my hips, filling every inch of her.

Orianna cried out my name over and over as I pressed my thumb to her clit, circled it lightly at first, then added more pressure. I continued the bump and grind, a rapid thrust and retreat as I slammed my hips forward, burying myself in her slickness, feeling the walls of her pussy grip me until my spine tingled, the electricity shooting through every nerve.

"Orianna ... oh, fuck..." It was too much, the intensity overwhelming me, sucking me into the vortex, suspended somewhere between sheer ecstasy and mind-numbing pleasure bordering on pain.

I drove into her once, twice ... on the third, I threw my head back and roared, my release barreling through me, shattering my sanity for precious seconds.

And when we were finished, it was Orianna's contented sigh that brought all my pieces back together, made me whole once more.

26

KAJ

———

"Christ Almighty!" I kicked the blankets off my legs. "How the fuck do they handle this shit?"

I fisted my cock as I flopped onto my back, that dreaded sexual energy slamming into me, pulling me from a deep, peaceful sleep. I was no longer curious about what caused it—Obsidian had so kindly filled me in via a warning that it would likely occur frequently—but that didn't mean I could ignore it. Oh, no, I was powerless against the onslaught of sexual heat that burned my body from the inside out.

Fucking angels. If I didn't like them so much, I would damn them all to Hell.

I grunted, gripping my cock firmly, dragging my palm up and down in an attempt to assuage the beast.

Kaj. I need you, Kaj.

Lifting my head, I scanned the darkness, looking for Acadia, whose voice was beckoning me. I knew the words were sent into my mind, but I hoped to find her at my bedside. She wasn't, but I sensed she was close, likely in her own bed, touching herself the same way I was.

I'm here, balisra.

Come to me, Kaj. I can't...

It took effort—like walking against hurricane-force winds —but I managed to get to my feet, intent on answering her plea. Vanishing wasn't an option, my mind plagued by the urgent need to come, making it impossible to focus. Since I was relegated to taking the long route, I snagged my boxers, dragged them on even as I took the steps toward the bedroom door. Another blast of heat drove me back a step when I reached the hallway, but I forged ahead, intent to get to my female. My body led the way, my cock like a metal detector, seeking the one and only thing that would ever sate me fully.

The trek down the hallway was like trudging through quicksand, but I finally reached Acadia's door. I raised my hand to knock when the door flew open. Inside, Acadia was on her bed, gloriously naked, back bowed, breasts thrust upward as she whimpered, her hand tucked between her thighs as she attempted to ease herself.

Whether it was my sheer will or the sexual energy abating, I didn't know, but the rest of the trip was easier. I crossed the threshold, shut her door with a thought, then stalked toward her as I disposed of the damn boxers. Acadia's amethyst eyes opened, hot and glowing as she watched me. I didn't waste time, knowing exactly what she needed when she spread her thighs and invited me to join her.

I crawled onto the mattress, inching closer, my mouth

dropping to her knee, sliding higher, over her thigh. I would've stopped to savor her sweetness, but Acadia had other plans for me, her small hands clutching at my hair as she dragged me up her body.

"You sure, *balisra*?"

"Yes," she hissed, arching her back once more as I dragged my aching cock through her slick folds.

Holy fuck, she was so wet, so hot.

Without preamble, I pushed inside her with enough restraint not to hurt her. It only took a moment for her body to acclimate to my size, her slickness coating me, easing the way. Sweet mother in Heaven. Acadia felt so fucking good, her body sending warmth radiating through my own. The only other feeling as amazing as this was coming home to her after having been away for so damn long.

"Take what you need," I snarled as I propped her knees over my forearms, then planted my hands on either side of her head and began pumping my hips.

Acadia's eyes remained locked on my face as she placed her palms flat on my chest, one directly over my heart. I watched, impaling her deep and hard as her purple irises glowed, cutting through the darkness, my energy being drawn into her, fueling her.

The first time she siphoned energy from me, I hadn't been able to explain it. I hadn't expected the intensity or the strange orgasmic sensations that resulted from it. And though the action weakened me for a beat, I couldn't imagine not giving this female everything she needed. It was my duty as her mate to take care of her, to feed her.

My thoughts got hijacked by images of her feeding from the other males in the house, and I could feel the shift in my body. All of my senses were heightened, every single one of them focused on the female beneath me. My fangs punched down and my eyes lit up, allowing me to see everything in super high-def.

"Kaj…"

I growled softly, fighting back the urge to mark her as mine. It was an instinct not easily shoved down but one I was growing intimately more familiar with.

Acadia's nails dug into my pecs as she drew on the sexual energy.

Fuck. Just the sight of her was enough to send me spiraling closer and closer to that blissful explosion that would sate me, albeit temporarily.

Acadia whimpered. "Kaj…"

I was gearing up to send us both into hyperspace when another blast of energy nearly knocked me over.

Acadia screamed, her sex clutching me, milking my cock as her hands fell from my chest.

I leaned forward, my mouth hovering over hers. "Kiss me," I demanded.

She did. And Heaven have mercy on my soul, I felt that kiss through my entire being. A cataclysmic mating of bodies ensued as Acadia took as much as she gave. I drilled into her. Hard, fast, deep. Over and over with startling force and over-whelming power. It wasn't so much sex as it was a claiming. My body, hers. My soul, hers.

When I pulled my mouth away, it was to stare down into her face. I wanted to see the submission in her eyes.

"Tell me," I growled. "Who do you belong to, Acadia?"

"You," she whimpered.

"Say my name," I demanded, punctuating the words with vicious thrusts that rocketed us both closer to orgasm.

"Kaj."

"Say it," I insisted.

"I belong to you, Kaj. Only you."

Her admission was what sent me over. The rumble tore up from my throat, an animalistic sound that no doubt could be heard for miles preceded the explosive orgasm. Mine. Hers.

When my body stilled, our eyes remained locked. I sensed her need to retreat, and I respected it, but I wasn't willing to let go just yet. Been there, done that, didn't fucking like it the first time. It was selfish of me to back her into that corner, to force her to say the words aloud, but I didn't regret it. Deep down, I knew Acadia belonged to me. But it would take time before she was willing to accept it fully.

Rather than walk away the way she wanted, I rolled us so that she was straddling me, my cock still buried to the hilt inside her.

"Now it's your turn, *balisra*. Take me, Acadia."

And she did.

ORIANNA

I wasn't startled when I was awoken by the soft mechanical whir. Not when the drapes started their tedious retraction or the interior shutters unlocked and began their slow, methodical ascent and not when the outer ones followed suit. In the short time I'd been at the mansion, I'd gotten familiar with the sounds of the day giving way to night, the mansion coming alive with those who were forced to live in darkness.

"Have you ever been in the sun?" I asked Eclipse, trailing my finger over his bare chest as we lay in his big bed.

"No."

"I assume there's no sun in Heaven?"

"It's always light there and it maintains a consistent temperature, but not from the sun, no."

"You said you've been here … on Earth … for fifteen hundred years, right?" Just saying the words brought a smile to my face. It seemed so outrageous to think of Eclipse as an angel, having existed for an eternity. It made me wonder if his memories extended back that far. Could he remember the events of his life so long ago?

"Correct."

"And before that?"

"I was training." His hand came up and covered mine where it rested over his heart.

"For?"

"Protecting humans."

"From what? I take it vampires aren't your enemies."

Eclipse chuckled. "No. Vampires are here for the same reason we are."

"To protect humans?"

"They're responsible for eliminating Lucifer's creatures, and we—my brothers and I—handle the demons who create those creatures."

"That sounds like a full-time job. There are only seven of you?"

"Technically, no. But last I heard, Michael hasn't yet released the other factions."

"Who's Michael?"

"The archangel who created us," he said easily.

"The tatted guy with wings?"

Eclipse chuckled. "Angel, but yes."

I lifted my head, peered at him in the dim light from the fire. "I thought you said you have parents."

"I do. But Obsidian does not. He was Michael's first creation. God didn't like that Michael had encroached on his style, so he forced Michael to utilize traditional reproduction manners using archsires and archdams."

That sounded far too clinical for my taste, but I didn't interrupt.

"Michael has a dedicated pool of angels who reproduce for him. The strongest, fastest, most intelligent beings he can find. They raise the offspring until they've reached puberty, then send them to Michael for training."

"At what age does an angel reach puberty?"

"Puberty is roughly after the twenty-fifth year, when they stop aging. As for full maturity, that depends on the upbringing, but generally close to the century mark."

I smiled as I lowered my head once more. "And you've been alive for seventeen centuries?"

"I have." His hand caressed my arm, warm and comforting.

"Is Penelope an angel?" I asked after a few beats of silence.

His hand paused briefly, then resumed its slow, easy caress. "She is now, yes."

"How did that happen?"

"Obsidian mated her."

I thought back to that vision of myself lying cold on the floor with Eclipse hovering over me. How I knew, I wasn't sure, but it made sense. That was a premonition of the day I would die, and the reason it didn't scare me was because it wasn't the end.

"I'm going to die," I told him. "I've seen it. You're going to kill me to bring me back so I can be at your side for eternity."

His hand stilled, squeezing gently, though I wasn't sure he realized he was doing it.

"I've seen it," I explained. "In a vision. I've wondered about it because it doesn't scare me." A soft chuckle escaped me. "I guess it probably should, huh?"

Eclipse moved then, his body shifting so I was forced to my back. He propped himself on an elbow and stared down at me. I loved the way he looked at me, as though I was the most important thing in the entire universe. It was a feeling I'd never experienced before. Not even with my own parents. Amber had always been our parents' favorite, and honestly, I never really cared. But here, with Eclipse, I wanted to be his everything.

"You are," he whispered, his eyes wandering my face. "You're my everything. My light in the darkness, my heat source in the blistering cold."

God, how I wanted to believe all those sweet words. Based on my experiences thus far, I had no reason to doubt him, but it wasn't easy to shed the tough skin calloused by years of being alone. Before Eclipse, I would've run screaming from the room if a guy even looked at me as though there was something more he wanted than sex. With Eclipse, I had no desire to run, but I wasn't letting all those walls around my heart crumble. However, the foundation was weakening with every minute I spent with him.

When his palm cradled the side of my face, gently urging me to turn my head, I did. I watched as his head lowered, felt the warmth pool in my core when his lips brushed mine. The slow stroke of his tongue inside my mouth dispersed that warmth through my entire being until my hands were sliding over his naked shoulders, pulling him closer, needing to be one with him.

But he didn't rush, simply kissed me with long, luxurious

strokes of his tongue against mine, soft, sweet touches of his lips until the heat consumed us both. And when it did, I gave in to the passion, the excitement. But there was something else I gave in to in that moment, something I would never be able to walk away from.

Him.

He was everything I'd ever wanted in this life.

Eclipse was my salvation.

27

ECLIPSE

Three days later, when the tension started to escalate within the mansion, the mission to find Asmia the sole focus, I knew Orianna and I needed a break from it all. Our efforts to contribute collided with everyone else's, ultimately making things more difficult. Not the intention, no, which was why I opted to slip out of the mansion with my female.

"I have to admit, Barin wasn't what I was expecting."

I shot a quick look over to the passenger seat and the beautiful female sitting there. "No? What'd you expect?"

She shrugged. "Something more ... angel-like, I guess."

I chuckled. "Wings? Halo?"

"Yeah. Maybe." Her soft giggle was a welcome sound.

We left the mansion as soon as the sun went down,

intending to make a quick trip to Grand Junction, aiming to cut the two-and-a-half-hour drive down by at least an hour to give us plenty of time to make it back to Darkness before sunrise. Though we weren't exactly sure what we were looking for, Barin informed us that Amber had spent quite a bit of time there before she disappeared off the grid nearly a year ago. Since Orianna had yet to search this particular patch of Colorado real estate, I offered to take her.

What I was really hoping for was to come back and find the *fiestreigh* had taken down Perfidious, and Asmia was back safe and sound at the mansion. Now that we'd passed the seventy-two-hour mark, everyone was beginning to worry we wouldn't be bringing her home safe and sound.

"You're worried about her, aren't you?"

The soft, empathetic tone of my *amsouelot's* voice had me sliding my hand over and linking my fingers with hers.

"I'm worried," I admitted.

"Everyone's doing the best they can. I even noticed Oliver was helping out."

Yeah, the human had come in rather handy. Reidar put him to work, and rumor was, Oliver had spent more time in the war room in recent days than he had in his own room. Seemed the male simply needed a mission to prove he was more than just a disgruntled asshole. Add to that the fact Bijou was keeping him company, and Oliver appeared to be in his element.

"We could've stayed there," Orianna said softly.

I peered her way, saw the concern etched between her brows. She'd taken my silence to mean I didn't want to be there.

"There's nothing I can do for them right now. This is where I need to be."

"That's the truth?"

I grinned. "I'm unable to lie to you."

"Says who?"

Squeezing her hand, I kept my eyes on the darkened road. "Says the Fates."

"The Fates are a *who*?"

"Angels, yes. Nevaeh, Karma, and Adorah. Sisters."

"Wow. The Fates are real and guardian angels aren't a myth. Next, you'll tell me dragons aren't merely fiction."

"Actually..."

"Oh, my God! Seriously?"

I laughed. "I've never encountered one, but yeah."

"They're real," she breathed out, sounding shocked.

"As real as vampires and angels, but long since extinct."

"Wow. That's... Wow."

B y the time we reached Grand Junction, I was in desperate need of stretching my legs. While I loved my car, the Bugatti wasn't the most comfortable when it came to long-distance travel. However, it worked to shave a full hour off the one-way trip, and I intended to do the same with the return. Which gave us almost seven full hours of night to unearth whatever secrets Amber might've left behind.

"Barin said she rented an apartment over the garage," Orianna mentioned as we exited the vehicle. "The man who owns the house said he'd leave the key under the mat. It's vacant right now."

I kept my eyes peeled as we made our way up the narrow wooden stairs to the door on the second floor. Orianna flipped up the rug to reveal a shiny brass key, as promised. While Orianna shoved it in the lock, I took the opportunity to scan the area for souls. When I came up with nothing, not even in the adjacent house, I breathed a little easier.

"How long did she stay here?"

"Nearly four months. Which is possibly a record for her," Orianna said as she pushed open the door and scanned the dark interior before stepping inside.

I flipped on a light and followed her in, closing and locking the door behind me.

"No one's staying here, but he said he's had a couple of tenants since she left. He also said there's a storage closet where he keeps anything left behind. Thought maybe I'd get lucky."

"Lead the way."

I was merely along for the ride, showing my female I was willing to do whatever it took to bring her closure where her sister was concerned. She'd spent so much time with Miklós, searching the message boards and tracking down virtual leads in between helping with the search for Asmia, I figured she needed this. While I sensed she'd come to accept her sister was dead, I knew how powerful hope could be. And until we located her body, I couldn't very well blame her for wanting to keep searching.

"This is a nice place. I wonder how Amber found it."

I scanned the interior. White walls, beige carpet, decent furniture. It was a vast improvement from the apartment we'd visited previously, that was for sure.

After we'd given the living room a quick once-over, I followed Orianna down a narrow hall. She flipped on more lights as she went. Coat closet, bedroom, bathroom, another small room with a desk, which I assumed was meant to be an office. Felt more like a closet to me, but hey, we were used to space.

Orianna pointed toward a door in the room. "I'm guessing that's where he stores the stuff."

Using another key, Orianna unlocked the knob and pulled open the door. Well, that explained where the other part of the room went. Looked like someone split the space in half to create this handy storage area. Evidently, the owner had an issue with people bailing and leaving their shit behind. Inside, there were several rows of boxes, all neatly sealed up and labeled.

I held my position at the door, keeping my ears tuned to the other rooms, ensuring no one came along to surprise us while Orianna searched the boxes.

My mind drifted to the conversation I had with Obsidian early that morning. My brother had reminded me that the next full moon was only a few days away—three and a half, to be exact—and wanted to know if they needed to prepare for the *lintamair*. In an effort to appease my brother, I pretended to give it some thought, although I had no intention of under-going the official mating ceremony this go-round. The mere thought of taking Orianna's life ... even thinking about it made me feel as though I was buried underground, the weight of the world focused on the center of my chest.

I remembered how Obsidian came apart at the seams before his ceremony, the terror of what he had to do weighing heavily on his heart. My palms were sweating just thinking about it. Nope. We'd have to wait. How long, I wasn't sure. But I figured I would know when the time was right.

"Here it is," Orianna said, leaning over one stack of boxes.

"I'll get it."

It was the work of a moment to retrieve the small box from the bottom of the stack, and as I stepped back to give Orianna space, I couldn't help wondering if I was putting her in even more danger by not going through with the ceremony.

REIDAR

"What are you doing?"

I took stock of the boxes piled in a row along the wall near the door. My private quarters looked more like a storage room than a peaceful place to rest my head.

"What does it look like I'm doing?" Winnie muttered, not bothering to look up at me. "I'm leaving."

Well, that was fairly obvious based on the boxes of shit. Her shit. All the things we'd moved from her apartment in California just two short months ago were being loaded back up.

"Winnie..."

"Don't 'Winnie' me, Reidar. You don't want me here any more than I want to be here."

I swallowed, the sound overly loud to my ears.

"Yeah." Her disappointment rang heavily in that one word. "That's what I thought."

Before she could storm back to the bathroom, I reached for the female, carefully curling my hand around her arm. I waited for the impact of touching her. Some sort of feeling, an urge to fight for us. I got nothing. Which had been the case for the past

few weeks, ever since she started harping on me to go back to California with her.

"We need to talk."

"Time's past for that," she snapped, trying to pull away.

"What about Penelope?" I asked.

"What about her? She'll be fine without me, Reidar. She's *been* fine without me. Before I came here, I hadn't seen her in a year." Her eyes narrowed. "Did you think that's why I came? For her?"

Honestly, I hoped it was the case because the thought of her uprooting her life for me...

"Oh, my God," she whispered heavily. "You did think that."

Meeting her saddened gaze, I tried to put the words in a sentence. I needed to tell her that if she left, her memories would be scrubbed. She would have no recollection of me, of the time she'd spent at the mansion. In fact, Penelope's entire existence would be erased from Winnie's memories, a huge part of her past gone forever.

"You can come with me," she said softly.

No, I couldn't. Not only because she deserved far better than what I could offer her, either. As much as I wanted to believe she was my *amsouelot*, I knew that wasn't the case. But I'd been biding my time, trying to figure out how to protect Winnie. She didn't deserve to have big gaps in her history, but since she was bound and determined to leave, it was inevitable.

"Do you love me? Even a little?"

Pulling myself from my thoughts, I focused on her face. She was a beautiful female, and perhaps that was what I got so caught up in when I was sent to protect her. That and I'd spent so long hoping to find the female I would spend the rest of my existence with, only to come up empty so many times. Five hundred and twenty-one years of existence, and I had yet to have anything or anyone who was mine and mine alone. Sure, I had the *fiestreigh*, my family. I had Obsidian, the male I looked up to, vowed to protect. But I'd always wanted more than that.

Truth was, I'd been willing to accept what Taayin and Asmia had. Their souls weren't destined to be together, but I'd seen their love for one another, knew it was possible.

"I care about you," I admitted because lying to her wasn't fair to her.

Her face fell, and I could see it in her eyes. She just realized what I'd been hiding all along. My love for her had never been real. It was a figment of my imagination, something I attempted to build up in order to create that perfect place in my mind where I felt I belonged. But the problem was, I had dragged her along with me, given her hope when, in actuality, there was none.

Tears glittered on Winnie's lashes as she took a step back from me. Her mouth opened, closed. Nothing came out. She was as speechless as I was, but deep down, I knew she wasn't heartbroken. Our love hadn't been real. For her, it was likely built on the heat of the moment. Me coming in and whisking her off to safety, taking her away from her life in an effort to protect her from this world she never knew existed.

"I'm sorry," I told her, knowing it wasn't nearly enough.

Winnie's eyes narrowed. "Yeah. You should be."

ORIANNA

ll I had of Amber's was a broken hair clip, a Colorado Mesa University T-shirt, a couple of dollar-store hand towels, a diary with exactly zero entries, and a red pen.

Not much of anything and exactly nothing to help me in my search.

But it was more than I had before we came here.

And while my disappointment continued to pile up, I felt a sense of peace. I knew it had to do with the fact Eclipse was there with me. He brought me there, giving me the chance to chase every lead in an effort to get the closure necessary to move on.

"I'm sorry, *sezari*," he whispered, pulling me against his chest, his big arms circling me, providing the comfort I'd come to expect from him.

Maybe that was the reason I suspected this would be my last venture in what had become my entire life's purpose. Finding Amber was all I'd focused on for so long that I had stopped caring about myself entirely. That wasn't easy to do these days, what with Eclipse giving me so much to live for.

But it wasn't just him. Penelope, Obsidian, Acadia, Miklós … they gave me something I hadn't had in a long time: contentment and a sense of belonging.

Despite the fact my heart was still cracked from the loss of my sister, I had something to live for now. People who cared about me, worried about me. I wasn't even sure the last time my mother and father had worried about me. Sure, Elizabeth asked about me every time we spoke, but I felt a detachment between us, likely brought on by time and distance.

"Anything else you want to check out while we're here?" Eclipse asked, his warm hand sliding over my hair.

I breathed him in, felt my body warming from his touch. I'd been on a constant simmer since we left the mansion several hours ago, and with every passing minute, I felt the need for him building.

"Are we safe here?" I asked, peering up at him.

His eyes locked on my face, the silver churning so beautifully.

"Safe how?"

I smiled. "For a few minutes of privacy?"

I noticed the instant those words registered because his silver eyes turned molten. Probably didn't help that I slipped my hands beneath his T-shirt, my palms sliding over his smooth flesh. I gave him a gentle nudge that had his back meeting the wall. We were still inside the storage room, the buttery-yellow glow from the ancient lightbulb providing the perfect ambiance.

When he didn't object, I lifted his shirt higher, my lips resuming the exploration my hands had been taking seconds before.

"*Sezari...*"

His skin was warm against my lips as I skimmed my mouth over him. The muscles beneath flexed, hardening his abdomen.

"Just a few minutes," I whispered, my hands shifting to the button on his jeans.

A soft thud sounded when he dropped his head back against the wall. I took that as permission to explore. Just a few minutes. That was all I needed. Some time to remind herself I was alive and had so much more to live for now. Just because one chapter of my life was coming to a close didn't mean I had to wait for the next. For the first time, I was ready to move forward, to live.

"I ... oh, fuck, *sezari*."

I smiled as I revealed the thick column of his erection. He was velvety smooth and hard as granite, a perfect combination. His breaths grew a bit labored as I continued my exploration, my lips traveling lower as I worked toward my goal. I wanted to feel him in my mouth, to taste him, to hear that rough growl that would eventually come when I took him between my lips.

Cognizant of where we were, I maintained my focus, dipping my head down and licking the swollen head, his salty taste exploding on my tongue. I moaned as I opened my lips and slid them around him, easing down slowly. He didn't rush me, one hand resting on my head, the other curled around the back of my neck as I caressed him with my lips and tongue.

In that moment, nothing existed except for the two of us and this intense heat we generated when we were together. Thanks to my conversations with Penelope, I learned a bit more about it. It was what the angels called *amnigh*, a phenomenon that encompassed two souls that were destined to be together. Our need for one another was spurred by destiny, but I fully believed it was more than that. I couldn't imagine wanting anyone more than I wanted him.

Eclipse's hips jerked forward, a deep guttural sound rumbling in his chest as I used my hand and mouth to tease and entice. I was driven by this insane need to pleasure him, to let him feel all those crazy sensations he instilled in me, to let him know I had an overwhelming desire to worship him.

"*Sezari* ... you're too good at that."

His praise made me smile, but I didn't stop my ministrations, continuing to take more of him in my mouth, my tongue exploring, laving, tormenting.

Eclipse's hand tightened on the back of my neck as though warning me if I continued, he wouldn't be able to hold back. That was exactly what I was working toward, sending him over the edge, knowing I was the one who could do this to him. The only one.

"Oh, fuck ... *sezari* ... I'm gonna come in your mouth."

The promise had my grip on him tightening as I stroked in rhythm to the suction, my mouth meeting my hand again and again. His erection pulsed and flexed, his hand tightening on my neck until...

"Fuck!"

He exploded in my mouth. I doubled my efforts to drink him down, not quite ready to stop. I loved the taste and feel of him, but it was more than that. It was the intrinsic trust required between two souls to allow this sort of intimacy. Bodies could mate, that was a given. People did it daily, some without thought or regard for the repercussions. But when love was involved, when one was willing to surrender mind, body, and soul to another, that was transcendent. It was the very reason I didn't fear my future anymore.

Eclipse was the one who stilled me, his hand fisting in my hair as he lifted my head. I smiled up at him, licking my lips as his silver stare pinned me in place. The world spun briefly as he switched our positions, my back meeting the wall as he leaned down, his lips finding mine. I sealed my mouth to his, loving the way his tongue caressed mine even as his deft fingers quickly unbuttoned my jeans. A sharp cry escaped when his hand dipped between my legs, his long, thick finger piercing me. Another joined as he fingered me, sending my brain spiraling.

I threw my arms around his neck, holding tightly as he worked me to the edge within seconds. I held on for as long as I could, but it wasn't long at all. Every muscle in my body tightened as my core shattered, the orgasm rocking me on my very foundation. It wasn't about my physical being, either. No, Eclipse had the ability to reach the very heart of my spiritual existence.

When I relaxed, his hand curled around my neck, his tongue still stroking inside my mouth, his lips softened as a smile pulled at both our mouths.

I forced my eyes open when he pulled back. His were glowing brightly, something I noticed more lately. It seemed the closer we got—both physically and emotionally—the more brilliant the light became.

"What do you say we take this back to our bed?" he suggested, his words a rough rasp that stirred more than my desire for him.

Our bed.

I liked the sound of that.

So, so much.

28

ECLIPSE

———

"There's no sign of her anywhere," Søren grumbled, his frustration as apparent as every other soul in the mansion.

It had been four days since Perfidious pulled the snatch-and-grab with Asmia, and despite our nightly searches, no one had uncovered so much as a single hint of where the demon had taken her. Because of that, tensions were high, and my anger was growing tenfold.

Though I had dedicated last night to Orianna's search for her sister, tonight, I was committed to the mission to search for Asmia. Surprisingly, Orianna suggested we both focus our efforts on the Fae for the time being. I wasn't sure what exactly happened last night, but Orianna had been different since we left that small apartment. Not only because of what we'd done, either. No, I noticed a shift in my *amsouelot*, as though she was finally coming to terms with the fact Amber was not coming back.

"Tell me who's out tonight," Obsidian demanded when he strolled into the war room where I had been monitoring the efforts for the past three hours.

"All *ladeares* are out right now," Søren told him. "The Fae have teamed up with them, as well."

The *lieterra* motioned toward the whiteboard, which outlined the current alignments.

"Where's Taayin?"

I decided to answer that one. "He asked to go out, so I approved it. He's with Viator and Basker." The two male Fae offered to tag along because they had more abilities when it came to subduing Taayin should it be necessary.

Obsidian's concern was palpable, but I was prepared to defend my decision if and when my oldest brother tried to nail my balls to the wall. The fact of the matter was, we couldn't keep Taayin locked up indefinitely. The male would go fucking crazy, and if anyone deserved to be out there looking for her, it was Taayin.

"Anyone else with them?"

"Raksa's keeping close but out of sight," I told my brother.

"Probably a good idea."

Yeah. Maybe. At this point, I couldn't blame Taayin for any outbursts that might arise from his search for the female he loved. Hell, I wouldn't be surprised if Taayin went on a rampage and burned down the entire town. Granted, I hoped it wouldn't come to that, but again, I wouldn't blame the male.

"Penelope and Bijou are with Orianna," Obsidian said, his eyes reflecting a hint of concern I hadn't noticed until now.

I turned to face my brother.

"She had another vision," he said softly.

Without waiting for more details, I let my senses flare out to locate my *amsouelot* before I evanesced and took form in the sunroom.

Anxiety spun in my veins as my brain worked to puzzle out the scene before me. Penelope and Bijou were sitting on one of the leather sofas, the females flanking Orianna, who had her head in her hands, her full attention on her feet.

My breaths rasped in and out of my lungs as true fear took root. Didn't matter that my brain had determined she was alive and breathing, I needed to hear her voice, see her eyes, touch her skin to know for sure.

Penelope looked up, her golden eyes sympathetic, the small smile hesitant. "She's all right."

I wasn't sure how she could be so calm and collected when every neuron in my brain was rapid-firing, and the damn things weren't in sync. Just the thought of something happening to her had my nervous system threatening a shutdown.

This was the third vision she'd had in as many days, none of which were about Asmia, rather focused solely on Obsidian, just a constant repeat of what she'd already seen. We opted to keep from sharing the details with my brother mainly because we didn't know what it meant. Until we could translate them into something we could shape and mold into a plan, I figured there was no reason to put everyone on high alert.

Bijou hopped to her feet, stepping out of the way as I approached. I took a seat beside Orianna, sliding my hand up and down her back. When she instantly leaned on me, I felt a comfort I'd gotten used to over the past few weeks. Although we were battling the *amnigh*, which seemed to be intensifying with every passing minute, we were growing closer in other ways, too. I found pleasure in taking care of Orianna, even being a shoulder for her to lean on when necessary, and it warmed me to know she was doing so more frequently.

"It wasn't about Asmia," Orianna said softly. "I hate that I'm disappointing everyone."

Frowning, I pulled away and looked into Orianna's lovely blue eyes. "No one's disappointed, *sezari*. Not even a little."

A small smile appeared, and I knew it was forced. "Then I'm disappointed in myself." She lifted her hand to show me the hairbrush she was clutching tightly. "I've kept this with me, and still nothing."

Penelope shifted, repositioning so she could face Orianna more fully while placing one hand on her ever-growing belly. "We don't expect you to be able to find her, Orianna. But we appreciate that you're trying."

I saw the sincerity in Penelope's face, heard it in her words. Without looking, I could feel Bijou's concern, her need to comfort, though she wasn't sure how to do so. The females in the house had shared some conversations recently, spent a bit more time together in an effort to pass it while Obsidian and I went out with the *fiestreigh* doing our part to locate Asmia. As much as everyone wanted us to sit on our asses, we just weren't built that way.

"I wish I could do more."

"We all wish we could do more," Penelope said, giving Orianna's knee a friendly pat. The move made Orianna jerk against me. I instantly reached for her as her eyes rolled back, her body going limp.

Okay, not the patting that sent her into those strange seizure-like convulsions. Like every other time, Orianna was unable to hold herself up, her body flopping as her eyes fluttered, only the whites showing. Didn't matter how many times I witnessed it, I was still scared shitless. Not for the first time, I wondered how Orianna had dealt with these when she'd been on her own, traveling the country in an effort to locate her sister.

"She's having another vision," Penelope whispered. "This is what happened earlier."

I felt a sudden panic flare in my chest as I eased her back on the pillow, watched helplessly as her body trembled.

A fluttering sound drew my attention away momentarily. When Michael appeared, I wasn't at all surprised to see him, but the worried expression on his face did concern me. Unfortunately, I didn't have time to deal with the archangel, turning my attention back to my *amsouelot*.

Orianna's eyes fluttered open as she exhaled. Her gaze instantly shot to me.

"She's his mate," she whispered, her voice rough.

"Who?" I asked, brushing her hair back from her face.

"Asmia. She's—"

"Taayin's *amsouelot*," Michael said sternly. "We have to bring him in now."

Without hesitation, I shot off a telepathic message to Obsidian so my brother could deal with the archangel's impromptu appearance. Before I even finished, Obsidian appeared, his eyes scanning the room, clearly looking for Penelope before shifting to Michael.

"Michael wants us to bring Taayin in," I relayed.

"Now," Michael tacked on. "Do not waste time."

"I'll go get him," Obsidian said, pivoting away from us.

"No." Michael shook his head. "Not you." His hard stare locked on me. "You."

"Go," Orianna urged, the word a broken whisper.

Because one didn't question an order from the archangel, I stood.

"I'll stay with her until you're back," Penelope stated,

taking Orianna's hand and giving it a gentle squeeze while Bijou took the position I vacated.

"Me, too," Bijou added.

Content my *amsouelot* was being taken care of, I headed out of the room. I didn't bother with my phone; instead vanished at the same time I ventured above Darkness, scanning the surrounding area until I locked onto Taayin's location. Before taking form near the abandoned warehouses the male was currently moving through, I reached out to Magnar and told my *ladeare* to meet me.

A minute later, with Magnar by my side, we strolled into the warehouse to find Taayin standing stone still, eyes glowing brightly.

"What's wrong with him?" Magnar asked, his question directed at the two Fae standing near him.

"No idea." Basker's amethyst eyes were wide, his pale face even whiter than usual. "He was walking, and then he wasn't."

"How long's he been like that?" I prompted.

"A few seconds. A minute at most."

"I want him back at the mansion," I ordered the Fae. "And I need your assistance in making that happen."

Using two fingers, I touched Taayin's forehead. The move had the male's knees giving out, his body crumbling. Magnar reached for him, easing him down to the floor.

"Where should I send him?" Basker asked, moving to stand over Taayin.

Dungeon, said the voice in my head.

With a sigh and a bit more animosity than was probably appropriate, I relayed Michael's command.

"The dungeon?" Magnar asked, his voice steely. "What the fuck are we putting him down there for?"

"His own safety." Not the first place I would've picked, but again, we didn't have the luxury of questioning the archangel's motives. "Now get him there."

Because I knew the Fae would do what was necessary, I relocated myself back to the mansion, this time taking form belowground, at the entrance to the rooms we'd allocated for prisoners. No one aside from Michael referred to it as a dungeon, but for all intents and purposes, that was basically what it was. A handful of ten-by-ten cells lined with stone on three sides and iron-over-titanium bars on the front. The iron was for strength, the titanium to keep anyone from materializing in or out.

"Where is he?" Michael asked, his voice as cold and hard as the rock lining the inside of those rooms.

"Basker is—"

Suddenly Taayin's lifeless body appeared, flat on his back on the unforgiving stone. Good thing he didn't know where he was.

When Basker stepped out of the cell, Michael immediately closed the door, locking it with his mind.

"Why the urgency?" Obsidian asked, appearing beside Michael.

Before the archangel could answer, Taayin's eyes flew open, and a blue light filled the space. The male shot to his feet, body braced for a fight. His fangs were descended from his jaw, and there was an air of menace surrounding him.

"That's why," Michael said when Taayin let out an earsplitting roar.

I took a step back when Taayin rushed the door, the thick iron bending under the impact.

Michael waved a hand, and the bars returned to their original form. "Reinforced now. It's for his own safety."

"Orianna said Asmia's his *amsouelot*," I told Obsidian, not sure if my brother was aware of the new development.

"The Fates confirmed," Michael stated. "It's the reason I'm here. Their souls have been aligned."

"I don't understand." I turned to face Michael. "They've been together for a long time. Why's this just coming to light?"

"Because it's a recent development," Michael said, glancing between Obsidian and me.

"You did this," I accused.

There wasn't a hint of remorse on the archangel's face. "I did."

"At my request," Obsidian interjected, his concerned gaze trailing over Taayin, who was now pacing like a caged animal.

I spun around. "What? Why the fuck would you do that?"

"To protect them both."

I motioned to the male behind the iron bars. "How the fuck is this protecting him?"

Obsidian stood tall, clearly ready to defend his actions. "Perfidious was going to claim Asmia as his mate."

"And this"—Michael motioned toward Taayin—"keeps Lucifer from taking her soul."

I glanced between the pair. "I'm confused. The reason we have to locate our *amsouelots* is so Lucifer can't get his hands on *our* souls. Why is this different? Won't he now get a two-for-one?"

Obsidian was the one to answer. "The Fae..." He swallowed, as though the words were bitter on his tongue. "Their souls belong to no one, Eclipse. Because of their race's past transgressions, God won't claim their souls or permit them in Heaven."

I felt a cold pit opening in my stomach. Why would the Almighty do that? And why the fuck didn't I know that?

"By aligning their souls, my father has no choice," Michael explained.

"With her soul aligned with Taayin's," Obsidian continued,

"we can safeguard her. For the time being, he can't take her to Hell. As long as we keep Taayin safe, essentially, Asmia is as well."

From behind the bars, a strangled sound came, drawing all our attention. Taayin dropped to his knees on the floor, head hanging down as though he'd been drained completely.

"He won't survive without her," I warned, turning my attention back to Obsidian as my anger renewed. "And what did you have to give up in order to make this happen?"

I knew Michael, like the Almighty, didn't do anything for free.

"That's not for you to worry about," Michael inserted.

"We're going to sedate him," Obsidian said, clearly sensing my need to argue and wanting to change the subject. "Until we can get her back."

Glancing between the two, I heard what they weren't saying: *which won't be anytime soon.*

29

ORIANNA

I had no idea what was going on, but something happened. Whatever it was, it had everyone in the mansion on edge, where they'd been since last night when that archangel appeared and ordered Eclipse to bring Taayin back. I had yet to see the angel in question, but there were rumors he was being kept in a cell below ground.

A cell. In the dungeon, to use Bijou's words.

As for Eclipse ... well, he was fit to be tied. Had been ever since his return, and I was a bit hesitant to ask what was wrong for fear of setting him off.

Which was why I was feeling a bit selfish. No, make that needy. Yes. That was an apt way of describing it. Needy. As had been the case every single day for the past few weeks, that lingering desire continued to build, growing steadier and more constant. Only these past couple of days it had intensified twofold. I couldn't seem to shake it no matter how many times Eclipse and I made love.

There was hardly a reprieve from when it abated to when it came back with a vigor that shocked me. I hated that I was constantly disrupting Eclipse's night, seeking him out in an effort to assuage the heat that had become part of my chemical makeup. It didn't help that I knew what it was, either. Nor did it help when Penelope warned me it would get significantly worse as time went by.

Perhaps a shower would help.

After hopping up from the chair I was occupying in the second-floor library—which was quite honestly the most impressive library I'd ever seen—I made my way up to the third floor. Thankfully, I could come and go as I pleased, not having to wait for Eclipse or someone to let me in the door. It felt strange having full access to the mansion, but I appreciated the fact that they trusted me enough to give me the ability to roam freely. Then again, from what I'd seen, they could monitor my every move thanks to the many cameras mounted throughout. Not to mention all the nifty powers these angels were programmed with.

When I stepped into Eclipse's bedroom, I came to a halt. I could hear something ringing, and it sounded—

"Shit." I raced to the nightstand, my hand slipping on the handle when I tried to open the drawer.

The second attempt proved successful, but then I nearly dropped the vibrating device in my attempt to answer.

"Hey, Mom," I said on a rush of air.

"Orianna? Are you all right? I haven't heard from you in a few days. I was worried."

Worried seemed an understatement based on the fear I heard in my mother's tone. Worse was the guilt that flooded my chest because my mother was right; I hadn't called. I was so caught up in all that was going on I'd neglected my own mother.

"I'm so sorry, Mom." I perched on the edge of the bed, crossed my legs in an attempt to stave off the heat. "I've been busy. It's no excuse, I know. I'm sorry. I meant to call you this morning."

"Please tell me you've found Amber."

A pain ghosted through my chest. It was the phantom reminder that I had yet to tell my mother what I'd learned about my sister. Looked like I was in the running for the world's shittiest daughter award.

"Not yet. But I'm still looking." The lie tasted terrible on my tongue, but it wasn't like I could tell my mother over the phone, even if I wanted to deliver the gut-wrenching news.

"I heard from your father."

My back straightened. "You what? What did he say?"

"He was calling to check in. To see how I was doing."

I grunted. Check in. Right. More like Erik ran out of money and was hoping to hit up Elizabeth for a loan. That was how it worked, and for whatever reason, my mother always came through for him. Didn't matter that the man would rob her blind if he thought he'd get away with it. The only reason he hadn't was because I threatened him within an inch of his life.

I stared around the room, eyes bouncing across all of Eclipse's things.

What was I going to do about my mother? It had always been my intention to take care of Elizabeth once I found Amber. To go back to Oklahoma, move in with my mom so I could help her with her day-to-day as well as find a way to get her weaned off those damn pain meds that had stolen her mind. Was that still the plan? Could I leave Eclipse? The thought of never seeing him again ... yeah, that wasn't something I wanted to ponder. Not now, not ever.

"Honey, I miss you."

My shoulders slumped, another fissure forming in my heart. I could feel my mother's pain, or it seemed like I could. I couldn't imagine what it was like for Elizabeth to be trapped in her own body, relying on others to take care of her because her own family had abandoned her.

"I miss you, too, Mom." And that much was the truth. No matter what I was dealing with, I always missed my mother. I wouldn't go so far as to say we were close. I had been gone so long that wasn't even a possibility. However, for the most part, my mother was the only family I had.

"I promise I'll call you in the morning, let you know if I've made any progress."

It pained me to lie, but I knew the truth would only cause Elizabeth more anguish. Worse was the idea of explaining to my mother how I called off the search, giving in to the fact that Amber was dead. Even Barin confirmed as much, and I was apt to believe the guardian angel. Why would he lie to me?

"I love you, Orianna. Call me tomorrow."

"I will. I love you, too, Mom."

The call disconnected, and I tossed the phone onto the nightstand. The instant I was on my feet, that damned heat washed over my entire body. It started in my chest, then bloomed to my extremities before centering at my core. Desire —far stronger than it had ever been—took root, flooding me with need. I stumbled in my attempt to remain steady, catching my weight with my hand on the mattress. Whatever this was, it had its own pulse, raging like a wildfire inside me.

Figuring a cold shower was in order, I tried to get my legs steady. Before I made it three steps, my clothes became unbearable against my oversensitive skin. I shed each piece as I trudged forward. By the time I reached the decadent shower, I was naked and burning from the inside out.

"*Sezari?*"

"In here," I answered, surprised when the words came out on a whimper. "Eclipse..."

"I'm here, *sezari*. Right here, love."

Still completely dressed, Eclipse joined me in the shower, the water plastering his shirt to his chest, flattening his mohawk. He made quick work of removing the soggy cotton, ignoring his hair after brushing it back from his face.

God, he had a beautiful face. All the stark angles, the black slashes of his brows, and those mesmerizing eyes.

Get with the program, sista!

Yep, that needy chick inside me wanted Eclipse naked, so I began ripping at his clothing, desperate to get to bare skin.

"I need you. It ... hurts."

When Eclipse shifted my fumbling hands away so he could remove his jeans, I stepped back, leaning against the tile, my hands instantly roaming to my breasts, squeezing, kneading.

What the hell was happening to me?

"Please ... do something," I pleaded as Eclipse dumped his wet jeans on the shower floor.

A lightning bolt of desire pierced me when he went to his knees. With all my inhibitions obliterated by this over-whelming ache, I didn't even blink when I placed one leg over his shoulder, opening myself for his mouth. I cried out when he sealed his lips to my pulsing clit. My brain barely registered the exquisite sensation when I detonated, my orgasm rocketing through me. It was the first of many to follow, but no matter how many times he made me come, the heat didn't dissipate. In fact, I was pretty sure it was growing stronger.

Praying he wouldn't stop, I grabbed his hair, tugging firmly as he feasted between my thighs, fireworks going off behind my closed eyes as I orgasmed in rapid succession. When my supporting leg became too weak to hold me, Eclipse was suddenly on his feet, and I was no longer on mine. He lifted me easily, my back still pressed to the tiled wall, as he aligned our bodies and pushed in deep.

"Oh, God, yes," I hissed.

I ringed my arms around his neck and held on, loving the way he filled me, stretching me so perfectly. Finesse wasn't even an option as I tried to find his lips with my own, needing more from him, something to quell this ache I couldn't seem to sate.

"Relax, *sezari*," Eclipse rumbled against my neck, his warm lips blazing fire across my skin.

"I can't." I squirmed, trying to get him to go deeper, although I could feel every delicious inch of him inside me.

Eclipse pulled back and met my gaze. I knew what I looked like. Hair plastered to my head, eyes likely crazed with this ridiculous desire threatening to drown me.

"Look at me," he ordered.

When I managed to stop writhing, I met his eyes. They were glowing, brighter than I'd ever seen before. It was there I saw the intent in the silver swirl. Eclipse took over, driving into me with quick, shallow thrusts that soon took a turn. Long and deep, he pummeled me, and as I watched him, I realized he was close. Suddenly desperate to watch him come, I gripped the sides of his face and held him there.

"Come for me," I pleaded. "Deep inside me."

As though my demand was the trigger, Eclipse's head fell back, and he groaned, his hips stilling as he filled me. It was in those blessed seconds that the ache eased, the need going from rapid boil to steady simmer, giving me some semblance of control.

"How long does this last?" I asked when Eclipse's breaths evened out, his eyes returning to their normal light.

He didn't answer, nor did he move to put me down, and I was content to remain right where I was. Despite the fact I could breathe again, I got the feeling this was far from over.

"It seems to be getting more intense."

And Penelope told me it would only get worse. Until when?

Now that I thought about it, we were having sex roughly three or four times a day. I hadn't put too much thought into it —aside from how much I seemed to be interrupting Eclipse— because I was attracted to him, and this thing between us was new. It made sense that I would want him, that our sex life would come charging out of the gate at a full gallop. But at what point did it start to ease up? I seriously doubted most couples were doing the horizontal mambo all the damn time. How would they get anything else done?

Eclipse's hold remained firm, bracing me against the wall as he plunged into me, just a steady shift of his weight on his feet, pushing him in deep. He repositioned me as though I weighed nothing, the muscles in his shoulders and arms flexing beautifully. But that's what he was. Beautiful. In every way. Sometimes I would find myself staring at him, completely in awe of how perfectly he was built. Then again, he was an angel, so it made sense.

I sighed, gripping his shoulders as my body tingled, another orgasm on the horizon. I noticed Eclipse's eyes dropping to my neck, and I knew what he needed. He'd been feeding from me daily, ever since that first time when I offered myself up to him. Oddly, it brought me pleasure to know I could give him something he needed. Eclipse had been taking care of me since that night at the club all those weeks ago, and I had nothing to give back. Nothing except for my blood.

Tilting my head to the side, I offered myself up to him once more.

Eclipse growled low in his throat, a sound that was so deliciously sexy it was a wonder I didn't orgasm right then.

Before he leaned in, I caught a glimpse of his fangs. The sight of them warmed me from the inside out, had my inner muscles locking on his erection as he continued to fill me.

Another deep rumble came from Eclipse before he latched on to my neck. The sharp sting lasted a fraction of a second before it was replaced with what I assumed was the best high known to humans. My body tightened, my muscles locking as my body shattered, the electrical energy pulsing out from my center to my fingers, my toes.

It could've been minutes or hours or, hell, days that Eclipse fueled his body with my lifeblood, and the entire time, I was swamped by pleasure so intense the friction of our bodies wasn't necessary to keep the orgasm rolling through me. It didn't subside completely, either. No, the tremor remained inside me, a blissful hum that continued as long as he was drinking from my vein.

I felt my body weakening, but I didn't care. I trusted him implicitly, knew he would never harm me. As though he knew I couldn't stand to lose any more blood, he broke the seal on my neck, his tongue swiping over my skin to close the wounds. And then Eclipse let loose on me, pummeling me again and again as I rode out the orgasm that seemed to go on forever. When another hit, shattering the other one, I cried out his name and felt him let go.

It was then the constant ache subsided completely, draining out of me and leaving a sense of satisfaction in its wake. There was no doubt it would return, probably sooner rather than later. It always did.

When Eclipse set me on my feet, I remained where I was,

allowing the wall to hold me up while my sexy angel went to work, soaping us both. I could barely move but managed to smile as his big, warm hands moved over me.

"Keep that up, and we'll have to do that again," I warned, my eyes closed as exhaustion pulled at me.

Eclipse stood tall and leaned down so his mouth hovered over mine. "Just say the word, *sezari*, and I'm there."

I chuckled, realizing I felt lighter than I had in ... well, ever.

30

KAJ

The moment the sun went down, I slipped out of Angel Central, ensuring no one saw me.

For the past five days, ever since the Fae Asmia went missing, the place had been sullen, full of angels attempting to find one of their own. Since I couldn't do much in the way of helping, aside from what little I contributed by reaching out to my clans, I figured now was the perfect time to address an issue I put off for too long. While I was all for helping the angels, I had my own race to contend with, and right now, they could ill afford me neglecting them.

With the sun well below the horizon, I maneuvered through the Dungeon, the place empty of patrons on a Sunday night. As I made my way to the hidden door behind the bar, I peered around and smiled. I never considered what a popular nightclub looked like when it was empty. It sort of reminded me of a corpse, completely drained of life and in desperate need of resuscitation. To put it simply, it looked a hell of a lot better with dim lights and bodies to hide all those blemishes.

As I lifted the bar top to step behind it, I noticed a set of scratch marks running down the wall near my head. Someone had been having either a damn good night or a really shitty one. In this place, it could go either way. Not that I much cared what went on here. As long as the humans weren't harmed and Darko didn't draw any unwanted attention from the locals or the winged police upstairs, the male could do as he pleased.

Following Darko's instructions, I pressed my palm to the stone on the left side of the door. The wooden rectangle opened slowly, disappearing into the wall. A row of lights lit up along the floor to reveal the three feet of space that gave way to a spiral staircase leading deep underground. The moment I cleared the doorway, the door slid shut behind me, sealing me inside. With my hand on the gun tucked in the holster on my hip, I made my way down the stairs, listening for any sounds to signal danger. Thanks to my keen vampire senses, I could hear everything, from the repetitive drip of a leaky pipe in the wall to the soft rasp of breaths coming from the dungeon, even a large truck rolling down the next street over.

I paused at the base of the stairs, allowing my senses to expand, ensuring there were no threats coming from the room. It wasn't that I was paranoid, but after what happened to Kardobahn and the rest of my family, I wasn't taking any chances these days.

I was able to discern how big the space was—roughly thirteen hundred square feet—and the count of bodies it contained. That was when I realized there was a problem. From what Darko told me, only five prisoners were being held in the cells beneath the club, but there were six souls contained within. Since Darko had passed on meeting me due to another obligation, I could only assume the extra was not the male who lured me there.

"If you're interested in continuing to breathe, you'll make yourself known," I said, pulling my Sig from its holster.

"I am no threat to you, *phaal*."

Alpha. It was so odd to hear someone refer to me that way.

I stepped out of the stairwell to see the enormous male on one knee, head bowed, the steel tip of his beloved dagger pressed to the concrete floor.

"Mirakel," I whispered, not believing my eyes. "What the fuck?"

I scanned the rest of the space: two females, three males, five cots, five blankets, an empty wooden chair, a set of keys, and a copy of *Guns and Ammo* were all it contained. But I didn't give a shit about the prisoners or the reading material of the absent guard. Nope. My attention was drawn right back to Mirakel, one of the four males I thought I lost back when Kardobahn had been murdered in the raids by the shadow beasts.

Tucking the gun back in its holster, I took a hesitant step closer to Mirakel. "Stand, warrior."

The male was all power and grace as he lifted his six-foot-seven-inch frame, his neon blue eyes glittering with emotion. Although he looked a little worse for wear, Mirakel appeared healthy and strong, still thick as a sequoia, his shoulder muscles flexing beneath the black T-shirt he wore.

I didn't give a shit that there were a handful of vampires observing this moment. I stepped forward and pressed my hands to Mirakel's hard, chiseled face, letting my eyes shift over his features. Still as rough and rugged as always, and most definitely alive.

"I thought you were dead," I whispered, swallowing past the emotion thick in my throat.

"You and me both," Mirakel said, his deep, guttural voice holding an edge of amusement.

With a relieved laugh, I pulled Mirakel toward me, hugged him roughly before releasing him.

"Darko didn't mention you were here," I acknowledged.

Mirakel's face hardened. "The male doesn't know."

I frowned. "How'd you get down here?"

"You're not the only one with tricks up your sleeve, *phaal*." His gaze swung around the dungeon before landing on me once more. "We need to get out of here."

"I've come to interrogate the prisoners," I explained. "Darko was delayed, but he's on his way."

"Darko's not coming." Mirakel's gravelly voice was full of derision. "We need to go, *phaal*, and we need to go now."

Having spent centuries with Mirakel at my side, along with the other warriors who had vowed to protect the race's Alpha at all costs, I knew the male wasn't prone to paranoia. And if he said we needed to go, there was no time to waste.

"Back the way I came?" I asked, figuring Mirakel already had an exit strategy.

The relief on his face was instant, as though he hadn't expected me to follow. "This way."

I spared a quick glance at the caged vampires—those who betrayed their race—and figured they were better off where they were. I fell into step behind Mirakel, who led the way to the far end of the space. Mirakel twisted a stone sticking out of the wall, and a moment later, it retracted, similar to the way the one upstairs had. Before the two of us stepped into the dark, musty space, I heard footsteps overhead. A lot of them.

"We've got to move," Mirakel said firmly, shoving me in front of him as the stone slid closed, sealing us in the darkness.

Good thing vampires didn't need light to see. In fact, our eyesight was designed for darkness, which allowed me to move through the tunnel with ease. Couldn't have been more than three feet across, seven feet tall, lined on both sides with rough stone, which was weathered from water seeping into the earth.

My quick scan told me there was no one ahead of us, only a few spiders and other creepy-crawlies that had set up shop down there. I followed Mirakel's clipped commands, jogging headlong into the pitch-black, the sound of our footsteps the only thing accompanying us in our hasty exit.

"Probably should've asked this before now, but what the hell is going on?" I ducked to avoid a web filling the circle of a split in the tunnel.

"Stay to the right," Mirakel barked. "There's an army of vampires back there." Mirakel's voice was cool and collected, as though he was relaying the weather. "They've come to assassinate you."

Oh. Was that all they were doing?

I exhaled heavily. Sometimes this whole Alpha thing sucked. I was always looking over my damn shoulder, wondering who was standing there, ready to plunge a knife in my back simply to step into my role. Granted, the Alpha gig wasn't all it was cracked up to be. Not an easy feat being the leader of an entire race, looking out for their well-being while still attempting to get a grip on what was going on. Hell, I was the first to go it alone. Even Kardobahn had relied on those closest to him.

Unfortunately, those I was closest to were all dead. I glanced back at Mirakel. Or at least I'd thought they were dead.

"Not much farther," Mirakel told me. "This exit leads into the forest. From what I can tell, they haven't used it in some time."

"They?"

"Darko and his group of traitors."

I stopped, spinning around to face Mirakel. "You're telling me Darko's a traitor?"

The male looked pained as he nodded. "Unfortunately, yes."

Son of a bitch.

Mirakel gave my shoulder a shove, urging me to keep going. "We're not safe until we're out of here. There's no way to vanish within the confines of this space."

Which meant the walls were enforced with titanium. It was the only material we couldn't move through.

I heard the sound of voices coming from behind us, so I hurried my pace. It took another few minutes before we came to a set of rusty bars that led up through a hole barely big enough for our shoulders to squeeze through.

"I don't know what's on the other side," Mirakel warned. "But I need you to go first so I can watch your back."

Without hesitation, I crawled up the rusted metal rungs, then pushed open the thick iron cover that sealed off the tunnel. Before I leveraged myself out, I scanned my surroundings. I sensed two males moving our way, probably a good mile off. Aside from them, there were a handful of forest animals skittering about, but no additional threats. For now.

Once I was out, I waited for Mirakel. The male launched himself up and out, then shifted the cover back in place.

I waved my hand over the metal plate, melting the edges so that it sealed in place. "They won't be getting out that way."

"We need to get out of here before Darko's reinforcements figure out where we went," Mirakel warned.

Had I been alone, I would've gone back to Obsidian's residence; however, that wasn't an option. While I wanted to trust Mirakel, the fact that I hadn't sniffed out Darko's betrayal told me I needed to take this slow. Last thing I would do was put my daughter in danger. Or Acadia.

"I know a place." I drifted into molecules, projecting the coordinates into Mirakel's mind as I did.

When we took form, it was in an abandoned warehouse in a small town south of Darkness. I had secured the place before I ventured to the mansion in the event Obsidian turned me away.

Although we were alone, Mirakel didn't relax as he strolled through the vacant metal building, checking locks on windows and doors. The most those would do was stall a human, damn sure not a vampire.

Mirakel turned to face me. "The others are waiting."

"Others?"

"With your permission, I'll let them know where we are."

"What others?" I insisted, moving toward the enormous male, one hand on my gun, the other on my dagger.

"Four of us survived, *phaal*," Mirakel said softly. "Barely."

Unable to believe the admission, I could only stare. Completely and utterly … relieved.

31

Two days later...

PERFIDIOUS

———

H aving spent the past week holed up here with the female, I was hoping tonight would be the night she would come around. Then again, that was my thought every single night when I came to visit her.

No, the accommodations weren't at all what I envisioned for my queen, but until Asmia got with the program, I decided this would be her new home, this cage deep in the heart of the mountain, not too far from where I found her. It was far more secure than the abandoned warehouse I'd initially taken her to, providing more security as well as privacy. No risk of those pesky humans stumbling upon us.

Unfortunately, it seemed my beloved Asmia and I continued to endure one setback after another, the latest being her illness. I had no fucking clue what was wrong with the Fae, but for the past couple of days, she'd been under the weather.

"Do you find these accommodations more suitable?" I asked, motioning toward the enormous king bed I had delivered to her cell just that morning.

I was outfitting the space with the nicest things money could buy. After all, it was my pleasure to treat her like the royalty she was. Asmia was my queen, even if she denied her position. She would come around. She simply needed time and perhaps a bit more persuasion on my part.

Asmia glared at me but didn't speak. Her usual response. The good news was, she was looking at me now.

I glanced at the padlock, then clicked it open with my mind before willing the door to swing wide. I stepped inside, wanting to be closer to her.

"I figured you'd want a status update."

She continued to pace, her body looking a tad thin beneath the white gown I picked out for this evening. I had taken great care in selecting the virginal silk, wanting only the best to touch her lovely flesh. As of yet, Asmia hadn't thanked me for my forethought, but she wasn't rejecting me outright, so I considered that a win.

"You have to admire their loyalty." I moved toward her, enjoying the way she flinched as I approached. You could make a male fall in love, but you couldn't kill the demon completely. "They're still out looking for you, but they have slowed their efforts quite a bit. Perhaps we should give them a call."

Asmia hissed.

"What? You don't want them to know you're all right? That I'm taking care of you the way you deserve?"

I stepped into her path, blocking her movements.

She was a lovely creature, I had to give her that much. Even pissed, she was beautiful. I reached out and fingered one long, silky lock of her hair.

"Don't touch me," she seethed, doing the pivot and pace once more.

At least she wasn't clawing at me anymore. I'd left the cell covered in scratches and bruises the first few days she was with me. It wasn't until I shackled her naked to the wall that she learned the error of her ways. Since ... well, Asmia continued to hiss and seethe, but she stopped being violent. It saddened me a bit, to be honest. I was looking forward to the feisty Fae. I knew our relationship would bring out the best and the worst in both of us.

"Still on that, are you?" I crooked my finger, urging her over when she stopped on the opposite side of her new room.

"I will never let you touch me. You might as well kill me now."

I chuckled. Kill her? Never.

Oh, no. What I had in store for my sweet Asmia went far beyond death.

When I reached for her, she slapped my arm away. She was far stronger than I'd given her credit for, but I did admire her fight. In fact, it turned me on. I enjoyed the game up to this point, but I was hoping we would've made more progress than we had.

"Come here, gorgeous," I instructed. "I think it's time for us to establish a few rules."

She glared at me, her lips sealed closed as though she didn't trust what might come out of her mouth.

When I reached for her again, she slapped my arm away.

Too bad she was no match for me.

"I was trying to be nice. Clearly you like it rough."

"What are you—"

With a smirk, I used the powers of my mind to send her flying backward into the wall. I pinned her in place with invisible chains, arms out wide, legs spread.

"I hate you," she snarled.

"One more word and you'll be naked again." I glared at her as I came closer.

Her lips clamped shut instantly.

"Now *that* is a fascinating pose." I moved closer, trailed my nail along the smooth curve of her jaw. "Makes you easily accessible. Perhaps this is what you've been waiting for? For me to take control? Hmm?"

Her eyes narrowed, as though she could singe me with a scathing look.

"I see it's going to take a bit more persuasion."

I snapped my fingers, her clothes disintegrating, leaving her naked to my hungry gaze.

"I hate you."

"I know." I took pride in that.

I took a step back and openly ogled her luscious body. Those beautiful full breasts tipped with rosy pink nipples, the flat belly, and the succulent spot between her trim thighs. She was tall and lean, her sinful body perfectly proportioned. I ached to feel her against me, to have those mile-long legs wrapped securely around my hips, but I refrained. As much as I wanted to claim her now, I sensed her hunger, knew she desperately needed to feed. How she'd lasted this long without siphoning my energy, I didn't know.

And while I didn't mind punishing her, I damn sure wouldn't allow her to starve herself to death. If I had to guess, that was her plan.

"I will kill you," she ground out.

"Doubtful, but I'd love to see you try." Turning, I paced away from her. "I figure it's best we get a few things straight." I smiled as I pivoted, moving toward her once more. "I'm sure it'll take some time for me to break you, but gorgeous, I've been looking forward to it. The more you fight me, the hotter I get."

I cupped her chin, dug my fingers into her jaw. Asmia attempted to jerk her head away, but I held it still, immobilizing her completely.

"The first step is for you to accept your new place. Here. With me." I motioned around the concrete prison. "Don't worry. I've got much finer accommodations underway. In Hell. You'll like it there. So much to do, souls to torment. Always keeps me busy."

I raked my gaze over her lovely curves, ensuring she saw my intentions.

"What was that? You'd rather stay here?" I shrugged. "Perhaps we shall. For a while. Now that Eevuhl's off on his mission, there's plenty to do to keep us entertained. Since Eevuhl felt compelled to take Seraphina on a road trip, it's just you and me. Of course, Sirius has to go. I'm not big on sharing. Certainly not you."

Stepping up so that we were nose to nose, I tightened my grip on her jaw. "But you are going to have to feed from me."

"Never," she snarled. "I'll starve before I touch you."

"You're so loyal, aren't you? Ready to forsake yourself for your family. I admire that." I trailed my fingers down her neck, her chest, paused between her breasts. "In fact, I'm eager to have that all to myself."

"I'll never be loyal to you."

Grinning, I tilted my head to the side. "See, gorgeous, that's where you're wrong. I figure if the angels can mate, so can I. After all, they're about as deserving as I am, are they not? At least I don't pretend to have a decent side."

"They *are* decent."

I snarled. "Bullshit. God has no mercy. No decency. He cast

his own son out of Heaven. How is that decent?" I took a deep breath, calmed myself. "But we do have one thing in common. None of us are above using our own powers to get what we want. And you, gorgeous ... I want."

"Never."

This time, when I gripped her chin, I forced her to hold my gaze as I locked onto her mind.

"I've given you more than enough time to get used to this. From this moment forward, you're mine, Asmia. Your love, devotion, that pitiful loyalty, it belongs to me. All of it."

Her eyes widened, some of the anger burning away as the mind control settled in.

"You are my queen, Asmia. My lover, my mate. From this moment forward, you are dedicated only to me. You'll remain by my side, bowing at my feet, begging to do anything I desire. It's no longer a request. It's a command. One you'll follow without complaint. I am forevermore the only male you need, the one who will sustain you. My energy force will keep you breathing for as long as I choose."

Testing the strength of my command, I leaned in, pressed my lips to hers. The female didn't try to move away, her mouth softening beneath mine.

Pulling back, I met her eyes. The amethyst orbs were no longer glowing, the purple morphing to an inky black, her very soul being shadowed by my own. As long as I kept it shielded with my powers, the angels would believe she was dead and gone, lost to them forever.

"You'll forget all about them, Asmia. They mean nothing to you. And should any of them ever approach you, you'll rip their pathetic heart out without thought or care. You're devoted only to me. Now say it."

"I'm devoted to you, Perfidious. Only you," she whispered softly.

"Good girl."

I released the hold on her body, allowing her to relax while still maintaining eye contact.

"You're my mate, Asmia. My one and only. From now until eternity."

"I'm your mate," she repeated, her sweet agreement making my dick hard.

"The first thing on our agenda is to feed you." I reached for her wrists, lifting her limp arms and settling her hands firmly on my chest.

Asmia didn't flinch, didn't pull away.

"Feed from me, Asmia. Take what you need to build your strength."

She stepped closer, my body tensing instinctually, preparing to fight her off should she turn feral.

But she didn't.

Her hands slowly lowered. She began tugging my shirt from my slacks while I watched, waited. When she'd freed the tails, she lifted the designer silk, her palms resting flat on my stomach, then inching higher.

Asmia's eyes closed with a gasp. My muscles locked up tight as I held myself still. I could feel it. Through her touch, she was siphoning my energy, taking it into herself, using it to fill her reserves.

"Fuck," I rumbled.

The sensation was mind-numbing, all-consuming. Though I could sense my energy waning, I was still powerful. Perhaps more so than ever before. If she could draw off me like this, I couldn't help but wonder what it would be like during sex.

Asmia moaned softly as though she'd read my mind.

Before I did something stupid like lose my focus, I gripped her wrists and jerked her hands from me. I'd never had a Fae feed from me, and I had no idea what the side effects might be.

For all I knew, she could be trying to kill me, draining the life right out of me.

When her eyes opened, Asmia's irises glittered black, her cheeks once again rosy, the gray tinge gone as her strength returned.

"Who am I, Asmia?"

"My king, my mate." The soft smile that tilted her lips sent a bolt of lust ripping through me. "The male I will serve forevermore."

Oh, how I loved mind control.

TAAYIN

I lay in the darkened cell, my arms too heavy to lift, legs too weak to move.

That had been the case since they brought me back here, forced me into this godforsaken hellhole.

But the good news was, my mind continued to float, drifting in and out of consciousness. I was never awake long enough for the pain to break through, which was both a blessing and a curse. My mind was clear enough—at times— to know what they were doing to me, to realize they were keeping me sedated so that the cold, painful longing didn't make me do something stupid, like venture out into the sunlight.

Oh, I'd considered it. More times than not, in fact. With Asmia gone, I had absolutely nothing to live for. She was my *amsouelot*, I knew that now. Which made me a stupid asshole for turning my back on her when she'd needed me most. But I was hurt by her betrayal. The fact that Perfidious had slipped into her mind, manipulated her into wanting him... I recoiled at the thought, though my body didn't move with my brain's direction.

The sane part of me knew it wasn't her fault, but the irrational part of me, the portion that housed my heart, had blamed her somehow. And look where that had gotten me.

Now that my female was gone, I had nothing left. Nothing mattered anymore. She was out there somewhere, I could sense it. That connection we had ... sometimes it was powerful enough to break through the drug fog, though not often. She was alive; that was all I was entirely sure of. Alive and with Perfidious.

The thought of her with that evil demon made my chest ache. Not even knowing she was still alive was enough to take the edge off the pain. She wouldn't choose to live like that. The female was so full of life, of joy. To live out eternity with that demon...

"I need to get out of here," I muttered, knowing Obsidian was there with me, leaning against the wall. The male visited me nightly, returning again and again to watch over me.

"You know I can't do that," Obsidian replied. "We can't lose you, too."

"It's too late for that." I was useless without Asmia. We both knew it. The least they could do was give me a chance to find her.

"We will find her," he declared.

Had I said that out loud? Maybe my brain was more fried than I thought.

"We'll find her and bring her home to you, Taayin."

Promises, promises. I no longer believed anything. I was completely defeated, ruined. Here I lay, void of feeling, mourning the love of my life and knowing there was no reason to forge ahead because what was left? Though Perfidious wasn't invincible, he was a demon. One with power at his disposal. It would be the work of a moment to turn Asmia against us, to have her offering her love and loyalty only to him. She wouldn't be able to stop it, nor would anyone else.

The notion had bile inching up my throat, but I swallowed it down, the thought of retching worse than the idea of dying on the cold, hard floor of the cell I now called home.

"I need you, Taayin," Obsidian growled. "Penelope needs you. This *family* needs you."

Obsidian's pain hit me square in the chest. Up to this point, I had never wavered in my loyalty, and I'd never questioned how much Obsidian cared for me. It was true, we were family. But that wasn't enough to ease the ache of Asmia's absence.

"We'll get through this," Obsidian said softly. "Together. It's not over, Taayin. She's not lost forever. We will get her back."

Though I wanted to rip him a new one, to insist he couldn't even fathom the loss I felt with Asmia gone, it wouldn't be true. Obsidian had mated Penelope. If anyone knew what I was going through, it was him. After all, Obsidian had endured it, living through the twenty-four hours after Penelope died at his hand.

I tried to move my lips, but nothing was coming out. I was drifting again, the floaty feeling renewed thanks to the needle they'd put into my arm, keeping me under. According to Obsidian, it was for my protection, to keep me sane. I had to wonder if sanity was fleeting. Without Asmia, did I care whether or not my brain was mush?

The answer was no. Nothing mattered. No one mattered.

"We will find her," Obsidian promised, his face appearing above me.

I let my eyes move over the male's face, but my tongue wouldn't work to respond. I tried to nod, but even that failed. I was so tired.

Maybe this time my eyes wouldn't open. I could go to sleep once and for all, spend eternity in peace.

"I've got you," Obsidian whispered. "I've always got you."

I heard only truth in his words, even as I wished my life to end, for the pain to fade.

32

ECLIPSE

———

"Have you ever considered we might need our own places?"

I shot a quick look at Reidar. "What the fuck are you talking about?"

"Man, it's fucking brutal."

"What is?" I turned north down an alley in the section we'd been searching for the past half hour.

"That damn *gathenya*. Fucking hell. I'm starting to think you're trying to kill us. I mean, seriously, how many times can you—"

"Don't go there," I warned.

"Trust me, man. I'm trying my damnedest not to. But shit.

It's been nonstop these past few days. It's a fucking wonder the walls aren't crumbling around the two of you."

I hid my grin. I heard something similar from Miklós yesterday, the male bitching about the fact he couldn't focus on work when that sexual energy kept slamming through the mansion like a tidal wave. Evidently, those who'd been through the same with Obsidian and Penelope were starting to hold a grudge.

Not that I could do anything about it. The *amnigh* had kicked into high gear, yes. Aside from easing my *amsouelot*, there wasn't much I could do about it. And I damn sure wasn't going to apologize because the *fiestreigh* were having a hard time.

I chuckled at the double entendre.

"You're laughing," Reidar grumbled. "Try being on our side of this shit, bro."

"Last I checked, you had a female to take care of business."

"Winnie and I haven't... Fuck, never mind."

"How're things with her, anyway?"

"She's leaving."

I shot a sympathetic glance his way. "Sorry to hear that."

"Yeah, well. I've asked her to stay until I can get Cimmerian back to the mansion."

"Why Cimmerian?" I paused to listen, trying to pick up the trail of the *impietans* we detected wandering the streets of Telluride.

"Because he won't scare the shit out of her when he wipes her memory."

I frowned. "You're saying I'd scare the shit out of her?"

"No. But I'm not about to ask you to put your hands on her. Could you imagine the shit Orianna would go through when you scrubbed Winnie's mind?"

True. I hadn't thought about that. In order for us to wipe

the mind of a human, we were required to be hands-on about it. Though the pain it caused was bearable, I damn sure wouldn't want Orianna to experience it.

"Same reason I can't ask Obsidian."

"I'm sure Cimmerian'll drop in if you ask him. Or you putting it off for another reason?"

"Nah. She's done with me, and I've run out of excuses to have her stay."

"So I take it she's not your *amsouelot*."

Reidar shook his head, then peered over his shoulder. "It's about fucking time."

The cheer in Reidar's tone spoke to the male's desperate need to get out some of his frustrations. I couldn't say the same. While I always longed for a good fight, I wasn't so much in the mood for one right now. In fact, I would've preferred to be back at the mansion with Orianna, preferably naked, curled up in my warm bed with my female draped over me.

Not out here in this nut-shriveling cold looking for the mindless, soulless bastards who'd started appearing more and more often around these streets in recent days. The only positive was that their presence meant Perfidious was still close. The demon had a penchant for transforming humans and considering the *impietans* only lived for three days, it meant he was hard at work with his turnabout army.

"How many we got?" Magnar asked when he appeared at Reidar's side.

"From the scent, I'd say three, and they're def *impietans*."

"How about I leave you boys to this," I offered.

Reidar clapped his hands together with glee. "More for me. Perfect."

"Holler if you need backup."

"Will do, boss man," Magnar noted as he fell into a quick jog beside Reidar.

I didn't bother to stick around, returning to the mansion to check in. I'd been out since the sun went down, skipping over the evening meal to ensure I had a couple of hours of recon under my belt. As it was, the *amnigh* had kicked into high gear, leaving roughly four hours tops between the time it subsided and returned. Obsidian already warned me that he'd had to drug Penelope before they underwent the *lintamair* just to give her a brief reprieve. I hoped like hell it didn't come to that. Considering we had roughly a month before the next full moon, it was going to suck if I had to keep my female doped up.

After materializing on the back porch, I slid open the doors to the sunroom, stepped in, and closed them quickly to keep out the chill. I heard voices coming from the main-floor office, so I strolled that way, hoping to check in with Obsidian before I made a trip upstairs to see Orianna.

The voices on the other side of the door were clipped and quiet. Too quiet for me to make out, so I rapped my knuckles on the door and waited to be granted entry.

The door opened on its own, Obsidian and Michael squared off in the center of the room, neither looking happy.

"What's up?" I stepped inside, wondering briefly if I needed to weapon up.

"Nothing," Obsidian growled. "He was just leaving."

Michael never looked away from Obsidian. Instead, he offered a quick nod before vanishing.

Obsidian's shoulders lowered from his ears when the male disappeared, but he didn't make a move to leave.

"This about Taayin?"

I knew Obsidian was keeping something from me where the male was concerned. The fact that he'd talked Michael into aligning Taayin's and Asmia's destinies meant Obsidian now owed Michael a huge favor. As for what that might be, no one seemed to know, and Obsidian wasn't talking.

When I realized Obsidian wasn't going to answer, I huffed. "Fine. Just thought I'd let you know I'm back. If you need me, shout."

I paused my exit when Obsidian said, "You know anyone with experience delivering babies?"

"Uh..." I turned around to face my brother, smiled. "Yeah, that would be a big fat no. Why? You think she'll need someone?"

Obsidian shrugged. "No idea, but I'd prefer not to get down to the wire and realize she does, and we've got no one here."

Damn fine point. However, I didn't know any angel midwives and all the healers resided in Heaven since we rarely needed treatment down here.

"You ask Michael?"

My brother shrugged. "Not yet."

"Well, if you want me to tug someone's ear, just let me know."

Obsidian's gaze lifted, met mine. "Thanks."

With a quick wave, I strolled toward the back staircase, took them two at a time to the third floor. I was making tracks to my private quarters when soft whispers drew me up short, had me pivoting on my heel and heading in the opposite direction. I found Penelope and Orianna sitting in the conference room, their heads together.

"Well, doesn't this look like trouble."

Both heads popped up, mirroring smiles on the females' faces.

"Hey," Orianna greeted.

"What's going on?" I asked, walking around to stand behind her so I could see the computer screen they were looking at.

"We were just tossing around a few ideas," Penelope explained, lifting a hand to point at the screen. "We were thinking maybe we should do some remodeling."

I leaned in, scanned the screen. "I think you mean construction because that sure looks like you're changing the floor plan."

Penelope giggled. "Just a little."

"To what?" I asked, gently squeezing Orianna's shoulders. "That looks like a living room. Don't we already have one of those up here?"

"*We* don't," Penelope said. "Y'all do. We were thinking maybe we could have a space of our own."

"Ah." I grinned. "So, that's a girly space?"

"We prefer to think of it as a male-free zone. Once all the *amsouelots* are in residence, we girls are going to need our own space. Not to mention, you boys'll be taking over when you're all back together."

I was about to offer my rebuttal when Orianna's shoulders tensed beneath my hands.

"Well, I think that's my cue!" Penelope said, popping up from her chair and smiling. "I'll catch up with you in a bit."

Orianna chuckled. "Yeah. Okay."

By the time the door closed, I was gearing up to make fine use of the conference room table.

OBSIDIAN

I figured this was payback.

After all, I had found it amusing that the *gathenya* had affected Taayin back when Penelope and I first got together.

Granted, *amusing* wasn't quite the word I would use to describe it now. Despite the inconvenience, it was still a pleasurable experience. At least times like this when my *ereswa* sought me out beforehand. When Penelope texted me and requested I come to our mated bed, I hightailed it upstairs, confused and more than a little concerned, only to learn she was planning ahead because Eclipse and Orianna just locked themselves in the third-floor conference room.

It didn't take long before I realized why.

The energy that swept through the mansion would've leveled me if I hadn't already been on my back. Even then, I had to grip the comforter to keep from tossing my *ereswa* to the mattress and mounting her like an animal.

"*Ayreme* ... fuck," I groaned as she stroked my cock with both hands, her gold eyes glowing brightly as she watched me. "I need ... *in* you. Now."

Her mouth fell open, her back bowing as though my words alone had set her off.

Unable to resist, I reached up, palming her heavy breasts, admiring her beauty as she continued to tease and torment. I loved her like this, naked and available, demanding.

Truth was, if Penelope didn't insist I sate her urges, I would've held out until after the baby was born. As it was, I was terrified that I would hurt her or do something to harm our unborn child. Though she swore that wouldn't happen, I wasn't sure how she knew. Everything she'd read about pregnancy and childbirth was for humans, something that didn't apply to us. Considering there was no record of an angel birth ever taking place on Earth, no one knew what might happen.

Penelope moaned, dragging me out of my thoughts and back to the moment.

"Put me inside you," I growled, kneading her breasts and tugging her toward me.

Her soft moan was the signal I was waiting for. She always did that right before she gave in to my gruff demands.

"Ride me, *ayreme*. Let me watch you."

A rumbling growl escaped me when she pressed the head of my cock against the wet juncture between her thighs. And when she sank down on me, I groaned loud and long, my cock jerking and twitching with the need to come inside her, to claim her a million times over.

Penelope reached for my hands, and I obliged, allowing her to twine her fingers with mine as she used me to steady herself, her hips doing that delicious rock-and-grind.

"Beautiful," I whispered, watching her breasts sway as she did. "Come for me, *ayreme*. Let me feel you come."

My beautiful *ereswa* whimpered softly, her hips beginning to rock faster. I assisted, releasing her hands so I could guide her hips, pushing up inside her as I held her above me. I didn't stop until she cried out my name, her sex clenching around me, dragging my orgasm out of me in a rush.

When her body went limp, I shifted, gently laying her on the bed as I curled up behind her, my hand covering the swell of her belly, my lips pressing to the back of her head.

"I love you, *ayreme*. Now and forever."

She muttered something that sounded similar, making me smile.

BIJOU

I was minding my own business, as was usually the case, when I felt that sweltering energy plow through the mansion.

Luckily, I was in the game room this time. The last time I was down in the kitchen. It had been hell getting to the second floor and hiding myself away as the rest of the mansion succumbed to what sounded like a heated orgy.

Straightening my spine and gritting my teeth, I put one foot in front of the other and made a hasty retreat for my bedroom. It was only three doors down on the right. It should take no time whatsoever to get there. Once inside, I could shut the door and ride out this heat wave with the help of my trusty vibrator. Heaven knew there was no one else here I wanted to help me assuage this overwhelming ache.

Okay, that wasn't entirely true. There was one person. Oliver. However, I got the feeling he was quite content with the status of our friendship. And that was exactly what we'd established during the few weeks I'd been there. The two of us spent quite a bit of time together watching movies, playing pool, swimming, sharing meals, more movies, more pool, more swimming.

And fine, it was my idea to be friends. It was what I

wanted. In the beginning. But I had to admit, I had a slight crush on the human.

A soft moan escaped me as my core clenched tightly. I paused with my hand on the wall as I continued my trek to my room.

If it weren't for what the angels called *gathenya*, I figured I would be fine and dandy with my friendship with Oliver as he was. But this ... whatever stoked these damn flames made it nearly impossible not to want something a bit more ... beneficial. Yes. That was a good word for it. Friends with benefits. That was a thing, right? I was sure plenty of people did it. Humans, vampires, didn't matter. The angels and Fae certainly had a good thing going for them. They alternated hookups the way I changed socks, a different pair every day.

Someone's deep groan had me pausing, glancing over my shoulder to ensure no one was behind me. The hallway was clear in both directions, thank God.

Swallowing, I continued toward my bedroom, but just as my feet were finally getting with the program, I drew up short when I noticed the door to Oliver's bedroom was partially open.

Don't look inside. Don't you dare look inside.

I looked.

Damn it.

Through the crack in the door, I could see Oliver on his bed, head propped up on navy-blue pillows, shoulders and chest bare, the rest of him covered by a navy-blue sheet. But it wasn't the linens that caught my attention. No, that was credited to the way Oliver's hand was moving beneath that thin fabric. There was no disguising what he was doing, either.

Another groan drifted from his mouth to my ears, and I swallowed a moan of my own.

"Fuck," Oliver hissed, kicking the sheet off.

My eyes widened when I got a look-see at the thick flesh between his legs, the firm hand that glided up and down it.

It was so very wrong of me to be watching him, but no matter how hard I tried, I couldn't look away. I was mesmerized by the way he touched himself. His hand firmly gripping the rigid flesh, stroking up, down, up, down, a steady rhythm that matched the race of his breaths in his lungs.

I'd never been a voyeur, but I wanted to see this male pleasure himself, to watch as his body kicked and twitched as the pleasure of his own touch consumed him. Having never been intimate with a male, I wasn't familiar with what it took to bring one pleasure, but based on the way Oliver roughly tugged on his flesh, I had to believe even humans could handle the dark urges I'd been plagued with since I hit puberty. I remembered Reve, the way that male had wanted me to save myself for him. We had to be mated, he'd told me many times. I never believed in that. For one, I was a bastard. Living proof that two did not need to be mated in order to be intimate.

It was a romantic gesture, sure. But who needed romance? That was for idiots, just look at me. I got caught up in all of Reve's sweet promises, only for the male to walk away as though he had never cared for me at all.

"Oh, fuck," Oliver groaned loudly, his back arching, his erection punching through his fist.

I held my breath, willed him to let himself go.

When he finally did, I felt an echo of pleasure shoot through my lower extremities. Not wanting him to know I'd seen him, I hurried to my bedroom, closing the door behind me.

And as I brought myself to orgasm with my trusty pink vibrator, I closed my eyes and thought of Oliver, wondering...

What if?

33

ECLIPSE

———

I woke to the sound of a phone ringing.

Knowing it wasn't mine, I rolled over, reached for Orianna, nudged her shoulder. "*Sezari.*"

"Hmm?"

"Your phone's ringing."

She bolted upright like I'd taken an electrical wire to her skin. I sensed her panic, smelled her fear, and it had sleep crumbling away as I pushed myself upright, leaning against the headboard. The wood was cold against my back, and I peered over to see the flames from the fire had subsided while we were asleep. I was tempted to get it going again but held off when Orianna answered the call.

"Mom? Are you all right?"

I couldn't help it, my hearing was too acute not to catch the words coming through the phone. The panic in Orianna's mother's voice was evident when she requested Orianna go home immediately. Apparently, Orianna's father was threatening to have her committed to a hospital for treatment—drugs, I surmised, based on the slur in her mother's words—and Elizabeth feared he was trying to take the house.

"Mom, it'll take me some time to get there, but I'm on my way." Orianna paused, listened. "I know, Mom. I'll hurry. It's a nine-hour drive."

I knew from the sound of Orianna's voice, she wasn't going to listen to reason. Despite the danger that resided outside the walls of the mansion, she was going to see her mother, with or without me. Which meant I was going with her.

I immediately thought of Asmia, of the mission we were on to locate the Fae and bring her home. It had been our sole focus since the day Perfidious pulled his shit-tastic snatch and grab. But while I wanted to dedicate all my attention to Asmia, I couldn't put her above Orianna. It wasn't the way I was programmed, no matter how shitty it seemed.

I waited patiently for her to finish the conversation, to disconnect, to set the phone down.

"I'll take you," I said softly, my mind whirling with things I needed to take care of before we hit the road.

Orianna twisted, peered back at me over her shoulder. "You've got so much going on here."

There was fear and anguish in her eyes, and it broke my heart to see her in pain.

"You're my priority, *sezari*. Where you go, I go."

Orianna shook her head. "I ... I can get there faster if you stay here. I can't afford to stop for the daylight, and since..."

"Your argument won't change my mind," I told her, my voice firm.

I saw the relief on her face, and warmth spread through me. It humbled me to know she wanted me at her side. Despite this whirlwind we'd been spinning in for the past month, we were growing closer. Minute by minute, hour by hour, day by day. Having Orianna at my side made it easier to breathe, to exist, even if neither of us knew what the next night would bring.

"I need to talk to Obsidian," I told her as I dropped my legs over the side of the bed. "Why don't you shower and get ready."

She nodded and wasted no time heading to the bathroom.

I dragged on my jeans from that morning and snagged my T-shirt. I pulled it on as I stepped out into the hallway. I could hear voices coming from the third-floor living area. I padded barefoot down the hall, turned the corner, and found Obsidian and Stygian reclined on the sofas, staring at the television.

I figured ripping the Band-Aid clean off was the best approach. "I'm taking Orianna to Oklahoma. Something's up with her mother, and she wants to go."

Obsidian sat up, worry instantly pulling his face tight.

"I know the dangers," I assured my brother. "I'll protect her."

Of course, that was so fucking easy to say, not nearly as simple to do, but I would keep her safe at all costs.

"Take Miklós and Magnar with you," Obsidian ordered.

Figuring it would be ignorant to refuse additional protection for my *amsouelot*, I nodded.

"I'll have Kandarie assigned to you from here," my brother continued. "I'll have him monitoring your movements and keeping an eye out for demons."

I could only nod. I knew Obsidian would do what he wanted when it came to protecting us. Now that Penelope was with him, our oldest brother was on a mission to ensure we were not in harm's way, our *amsouelots* located, their souls safe and secure, and out of Lucifer's nasty clutches. It never failed, Obsidian was the one who kept us together, the leader, some might say.

I let Obsidian worry over us for a few more minutes with his *be careful*s and *keep me informed*s. When I returned to my private quarters, I found Orianna already dressed, her wet hair hanging down her back.

"It's cold out. You need to dry your hair," I insisted. "By the time you're finished, I'll be ready to go."

Though she harrumphed at my request, Orianna made her way to the bathroom while I made a quick pass through the shower. As promised, I was dressed and tossing a few things into a bag when she emerged from the bathroom.

"I don't plan to stay," she told me. "So you don't need to pack much."

I grinned. In lieu of socks and underwear, I was packing weapons. An arsenal, in fact. I was taking no chances with Orianna's safety, and I seriously doubted the vampires had lost her scent. I still imagined them hovering on the perimeter of Darkness, waiting for her to emerge so they could get their nasty little claws in her. No doubt, the fact we hadn't encountered any on our last two trips out made my decision to take her easier. I could only pray if those bastards did catch up to us, we could outrun them at the very least because I could feel the determination coming off Orianna in waves. She was hellbent on coming to her mother's rescue, and no demon was going to get in her way.

. . .

Roughly twenty minutes later, armed to the teeth and weighed down with a care package hand-prepared by Phillip, I was steering the Bugatti out of the garage while Miklós followed in the Range Rover, Magnar riding shotgun. Neither my *lieterra* nor my *ladeare* had batted an eyelash when they learned of their new assignment. If I had to guess, they were eager to get out from under the weight of the mansion and the doom and gloom that lingered heavily throughout.

The silence in the car was the equivalent of a drop in cabin pressure at thirty thousand feet. When it got to be too much, I flipped on the radio, "Crooked Halo" by Stitched Up Heart choking out the hush-hush. Relaxing evidently wasn't an option because no matter how hard I tried, my senses were hypervigilant, tracking everything within a mile radius. Not an easy feat when we were averaging speeds around ninety miles per hour.

Orianna's frustrated exhale pulled my full attention back into the vehicle. "I can't believe Erik's doing this."

"You refer to your father by name?"

She peered over at me. "I figure he hasn't earned *Dad*, so yeah. When I refer to him at all." Orianna sighed, shifted her gaze out the window. "He must've hit rock bottom. That's the only reason I can figure he'd go after my mother. She told me a few days ago he stopped by. Probably realized she was low on funds, figured shipping her off would allow him to sell the house."

"He wants to hospitalize her?"

"Yeah." Orianna leaned into the seat, stared straight ahead. "I'm not oblivious. I know my mother's addicted to painkillers. But the doctor keeps prescribing them, so who am I to intervene? And who the hell made Erik her boss? I always figured he'd use her weakness against her, but this is lower than low." Her voice grew more tense with her agitation. "He's never given a shit about her. He's too selfish for that. And now he's going to what? Upend her world, ship her off? Fuck that."

"We can bring her to Darkness," I offered before realizing the words had been hanging on the tip of my tongue.

Orianna's head snapped over, her mouth hanging open, shock stretching her delicate skin tight around her eyes.

"She's your mother, Orianna. I know you've taken care of her most of your life. If you want her close, we'll bring her to Darkness."

A strangled laugh escaped. "I'm not sure how well that'll go over. Elizabeth might live in a drug-induced haze, but I'm pretty sure she'll catch on to the fact there's a house full of angels."

Yeah, that was where the problem lay. "She won't live in the mansion," I said softly. "But we can get her a place of her own. The *heurosp* don't reside in the mansion. We'll design a house for her. Get her a few *heurosp* and a nurse or two to take care of her."

"I can't tell her about you, can I?"

I cut my eyes to her, saw the worry on her face. "No. We're restricted from interacting with humans."

Although, I wasn't sure the rules for family. Perhaps there was an amendment I hadn't read. One that said it was cool for the mom-in-law to know about Heaven's warriors on Earth.

"What about Oliver and Winnie? You interact with them just fine."

"We overstepped," I admitted. "Obsidian brought Oliver because he worried Perfidious would use him against Penelope. And Winnie ... that was a fluke. No one could've known she was Reidar's *amsouelot*." Or *not*, as seemed to be the case.

"So why isn't she an angel now? Like Penelope?"

I found it fascinating that she could talk so easily about this.

"What?" she asked. "Penelope likes to share her thoughts."

Yeah, that was what I was worried about.

"That's a question for Reidar," I told her. "As for your mother ... just because we can't bring her into the fold doesn't mean she can't be a part of your life. She needs you, and you need her. Bringing her back to Darkness makes sense."

I briefly glanced at Orianna when there was no response, and my heart squeezed. Tears were rolling down her cheeks in a flood.

"I'm ... sorry." She sobbed. "I don't know why I'm blubbering like a baby."

I knew why. Orianna was used to doing things on her own. Had been all her life. Between looking for her sister and taking care of her crippled mother, she was the one giving everything she had. She wasn't used to having someone want to do things for her.

Turning my attention back to the road, I reached over, took her hand, and brushed my thumb over her smooth skin. "Orianna, I'd do anything for you. Anything at all. I hope you know that by now."

Another sob. "I..." Her hand squeezed mine. "I love you, Eclipse."

I had spent my entire existence living in darkness, never experiencing what it felt like to have the sun on my face, but in that moment, the warmth and light were upon me. Those few words turned my world from dark to light.

Orianna chuckled, a hint of hysteria in the sound. "I'm sorry. I didn't mean to make you uncomfortable."

I pulled her hand over, kissed her knuckles. "I'm not

uncomfortable, *sezari*. Definitely not uncomfortable." *I'm whole for the first time.*

ORIANNA

I hadn't meant to break down like a sappy girl, but that was exactly what happened when Eclipse was talking about bringing my mother to Darkness. Honestly, the thought never crossed my mind, but admittedly, I never depended on others to take care of me or my mother. Good thing, too, considering no one had ever been there.

The last people I remembered who gave a shit at all were my grandparents, but Elizabeth's mother and father passed away a couple of years after their daughter's accident. My grandmother died from complications from pneumonia, and my grandfather ... well, I believed my grandfather died of a broken heart, even though I knew that wasn't possible.

Because Erik had already shipped me and Amber off to boarding school, we didn't get to spend time with either grandparent during their last days, having only been given a pass to go to the funerals. Not surprisingly, Erik didn't attend either one, but he was the first to ensure Elizabeth got the money she was promised in their will.

The bastard.

"We're going to make it to your mother's before sunrise," Eclipse said. "But it'll be close. We'll need somewhere safe to go."

I knew he was referring to him, Miklós, and Magnar. They needed somewhere safe from the sun. "The basement's not the greatest space, but it's mostly finished. And there's no sunlight. No exterior windows or doors."

"I don't suppose I'll be lucky enough you'll stay with me."

I felt his eyes on me. "I figure my father's planning to show up during the day."

"You need to know I can't protect you when the sun's up."

I heard the pain in those words. He hated admitting a weakness. "I know. I'll be fine."

Based on his expression, he didn't agree with me, but Eclipse didn't argue.

"Why don't we see what's going on when we get there," I suggested. "If my mother's all right, I'll stay with you."

Another nod was his only response, The Pretty Reckless filling the space, going on about a house on a hill.

It wasn't until the last fifty miles or so that I felt the tension growing in my body, and it had nothing to do with the situation that lay ahead of us. No, this was a sexual tension that was growing infinitely more intense with every passing mile until I was flushed from the heat consuming me.

Eclipse must've noticed because his hand shifted along my thigh. "Only a few more minutes."

I could tell he was feeling it, too. His breathing had become a bit heavier, the weight of his hand settling on my leg as though it took effort to hold it up. If we kept this up, neither of us would be able to walk by the time we got to my mother's.

"I'm not sure I can last that long," I admitted, tugging at my sweater, attempting to keep it from brushing against my hypersensitive skin.

NICOLE EDWARDS

I was barely aware of Eclipse hitting a button, Magnar's voice sounding through the speakers. Something about them going on ahead, checking the perimeter of the house once they arrived. The words droned on, an irritation that had nothing to do with Magnar and everything to do with this frustration within me, the desperate need to fuck.

A whimper escaped, pushing right past my attempt to swallow it. I was seconds from writhing against the seat when Eclipse veered off the main road.

"Where are you going?" I rasped. "We're almost there."

The car came to a stop, and I forced my eyes open. Eclipse had parked beneath an enormous oak tree. The branches had shed most of their leaves with the coming of winter but still had enough to shield us from the road in the distance.

Not that anyone would be looking. It was four-thirty in the morning and black as pitch out there in the country. Then again, the farmers would be getting up soon, and if we weren't careful, they'd be getting a peep show.

The driver's door opened, closed. Passenger door was next, and a breath later, I was in Eclipse's arms. He hip-checked the door, then strolled to the front of the vehicle. He rested my butt on the hood of the car as his lips fused to mine. In that moment, I didn't care where we were or who might see us, or the fact that my ass was on the hood of a three-million-dollar sports car. The only thing that mattered was Eclipse's lips on mine, his hands working my leggings down to my ankles. While he released the button on his jeans, I toed off one of my ankle boots and freed my leg.

The air was downright chilly but not enough to extinguish any of the heat churning in my bloodstream.

"Please, Eclipse." I peppered kisses along his jaw, loving how he smelled. "I need you inside me."

"Put your legs around me, *sezari*."

428

My bare butt squeaked when he pulled me closer to the edge of the hood. My legs followed his direction, wrapping around his hips, my ankles pressing against his ass. I felt the blunt head of his erection against my eager opening, and then...

"Oh, God, yes."

My head fell back as he began driving into me, bottoming out with every brutal thrust. No foreplay, no teasing. Just the exquisite feel of him sliding deep inside my body. The friction eased some of the pain sparked by the devastating need, but it wasn't enough. Still, I focused on how good he felt inside me, how perfect it was to have his thick arms surrounding me. I crushed my mouth to his and tried to climb him, wanting more, needing everything. My body rocked with every punishing thrust, the glorious friction dragging long, desperate moans from me.

"I love you," I whimpered when I pulled back for air. I wasn't sure why I felt the need to tell him, but I did.

He whispered something in return, and while I didn't speak his language, I heard the sincerity in the rough rasp of his voice, suspected he was returning the sentiment. It warmed me in a different way, had my insides burning brighter until ... an explosion of epic proportions had me crying out his name.

Eclipse grunted, driving into me several times before his body stilled, his muscles bunching beneath my hands as he jerked me toward him. He growled low in his throat, and I felt his release. It drove out every ounce of the ache I'd been plagued with and filled me with a sweet rush of love.

I was in a daze, barely noticing when Eclipse gently cleaned me before helping me back into my leggings, returning my boot to my foot. Then I was in the car, his hand in mine as he steered us back to the main road as though those perfect few minutes never happened.

H alf an hour later, Eclipse pulled into my mother's driveway, parking behind the Range Rover. The two ridiculously expensive vehicles stuck out like a sore thumb in the quiet neighborhood.

"I'll throw a cloak over them," Eclipse told me, clearly reading my mind. "No one will see them."

Eclipse snagged both our bags, then followed me along the thin concrete path to the porch. When I peered behind me, the vehicles had vanished in thin air. There one second, gone the next. Another one of his nifty little tricks.

I didn't see Magnar or Miklós as I made my way to the front steps. Rather than knock, I used the house key to let myself in, Eclipse right behind me. Within seconds, the other two angels were with us, following as I stepped into the dark interior of my childhood home.

Good news, it was clean. My mother had always been a stickler for cleanliness, and that was one thing she'd clung to since the attack. No matter her limitations, Elizabeth McKay kept the space she occupied spotless. Or rather, those who cared for her did.

"Check the house," Eclipse instructed Magnar.

I'd already given them a brief overview of the layout at Eclipse's request. If I had to guess, they'd memorized the three-bedroom, two-bath floor plan, the trek through merely a means of ensuring there were no uninvited guests.

"My mother's a night owl," I told them. "She sleeps during the day, so she's probably in her bedroom watching television."

"She's in her room," Eclipse confirmed. "I can hear her."

"Do you want me to let her know I have guests? You can stay out of sight and all..."

Eclipse shook his head. "Not unless we have no other option. We don't want to agitate her. If she's worried about your father, probably won't help to have the three of us here. Just lead the way to the basement."

I led the way to the kitchen, then through the single door in the wall beside the refrigerator. I reached in and flipped the switch on the wall, illuminating the lower level.

"Go check on her," Eclipse said. "Then come down when you can. I'll be waiting."

I nodded, but before I could turn away, Eclipse reached for my hand, pulling me into his arms.

"Do not answer the door for anyone other than your father," he said softly. "I don't care if you know them or not. Right now, I'm not sure who we can trust."

"Okay."

"I know you want to stay with her, but I'd feel much better if you were with me."

The admission filled me with warmth. "I probably won't be able to sleep without you anyway."

A small smile formed on his beautiful mouth before he kissed me softly and sent me on my way.

I made my way through the dark house, flipping on lights as I went. Magnar was installing a tiny camera in the hallway, high up on the wall and giving an optimal view of anyone coming toward my mother's bedroom. A bunch of eyes on me gave me the willies, but I figured it was wasted breath to argue with them. Three angels trapped in a basement would want to have a look-see. That I understood.

There's one in the kitchen, dining, and living room. Another at the front door.

431

I nodded at Magnar, assuring him I received the information.

When he disappeared, I took a deep breath. Now to see what I was dealing with.

I found Elizabeth in her bedroom, sitting in her power wheelchair. Her limp brown hair had recently been trimmed, falling just below her ears, and there wasn't a hint of makeup on her face. She looked old, I thought. Older than I remembered.

But she looked good, considering where she spent most of her time. Rarely did Elizabeth allow anyone to help her into bed or onto the sofa for fear no one would be there to help her out. Even when I had been living there, back before I went on my search for Amber, Elizabeth refused to get trapped in her bed. The only person she allowed to help her in and out of the chair was the physical therapist who came two days a week.

"Mom?"

Elizabeth's head turned slowly, a smile forming, her light brown eyes glittering with recognition. "Orianna. You came."

I stepped into the room, peered around. Bed was made, surfaces dusted, the oriental rug vacuumed. "I promised you I would."

The soft whirring sound of the chair's motor sounded as Elizabeth backed away from the television. "Has it been nine hours already?"

"It has." Or mostly, anyway. Eclipse shaved off nearly a full hour, even with our unplanned stop.

I stepped back so my mother could steer herself to the hallway.

"Have you heard from Erik again?"

"Not since last night. He said he's coming today."

"Did he say when?"

"Early." Elizabeth glanced around, as though she wasn't

sure where she was. "At least I think that's what he said." Her eyes shot to my face. "Did you find her?"

"Amber?" I shook my head, motioned for my mother to lead the way. "Not yet."

We ventured down the hall in silence, then into the kitchen. It looked the same as I remembered: same white refrigerator, dishwasher, and stove, familiar rooster border along the top of the laminate countertops, which had the same coffee cup stain that had been there for as long as I could remember. It wasn't the same house I grew up in, but it was the one we moved to after Elizabeth's attack. My mother had wanted out of Oklahoma City, and this had gotten her closer to her parents at the time.

"Would you like some coffee?" Elizabeth offered.

"I'll make it, Mom." Coffee was probably the worst thing for me right now, considering my agitation, but the caffeine would do wonders to help me stay awake.

While I went to work with the coffeepot, Elizabeth went for the refrigerator. She returned with a small bottle of creamer, set it on the counter.

"Did you find her?"

I paused, coffee grounds suspended over the filter as I glanced at my mother. The drugs did that, I reminded myself. Made her forget things that happened. Like conversations had not two minutes ago.

"Not yet." I dumped the grounds into the filter, closed the lid, and punched the button to start.

Once the coffeepot began its near-death gurgle, I turned to face my mother. "When's the last time the nurse was here?"

"Yesterday." Elizabeth glanced at the table, the counter. "I think."

Someone had been coming by, I knew that much.

"Your father called yesterday," Elizabeth said as she turned her chair around, headed to the refrigerator again.

I watched my mother, my heart breaking when I realized Elizabeth was attempting to find the creamer, which she'd already brought over.

"I've got it, Mom."

Elizabeth smiled. "Oh, good. You found the creamer."

Swallowing hard, I fought back the tears. There was no sense breaking down now. I would reserve that for later, during the hard conversation to come.

34

ECLIPSE

"Sun's up," Miklós intoned, his attention focused on the laptop he had perched on his thighs. "This is our new home for the next..." He peered at his watch.

"Twelve hours," Magnar stated.

As if I didn't already know that. The prickle on my neck was all the warning I needed, a reminder that dust and ash were my forever form if I didn't find shelter. It wasn't until I stepped into the musty basement that I realized how good we had it back in Darkness. At the mansion, we were protected from the sun, able to move about at will with all the luxuries at our disposal, never having to worry that a giant ball of fire might be our demise.

But the sun wasn't Orianna's enemy. At least not as long as she was human. She could wander around freely while I was forced to cower down here, doing my damnedest not to think about a backup plan if, say, the house was to burn to the ground.

Yeah. Best to dump the doom and gloom.

In an effort to hold on to my sanity, I listened to Orianna and Elizabeth talking upstairs in the kitchen. I smelled burnt coffee and the lingering aroma of lemon cleaner.

I was so in tune with Orianna I could feel the sadness that cloaked her. Her mother's condition pained her, though I wasn't sure if it was that she was confined to the wheelchair or that she was ensnared by the pain meds, a prisoner to addiction. I couldn't imagine either was fun. Not for Elizabeth or those who cared for her.

"Did you map the house?" Miklós asked Magnar.

"Just like Orianna said. Three bedrooms, two baths," the male responded. "Small entry inside the living room. Couch, television, old coffee table. I doubt anyone's been in that room in at least a year, maybe two. Kitchen just beyond that, separate hall leading to the bedrooms. The first on the left looks like it's been converted into an office. Next, on the right, appears to be their other daughter's room. Probably set up as a shrine when she skipped town. Next is a small bath, also on the right. Tub, sink, toilet. Nothing fancy and clearly not used. Last, straight ahead, is the master bedroom. Queen bed, television on top of the dresser, one nightstand, one lamp. Both closet and bathroom doors are on the left side of the room. That bath's been modified for her wheelchair, appears used often and meticulously clean."

I continued to stare at the door, mentally walking through the house using Magnar's description.

"And the cameras?" Miklós asked. "I see three. How many'd you get up?"

"Five." Magnar leaned over, peering at Miklós's computer.

"Yep, living room and hallway. That's the view from above this door"—he pointed to the entry to the basement—"and I got one pointing at the front door, another on the front porch."

"There they are," Miklós said, relief in his tone.

"She must have help around here," Magnar noted. "House is clean, but I'm not sure how she does laundry since it's down here."

I made a mental note to ensure Elizabeth had all the comforts when she moved to Darkness. *If.* If she moved to Darkness. I couldn't very well ship her off without Orianna's go-ahead, and I got the impression it wouldn't be an easy sell for Elizabeth. Then again, if Elizabeth believed Orianna wanted her mother close, perhaps she would jump on board. I was serious when I told Orianna we couldn't interact with the human. Not if it was at all avoidable. Well and truly sucked, if you asked me. I wouldn't mind having a mother-in-law, spending time with Orianna's family.

"Backyard's got a chain-link fence surrounding it," Miklós said, "a small shed that's padlocked. Looks like someone's been in and out of there frequently. Front door and back door are the only exits, and from a quick inspection, someone's painted the windows shut. Considering the age of the house and Elizabeth's inability to do the work herself, someone's doing right by it and her."

I didn't add anything to their conversation, and I tuned out when they shifted to discussions of who would sleep where.

I was far too twitchy for sleep. Probably had a lot to do with the fact that I was trapped now that the sun was rising higher in the sky, with no way of helping Orianna should she need it. I didn't like the helpless feeling at all. Not being able to protect my *amsouelot* was my worst fear. A month ago, I would've been content to believe she was safe in that shitty little apartment with the *fiestreigh* keeping tabs on her. Now that I'd held her while she slept in my bed, woke with her next to me, I couldn't bear the thought of not being right there to ensure no harm would come to her.

The only positive was that the vampires and demons were trapped, as well. Except for the shadow beasts, but I'd yet to encounter any who had Orianna on their radar.

However, humans were just as capable of raining hell as any of the supernatural. Namely, Orianna's father, who seemed to be intent on hurting Elizabeth, even if it was only financially.

Turning, I peered back at Miklós. "What do you know about Erik McKay?"

The *lieterra* snatched up his laptop once again. "Last known residence was Phoenix, Arizona. That was three months ago. Looks like he's been drifting for quite some time. No employment records for the past eight years, but that doesn't mean he's not working for cash. He's managed to stay low, keeping off the government's radar. Oh, and he's got no bank accounts that I can find. None after he left several in the red back when he left Elizabeth high and dry after he shipped Orianna and Amber off to boarding school, paid for by Elizabeth's parents."

"What about that place we went to in Telluride? Not recent?"

"Kandarie did some digging on that and found he'd first been in the area about three years ago. Same time as Orianna's sister. We figure that's how she tracked him down, followed him back. It looks like they tried to establish a relationship, but dear old Dad left Amber high and dry in that shitty apartment after a month and a half. He rented it again but bailed shortly after the eviction was processed. We were able to track Amber's movements until seven months ago. Came to the same conclusion her GA did."

That she was dead, I knew. Amber's guardian angel had documented it after having lost his connection to her.

Footsteps sounded above us, causing me to turn toward the noise. The basement door creaked as it opened, and then Orianna appeared at the top of the rickety staircase.

I moved toward her. "Everything all right?"

Orianna nodded, carefully moving down the wooden treads. "I'm hoping she'll sleep now that she's taken her meds. Once she does, I'll check in, but I need to stay up there to greet Erik if he does show up."

A soft growl escaped me, but I couldn't help it. The thought of Orianna going up against her father without me at her side ... it bothered me immensely.

"I'll be fine," she said softly. "He won't hurt me."

She didn't know that. Depending on what Erik McKay was after, it was quite possible he was a loose cannon. If the guy owed money, chances were he was being hassled for it. If he didn't pay, that put anyone in his life in harm's way.

Orianna took my hand and tugged. Confused, I moved with her.

She stepped into a small alcove beneath the stairs, giving us a modicum of privacy, though Magnar and Miklós could still hear everything we said.

"I'm not sure I'll make it through the day..." Her eyes completed that sentence, filling in the blank spaces and sending warmth through my bloodstream.

She was referring to the *amnigh*. There was no denying it was intensifying. The fact that I was feeding from her had robbed us of the slight reprieve we would've had once it became too much to bear. There was no timetable that outlined how long we had before it overtook her the way it had Penelope right before Obsidian had mated with her.

Personally, I was hoping for time. A lot of it. I wasn't eager to undergo the *lintamair*. Didn't matter that it would forever tether Orianna's soul to mine, the mere thought of taking her life wasn't something I could contemplate. I remembered seeing Obsidian in the moments leading up to the mating ceremony. My brother had been a mess, a complete and total wreck. No doubt in my mind, it was his reaction to doing the most difficult thing he would ever have to do.

Orianna's soft blond hair felt like silk as I brushed it back from her face, my fingertips moving to the warmth of her cheek. "If you need me, I'll be right here."

I didn't bother to mention that I would need to feed before sundown. My strength was already waning, but I would hold out for as long as I could.

As though programmed to respond to the thought of her blood, my fangs descended, throbbing with the urge to sink into her vein.

"You need to feed," she said softly, her arms sliding around my waist.

I shook My head. "I'm fine for now."

I knew the impact it had on her. Orianna's entire body responded to me feeding from her, and right now, we lacked the privacy I required. No way would I allow Miklós or Magnar to listen in on our private moments. Not if I could help it.

My ears perked up at the sound of Elizabeth's voice coming from upstairs. "Your mother's calling you."

"Shit." Orianna sighed. "Okay. Let me sit with her. Once she's asleep, I'll come back down."

Because I had no other options, I released her, then watched as she made her way up the stairs. When she opened the door, I saw the glint of light coming into the house.

Another shitty reminder that I was trapped and the female I loved was out of reach.

KAJ

I paced the storage room beneath the empty warehouse, my gaze continuing to swing over to Mirakel, Huracān, Blāz, and Kidel. They were what was known as the Zenith, the group of warriors whose sole responsibility was to protect the Alpha of the race. Or rather, they were what was left of the group, anyway. At one time, I'd been one of them, a warrior amongst an army of invincible vampires. Now there were only four remaining.

I still couldn't believe the males were there, alive and well, from what I could tell. The last time I saw them was right after the raids on Kardobahn's camp. Despite all our efforts, we were too late to save my father, my baby brothers, but just in time to encounter a second wave of shadow beasts that had come to set fire to the camp, ensuring no lives were spared. At the time, I thought the warriors had died in their attempt to save me, their recently appointed Alpha.

It had been a solid week since I stumbled upon Mirakel in that dungeon, and since then, I had been trying to understand how I had lost touch with them for so long, how I hadn't known they were still alive. More importantly, why they didn't make every attempt to meet up with me.

"Why'd you stay gone?" I asked, still trying to come to

terms with it all. While I was grateful they were alive and kicking, I still had reservations about who I could trust.

"We got separated that day," Mirakel explained. "When the fires were burning, I didn't know whether they"—he motioned toward the others—"were alive or not, but my mission is to protect my Alpha, so I went in search of you."

"Did you go back for them?" I inquired.

Mirakel shook his head, misery glittering in his neon blue eyes. "I wanted to, but my objective was to find and protect you, *phaal.*"

Yes, I understood all too well their mission. The Zenith were trained to lay down their lives for the ruler of the race. When Kardobahn was killed, we'd been leveled. Hard not to be when our only objective was to ensure the Alpha's safety and that of his family. In that regard, we'd all failed my father, even though we nearly lost our own lives in the process.

That day... Fuck, I could still see the aftermath in my mind as though the image had been superimposed on the backs of my eyelids. The devastation—

"I did the same," Huracān said, pulling my mind back to the present. "Went in search of you. But I found Kidel instead. Injured, nearly dead." The male lowered his eyes. "I couldn't leave him, *phaal.*"

I stopped, turning to face Huracān. "No, you couldn't," I agreed. "And I'm glad you didn't."

It had been hell thinking I'd lost them. Because of their roles as warriors protecting their Alpha, I had always considered them family. I'd fought alongside them and would've given my life for theirs. To think that they would put my life above their own was a humbling prospect, one that would take time to get used to now that I was their Alpha.

"I got word that Huracān made it out," Blāz stated. "By

then, I'd already caught your scent but figured we'd do better together, so I went looking for him."

Blāz's words rang with disgrace, as though he despised the fact he'd diverted from his mission, choosing to save his family when he thought all was lost. I never believed in that particular objective of the Zenith. While I understood the need to protect the Alpha, I always thought it made more sense to protect all vampires, to ensure the race's survival above all else.

"That's ultimately how we found you," Mirakel said. "Misplaced Halos came back online, and there was word you'd been sighted. I followed the message boards and found one Huracān left for you."

I should've looked there, but I hadn't.

"That was where we learned of your daughter," Blāz stated. "So we tracked her to you."

A ghost of a smile formed on my mouth. "I thought someone was following us, so I shook the tail. That was you?"

Mirakel shook his head. "It was Darko's males. Ultimately, we found you when we stumbled on their scent."

I exhaled heavily. Mirakel had explained what he'd overheard regarding Darko's intention of taking the reins as Alpha. Evidently, there were quite a few factions who were not happy with the thought of me ruling the race, and they decided to side with the enemy. Not that it surprised me. There'd always been those who didn't want Kardobahn at the helm, but my father had ruled for seven hundred years, surviving multiple attempts on his life. As for whether or not he'd been a good ruler, that wasn't for me to decide. My father and I rarely saw eye to eye. We had many differences of opinion, and no doubt, those would be noted by my enemies, as well.

"We failed you, *phaal*," Huracān said solemnly.

For fuck's sake.

I should've known that was coming. The Zenith held themselves to a higher standard than all other vampires, and because of that, they were harder on themselves, seeing failure when there was none.

"You did not," I snapped, waving my hand dismissively. "I'm alive, aren't I? You're alive. That's all that matters." I peered over at Mirakel. "Well, aside from taking down Darko before he gets his hands on me."

Or those I cared about. I knew Darko well, and I was aware the male would stop at nothing to continue to climb the ladder toward power. I'd felt it when I visited the Dungeon, knew something was brewing, but I'd shrugged it off.

"May I ask where you've been staying?" Mirakel questioned.

I studied him momentarily. At my core, I knew I could trust these males. In fact, they were the only ones I could do so implicitly. They would have my back and me theirs.

"I took refuge with the angels," I admitted. "I needed a place for Bijou."

"That explains why you fell off the grid," Huracān stated with a smirk. "Obsidian's good at blending."

He was that.

Resuming my pacing, I considered our options. "When the sun goes down, I'll pay Obsidian a visit. The angels have another residence in Darkness. It's been abandoned for a few years since they built their new fortress. I'll see if they'll allow us to stay temporarily." Or perhaps indefinitely. I got the feeling Darkness was exactly where I belonged, close to Bijou and Acadia.

"As long as you're aware we go where you go," Mirakel stated. "It's our duty to protect the Alpha."

I nodded. "Understood. And for as long as I'm in that role, I'd trust no one else more to have my back."

The question was, how long would it be before Darko or another traitor overthrew me?

MIRAKEL

As I stood facing the Alpha I was sworn to protect, there was no way of denying my job had gotten immensely more difficult with the changing of the guard.

I'd spent three hundred and fifty of my three hundred eighty-two years fighting alongside Kaj. The male had trained me from the time I was old enough to wield a sword, trusted me to keep Kardobahn safe, and proved it by inducting me into the Zenith despite my lineage and lack of blueblood running through my veins.

Of course, if you measured my life with successes and failures, the scales of justice would no doubt weigh heavier on the latter. After all, Kardobahn, our Alpha for the past seven centuries, was dead. I had failed Kaj in that regard. Hell, I'd failed them all because I could not stop the shadow beasts from wiping out the entire camp.

Here, as I stood before the race's new Alpha, it was impossible not to notice the transformation that had taken place in the male who was now the most powerful vampire in existence, the ruler of our race. The past year and a half had taken its toll on Kaj, worn him down. Those brilliant green eyes held shadows of his loss, the pain he'd endured. I felt responsible for some of those shadows, for some of that pain.

"We should move below ground," Kaj said. "The space isn't much, but we'll be safe there until nightfall."

I glanced at Blāz, nodded.

The male was on his feet, marching to the door in the floor that led down to the space below. A few minutes later, Blāz returned, nodding his approval. We would be safe there for the time being. A vacant metal structure in the center of a town populated by humans wasn't the best of accommodations as far as protecting Kaj went, but beggars couldn't be choosers. For now, this was our only option. In a way, it was better than the last building Kaj had taken us to before we separated so I could gather the others. A bit easier to defend, in my opinion.

"Can I speak to you for a moment, *phaal*?" I requested once the other three males had gone below to get settled.

Kaj turned to face me, smiled. The breath he released was one of relief, not frustration, but it drew me up all the same.

"It's so fucking good to have you here."

Those few words did it, spoken in that grateful tone... I was overwhelmed by emotions, the ones I'd been shoving down deep for so long now. Concern, uncertainty, sorrow, even fear. I'd never given up on his search for Kaj, never would have, so this was a relief beyond anything I could've expected, and it was almost too much for my brain to process.

Dropping to my knee before the leader of the race, I ducked my head. "*I'm not worthy of you, my Alpha,*" I said in our native tongue. "*I have failed you, but should you find it in your heart to forgive me, I pledge to you my loyalty, my strength, my very soul, from now until my dying breath.*"

A firm hand rested atop my head, and I inhaled a deep breath.

"There's nothing to forgive," Kaj replied softly. "You've never let me down, Mirakel. You couldn't. Now stand, warrior."

I drew myself up to my full height, met Kaj's warm stare.

"I won't fail you," I promised, the words pitched low and laced with the gravelly emotion that coated my throat.

Kaj nodded. "As of this moment, I'm appointing you as my *adighrielin*. Do you accept the position that is bestowed upon you?"

Adighrielin. The Alpha's advisor, his right hand. More importantly, the most honorable position within the Zenith, that which was the first line of defense to the Alpha.

I had to clear my throat even as I bowed before Kaj. "It would be my honor, *phaal*."

There was a bit more throat clearing, but I noticed it wasn't only me. Kaj seemed to be having the same problem.

A firm hand curled around my neck, pulling me toward Kaj. Our foreheads met.

"I thought I lost you. I've missed you, brother," Kaj whispered in our language.

"I'm not that easy to get rid of," I said lightly, my chest tight, my throat clogged by emotion.

Though I'd pledged to serve the leader of my race, Kaj was more than that to me. I had looked up to him my entire life. It wasn't until our lives had intertwined that I felt whole for the first time. As though I belonged. Having been turned out at birth, discarded by those who should've cared for me, I hadn't had a family until Kaj. These past few months, the only thing that kept me from walking right out into the sun and letting that blazing ball of fire claim me was my desire to find him. I'd held on to hope that he had not been stolen from me and that hope had paid off.

"The sun'll be up any minute," Kaj said, his voice a bit

steadier than before. "Let's get below ground. We need sleep if we plan to tackle the future come nightfall."

I nodded and squared my shoulders. "After you, *phaal*."

35

ORIANNA

I hadn't realized how disconnected I was with this house. Made some sense, considering I didn't grow up there.

No, when I thought of home, it was always the house we lived in before my mother's attack. The home we'd come to directly from the hospital. The one my mother had loved from the moment she saw it shortly after she married my father.

This house was nothing like that one.

It was familiar, sure, because I had visited my mother through the years, even come here during our approved leaves back when I was in school. It had never been my home, though, and that was never more apparent than now, when I found myself trapped there.

Well, technically, I wasn't trapped, but Eclipse was, so it was almost the same difference. It pained me to know that he was in the basement, unable to leave until the sun went down in—I peered at my watch—nine more hours. Lovely. I wasn't sure which was worse—him having to be down there or me having to be up here. Neither was a comforting thought.

"This sucks," I muttered as I strolled through the living room, the kitchen, down the hallway, back.

It had been my routine for the past hour, ever since Elizabeth finally drifted off in her chair. My mother looked so uncomfortable, but I wasn't about to suggest she get in bed. I'd done that once already, and my mother's ire had surprised me. Evidently, Elizabeth still believed she would be trapped indefinitely if she were to do that.

So, while she nodded off, I chose to wear the carpet and linoleum thin, pacing back and forth in an effort to stay awake. I probably should've taken the opportunity to sleep, but my brain was wired for sound, and I knew it wouldn't matter if I got horizontal, sleep wouldn't find me.

When I made another pass through the kitchen, I paused at the door to the basement. I wanted to go down, to see Eclipse, but I was fighting that urge, knowing if I did, the ache that had become an incessant throb within me would only get worse. The sexual tension seemed to have settled in, making me crave him more so than was appropriate. And it was constant, not abating completely, not even right after we made love.

Made love.

I honestly never thought I'd *make love* to anyone. Hell, I never figured I'd *find* love, but I had, hadn't I? With Eclipse.

Every so often, I found myself imagining a life with him. Waking up to him each night, falling asleep with him every morning. Breakfasts, dinners, holidays. The basics seemed simple. Coexisting in his world would be easy because I wanted to be there. But how could I possibly contribute? I had no skills, so what would I do for work? A convenience store clerk didn't seem appropriate, but not because I was above it. No, more so because of the dangers lurking out there. I didn't truly understand what the vampires wanted with me, why they had lured me to that club, but based on Eclipse's reaction to the news, it wasn't so they could get their swerve on.

I paused in the kitchen, my gaze swinging to the basement door. The heat was building, and I knew it had nothing to do with me hoofing it from one room to another. My body longed for Eclipse's, and ignoring it would only make me insane.

Ah, damn.

I opened the door to the basement, slipped inside, and carefully maneuvered down the rickety stairs. It was dark, save for a glimmer of light coming from Miklós's laptop in the far corner. Part of me expected to find all three of them passed out cold, sleeping because it was daytime, and that was when the mansion usually went into dream mode.

"Is everything all right?" Eclipse's voice came from the alcove beneath the stairs.

The glow of his eyes was what I used to see by. "Yes."

"You've been pacing," he said, motioning for me to join him.

I took his hand, allowed him to guide me down onto his lap. I straddled his extended legs, sliding my hands over his rock-hard chest, up to the warm skin of his neck. Just touching him settled something within me even as it fanned the flames of my libido.

"My mother's finally asleep, and I've been keeping an eye out for my father."

His warm hands caressed my face gently, as though he'd missed me in the short time I'd been away from him. His touch soothed while, at the same time, sending my heart into a gallop. It was insane how much I wanted him, how desperate I could feel. When he guided my head toward his, I shifted, angling so my lips could find their mate. I loved how I fit against him, how perfect it felt to be in his arms, as though he was made just for me.

Eclipse's kiss was gentle but persistent. I could taste his hunger, and it started that familiar hum beneath my skin. The way he penetrated me with his tongue, slipping inside, grazing mine. Reverent, sweet, but underneath was an undeniable hunger. I relished the moments we could do this. Make out like teenagers, hands roaming, tongues dancing. The amount of time I'd been with him felt more like years than mere weeks, every passing hour solidifying my feelings for him to the point I could no longer see a life without him in it.

When he pulled back, his hands went to my face, holding me so I was peering into his eyes.

I need you, Orianna.

I heard the words in my mind, knew he was projecting them there.

Despite the fact my body was clearly on board, my brain shifted to Magnar and Miklós, who were on the other side of the room, probably not even ten yards away.

Do you trust me, sezari?

Of course I did.

I nodded, held his stare.

Take off your shirt.

Giving myself over to Eclipse was easy. I did trust him. Not only with my body but also with my heart.

It still felt taboo because there were others nearby, but I couldn't refuse his request. I pulled back enough to do as he asked, loving the way his silver eyes glowed as he watched me. Without him having to ask, I discarded my bra as well.

A soft rumble escaped him as his eyes caressed me like a physical touch. His approval was what I longed for, and when

456

he gave it so freely, I knew I was lost, completely and totally done for.

His eyes shifted to my face momentarily before he cupped my breasts and lifted them. His lips met mine as he teased, his big hands kneading, plumping, sending my nerve endings toward an inevitable riot. He kissed my lips, then glided them over my jaw, my neck, lower. A gasp escaped me when his tongue glided over one nipple, then the other. I sucked in air, the warmth of his mouth making chills dance over my skin. It took effort not to cry out when he nipped me with his teeth, but I could do nothing to stop the rasp of my breaths. Eclipse feasted on my breasts for long, delicious minutes while I ran my fingers over the shorn hair at the sides of his head.

He paused long enough to instruct me to remove my leggings, which I did awkwardly as I straddled his thighs, my breasts still pressed to his mouth. Eclipse assisted, dragging the stretchy fabric down, making it easier for me to get them off.

"Panties, too," he whispered.

My eyes widened, fear that Miklós or Magnar would know what we were doing.

"They can't see or hear us now, *sezari*."

I wasn't sure how he managed that, but I wasn't about to question him.

When I was naked, he resumed laving me, licking and sucking my nipples, working me into a frenzy until I was desperate for him. He continued to torment and tease while I freed the button on his jeans, but that was as far as I could go because of his position. Thankfully, Eclipse took over, shoving his jeans down while I yanked his shirt up.

I was in awe of his hard body. All that sleek, bronze skin stretched over so much muscle and sinew. He was perfection, all smooth planes and hard angles. I recalled all those hours spent in his bed, my hands wandering and roaming, exploring.

"Ride me, *sezari*," he whispered against my ear. "I need to be inside you."

I was surprised I didn't orgasm from his words alone.

He guided his erection against my hot center while I sank down on him.

A moan slipped up my throat as my body adjusted to his glorious girth. He filled me easily, my pussy slick and eager for him. Once I was seated with him fully inside me, I began to move, bringing us both the ecstasy we sought. It started with me lifting and lowering on him and ended with me rocking my hips forward and back while Eclipse latched on to my neck, his fangs sinking into my vein.

Never in my life had I imagined so much ecstasy could be had. Thanks to human myths and lore, fangs were there to score and drain, vampires the epitome of evil and death. Knowing what I did, I wondered who had put those rumors in play. Because this ... Eclipse's fangs in my neck ... oh, God, it was heaven.

I sighed as the exquisite sensations washed over me. There was no stopping my orgasm, my body suspended in that sublime state for long minutes as he fed from me and filled me at the same time.

By the time he was licking the wound closed, I was hanging by a thread, in desperate need of more. Eclipse must've felt it, too, because he quickly shifted our positions. There was a brief chill as he separated our bodies, turning me so I was facing away from him. When I was on my knees, Eclipse behind me, he pushed deep inside me again and drove us both to the precipice. His fingers curled around my shoulders as he held on, this time riding me. I hung there, suspended on the razor's edge for long seconds, and when Eclipse slammed into me one final time, his fingertips digging in, I came as he did.

Due to our circumstances and location, there was no cuddling afterward. Just the cold separation of our bodies. Feeling slightly exposed because we weren't alone, I fumbled around for my clothes. When I located them all, I hurried to dress, then returned to Eclipse's arms, where I wanted to remain for the rest of the day but knew I couldn't.

"You should get some sleep," I told him, running my fingers over his cheeks, enjoying the feel of his stubble.

"Can't sleep," he mumbled against my neck. "Not without you beside me." Eclipse lifted his head. "When night falls, we need to head back. Do you think your mother will go with us willingly?"

I shrugged. It was what I hoped to talk to Elizabeth about, but I needed my mother to be alert, not immersed in that drug-induced fog she lived in.

"She needs you to look after her," Eclipse said, as though reading my mind.

"I want to introduce you to her. When night falls. I know that's against the rules, but..." I smiled. "I really want my mother to know you, Eclipse."

"I can persuade her to go with us if you'd like."

I should've probably been surprised that he was willing to break the rules for me. I wasn't. If nothing else, I trusted what we felt for one another.

I knew he had all sorts of magical abilities, and though I was hesitant for him to use them to manipulate my mother, I wasn't sure there was any other way.

Suddenly Eclipse pulled back, his eyes closing. "There's a male here," he said softly. "Just pulled in the driveway."

It pained me to pull away, but I needed to be upstairs when

Erik came to the door. I wasn't about to let him in if I could help it.

"Orianna."

With one foot on the bottom step, I turned back. The tortured look on Eclipse's face spoke volumes. He hated not being able to protect me and it physically hurt him.

"I'll be fine," I assured him. "I've been on my own for a long time, Eclipse. I know what I'm doing."

His silver eyes caressed my face before he offered a clipped nod.

Without looking back, I hurried up the stairs, my stomach wobbling when the stairs seemed to do the same. When I reached the door, I exhaled my relief, then stepped into the house.

No sooner had I closed the basement door than a heavy knock sounded from the front of the house. The knob was turning as I approached.

"What do you want?" I asked, yanking the door open before Erik could.

My father's eyes widened as he stared back at me, clearly surprised to see me. "Orianna, baby." A smile pulled at his haggard face. "It's so good to see you."

Using my body, I blocked his entrance. "Why are you here?"

Erik peered beyond me into the house. "Your mother asked me to stop by."

"No, she didn't."

His blue eyes lowered to my face, and I saw the shift. Gone was the pleasant father who missed his daughter. In his place, the desperate, angry man who'd bled my mother dry, stealing her money so he could fund his addiction to booze and gambling.

"I need to talk to my wife," Erik demanded, stepping forward.

I didn't budge. "She's asleep right now."

His eyes narrowed. "You mean she's doped? Because that's the only state she's ever in, Orianna. You'd know if you cared to stay with her."

Fury raged in my veins; this altercation was a long time coming. "Fuck you," I snapped. "I'm the only one who's taken care of her."

His lip curled in a snarl. "Yeah? Traipsing across the country looking for your failure of a sister? That's what you call taking care of her?"

"Well, while we're laying blame"—I met his hard stare—"who's the one who put her in that fucking chair?"

"That's not fair, Orianna. I had nothing to do with that."

"Bullshit. You're the reason for all of it, *Dad*. You single-handedly tore this family apart. And now look at us."

Erik's eyes narrowed, but he didn't say a word.

I was about to scream at him when I heard car doors shutting outside. I managed to peer around my father just as two police officers were stepping out of their vehicles. Their keen gazes were scanning the area, searching for a threat.

Erik grinned. "I do believe they're here for a welfare check. Perhaps we should be the ones to decide whether or not it's safe for her to be here."

Fucking hell.

36

ECLIPSE

I shot upright, shoulders tense, fangs extending from my jaw. For the past forty-five minutes, I'd remained still, my senses scanning the goings-on upstairs. I listened to two males converse, one calm, the other demanding, while a third talked in soft tones with Orianna.

The topic: Elizabeth, of course.

More accurately, Elizabeth's need for help for her addiction and the fact it wasn't safe for her to remain in the home by herself.

Orianna had been livid, but my *amsouelot* had controlled her temper, remaining rational in her attempt to sway them to her side.

It hadn't worked.

"She's gone," I growled, the words sounding feral.

"Eclipse..." Miklós's tone was firm, as though he could possibly keep me in control by simply saying my name.

"She's. Gone." My eyes burned so bright the entire basement glittered in the silver hue.

"We will get her back." Magnar's words were a promise.

From the instant I heard all those footsteps banging around upstairs, I knew I should've done something. At the very least, I could've erected a barrier around the house, making it impossible for those fucking cops to leave. Instead, I'd considered Orianna's feelings on the matter, and now they were all fucking gone. Orianna, her mother, that bastard father.

"Breathe," Magnar growled, the command harsh.

I attempted to do just that but failed. I was fucking trapped in this godforsaken basement for the foreseeable future, and I had no fucking clue where Orianna was. I had no way of getting in touch with her despite the fact all three of us had cell phones. No one had the sense to give her the damn numbers.

"Hey, man, I'm calling to let you know of a situation."

I was barely aware of Miklós rambling on, getting whoever was on the other end of that call up to speed. Not that it would matter. No one at the mansion could go out in the sunlight, either. Not unless they wanted to coerce one of the *heurosp* into helping out. And the last thing we needed was another human in the mix.

I paced over to the far side of the basement, planted my hands on the washing machine, and braced myself there. It wasn't until Magnar shouted from behind me that I realized I was denting the damn thing with the strength of my hands.

This wasn't happening. Orianna was not gone. She was just ... out there somewhere. With her mother. Taking care of the situation.

I breathed in through my nose, out through my mouth.

What if the demons planned this? Without my soul tethered to hers, they could claim her as theirs, essentially taking me with her. Not that I gave a shit about the last part. Without Orianna, my world would cease to exist. Precisely what Taayin was going through now.

"Thanks, Reidar. Let me know what you find out."

I turned to look at my *lieterra*, waiting for some fabulous news that would get us all out of this fucked-up situation.

"It's not the best plan in the world, but..." Miklós moved closer. "Kaj knows a couple of humans who've helped him out in the past. They can be here in an hour, which is a hell of a lot sooner than we can get out of here."

"Kaj?" I frowned.

Miklós nodded. "When he didn't come back this morning, Obsidian called him to check in. The male asked for a favor. Wants to take up residence in the old mansion. Obsidian gave him the go-ahead but told him to expect him to call in a favor. This is him calling it in."

Lovely. I could only imagine what sort of humans dallied with the fucking vampires.

"It's the only option we've got," Miklós stated.

I hated that the male was right.

"Plus, I took the liberty of putting a tracker in Orianna's cell phone."

My head snapped up. "You can call her?"

"Not exactly. However, Kandarie is doing some work to get the number. In the meantime..." Miklós turned his laptop around.

"What the fuck am I looking at?" I grumbled.

"At least we know where she is. That's a city-run hospital. My guess is Orianna's father convinced them to hold Elizabeth for seventy-two hours. It's not surprising that Orianna would go with her."

Yeah, but she could've at least told me first.

Then again, it would've drawn attention to us, the police would've had questions, and since Elizabeth had no knowledge of our presence ... yeah, it could've been ugly. No wonder Orianna caved to their request.

I managed to breathe in deeply, exhale slowly. Some of the fire in my blood simmered down, the risk of an inferno being snuffed out. At least temporarily.

The sound of a door opening overhead drew our attention upward.

Miklós closed the computer lid at the same time I killed the lights with my mind.

"My name's still on the deed."

Orianna's father. He was back.

"Yep. Free and clear."

I had no idea who the human was talking to, but based on the muffled response, he was alone. Which meant he was on the phone.

"The house is paid for. It's got to be a quick sell. Cash only. As-is."

Son of a bitch. The bastard was a real tool. Selling the house right out from under his crippled wife.

"Between that and the life insurance policy I've got on Amber ... yeah, I'll be able to cover my debt."

The bastard. He knew Amber was dead?

More muffled chatter ensued.

"Then we'll be square, right? And since Amber's no longer a problem, you'll call off your dogs?" There was a lengthy pause, followed by, "No. Orianna's not gonna be an issue. If she tries to interfere, I know who to call to get her out of the way." More air. "Yeah. I know. You won't see or hear from me again."

No one would. I would make damn sure of it.

I glanced over at Magnar. Without saying a word or

implanting any thoughts, I expressed exactly what I felt about the subject. Magnar nodded, the only response needed to confirm he understood what I expected once we got out of this fucking basement.

By the time the sun lowered enough that I wouldn't be turned to ash, I was hanging by a very fragile thread. Without giving a shit as to who might be waiting upstairs, I slammed my way through the door and into the kitchen.

"I want everything packed up. Fast. Get it back to the mansion," I ordered Miklós. "And Magnar...?"

"Got it, boss."

With a nod, I vanished, taking form at the coordinates my *lieterra* had given me. It was all I could do to cloak myself when I walked into the hospital, ensuring the humans weren't aware of my presence. I stormed through the main waiting room, then went one by one in the various sections of the hospital until I found Orianna. She was sitting in the cafeteria, staring down at her phone as though she could will it to ring in her hands.

I backtracked to a vacated hallway and dropped the cloak before returning to her.

I wasn't quite ten feet away when two human males stood from their spots and headed right for me. Beneath those leather dusters, I could see the outline of their weapons. And based on the way they moved, they knew how to use them.

It was then that Orianna lifted her head and glanced over, tears pooling in her eyes as she shot to her feet and raced into my arms.

The two males backed off instantly but didn't leave.

"I didn't need bodyguards," she said, her face pressed against my chest. "But thank you, anyway."

I met the gaze of the taller one, nodding. There were no words, but their expressions said it all. They'd fulfilled their favor to Kaj.

"They refuse to let her go, Eclipse," she said when we were alone. "Forcing her to do all these tests. Like an animal. I can't believe he would do this to her. After all the shit he's put her through."

"We'll get her out of here."

"They said they can hold her for seventy-two hours."

When she pulled back and met my eyes, I offered the hint of a smile. "I've got ways around that, *sezari*. Don't you worry about it."

The way her eyes lit up settled something in my chest. It erased the anxious worry that had plagued me for hours. But at the same time, it solidified a few things for me, and I knew once we got back to the mansion, there were things I had to address with her. Things that would ultimately change Orianna's life forever.

"I've got Miklós packing up your mother's house." I went on to explain the conversation I overheard, leaving out the bits about Amber.

As expected, Orianna's response was arctic. Her anger was so potent I could feel it coming off her, washing over me.

Tilting her head up with my finger on her chin, I met her gaze and held it. "Trust me to take care of it, *sezari*."

"I do," she whispered. "I do trust you, I just..."

I could see a million questions brewing, but I shook my head. "It's best you don't know the details. But we do need to get your mother out of here. I've got Echo on the way to escort her back to Darkness."

"I should go with her."

"It's safer for both of you if you don't."

"I can take care of myself," she countered hotly, clearly not amused by my desire to handle the situation.

"And I'm not arguing that point. But we've got some issues going down with vampires right now that directly affect the *amsouelots*. The less time we're away from the mansion, the better off everyone is."

"What issues?"

I didn't have all the details on the vampire traitors, but I told Orianna what I'd learned from Obsidian regarding Darko and his attempt to overthrow the Alpha. Thankfully, it seemed to be enough to appease her, if only temporarily.

"Your mother's safe with Echo and Cayden. They'll get her back with as little interaction as possible. If they leave now, they'll make it to Darkness before sunrise."

"And us?" Orianna asked.

"We're not driving this time, *sezari*."

"Then—"

Taking her hand, I cut her off with a request for her to take me to her mother. I figured it was probably best not to let her know that I intended to evanesce her physical form and return her to the mansion that way. Not only was it not a traditional form of travel, it was also going to be slightly painful. For her.

But it sure as hell beat the alternative.

ACADIA

I was surprised there wasn't a cloud of arctic air in my wake as I marched through the mansion, down the stairs, and along the wide hallway that bisected the subterranean chambers. I'd spent the past half hour talking myself into this confrontation, and the moment I set my mind to it, I felt the shift within me.

"Where is he?" I demanded when I stopped directly in front of the war room entrance.

The enormous male currently commanding those within slowly glanced back over his shoulder.

"You're up early," Obsidian said, his tone casual, as though the demand hadn't actually snapped from my mouth.

"Where is he?" I repeated.

There was enough icy chill that time to have all eyes shifting to me. Expressions ranged from surprise to disbelief.

Good. My goal was to get their attention. It wasn't like me to make demands on the males I serviced, but I'd spent the entire day attempting to sleep while knowing Kaj was some-where else. The male didn't return to the mansion last night, though he promised me he would return before he ventured out on whatever clandestine mission he'd set in motion.

"Acadia?" Obsidian sounded like he was attempting to soothe a wild animal.

"Don't placate me, Obsidian. Where is Kaj?"

After rumbling something to the others, the male raised a hand, motioning me toward the hall. Lifting my skirts, a move that was second nature, seemed strangely stifling at the moment. Why did I wear these dresses again?

Once Obsidian made his way over, I pivoted, then stormed out of the war room. Probably would've had more impact if I had shoes on, but ... well, I didn't like shoes. Never had.

"What's wrong?" Obsidian's voice was low and edged with concern.

"Kaj. He's gone. Where is he?"

"I talked to him early this morning," he explained, his tone soothing, relaxed. "I called to check on him. He wasn't able to make it back before the sun came up. But he's fine. He'll probably stroll in any minute now."

I hated that I was worried about the male. It angered me that he brought out these feelings, made me actually care about him. I didn't want to have feelings for him. Of any kind. Least of all ... love.

"I expect you to keep me apprised," I insisted.

Obsidian's eyebrows rose above the dark shades that covered his eyes.

"I apologize," I added quickly, lowering my gaze respectfully. "I don't mean to be ... like this."

"Is there something between you and Kaj?"

I knew the question would come sooner or later. "Of course not."

It was a lie, something I swore never to do to Obsidian, but I had no desire for him to know what was going on—not that there was anything. But still, I had a strange desire to keep my ... whatever it was Kaj invoked in me ... from unraveling. The more people who knew, the more chaotic things would get.

"You know I can read you, right?"

I huffed. It was a truly un-Fae-like thing to do, but I couldn't bring myself to care.

"Fine," I blurted. "I've been feeding him. And I ... well, I got the sense he was in trouble. So I wanted to be sure."

Obsidian stared at me, clearly not believing a word coming

out of my mouth, but oh, well. I was in a mood, and he would just have to deal. He knew me better than anyone else because I'd been with him since the beginning of our mission, some fifteen hundred years ago. We'd been through everything together, all the ups and downs. Granted, most of my ups and downs were more like gently rolling hills, not this mountain-versus-valley thing I had going on now.

"I've known Kaj a long time, Acadia. And I've been immersed in the vampire world, so I know what happens when—"

I lifted my hand. "Do not say it." I shook my head. "Do not tell me he's bonded with me. It's just not true, and I'm—"

"He's asked to move into the old place."

My eyes widened, my jaw falling open. "What?"

"Kaj wants to reside outside of these walls."

"Why?"

"Because he's the vampire Alpha, Acadia. Being under this roof with males who will not, under any circumstance, submit to his will... For a vampire, that's not easy. Especially him. He needs space from us, but he wants to remain close."

"And Bijou?"

"He'd prefer she stay here. At least until he can get back to some semblance of normalcy."

"Who'll live there with him?" Not that I cared. Really. I didn't.

"From what I gather, he's located some of the Zenith."

But I thought they'd all been killed in the raids. At least, that was what we'd learned on the Misplaced Halos message boards. Not exactly CNN, but it gave us insight into what was happening for those species that humans didn't know existed.

"Hey, Obsidian? You got a minute?"

I waved him off. "Go. Take care of that. I ... uh ... I just need some time to myself."

"You sure? I'm here, Acadia. Anytime you want to talk."

"I know."

I turned away from him, needing a minute for everything to sink in. Although I wasn't convinced any amount of time would allow for that to happen, it was imperative I get my thoughts in order.

Otherwise, I had no chance of confronting Kaj. About anything.

Least of all, whatever this was between us.

37

REIDAR

"She cool?" I asked Obsidian when the big boss man strolled back into the war room.

Obsidian waved me off, as usual. "She's fine. A little antsy, but she's worried about Kaj."

"That male can take care of himself," I assured him.

"I know that, and you know that, but Acadia ... she's not seeing him the same way we are."

Because she was looking through the rosy veil of her feelings for the male. I got it. More so than I wanted to admit. The way things stood between me and Winnie had me feeling like I was free-falling without wings to slow my descent. And though I'd managed to hold Winnie off for the time being, I was merely biding my time. Or wasting hers, as Winnie had told me that evening when I woke.

Not that she was wrong. However, wiping out entire sections of her memory wasn't something I was looking forward to. I blamed myself for jumping the gun, for getting her into this mess in the first place. If I'd simply done my damn job and kept an eye on her from afar, Winnie never would've known I existed, and she damn sure wouldn't have been immersed in a world that technically wasn't supposed to be real according to human lore.

"Can you get me a location on Kaj?"

Obsidian's voice registered, pulling me out of my scrambled thoughts and back to the task at hand.

"Last we picked up on him, he was hunkered down in an abandoned warehouse nearby," I informed him.

"Good. That means he's close. And Michael?"

I peered over at the male. "What about him?"

"Is he here?"

I frowned. "Why would he be?"

Obsidian exhaled heavily. "I need some face time with my brothers. By the end of the week."

"Can I tell them what it's about?"

"I'll let it be a surprise."

Great. I knew how much the warriors enjoyed surprises.

It was the work of a moment to get the schedules aligned so that the brothers would all be under one roof and the missions to find the *amsouelots* would not be interrupted more than they already had been. As it was, the search for Asmia had taken precedence, but the urgency for finding those females belonging to the warriors was equally important. Considering the repercussions if Lucifer were to get his hands on one of them...

Why was it that everything seemed to be out of control right now? It was as though chaos had settled over the mansion and was doing its best to stir shit up. Not quite a year ago, we'd spent our nights fighting demons, seeking them out rather than being on the defensive. These days, demons were the least of our worries, save for those who were slated to find the *amsouelots*, Perfidious having been at the top of that most-wanted list. Now, we were looking for him for an entirely different reason.

I thought back to Winnie's demand that I leave the mansion, otherwise she was going without me. I had to wonder whether I would've been able to agree even if she was my *amsouelot*. The thought of leaving my family behind...

With a heavy exhale, I turned my attention to the others in the room. Now was not the time for my personal bullshit to get in the way. I'd deal with that later.

Much later, if I was lucky.

PERFIDIOUS

"You look lovely this evening," I told Asmia when the female stood to greet me.

Although it'd been nearly a week since I started with the mind-control efforts, I wasn't taking any chances with my sweet Fae. Until I could trust she wasn't going to slit my throat while I slept, I figured it best she remained behind these solid bars, protected deep within the mountain. Which meant I was still sleeping alone, something I wasn't all that fond of.

"I'd prefer to see you without the dress, though," I told her.

Asmia's black eyes glittered as a smile pulled at her mouth. Without hesitation, she quickly slipped the black silk from her body. The fact she wore nothing beneath pleased me immensely.

It was all I could do not to shove her to the ground and mount her from behind. My cock raged with the need to claim her, but I was refraining for now. The first time I took her would be something we would remember for the rest of our days, so I figured there was no reason to rush. This was just the beginning for us.

"The angels have called off their search for you," I lied, keeping my voice even. "They've cast you aside, moved on to more important things. I thought you should know."

There was no reaction on her part. Not so much as a grimace on those lovely features.

"You knew that was going to happen, though. You're nothing but an employee to them, a servant." I paused behind her, sliding my finger down her spine. "How does that make you feel?"

"It doesn't," she replied softly.

"You don't care about them anymore?"

"No."

I smiled, then leaned in and brushed my lips to her shoulder. "That's good. I'm the only one you should be worried about. I'm the one who'll care for you, Asmia, keep you safe. You know that, right?"

"Yes."

I tried to pretend the robotic responses didn't bother me. It was temporary. For now I would continue to control her mind, keep her enslaved to me that way. It was necessary while I chipped away at those loyalties of hers. Before long, I would have her defeated, feeling like she was nothing. At that point, I planned to build her back up, mold her into the perfect queen.

In the meantime, I was waiting for my request to be approved. It was a gamble, but I sought Lucifer's approval in aligning our souls. The king of Hell hadn't gotten back to me yet, but I knew my request was being considered.

"Are you hungry, gorgeous?" I strolled around to stand in front of her. "Would you like to feed from me?"

Her eyes remained straight forward, locking on my face. "Yes."

"Say please."

"Please, Perfidious, may I feed from you?"

I untied the sash that held my smoking jacket closed, then let the silk fall open, revealing my chest. I happened to be quite fond of the human I acquired recently. One of the best I'd come across in quite some time. However, I was starting to wonder why I even bothered. Eventually Asmia would need to get acquainted with my true form. The human husk wouldn't survive in Hell, so I would have to leave it behind.

"Come to me," I ordered, maintaining my position a few feet away.

When she stepped forward, I braced myself for her touch. Those soft hands flattened on my chest, and no sooner did they make contact than I felt that flood of euphoria. It was almost better than sex, the way her body siphoned my energy. I'd done some reading on the subject and learned that the Fae fed from emotional energy, not merely strength. It was a peculiar phenomenon, but it intrigued me.

As I stood there, my cock throbbed, tenting the fly of my silk pants, pulsating with the need to find entrance into her lovely body.

Soon, I reminded myself. Only a little while longer, and this gorgeous female would be ripe for the taking. In the meantime, I was going to keep her nourished and under my spell.

"Stop," I demanded.

Her hands instantly fell to her sides, her eyelids lifting to reveal her black irises. That beautiful amethyst color seemed to have disappeared completely beneath the shadow of my mind control.

It wouldn't be much longer before her entire existence would be erased, hidden from those who were still beating feet to find her. Those angels were like bulldogs. They didn't seem to know when to quit, which had caused only a few problems for me in recent days. Luckily, I had access to humans who were keeping the angels busy and looking the other way.

Sooner or later, they would realize the same thing I did: this creature belonged to me.

And I damn sure wasn't about to let her go. Not without one hell of a fight.

38

OLIVER

"Nope," I said with a chuckle. "Not that one. The eight ball goes in last."

"Why?" Bijou asked, her gaze cast over the pool table.

"Those are the rules."

I watched as she considered her next move, her hand curled around the end of the stick as she studied the solids and stripes on the table. We'd been at this game for a good hour, mainly for this very reason. Bijou spent more time planning than doing.

Not that I minded. In fact, I found it fascinating. Then again, I found everything about Bijou fascinating.

There was no denying my mood had vastly improved since she moved into the mansion. Seeing her every day, even if it was just in passing, had given me a new lease on life. Almost as though I'd finally found where I belonged.

Of course, that was stupid. I was like a square peg being shoved into a round hole. I had nothing in common with a single soul here, but that was no longer something I focused on. I wanted to say it was all thanks to Bijou, but I wasn't sure that was the truth. Since Reidar had given me a job to do—a true-blue paying job—adding additional tasks day by day, urging me to think outside the box and contribute to their mission, that odd-man-out feeling was starting to abate.

"What about this one?" Bijou pointed at the three-ball.

"Sure. Go for it."

I admired her as she leaned over the table, her lean body shifting and moving until she was where she wanted to be. Bijou was, by far, the most beautiful woman ... *vampire* I'd ever set my eyes upon. Quite the opposite of any of the women I'd ever been attracted to. I could admit I'd always had a thing for chicks with an edge. Probably the reason I'd taken to Seraphina. Because I'd mistakenly believed her to be a stripper, I hadn't worried I would offend her delicate sensibilities.

With Bijou, I found I wanted to be a better man. In the short time we'd been hanging out, I managed to cut back on the cursing, and though I was still polishing off every bottle of Belvedere I could get my hands on, they were lasting a little longer than normal. Cold turkey wasn't my thing, but I figured I'd earned an A for effort.

I smiled when the cue ball sailed toward the three, sending it to the right corner pocket ... just not quite *in* the pocket. Had she put a little power behind that shot, Bijou would've sunk it. Then again, we'd already had to replace two cue balls when she impaled them with the stick. Her strength had shocked me.

"I want to go for a swim," she said as she passed me.

"What's stopping you?" I asked, leaning over and taking

aim at the ten ball. I reared back and took the shot, sending it to the corner pocket.

"Will you go with me?"

I peered over at her. "I thought you liked to swim alone."

That was what she told me the first time I offered to go with her.

"I lied."

"All you have to do is ask, Bijou. I've got the night off, so I'm happy to hang with you."

Hell, I would've followed her anywhere. Which was the problem and the very reason I was keeping my distance. For my own sanity, really. I was well aware of my reputation when it came to women. *Slam, bam, thank you, ma'am* was my mantra. Or it had been. Then I met Seraphina, and I mistakenly believed there might be more than a quick roll. Then I learned I'd been banging a demon and...

"Are you okay?" Bijou's soft hand landed on my arm.

I gently eased my arm away from her touch. "Fine."

"You look pale."

Yeah, well, thinking about Seraphina tended to do that. Especially since I'd gotten a glimpse of what she looked like without the skin of a human covering her. I still saw that image in my nightmares, woke up in a cold sweat because ... that was just nasty.

"So you'll swim with me?"

"Sure."

Her smile was so wide I got a flash of fangs. That strange sensation—like someone had tossed sparklers into my chest cavity—had me gripping the side of the table. I figured it was some strange fetish because that would be just like me. I was a man-whore, no doubt about it. Never mind that I was doing my level best to keep my sights off the sweet, lovely vampire I was spending my time with. So it made total sense that I'd find some kind of sexual fascination with those sharp canines. The thought of Bijou sinking those razor-sharp teeth into my—

"I'm going to grab a snack first. Then I'll go get changed," Bijou said. "Meet you down there?"

Shaking off the crude image superimposed in my head, I nodded. "Yep."

My gaze shifted to her denim-clad ass as she strolled out of the game room, disappearing into the hall.

I exhaled as I replaced the stick on the wall, then gathered all the balls into the rack, leaving them in place for whoever came to play after us.

I rubbed a hand over my stomach, attempting to ease my intestines. I wasn't sure what was causing the ruckus, but for the past few days, I'd felt ... I wouldn't so much say I was sick, but there was definitely something up. The more time I spent with Bijou, the worse it seemed to get. At first I'd mistaken it for desire. Because, duh, she did it for me in a major way.

But then the cramping started, as though my stomach was attempting to eat itself. It was almost like a hunger pain. On steroids.

"Probably nerves," I muttered as I stepped into my bedroom, closing the door behind me.

That made me smile. Me? Nervous? No way. Not when it came to chicks.

Then again, stranger things had happened.

ORIANNA

I hugged the toilet, my face pale and clammy, sweat beading on my brow.

It was the same position I'd been in for the past few hours, ever since we returned to the mansion. More specifically, ever since Eclipse turned me into a mist and relocated me back to his private quarters.

"*Sezari?*"

"Hmm?" No matter how hard I tried, I couldn't lift my head from where it rested on my forearm. It was hard enough to lift my eyelids, much less the heavier parts of my body.

"I am *so* sorry," he said for the thousandth time.

I wanted to tell him not to be, but until my molecules realigned to the same spot they'd been before he ghosted me out of Oklahoma, I couldn't string that many words together.

My stomach heaved, my head bobbing as I stared down into the clear water in the bowl. My eyes closed as my body attempted to expel my stomach. I was convinced that was all that was left because everything else was long gone by now.

A cool rag covered my forehead and I sighed, turning my head on my arm. The toilet flushed thanks to Eclipse, but I knew a *heurosp* was pacing the hallway, eager to get in here to clean up so neither of us had to.

I wanted nothing more than to fall into bed and sleep for a millennium, but until I could get my body under control, relocating was only going to make it worse.

Eclipse squatted down beside me. "I've got Reidar trying to find a human doctor."

I managed a smile. A human doctor? What were they going

to do? I seriously doubted there was a cure for motion sickness induced by teleporting.

And to think, Eclipse had warned me it might be uncomfortable.

That was the freaking understatement of the year.

Uncomfortable was wearing jeans to Thanksgiving dinner or riding a bus beside a woman with pointy elbows. This... It was as though my brain had registered that I'd been splintered into the ether, my chemical makeup splattered across time and space only to be pulled back together at the end. Yeah. I'd take sitting in a car for nine hours, thank you very much.

I couldn't imagine anything worse than this. Not the worst hangover in the world held a candle to having your body split apart and miraculously pieced back together.

The bad news? Well, that would be the fact that the magic reset button on my hormones had been pressed, and not only did I want to expel my innards, I also had a bad case of the wants. My body needed Eclipse's despite the fact I was in no shape to accommodate. Which I figured was part of the reason for the sweat on my brow.

A knock sounded, and then Eclipse was gone, leaving me to hug the toilet all by my lonesome. I could hear the soft rumble of voices followed by a click, more footsteps.

"I think we've got a solution."

I wanted to open my eyes to look, but my brain couldn't relay the information to my optic nerve, so I remained right where I was.

"It's morphine," he said simply. "It'll knock you out long enough for your equilibrium to return."

This time, I did conjure up enough energy to shake my head, rolling my forehead on my arm. No drugs for me. Nope. No way. Not after what I watched my mother go through for years.

A soft grumble was all I could get out.

"It'll help, *sezari*."

"No. Drugs."

I was feeling better. Really.

My attempt to lift my head resulted in another attempt for my body to expel my organs, but it didn't last nearly as long. Surely that was a good sign.

"If you won't take the drugs, let me put you under for a little while."

"No drugs," I forced through dry lips.

"No drugs. I swear."

I was about to ask what his intentions were, but then...

Lights. Out.

ECLIPSE

"She'll be fine," Aphotic said.

"Her body just needs to rest," Stygian added.

"Penelope survived it," Obsidian surmised.

I was aware of all the voices, but I had nothing to contribute. They could placate me all fucking night, wouldn't change the fact that I damn near killed my female. From the instant we'd taken form here at the mansion nearly twenty-four hours ago, I realized the error of my ways. Probably wouldn't have been a big deal if it hadn't been for the distance we covered in such a short time.

"It really wouldn't hurt to get a healer in here," Obsidian said, agreeing to my earlier request.

I peered over at my brothers as Aphotic spoke up.

"We can't afford another human knowing about us."

Stygian nodded in agreement. "He's right."

"Not a human doctor, then," Obsidian suggested.

I barked a laugh. "Then what? A vampire healer? How the hell will that help?"

"I was thinking more along the lines of an angel." Obsidian's tone said he didn't appreciate the fact we thought he was an idiot.

"And you know one?" Stygian inquired.

"No."

Which was the biggest issue of all. We'd never needed medical attention. Our powers were strong enough to heal one another, the need for an outside source unnecessary. The only time we'd ever run into issues was with the *fiestreigh*. From time to time, if me or my brothers weren't around, someone would require medical attention. Which was the very reason we kept the Fae on hand. Those males and females had more powers than me and my brothers and, thus far, had been able to manage taking care of any injuries.

"We've run into this issue before," Obsidian said, his silver gaze settling on my face. "When you were shot, remember?"

Oh, I remembered. I will never forget the sight of Penelope crumbling to her knees when Obsidian had removed the bullet from my shoulder. She had endured every ounce of my agony because it was transferred through her mate.

But Obsidian did have a point. Once we were all mated, we would be forsaking our females if we had to assist an injury. If we had someone in-house, so to speak, he or she could take care of whatever emergencies arose. Someone who was trained for that sort of thing.

"Not only that," Aphotic inserted, "but like it or not, we've got humans in our ranks now. Oliver, Winnie. We need someone familiar with the human makeup."

I didn't mention Orianna's mother, who was currently en route. Considering I had no place other than the mansion to put her, we were about to add one more to the headcount. But I'd be damned if I would apologize for it.

"Agree." Obsidian paced across the room, then paused.

I should've known what he was doing, but it wasn't until I heard the flutter of wings that I realized Obsidian had summoned Michael.

Heaven help us all. That male was spending more and more time here. In fact, I was surprised Michael hadn't commandeered his own crash pad so he could waste away the days, not only the nights.

The archangel took a quick look around, dark brows lowering. "Who died?"

I growled low in my throat, pinning the male with a hateful glare.

"Relax." Michael waved me off. "I'm well aware of the human and her ... issues."

Issues? I blew her apart, brought her back together, and now her body was rejecting itself.

Obsidian went on to explain the situation as well as tack on his request for a medical professional.

"Your request is for an angel to heal your humans?" Michael snorted as though the suggestion was ludicrous.

I planted my shoulder against the wall and listened as Obsidian made our case, listing out a handful of incidents that had required our healing powers in just the last couple of months. Though those seemed few and far between, to hear them laid out like that told me we required a healer far more often than I thought.

"Fine," Michael blurted, cutting Obsidian off mid-sentence. "You can have Apollo and Amethyst." Michael's silver gaze slowly slid over each of our faces. "Under one condition."

I rolled my eyes. The archangel never did anything without getting something in return. Which reminded me, I'd yet to learn what Obsidian put up as collateral for Michael's participation in uniting Taayin's and Asmia's souls.

"Our previous agreement still stands," Michael told Obsidian. "Within the time frame we previously outlined."

Clearly he hadn't forgotten about it.

"I know," Obsidian grumbled. "What's your stipulation?"

"You seven shall erect a training facility. Here in Darkness. Rather than undergo their training in Heaven, all new recruits will come here. Where the seven of you will bestow your knowledge and skills upon them."

I frowned, peering over at my brothers. Seriously? Michael wanted us to be … *teachers*?

"Each class will be made up of fifty to sixty males—"

"Why not females?" Shadow questioned, the words coming out in a snarl.

"Fine … and females, if there are any interested."

That last part was said on a huff of air, as though Michael couldn't believe there would be any females interested in taking up the fight here on Earth.

"You'll have one year for each class. Once they're in prime condition, they'll be returned for relocation."

"I'll need to discuss this with my brothers," Obsidian told him. "You'll have my answer by morning."

Michael nodded. His wings expanded and then he was gone.

"Training?" Aphotic snorted. "Is he serious? Us?"

I noticed Obsidian was peering over at Stygian. The two males had been responsible for training the rest of us, so they had the experience. Made sense that Michael would request them to be at the helm. But the rest of us? Who was going to hold up the fight if we were all in a classroom with our thumbs up our asses?

"Amethyst and Apollo?" Shadow grumbled. "Has anyone even seen them in the past five hundred years?"

"They've been helping with Michael's warrior offspring," Obsidian explained.

"That's why he wants us to resume the training down here?" Cimmerian noted.

"Yes," Obsidian agreed.

Unable to keep my mouth shut, I pushed off the wall, strolled toward my brothers, my eyes locked on Obsidian. "Before we take a vote, I think we deserve to know what agreement you and Michael came to. What did you have to promise him to get Taayin's and Asmia's souls aligned?"

All eyes turned to Obsidian, and I would go so far as to say they all weren't privy to this new development.

Obsidian held my gaze, but as was the case any time his back was to the wall, our oldest brother didn't say a word.

39

MICHAEL

"What ails you, sire?"

I cast a dismissive glance at the female. "You may go."

Her golden eyes widened, but she slid from beneath the silk sheets on my bed. In a hurry, she wrapped herself in her white silk robes and left me alone, per my request. With a sigh, I went to the windows overlooking the gardens below. Here in Heaven, everything was pristine and perfect, much the opposite of Earth, though, in some strange way, I could see the beauty of both realms. Oddly, I preferred the latter these days. Hadn't always been the case for me, though.

At one time, I had cherished my life in Heaven. But that

was long, long ago. I'd lost so much, and though I made efforts to fill the void in my heart, I knew I would never be as complete as I had once been. The closest I'd come to feeling whole was after Obsidian's creation. Those first years with the young male at my side had renewed my spirit, given me something to live for. Obsidian was my child for all intents and purposes, though I hadn't shared the birth with my female.

I swallowed the lump in my throat, forcing back the memories of my beloved. Those intrusive thoughts had no place here. My beautiful *ereswa* was no longer with me, lost forever despite the fact I knew she still breathed. Those breaths existed in Hell, alongside Lucifer, the male who had ripped her from my arms, only one of Lucifer's many betrayals but perhaps the most painful on a personal front.

Wispy white clouds drifted overhead, nothing more than smoke against the clear blue sky. Below was the expanse of the great mansion I called home. All white marble, sparkling in the never-ending light that contributed to its vibrancy. Inside its walls were thousands who had pledged their loyalty to God, the Almighty Creator, and had vowed to serve in whatever way necessary to ensure my father's creations led an oblivious existence. And as a means of repaying my debts to my father, I ensured their safety, cared for them, loved them. As much as I could, anyway.

My gaze shifted to the south. On the far side of the vast estate was the residence for those who devoted their existence to the creation of warriors. The strongest males and the most formidable females were hand-selected to reside there, paired by me, sometimes shifted around to suit my mood.

Time was irrelevant here, as was most everything else. I spent my days watching over my warriors, those I'd relegated to Earth, as well as those born to the archsires and archdams, the first hundred years of their lives molded so they were prepared for their duties.

Most of those males were soldiers, assigned to the *fiestreigh*, providing support to the seven males who proved stronger than all others. With the birth of every male, I prayed the young would be strong enough, resilient enough to lead an army of his own one day. Like Obsidian.

Unfortunately, my prayers had yet to be answered.

Or so I thought.

It wasn't until I observed Obsidian training with his brothers that I recognized the error of my ways. While I had given Obsidian life, I hadn't made him into the male he is today. No, Obsidian had thrived because of his brothers. It dawned on me that perhaps the way to build stronger males was to have them led by the strongest. While I wanted to believe I was that male, I knew that wasn't so. Not when it came to instilling those values that kept the males together, fighting for one another.

Perhaps it was deceitful, but I had grabbed hold of the opportunity that presented itself. I had waited centuries for Obsidian to call upon me, to request a favor. I should've known it would be one to save a member of his family, as I referred to the males and females who fought alongside him.

Now that his favor had been granted—Taayin's and Asmia's souls forever aligned—I could only wait while Obsidian maneuvered the rest of the pieces into position so that my plan would be set in motion.

It wouldn't be long now.

I hoped.

OBSIDIAN

I realized pacing had become a comfortable exercise these past few weeks. I did it to clear my mind, to process my thoughts, to deal with the frustrations that plagued me and my family. There seemed to be so many these days, but there was only one that had the ability to make me see red.

Small hands spread out over my back as I stared at the vast expanse of darkness laid out beyond the balcony where I stood.

"What's on your mind?" Penelope asked, her voice soft.

I breathed in deeply when she pressed her cheek to my back, her presence the only comfort I seemed to find these days.

"The future," I admitted. And all it encompassed.

There were so many changes coming for us, most dictated by Michael, laid at my feet so I could bring them to fruition.

Shifting, I drew Penelope to my side as I slid my arm over her shoulder, hugging her small frame to me.

"It's Michael, isn't it?"

I nodded, though she wasn't looking at me to see my response.

"What does he want now?"

"To reside here with us."

My *ereswa* pulled back, her golden eyes locking on my face. "Here? On Earth?"

Another nod.

"Have you told your brothers?"

"Not yet." Because I had no idea how to tell them I agreed to Michael's request to save Asmia and Taayin. In the grand scheme, it was a decision that would ultimately change everything. The structure of our very lives now rested on how I handled this.

"Why?" Her hand shifted to my chest. "Why does Michael wish to spend his time here?"

"I don't know."

"Perhaps he simply wants to be part of your life."

I peered down at Penelope. "I doubt that."

Her smile was sweet. "I don't. I know there's some animosity between your brothers and Michael, but as an unbiased bystander, I see how Michael looks at you. He doesn't see you as his creation, something he can control."

A disbelieving grunt was all I could muster.

"It's true." Penelope patted me over my heart. "Michael looks at you as a father would a son. I've seen it with my own eyes."

"Michael doesn't do anything without an agenda."

"Maybe not. But that doesn't mean his intentions aren't pure. At least as far as this is concerned."

"He wants my brothers and me to train the future factions," I told her. "I've requested he provide us with healers. In return, he expects us to train."

"But that's not what you want?"

I grunted. "I don't know what I want."

Aside from taking care of Penelope and our child, I was foggy about my future.

"You'd be a great trainer, Obsidian. All of you would."

"It's not the training that worries me."

"Then what does?"

I exhaled slowly. "We bring the trainees here, spend a year teaching them to fight, then what? I'm supposed to let them walk away, go off on their own? That's Michael's plan. He doesn't consider what comes along with all that time and effort."

"You'll worry about them," she said, hugging me tightly. "Tell him that. Let him know you'll expect to have a say in their future, not merely their training."

I didn't know what to say to that. I wasn't sure Michael would even care.

"It's the dawn of a new day, Obsidian," Penelope said, her voice laced with amusement. "And I don't mean that literally. However, might I suggest you look deeper into Michael's requests? Perhaps he merely wants what you have."

Staring down at my female, I frowned. "And what do I have that he doesn't?"

"Family. Those who care about you, who are loyal to you."

I lifted my gaze to the mountains in the distance once more. "Michael has that. In Heaven."

"Who? You told me his *ereswa* died. That means he's all alone, is he not?"

"He has plenty of loyal subjects."

"Not the same, Obsidian, and you know it. What you've built here ... this is a family. These aren't your subjects, the *fiestreigh* aren't merely soldiers in your army. They belong to you, and you to them. I wouldn't blame Michael if he wanted to experience that."

I understood where she was coming from. I could even understand why Michael might want that. The problem was my brothers weren't all on good terms with Michael. And I feared I overstepped by making decisions without discussing with them first. I'd already agreed to allow Michael within the walls of the mansion for as long as he desired. I agreed with the best of intentions, in an effort to save my family.

"What are you going to tell him about the training?"

"What can I tell him?" I countered, repositioning so I was standing behind Penelope. I draped my arms over her shoulders and pressed my palms to her belly. "He's promised to provide healers if I agree. How can I decline? We need them."

Perhaps now more than ever. And there was a significant amount of selfishness in that belief. Our son or daughter would be arriving within weeks, and the thought of Penelope enduring any complications that might cause harm to her or our child... The ache in my chest was all the answer I needed. Those healers were a necessity for all of us.

"Whatever your decision, I know it'll be the right one," Penelope said, her fingers curling over my biceps as she held on to me. "Your heart's in the right place, Obsidian. And we, as your family, will support you."

Yeah. That was what I was worried about.

40

KAJ

"It'll need a little work to get it back to its original glory," I told the males as we strolled through the kitchen to the dining room beyond.

"How many bedrooms?" Mirakel asked.

"Forty."

Blāz whistled. "Damn. Those angels don't play around, huh?"

I smirked. "You should see the new place." Compared to the new residence, this was little more than a shanty on steroids.

"What about the underground space?" Huracān asked.

Figuring it was easier to show than tell, I led them back through the main floor. It was open, with high ceilings, large windows, plenty of space to house us and those we determined worthy of the fight ahead. I wasn't sure how fond I was of the decor, but that was simple to fix. We weren't strangers to hard work, and fortunately, funds were not in short supply. We could bring civilians in to do the job, provided the angels agreed to shift their cloaking spell a few miles to the north.

It was a damn fine place to put down roots. Not only was it large enough to house us, it gave me options to expand the Zenith, grow them into the formidable army necessary to protect the race from everyone, including traitorous vampires.

"Right now, I want to get it furnished," I told Mirakel. "Hire someone to handle it. Check out their background first. But let's get some furniture in here. Bring on a handful of *vestrahn* to maintain it. We'll need a computer setup, get tied into the Misplaced Halos boards."

Mirakel nodded, no doubt making mental notes.

The five of us made our way down the concrete steps to the space beneath the mansion.

"Now that's more like it," Blāz noted.

Yes, the angels had spared no expense with the under-ground residence. If I had to guess, this area was designed and built long before the above-ground structure was added.

"Where do the tunnels go?" Huracān asked, nodding to a series of hallways that branched off in all directions.

"Likely through the mountain," I told him, though I wasn't sure where they went. Something told me they connected with the angels' current residence, but I wasn't sure I was ready to tell the others that. Not until I'd checked it out for myself and secured it so no one could breach the angel mansion without my knowledge.

"We've got our work cut out for us," Mirakel said, his words directed at the others.

"I need to check in with my daughter," I told them. "If you can spare me for a couple of hours."

Mirakel bowed. "Of course, *phaal*."

It still felt strange for them to refer to me as their Alpha, but I refrained from asking them not to. I knew it was important that they had a leader. Their very existence was based on it, in fact.

"I'll be back shortly."

I left the males to discuss the next steps beneath what was dubbed the Lair. Once I was upstairs, I stepped out into the crisp night air, vanished my form, and materialized on the front steps of Angel Central, as I'd heard the human male refer to it.

Speaking of the human ... I wasn't sure what to think of Oliver Calazans yet. I noticed the male's interest in Bijou, but I didn't have the heart to tell him Bijou's heart resided with another. For one, I hoped she'd move past that ill-fated crush. Reve, the male she'd given her heart to, was nothing more than an opportunistic little shit who wasn't even remotely good enough for my little girl. Then again, considering I was new to this father gig, I wasn't sure I had a right to suggest such a thing.

When I stepped into the main foyer, I expanded my senses, noting where the others were. It was oddly quiet, a few conversations taking place, but the majority of the energy seemed to be in the main room below. I figured I would locate Obsidian to thank the male for being so considerate in offering accommodations, but I didn't make it that far.

My boots were tracking over the rug when there was a distinct hum in my blood. I pulled up short, peering up at the ceiling as though I could see through it. My senses scattered once more when I managed to home in on the source.

Acadia.

Pivoting, I strolled to the stairway, taking them two at a time to the top. I made a hard left, a quick right, then three

505

doors down. I paused with my hand raised to knock. Rather than announce my presence to every soul in the place, I dropped my hand.

Let me in, Acadia.

The door swung open, surprising me. Honestly, I expected Acadia to turn her nose up at me. After our last conversation in the stairwell, when I all but claimed her as mine, I was waiting for her to put me in my place.

"Where were you?" Her eyes were wide, concern pulling on the corners, adding a wrinkle to her smooth brow.

I stepped into the room, eased the door shut behind me. "I've been taking care of some business."

"I was..." Acadia inhaled, exhaled.

I waited for her to finish, but right before my eyes, her expression smoothed out, giving away nothing. Just like her to tug that mask in place, pretend she didn't care about me.

Not that I blamed her. When I walked away, I knew I'd hurt her. It hadn't been my intention, but when she refused to go with me, I had no choice. And that was one of the main reasons I decided to settle down nearby. Perhaps if she could remain close to the angels, Acadia wouldn't keep pushing me away.

Daring to move closer, I took each step with caution. One foot then the other.

Acadia remained where she stood, her eyes locked on my face. I could see the wariness in her eyes. She wanted me but she didn't want to want me. I knew the feeling. It was what had plagued me for the eighteen months I was away from her. My heart had remained there while my duty was with the vampires. As it was, my absence had led to the demise of my father. I couldn't help thinking if I hadn't been injured, hadn't taken shelter there, that my father would still be alive.

Since I couldn't change the past, I had no choice but to make plans for the future. Taking care of my clans was paramount. Shoring up our armies and preparing for battle against the shadow beasts was critical to our existence.

But my heart was here with her, and it always would be.

"I've moved into the vacated residence nearby," I told her, watching her face to gauge her reaction.

"And this concerns me how?"

I smiled, stepping in close now that I realized she was not going to run from me.

"Because it's where I would like you to reside," I said softly, lifting my hand and brushing the tips of my fingers over her smooth cheek.

For a moment, Acadia closed her eyes. I could hear the rapid thump of her heart, knew she was affected by my nearness.

"I cannot abandon the warriors."

"No one's asking you to," I assured her. "When you're ready, you'll come to me, Acadia."

Her eyes opened, meeting mine. "I've been thinking about that."

"And?"

"And I'm not convinced this is a good mating. You and me."

I smirked. "*Balisra*, that is not up to you to decide. The Fates have already sealed it. My heart, my very soul shall always belong to you."

She shook her head as though that would void my statement.

I leaned in, pressing my forehead to hers, then reverted to my native language to express my feelings. "*'Tis true, my sweet love. My heart, body, and soul are forevermore yours. There is nothing either of us shall do to change that.*"

Because I knew she didn't understand, I relayed them another way, curling my finger beneath her chin and tilting her head back. I met her lips with mine, brushing them ever so softly.

"When you are ready, Acadia, know I am waiting for you."

"If you are not here, I shall have to feed from another," she said softly.

I pulled back, curled my hand over her cheek, and met her stare. "*Balisra*, it would be my honor as well as my pleasure to feed you. You must only ask."

"Will you feed from anyone else?"

"I would rather die before I touched the flesh of another female."

Which was part of the problem. I hadn't fed for a few days now, and my strength was waning.

"Would you oblige me now, *balisra*?"

Acadia nodded.

It was all I could do not to weep, her grace unparalleled. Despite the fact I hurt her, and she refused to believe I would forever remain true, my sweet Acadia still provided me with the gift of life.

ORIANNA

 he pain was unbearable.

Thankfully, the nausea abated a few hours ago,

but without that discomfort plaguing me, the ache within became my sole focus.

I ignored it for the longest time, waiting patiently for the *heurosp* to tend to me, cleaning the bathroom and tidying up while Eclipse met with his brothers. I even managed a shower, having grown tired of my own skin after nearly two days of feeling as though I was dying.

Now that I was finally alone, I was racked with a heat that encompassed my entire being.

Initially, I paced the room from one end to the other. Back and forth, back and forth. When my legs trembled from the weight, I settled onto the bed, laid out over the silky comforter. Then, the scrape of my clothing became an irritant I could no longer handle, so I stripped. The bedding beneath me cooled the heat for a few minutes, but even that was fleeting.

What I needed was Eclipse, but I was beginning to wonder if this persistent ache would ever be fully quenched. It seemed to be intensifying the longer we were together when, in reality, it should've been easing off. That was the way it worked in the human realm, at least. Fireworks and sparks in the beginning, then a steady simmer, and finally a cooldown when the other's familiar comfort overrode that unbridled desire. Or at least that was how I'd always thought it to work. Maybe some people went hog wild right out of the gate, and it lasted for eternity.

Of course, I knew this was some strange angel phenomenon, but *come on!* At what point did it give up the ghost? We were together, for goodness sake. What more did the ... whoever was in charge of this want? An eternal flame that engulfed us both, rendering us useless?

I wasn't sure I could handle that sort of flame. I was more of a gentle-flicker kinda girl.

A distressed moan surfaced, my back arching as my hands

slid over my breasts. The sensation of my touch sparked the heat, but I knew it would only make it worse. I needed Eclipse. And I wasn't sure I could wait.

When he didn't come, fear consumed me. He'd always come to me when I was in need of him. For weeks now, he'd offered himself up to me, soothing me as well as himself. Even when he hadn't been close, he'd seemed to sense my need.

So where was he? Why wasn't he helping me?

A tear leaked out of my eye, dripping down my cheek.

Had he abandoned me like everyone else in my life? Placed me on a shelf to collect dust? Maybe all that hurling had turned him off. He'd finally seen real-life closing in and decided it wasn't for him.

Then it dawned on me. I had told him I loved him, but he didn't return the sentiment. Not in my language, anyway. What if his words had been a gentle letdown, not a declaration of love? Maybe he thought I could take care of myself. After all, I had told him as much when I refused to stay with him in the basement of my mother's house. And I had handled the situation. Not quite well, mind you, but in a manner that hadn't allowed things to get out of control.

My core was aflame, like center-of-the-Earth hot, and there was no way I could cool it on my own.

Figuring I could explore my options since I had no other alternatives, I closed my eyes and slipped my fingers between my legs.

"Oh, God." That gentle brush against my flesh had chills racing down my spine, sending tingling sensations to every limb. I aimed for more, centering on my clit. If I could spark one good orgasm, perhaps I could rest for a while.

Before long, the whimpers and moans were more from frustration than satisfaction. I thrashed on the bed, anger bubbling up because I needed relief, and this wasn't helping.

"*Sezari?* Oh, fuck, baby."

My eyes shot open at the sound of Eclipse's voice. He was tearing off his T-shirt as he strolled toward me. My gaze settled upon all that smooth, rippling flesh, and my fingers suddenly itched to wander and explore. Though seeing him did nothing to quell the urge, it gave me a distraction. He was truly beautiful. The sexy mohawk, those iridescent eyes, the strong chin. And his body ... it was absolute perfection. Long, lean, thick with muscle.

"Eclipse."

"I'm here, *sezari*."

There was a thump, then another as his boots hit the floor. His jeans went next, and finally, he was crawling over me. Like the poles of magnets, my hands clutched him, arms sliding around his torso as I pulled him down to me.

"I thought you left me," I mumbled, burying my face in his neck as I let his warmth infuse me.

"Never, *sezari*."

"I'm sorry," I continued. "Sorry if I'm too independent. It was ingrained in me. I don't mean—"

"Shh, baby. You're perfect just the way you are." His lips grazed my forehead, my cheek, lower.

When his mouth fused to mine, I whimpered, absorbing him into every inch of me.

There was no foreplay, but I didn't need it. Right now, I wanted him inside me, filling me, consuming me. He slid his arm beneath my right leg, drawing it up, my knee curving over his forearm, and then ... mother of all things holy, he was sinking inside me.

"Yes," I hissed, biting his shoulder as pleasure overrode the ache. It wasn't enough, but it was exactly what I needed. I held on tightly as he pumped his hips, the friction bringing tears to my eyes, the relief so intense.

Eclipse's head lowered, his face pressed against my shoulder as he held himself over me and gave me what I needed. Thrust and retreat, again and again, until the only thing I knew was the feel of him surrounding me.

I wasn't sure how many times I came, but like every time his body molded to mine, it didn't matter. He shattered me on so many levels; physical was only a part of it. But it felt amazing, my hands running over smooth, warm skin, his back muscles flexing beneath my palms as he arched and bowed.

"You feel so good, *sezari*." His voice cracked, as though the emotion couldn't be contained by the vibration of his vocal cords.

Tears rolled down my cheeks as I held on for dear life. He was there with me, right there in that very moment. I could feel not only his physical presence but something more. It was what I'd needed all my life: someone who would care for me, love me. Not because I was a means to an end but because I was what he needed as well.

Eclipse's rhythm slipped, his erection driving deep inside me again and again, but I could feel his body vibrating beneath my palms.

"I love you, *sezari*," he whispered against my ear. "You're my everything. My here and now. My tomorrow. Don't ever think otherwise."

My nails dug into his back as those words pierced my heart, the heat swelling, encompassing my entire being until I was shuddering.

"Eclipse ... please..." I cried out as he drove into me one final time.

His muscles tensed, his head tilting back, and that familiar growl escaped him, a low, guttural sound that shattered me once more.

Eclipse collapsed beside me, pulling me into his body, his

arm beneath my head. He held me tightly to him, as though he feared I would slip away if he didn't. My breaths were labored, my body slick with sweat from the workout we just had, but I didn't care if he squeezed the life out of me.

"I love you, *sezari*, with all that I am."

Those words ... they were what I needed to hear. A balm to my soul.

I was right where I wanted to be, but more importantly, I needed the reassurance that I was right where *he* wanted me to be.

OLIVER

"What the fuck?"

"Seriously?"

The question rumbled through the mansion as the sexual energy slammed through everyone inside.

"Oh, fuck..."

Males and females began scrambling, searching for someone to assuage the ache. Those who'd yet to experience the phenomenon appeared dumbfounded by the over-whelming sensation, the desperate need to fuck, but even they had the sense to know how to handle themselves. I could hear their moans and sighs, flesh against flesh. It was the same sounds that encompassed the mansion whenever that strange energy flooded it.

As I stood at the edge of the pool, I inhaled deeply, trying to fight it off. My shorts scraped against my oversensitive skin, the urge to rip them off nearly too great to resist.

Had it not been for the female staring back at me with wide, uncertain eyes, I would've stumbled somewhere private, used my hand to release the frustration steadily growing into an overwhelming need. It wasn't ideal, but it was what I had to do whenever it happened. If I didn't, I feared my balls would explode.

"Oliver?" Bijou's green eyes were locked on me. "What is that? Why does it keep happening?"

Even as she spoke, she stumbled toward the sauna, where she'd been headed before the wave crashed.

"Oh, God!" Her head tilted back, the sleek line of her luscious neck beckoning me.

"It's okay," I urged. "Come on."

Summoning as much energy as I could, I helped her into the ten-by-ten room, eased her onto one of the teak benches. The thing was maintained at a steady temperature, so it was already ridiculously warm. Perhaps not the best place for someone whose hormones were obliterated.

When Bijou rolled onto her back, I fought the urge to mount her. It was an animalistic reaction, one spurred by whatever the phenomenon was. No one seemed to have the answers, and yes, I attempted to get them after the first time my body was assaulted by the overwhelming need to fuck. I knew if I sank inside her, it would ease the ache for both of us, but...

Truth was, I'd thought of little else since I first laid eyes on her in the dining room.

"Please…" Her head lifted, eyes pleading. "Oliver, please…"

Fucking hell. I wanted nothing more than to fall into her, but I knew that was stupid. We were only friends. Bijou deserved so much better than the likes of me. Even temporarily. Considering I'd fucked a demon … I couldn't fathom sliding inside her sweet, warm heat, tainting her with the darkness of my soul.

Never mind the fact we were of two completely different species. I wasn't even sure our biologies were the same, even if our instincts were.

Her hand lifted, reaching for me.

I wasn't even aware I'd moved, but the next thing I knew, she had pulled me down with her. The sweet scent of gardenias flooded my senses, made my head spin.

"Bijou…"

"I need you," she whimpered, pressing my hand to her breast.

Though I made no move to take advantage, the beautiful female thrust her chest into my hand, her hips rocking beneath me.

"It'll pass," I promised her. I'd experienced it enough to know. All we had to do was hold out, and it would dissipate. The lingering need would eventually subside.

Although I was starting to question that.

"Kiss me," she demanded, reaching for me.

I knew she would regret this, but my willpower waned, leaving me vulnerable to her desires and my own.

Gripping her hair, I kept our mouths separated by a mere centimeter. Our breaths mingled, the need consuming us both.

"Please, Oliver … I want you."

Lifting my head, I met her gaze, got lost in the sparkling green depths. She held my stare for long seconds, and within those phosphorescent orbs, I could see the approval, but I knew she wasn't thinking clearly.

"Fuck." I groaned low in my throat as my mouth crushed to hers.

A fury unlike anything I'd ever known ignited inside me, a desperate ache that had nothing to do with the energy cast off by whoever was responsible. This was something else, something more. I felt as though my skin was too small for my body, the flesh holding in a power too strong for it to maintain.

Bijou's soft hands slid over my wet skin, her cool fingers gliding down my back once, twice. When her nails sank into me, I hissed, the pleasure overriding any possible pain.

"We can't do this," I growled, trying to refrain, failing miserably.

"We have to," she countered, pulling my mouth back to hers.

She was far stronger than she appeared, her hands holding me despite my best efforts to retreat. Or perhaps that was my brain making excuses because there was no denying I wanted her more than I wanted air. This was the perfect opportunity, one the old me never would've passed up.

But I wasn't that man anymore. I'd changed in the short time I'd been here in the mansion. The last thing I wanted was to take advantage of Bijou, to rip through the fabric of our newly forming friendship.

In an effort to help ease her pain, I pressed my thigh between her legs, ground against the heat I could feel through her bathing suit. Fucking hell. She was so hot...

"Oliver!" Bijou cried out even as she attempted to slide her hands between our bodies.

Knowing only one way to sate her and not take advantage, I gripped her wrists, held them flat against the wood.

"Don't move," I ordered, the deep rumble of my voice catching her attention.

Though she trembled, she didn't move. Not even when I shifted to the end of the bench, lowering my knees to the floor as I settled between her thighs. The scent of her arousal had me groaning, my cock throbbing painfully, desperate to feel her sliding over me.

"Please, Oliver. Help me. Make it stop."

A dark rumble escaped me as I pulled her toward me, bringing my mouth closer to her pussy. Bijou accommodated me, placing her feet on the edge of the bench, her knees dropping open. Tugging the wet fabric of her bathing suit to the side, I used my fingers to spread her smooth, hairless lips before lowering my head. Her juices coated my tongue, sweet ambrosia flooding my senses as I used my tongue to sate her desire.

"Oh, God! Oliver … that's … oh … yes!"

Bijou's hand sank into my hair, holding firmly as I suckled her clit, eager to give her the release she was so desperate to achieve. Truth was, I could've spent the rest of my fucking life with my face buried between her legs. I'd never tasted anything as fucking sweet as her, and those noises she was making... Pain infused me, made my head swim. My balls ached, but I ignored my own body as I worked her closer to climax.

"More, Oliver..." The soft, tormented whisper nearly broke me.

Somehow, I managed to hold back. I pushed two fingers deep inside her, thrusting roughly as I flicked her clit with my tongue. The tiny nub pulsed as her body drew up tight. A beautiful cry escaped her as she came, her tight sheath clutching my fingers like a vice.

The moment the orgasm swept through her, she relaxed.

Completely drained by my body's needs, it took tremendous effort to adjust her clothing, covering her once more. When I got to my feet, I peered down at her beautiful face. In that moment, I realized I'd never wanted anyone or anything as much as I wanted her.

"Don't go," she whispered, her eyes beseeching.

"I assure you, I don't want to." I swallowed hard, resigned myself to what was necessary. "But I have to."

Knowing I was seconds from doing something we would both regret, I stumbled toward the door to the house, out of the sauna, past the pool. Once inside, the cool air chilled me, but I welcomed the sensation as I raced down the hallway, took the stairs to the second floor at a rapid clip. I managed to make it to my room, slamming the door behind me and leaning against the solid wood.

Within seconds, I had my cock in my fist, jerking roughly, attempting to ease the ache. Closing my eyes, I saw Bijou vividly. Only this was a fantasy, one where she was spread out before me in all her naked glory. Her dark hair draped over my pillow as I climbed over her. The instant my fantasy self plunged into the warmth of her, I came in a violent rush. I slammed into the door behind me, fell to the floor, every ounce of my energy drained from the efforts it had taken to resist her.

As I closed my eyes and dragged air into my exhausted lungs, an image appeared in my mind. Just an extension of my fantasy, only in this one, I was sinking my nonexistent fangs into her flesh.

What. The. Fuck?

41

ECLIPSE

"Thanksgiving with angels," Orianna said, grinning from ear to ear.

My smile formed as a direct result of hers. "You know, this is the first Thanksgiving we've ever celebrated."

It had been ten days since I brought her back to the mansion, two hundred and forty-some-odd hours since I nearly killed the female I adored beyond reason. And here she sat, smiling up at me as though none of that ever happened.

Sure, a lot had happened in the past week, including the ass-reaming I received when I moved Elizabeth into the mansion, settling her into one of the spare guest rooms on the second floor. To be honest, at the time, I was more worried about Orianna than the fact I was bringing a human into the mansion. Since I had nowhere else to safely put my *amsouelot's* mother, the mansion was the only option. Having witnessed Orianna's pure happiness at seeing her mother there, I would do it again in a heartbeat. Consequences be damned.

Her eyebrows lowered. "Your first Thanksgiving? Seriously? Why is that?"

"We don't follow human traditions," I admitted.

"Really?" Her gaze swung to the *heurosp* currently strolling in with dishes piled high with food. "They're human, aren't they?"

"Technically, yes."

"What does that mean? Technically?"

"Their biological makeup is human. They were born human, but ... well, to put it simply, they're immortal."

"Wow. How is that even possible?"

I shrugged. "One of Michael's doings."

Though I didn't know the logistics required to make a mortal immortal, I understood Michael's reasoning. It was in the interest of safety. The last thing we could afford was humans traipsing through the mansion, turning over every fifty or sixty years once they'd reached their maximum life-span. This way, they would forever remain in service to angels, and no one was the wiser.

"So why this year?" Orianna asked.

"Couple of reasons." I glanced over at Obsidian and his *ereswa*. "Penelope requested it."

I didn't tell Orianna that Penelope had asked because she knew this was going to be the last holiday she would have with Winnie. Though she'd been threatening for some time now, the time had finally come for Winnie to leave the mansion and go back to her human world in California. This was one last celebration before Cimmerian pulled the whole wool-over-the-eyes with her memories and sent her back out into the world.

"Penelope was human. Makes sense she'd want to celebrate those traditions." Orianna smiled, sliding her hand over my forearm. "I'm glad I'm here with you."

I leaned over, met her lips with my own. "Me, too."

"I wish my mother would've wanted to join us."

Dropping my gaze to my glass, I nodded. We had invited Elizabeth down for the meal, but she'd kindly declined the offer. Ever since her arrival, she'd remained in her private quarters, the *heurosp* seeing to her every need. Though she seemed somewhat content to be living closer to Orianna, it wasn't all roses and sunshine for her. We had to intervene a couple of times to calm her nerves because being in a new place had set her off. I figured the drugs weren't helping, but getting her settled in required we not change too much else. We'd yet to reveal the fact Amber was dead, and since that was Elizabeth's primary concern, it was likely Orianna's mother thought we were interfering with her daughter's mission. But until Orianna decided to tell her, it wasn't my place to intervene.

The sound of sterling silver clanking against crystal drew everyone's attention to Obsidian, the various conversations dying down around us.

"My *ereswa* has asked that I say a few words." Obsidian glanced from one face to another. "While I wish all the *amsouelots* were here with us now, there's still a lot for us to be thankful for. It's been a difficult year for us, and I don't expect that to settle in the near future, but I do hold out hope that we will all soon be together as we're meant to be."

A soft rumble of agreement came from the peanut gallery.

"As long as we continue to have each other's backs, there's no doubt this family will continue to expand and grow, exactly as it was meant to since inception."

I nodded when Obsidian looked my way.

"Today, we shall celebrate all we're thankful for in the tradition of the humans. And tomorrow, we'll resume our quest to protect those same souls from the evils they don't see."

"Hear, hear!" someone shouted.

Glasses clinked together in cheers, but my attention shifted to Orianna. I smiled at the female who completed me in ways I never expected. Reaching for her, I cupped the back of her head and pulled her in for a kiss.

In the ancient language of angels, I said, "*Forever my heart is yours, sweet love of mine.*"

Orianna's eyes glittered. "What does that mean?"

"Rough translation?" I pressed my lips to hers once more. "I will love you forever, *sezari*."

"Ditto."

"Let's eat!" someone shouted, which ignited a chant of the same.

I grinned. I found it interesting how much emphasis the humans, American humans in this case, put on this meal for which they gathered once a year to give thanks for all they had. It was a holiday to be celebrated for them. For me and my family, this was a daily ritual, something Obsidian had held up for centuries, ensuring we never drifted too far apart from one another.

For us, it was just ... normal.

ORIANNA

"Are you sure you're ready for this?" Cimmerian asked.

I wasn't sure who his question was directed at. Reidar or Penelope. Perhaps both.

After we finished the Thanksgiving feast, a.k.a. the morning meal, everyone remained in the dining room, swapping stories and jokes, laughing and drinking. All while Winnie sat beside Penelope, utterly oblivious to what was coming. By the time everyone made their way to their private quarters to sleep off the alcohol they'd imbibed and the food they'd put away, there was a sense of contentment throughout the mansion.

Now that night had fallen once more and everyone had come down to see Winnie off, there was a sorrow that choked out all the cheerfulness.

Truth was, I had been surprised to see Winnie at the Thanksgiving feast. During my time in the mansion, I'd seen her least of all, and those times I was in her company weren't exactly pleasant. According to Penelope, Winnie had long ago decided she wanted to go home, and the only reason she remained was because Reidar continued to stall. Despite the fact everyone had attempted to make Winnie feel at home, the woman refused their kindness, latching on to her unhappiness and clutching it like a lifeline. It had gotten to the point everyone began to avoid Winnie the same as she had them.

So, it seemed a good thing they decided it was time for Winnie to go home.

Turned out, going back to the human world after living

amongst angels wasn't an easy thing. Not for anyone, apparently.

The only reason I had been filled in was because I'd questioned Eclipse. It wasn't too difficult to pick up on the fact they were holding something back in their attempt to enjoy their last remaining moments with the woman. I almost wished I'd stayed in bed with Eclipse, not volunteered to be a shoulder for Penelope.

Then again, I wouldn't have turned my back on my newest friend.

"Can I say goodbye?" Penelope asked, her attention on Cimmerian.

"Of course. Just know that you'll have those memories, not her."

Penelope nodded, then headed up the stairs to the sunroom, where Winnie was currently standing, staring out at the pitch-black of the *dhira* the warriors maintained over the mansion.

"So, how's this work?" Reidar asked.

"When you give me the go-ahead, I'll filter out all her memories of Penelope and insert a stand-in. Winnie will know she and her best friend parted ways years ago on good terms. Everything else will remain as is for her. These past few months won't exist in her mind, and she'll believe she quit her job in order to find something better."

Wow. That didn't sound pleasant at all.

"How does she get back to California?"

I hoped it wasn't by means of teleporting. Having experienced that one for myself … yeah, that was a big hell no, thank you very much.

"Alden and Naos have agreed to accompany her. They'll need to leave as soon as possible."

Reidar nodded, as though that was reasonable, but I could

see the discomfort on his face. This wasn't easy for him by any means. From my understanding, Reidar had believed Winnie was his soul mate when they met, so he'd brought her back to the mansion. The months that followed had brought to light the error in his thinking, and now he had to deal with the aftermath.

"She'll be fine," Cimmerian assured him. "Just know you can have no contact with her going forward."

"Understood."

Feeling as though I was intruding on the angels' private moment, I opted to wander away from the group. I stood at the base of the stairs to the sunroom, staring up at the two women currently talking softly. For a moment, I tried to imagine a life where part of my memories had been scrubbed. Though I wouldn't know I was missing something, I wondered if there would still be a void.

Probably, I figured. After all, that was how I felt about Amber. My sister had been gone for so long it was difficult to remember the good times we'd shared back before our world had been disrupted. First, my mother's attack, my father sending us away. Those years we'd spent feeling alone and adrift. For a time, we'd leaned on one another, but even that didn't last long enough. In an effort to heal those wounds, we drifted apart until there was nothing left. The only thing I had left was my mother, but even that felt tenuous at the moment.

A warm body moved behind me, strong hands settling on my shoulders. I leaned into the familiar warmth and sent up another silent thank-you for Eclipse. I had no idea how our worlds collided, but now that they had, I couldn't imagine myself anywhere else.

For the first time in years, my mother wasn't the only thing I had left. I had Eclipse. He alone had filled that void, given me hope when I had none. I knew he loved me because I could feel it, but he was holding something back. I detected it recently. A disconnect, as though he wasn't ready to move things to the next level, whatever that might be.

I got the feeling it had to do with that vision. The one where I was dead, his enormous body hovering over me. When I'd asked him what it meant, Eclipse had avoided answering, which told me he knew but didn't want to say. The only thing that kept the fear at bay was the fact I knew that moment wasn't the end, it was the beginning.

Of what, I wasn't entirely sure, but I had my suspicions.

42

MIRAKEL

———

While Kaj was enjoying turkey and dressing with his daughter and the angels, the crew and I were busy making necessary improvements to the Lair.

Kaj took a few pointers from Angel Central, so we'd been busy getting the steel shutters fitted over all the windows. Installing the metal tracks and the steel sheeting on both the inside and outside was the easy part, I had learned. It was getting everything tied into the automated system Blāz was creating that proved to be the more difficult part. The male promised the Lair would be as automated as Angel Central by the time he was finished, maybe more so.

Needless to say, until we could eliminate all the bugs, we were forced to sleep down below.

Not that I minded. For the past eighteen months, I'd been on the move, most of the time taking up space in abandoned structures—be it houses or commercial buildings—so having a soft place to rest my head was quite nice. It wouldn't have mattered if I was below ground or in a cardboard box. As long as the sun wouldn't get me, I was content. My position within the Zenith had never involved living the high life of the noblemen and women I was in service to. I didn't expect it to be any different now, although Kaj didn't seem to understand that.

The biggest difference, though, was the food. Evidently, the angels' house staff got wind of our arrival and insisted on ensuring we were fed. At first, a casserole appeared in the kitchen, the next day another, along with place settings. Day after, more dishes, more food, some linens. Since ... well, I was pretty sure a couple of the caretakers had moved in permanently.

But it wasn't the food I was worried about. That was taken care of, but now it was the blood requirements that were becoming more of a necessity than a nuisance. While I had ventured out of the Lair once since we arrived with Kaj, I was holding off as long as possible. Now, I feared I'd waited too long, which meant getting to the next town over was going to require something more than my own body for transportation. Without access to vehicles, I was pretty much screwed unless Kaj came through for me, as he said he would. Something about a Fae providing for us. I wasn't sure. My brain was a bit foggy at the moment.

As I stared at the stone ceiling, letting my arms rest at my sides, I tried to sleep, but it wasn't happening. Despite the brain mush from the lack of feeding, there was a restlessness beneath my skin. Had been the case since I left the Seattle camp in search of Kaj. I'd lived with that unease for months, using it to fuel me in my search for the Alpha. Now that I'd found Kaj, seemed my body hadn't gotten the message.

Would probably help if we could get back to a regular fighting routine. We needed to shore up our ranks and get back to training on a regular basis. As we were now, I wouldn't be surprised if a group of *impietans* took us all out in one fell swoop. A year ago, I would've laughed at the thought. Now ... well, I had to wonder.

A soft knock had me looking over at the wooden door that sealed off the small concrete room.

"Yes?"

The door opened a fraction of an inch. "Might I come in, sire?"

I forced my legs over the side of the bed and sat up, the softly spoken words surprising me. "Of course."

When she stepped into the room, I wasn't exactly sure who she was or why she was there. The female was slight of stature and pale of skin, her red-blond hair pinned high up on her head, revealing a delicate neck and a body covered by a long dress made of silk. She was otherworldly. Part of me expected to see a halo perched upon her head, casting a heavenly glow around her.

There was no such light, but she was beautiful, nonetheless.

"Kaj asked that I come see you," she said, offering a smile as she stepped into the room, closing the door behind her.

"Whatever for?" I asked, unable to grasp why she could possibly be there.

The female's head dipped low. "I'm to be of service, sire."

"Service?"

"In any manner you might need."

Okay, what the fuck?

"Who are you?" I asked, figuring I'd get right to the point.

"My name's Briony. I'm Fae."

Ah. Okay. Now it was making a bit more sense.

Kinda.

"So you came to feed me," I muttered.

"I am here to take care of any needs you might have, sire."

Frowning, I met her gaze. "I'm not sure I understand."

"If there's something you might need of a sexual nature, I am here to please."

To please? What the fuck kind of brothel were those angels running over there? I got the gist of needing a blood source, but sex ... seriously?

"How about we stick to the blood for now," I said, pushing to my feet.

No sooner had I gotten vertical than the female stepped forward, the silky fabric covering her sliding off her shoulders and pooling on the floor at her feet.

My brain might've been a bit slow, but my cock damn sure wasn't. It rose to the occasion without hesitation, straining against the leather that the bastard was encased in as my eyes scanned all five feet nothing of her, from her high-tipped breasts to the delectable curve of her waist, the delicious flair of her hips. Delicate thighs, adorable knees, small ankles leading to tiny feet. She was exactly what I'd expected a fairy to look like, only more ... precious.

And to think she was offering me sex.

If I took her ... I would break her in half with minimal effort.

Forcing my gaze back to her face, I shook my head and looked away. "I ... uh ... I'm not sure that's appropriate."

"I don't understand, sire," she said softly.

I flapped a hand in her direction as though encompassing her nakedness.

Why I was acting like some virginal teenager, I didn't

know. It wasn't like I hadn't been with a female before. I had. Thousands of them in my years on this Earth. However, those encounters usually involved a dance of some sort. Not once in my life had I ever paid for sex, and I damn sure didn't intend to start now.

"Sire? Do I not please you?"

Hearing the uncertainty in her tone had me turning around. "You're quite pleasing," I assured her, then nodded to her robe. "But I'd prefer you remained clothed if it's all the same to you."

Her cheeks turned a pretty shade of pink as she reached down and retrieved her robe. As she slid it on, I found myself watching until all those smooth, gentle curves were hidden from view.

"Where would you like me?" she asked kindly.

Beneath me, I thought at the same time I said, "Let's sit."

Not quite a logical decision, considering the only piece of furniture in the room was the bed.

Fucking lovely.

I made the mistake of sitting on the mattress first. Briony came to stand before me, waiting patiently for my instruction.

Because I was too exhausted to put forth the effort to make this easy on either of us, I motioned for her to turn away from me. When she did, I pulled her down onto my lap, which was a huge fucking mistake. The instant her little ass settled on my thighs, my cock swelled, stretching the leather meant to keep him contained.

Son of a bitch.

Briony, clearly comfortable with this, leaned back against me, ensuring her hair was off her neck as she angled her head away from me. In anticipation, my fangs descended into my mouth, tingling with the urge to sink into her flesh.

Not sure where to put my hands, I wrapped my arms

around her. To hold her in place, of course. After all, I was a big male, much bigger than she, so it was as much for her comfort as mine.

Yeah. Uh-huh. Sure it was.

I leaned in, inhaling her scent, which I couldn't place but found I liked more than I should.

As I kept my body in check, I drew my arms tighter and pierced her vein, drawing her blood into my mouth. At that point, biology should've kicked in. Just like the millions of times I'd taken a vein in my lifetime, everything should've been hunky-dory.

So not the case.

Not by a long fucking shot.

The instant her blood hit my tongue, my body waged an all-out assault on my mind. Her blood was so rich, unlike anything I'd ever tasted before. As it slid over my tongue and down my throat, my muscles flexed, the power in my body surpassing what I was sure all those well-honed fibers could contain.

I was so focused on drinking I didn't realize my arms had shifted or that my hands had settled over her breasts, somehow finding them beneath the thin fabric that had been covering her but was now open down the front. At least I was gentle, I thought as I took stock of the situation, the way my palms were cupping her, my fingers lightly kneading the warm flesh.

My body had a mind of its own.

The soft moans that escaped the diminutive female in my arms weren't helping either. Nor did her placing her hands over mine, holding them to her breasts as I sucked on her vein. My head was buzzing, and I figured it was a combination of her sweet taste, the softness of her skin, and that delicate scent. Never had I encountered a female who affected me like this. Hell, not even a fraction of this.

When her hips began to shift, her ass pressing insistently against my erection, I had to release her breast and curl my arm around her hips to still her movements. As it was, I was rutting against her, my cock straining in an attempt to get to where it needed to be. But I couldn't fucking stop. I couldn't break the seal on her neck, and I couldn't stop the bump and grind of my hips as I held her to me.

Seconds felt like an eternity, and when my gut finally gave my brain permission to let go, I sealed the punctures on her skin, buried my face in her neck, and gave in to the inevitable.

"Fuck," I growled softly against her neck, my cock grinding against her. "Oh, fuck."

I came so hard it was a wonder we remained on the bed. I thought for sure I would've launched her across the room from the intensity of that explosion.

No. I was happy to see she remained where she was, perched on my lap, her breaths as labored as mine.

"I'm sorry," I said softly, adjusting her robe to cover her. "I'm so fucking sorry."

"Don't be."

"You should go," I urged, shifting so that she was forced to get to her feet.

"Of course, sire."

I couldn't believe what just happened. Never had I lost control like that. Not once in my life. Had I been naked … fucking hell, I probably would've mounted her like a goddamn animal, taken what didn't belong to me.

Realizing she was still there, standing near the door but making no move to leave, I lifted my head, pinned her with my gaze. "Go. Now."

Her amethyst eyes met mine briefly, and there was a flash

of something. Regret, fear? I didn't fucking know, and I didn't have it in me to figure it out now.

"Go!" I barked, fearful if she stayed for one more second I would strip us both and give in to that overwhelming urge.

Finally she slipped out, the door closing quietly behind her.

I stared at the wood for the longest time, trying to figure out if any of that actually happened or if I'd been dreaming. Based on the strength I felt flooding me, I knew it had been real. I'd fed from her, then physically assaulted her. Didn't matter that she'd offered when she came into the room. That wasn't my style.

That was...

What.

The.

Fuck?

43

REIDAR

Another week under our belts.

Forty-seven days since Asmia was taken right out from under our noses and a whole week since Winnie went back to California, resuming a life she had no clue had been on an entirely different course just a few days prior.

While we were no closer to locating Asmia, a fact that irked the shit out of me, I felt like I was back on track, my mind once again settled, not in flux now that the Winnie situation was settled.

Except, one of our own was still missing, and we couldn't do a goddamn thing to find her. No matter how hard we tried, every fucking lead led absolutely nowhere. I wasn't sure why I thought all would be right once I had a chance to get my head back in the game. Turned out, I wasn't a one-man show, and my distraction hadn't helped the situation, nor had it hurt. Unfortunately.

Needless to say, tensions were high at the mansion. Between that damn *gathenya* that had settled like a fog because it was obvious Eclipse and Orianna needed to fucking mate and get it over with and the loss of one of our own, everyone was getting antsy. Likely worse because no one had the ability to control either.

Of course, I had never been the sort to deal well with that sort of pressure. Didn't help that Winnie was gone and, in her absence, there was an ache that had settled within me. I hadn't thought it possible, but I actually missed her. More accurately, I missed what I thought we had. I thought she was my *amsouelot,* but I'd been sadly mistaken. The connection we shared when I met her ... I had been positive she was my other half.

How could I have been so wrong about her?

Truth was, I didn't know the first thing about tethered souls, but I'd undoubtedly jumped the gun on that one. Wishful thinking, that was what it had been. I'd held on to the hope that there was a female slated for me and there was more to my cold, lonely existence than fighting demons. Live and learn, right? Oh, yeah, I had lived, and I had most certainly learned, and I would be damned if I ever let that happen again. Until there was a bright neon sign flashing *she's the one*, I was going to stick with sating my baser urges with the Fae and moving on with my life. Much less complicated.

"Anyone seen Kaj?"

I pulled my attention away from the computer screen as Obsidian's heavy footfalls moved closer.

"Last time I talked to him, we were going over the plans for the tunnels that connected his residence to ours," I informed him.

"Was there an issue?"

I stood, wanting to be on a more even level with the male. "He wanted some additional safeguards to ensure no one could get through unless he'd cleared them personally. We're installing a fingerprint scanner and voice recognition for the locking system. We agreed he would give us the approval and we would put them into the system, ensuring we're all aware of who has access. So far, he's only given permission for Mirakel to come and go as necessary."

Obsidian nodded. "He's a good male. I trust him."

"Who, Mirakel? Or Kaj?" I joked, knowing he was referring to the vampire Alpha. After just a short conversation with Kaj, I understood the male's need to keep Bijou and Acadia safe. Since both females resided here, it made sense he didn't want just anyone to slip past our defenses.

"I think I'll head over there, see where they are with getting settled," Obsidian said.

I nodded, glanced down at my computer screen. "Mind if I go with you?"

Obsidian's silver eyes settled on my face. "Come on. We'll walk the tunnels."

Clearly he'd sensed that I didn't need to spend too much time locked in my own head. Didn't surprise me. Obsidian was astute, not to mention always keeping an eye out for us, though our job was to do that for him.

"Apollo and Amethyst should be arriving in a couple of days," Obsidian told me.

I nodded, falling into step with him. "Penelope's already working to get everything they'll need. She's going off the list Michael provided. And we've sectioned off a portion of the underground rooms to use as their medical facility. They've requested to have their rooms down here, as well."

Obsidian nodded. "God knows we've got enough space."

That we did. But then, that was the intention when we built the fortress we now resided in. We were determined we would not outgrow it for quite some time.

We traversed the winding tunnels beneath the mansion, the gas-powered lamps igniting when the motion sensors detected our presence.

"You doing all right, Reidar?"

"As good as can be expected," I admitted, figuring it probably wasn't a good idea to tell Obsidian I hated sleeping alone.

"We've been together a long time," Obsidian stated. "I can usually detect when your brain's on overload."

I kept walking as I gathered my thoughts, then paused, the move drawing Obsidian to a halt.

"When you met Penelope, was there ever any doubt that she was your *amsouelot*? I mean, I get that you knew she was because of the list and all, but ... was there ever any doubt?"

Obsidian's silver stare scoured my face. "None."

I sighed. "I was afraid you were going to say that."

"You made the right choice with Winnie." Obsidian's voice was laced with sympathy.

Meeting the male's eyes, I nodded. "I know. It's just..."

"It sucks?" Obsidian chuckled. "It's not supposed to feel good. Just because she wasn't slated as your soul's destiny doesn't mean you didn't care about her."

"I know." And I did, but that didn't stop all the what-ifs plaguing me. What if I'd treated her differently? What if I'd undergone the *lintamair* rather than hold out?

Obsidian cursed under his breath.

"I swear on my soul, Obsidian, I believed her to be my *amsouelot*. I've never felt that sort of connection with anyone before. But..." I exhaled heavily. "I found myself wanting space from her. Don't get me wrong, she's a great female. Kind, sweet, beautiful."

"But she's not your *amsouelot*."

"How will I know who is?" I blurted. "Is there some sort of sign that'll appear?"

Obsidian's big hand settled on my shoulder. "When your soul meets the one destined for you, there's no question. You simply know."

"Fucking hell." I stabbed the toe of my boot into the soft earth beneath my feet.

"You need to reset your focus, Reidar. We've got a lot going on right now. And I need you now more than ever. With the baby coming, this sitch with Taayin ... I have no right to ask more of you, but I need your head to be clear."

I stared into Obsidian's face. "It is." I shook my head. "It will be. I assure you of that."

Obsidian nodded. "Come on. Right now, let's check out this new Lair Kaj is bragging about. I'm in the mood to give him shit. We'll start with his choice of decor."

I chuckled. "And if it's nice?"

"We'll give him shit anyway."

Grateful for some space from my thoughts, I fell into step with Obsidian, my shoulders feeling a little lighter already.

NICOLE EDWARDS

ECLIPSE

I strolled down the hall, past the war room, beyond the storage areas to the new double doors. I pushed the bar on the door, smiling when they swung wide to reveal an expanse of clean white floors, bright white walls.

The new medical facility was almost complete. Considering Penelope was entering week sixteen of her pregnancy, we'd all been under the gun to get it finished before the baby made an appearance. Based on what I could tell, we were going to meet our goal with a few days to spare.

I heard the familiar sound of power tools, saw a dozen heads bent over various projects, finishing up before the healers arrived in a couple of days. But it wasn't the curtained spaces or the fancy equipment that had drawn me down here. While I was happy to see the progress, I was in search of my *amsouelot*. She'd been spending a significant amount of time down here, helping Penelope to design the space and secure all the necessary medical equipment to make it functional.

"I'm worried one recovery room won't be enough." Penelope's voice carried from beyond a newly constructed wall.

"I agree," Orianna replied. "I think two at the very least."

"I'll talk to Gryffyth," Penelope said. "Have him modify the blueprint to incorporate another space. What about the training suite?"

I stepped up behind Orianna, watching the two females as they stared out at the white tiled flooring laid out before us.

"Oh, hey." Penelope's gaze shifted over her shoulder.

I offered the female a smile, then planted my hands on Orianna's shoulders, leaning down and pressing a kiss to her cheek. "Didn't mean to interrupt."

"We're almost finished, actually," Penelope said, a grin forming. "In fact, I was about to head upstairs." Her hand rested on her swollen belly. "Figured I'd grab a snack before the morning meal."

"Don't run off on my account."

A knowing grin had Penelope's fangs flashing. "Why don't you give him a tour?" she told Orianna.

"I'll do that." Orianna turned to face me. "Although I'm not sure you need one."

I stared down into her beautiful face. "I wouldn't mind a tour."

"There's no privacy down here," she whispered, clearly picking up on why I'd sought her out.

"If you look in the right places, there's always privacy."

Taking her hand, I led her through the medical section to the rooms beyond. In an effort to give the brother and sister healers some private space, we'd turned a good portion of the underground rooms into their private quarters, including two separate bedrooms, a fully equipped kitchen, and an area for them to kick back and chill. I had no idea why Apollo and Amethyst wanted separate space, but I had agreed with Penelope that they might need time to acclimate to being on Earth. It was quite a change from Heaven.

"Is that why you came down here?" Orianna asked as I led the way into one of the empty bedrooms.

"To seduce you?" I pulled her against me, then backed her to the wall. "Absolutely."

Granted, it had only been two hours since I last had her, but that damn *gathenya* had its claws in us both. Getting ahead of the heat was the only option, the only thing keeping me even remotely sane.

Orianna moaned softly, her hands sliding up my chest to my neck. A chill danced down my spine when her fingernails sensually scraped my scalp.

Ever since the morning I went to our room to find her writhing on the bed, and I'd had no clue she needed me, I had been keeping my senses tuned to her. I had no idea how I managed to get distracted enough to have missed it, but I blamed Michael's appearance for part of it.

What bothered me most was that Orianna believed I had abandoned her. She had needed me, and I hadn't known; otherwise, I would've been at her side instantly. Those tears had broken my heart, reminding me how fragile she was. Not on the outside, of course. Orianna was a strong female, one of the strongest I'd ever met.

"Didn't we just do this?" Orianna's breathless words had me pulling my mouth from hers.

"It's been two hours."

She laughed, a sound that made my chest swell.

"Well, in that case..." She pulled my mouth back to hers.

"I want to put my tongue somewhere else," I whispered against her lips.

"Is that right?"

I slid my hand up her thigh, sliding higher until I reached the waistband of her leggings. I loved that she favored these things because they made it extremely easy to get her naked. Pretty soon, though, I was going to insist she wear skirts because ... yeah, that would take no effort at all.

The *amnigh* had all but consumed us, and though I knew what we needed to do for permanent relief, I was having a difficult time suggesting it. The thought of slaying the female I loved more than life itself was not something I could fathom. After the hell I'd put her through when I brought her back from Oklahoma, I couldn't imagine hurting her again. Knowing I was the one responsible for her pain had leveled me.

On the other hand, being the one who took her life... I wasn't sure I would survive it.

However, the alternative was going to be keeping her drugged, and I already knew her feelings on that. Obsidian assured me it was the only option aside from going through with the *lintamair*. We already agreed to discuss with the healers when they arrived to see if there was something we could do in the future, but that wouldn't benefit Orianna. Again, she wasn't going to succumb to being drugged.

As I tugged her leggings down her thighs, I went to my knees, trailing kisses over her hips as I uncovered the soft, smooth flesh beneath.

"Eclipse!"

I smiled. "I love when you say my name like that."

I looked up at her as I lifted one of her legs and draped it over my shoulder.

She cried out my name again when I dragged my tongue along her cleft. I loved the way she shuddered as I pleasured her. These moments were few and far between because of the *amnigh*. I spent more time easing than exploring, and I wanted the shift to be permanent. I wanted to spend my evenings with my tongue buried between her thighs, my mornings sliding into the warm haven of her body. And in between ... I wanted to make Orianna happy. Whatever that looked like. As long as she had a smile on her face, I would consider it a job well done.

"Eclipse..." Orianna squealed when her other leg gave way, but I was right there, holding her up with my hands as I worked her clit faster.

A soft, guttural moan escaped as her hand stabbed into my hair, tugging roughly as she came against my mouth.

After a quick shift to my feet, I lifted her and carried her over to one of the medical exam tables being stored there. Without fanfare, I set her on the edge, freed my erection, then aligned our bodies. My head fell back on my shoulders as fireworks danced behind my eyelids when I sank into her tight sheath. This was heaven, right here. My *amsouelot* in my arms, our bodies joined, the soft rasps of her breaths as she urged me to pump harder, faster, deeper.

And when her body shattered around me, I let myself go, filling her, marking her, claiming her. She was mine. From now until eternity, and there was only one way to ensure that would forever be the case.

As I caught my breath, I leaned forward, pressing my forehead to Orianna's.

"I want to mate you," I whispered.

"Okay." Her hands trembled as they trailed up to my shoulders.

"I mean ... I want to make this joining official."

"Okay."

I lifted my head, tilting her chin up so I could peer into her beautiful eyes. "I don't think you understand. I want—"

Orianna's soft fingers pressed gently to my lips. "I know what it means, Eclipse. And I want the same thing."

Fear trickled into my veins, strangling the elation.

Orianna's hand shifted to my cheek, the other one joining on the other side. "You're the only man"—she smiled brightly—"*angel*, who has ever made me feel this way. Like I'm ... valuable. I love you. I want to spend eternity with you. Not just the amount of time I have left here. Forever."

Her eyes searched mine as her thumb brushed over my cheek.

"I trust you, Eclipse. Together, we can get through anything. Even my death and my resurrection." Unshed tears glistened in her eyes. "Am I scared?" She nodded. "Terrified. But I trust myself as much as I trust you. I know this is the right thing. I know we're meant to be together. If it's any consolation, I've seen it in my visions. I know we get through it unscathed. I will return to you, and we will be together for eternity."

I wasn't sure if that helped, but I was past the point of talking myself out of it.

"I'm ready whenever you are," she whispered.

I wrapped my arms around her, yanking her to my chest. I was probably cutting off the circulation to her brain, but I couldn't let go.

It was all I could do to remain standing.

44

OBSIDIAN

———

One would've thought my *ereswa* had given birth by the way the mansion lit up with excitement on the day the healers arrived. Luckily, they'd opted to make their appearance at daybreak rather than nightfall. Had it been the other way around, last night would've been a complete and total waste, something we couldn't afford right now. Not with Asmia still out there.

I remained just outside the infirmary, what the *fiestreigh* had dubbed the "Torture Chamber", watching my female introduce the healers to their new workspace.

"We tried to think of everything you might need," Penelope told Apollo and Amethyst. "I'm sure we've missed something, but you need only ask, and we'll ensure you get it."

Apollo, ever the strong, silent type, merely nodded, his

silver gaze swinging across the vast landscape of gleaming white and stainless steel. The male's dark hair was shorn to the scalp, likely a style that was easy to maintain, and every so often he would run his hand over it as though it was a recent development.

The medical facility was complete, the patient rooms set up, the surgical suite holding every possible tool we could get our hands on, including what humans called an MRI machine. I knew nothing of human medicine, nor did I have any desire to get acquainted with it. The only thing I cared about was getting some assurance that my female and our baby would be in good hands once our son or daughter decided to make an appearance.

"We thank you kindly," Amethyst told Penelope, reaching out and giving Penelope's hand a gentle squeeze. "And we're glad to be here."

Based on the slant of Apollo's eyebrows, I wasn't so sure the male felt the same.

"I'll show you to your private quarters," Penelope offered, nodding to the far end of the hallway.

When the females departed, I turned to Apollo. "Are we going to have problems?"

The male turned to face me, silver eyes locking onto my face. "I don't anticipate any. You?"

Offering a half-hearted shrug, I held that stare. "I get the feeling you're not keen on being here."

A partial smile appeared, softening the male's hard-lined face. "As you can imagine, moving tends to take it out on a male."

That dragged a laugh from me. "I understand fully. I did the same fifteen hundred years ago."

"Then you've had a bit more time to settle in than I."

True.

"Not sure what you like to do in your spare time," I told him, "but don't feel like you have to remain down here. The entire mansion is fortified for access during daylight hours. There's plenty of recreation up there, including a fully equipped gym and an Olympic-size pool. Down here we've got a dedicated sparring room. Should you feel so inclined, simply let me know if you'd like a partner."

Apollo smiled, the tips of his fangs flashing. "I might just take you up on that."

I wondered if those fangs were a new development. Angels in Heaven didn't have the necessary tools to feed here on Earth, and the fact Apollo was sporting the new dental hardware told me the male was being held to the same rule: feed from the Fae so the Almighty could keep close tabs on you.

"I look forward to it." I motioned toward the end of the hallway in the direction the females went. "You've got a chef's kitchen, and while I've asked the *heurosp* to give you space, I can't say with absolute certainty they'll follow my command. They prefer to be of service, and I'm pretty sure they feel it's a crime when one of us attempts to do their job."

"These are humans?" Apollo asked.

"Immortals, but yes, biologically, they're still human. Is that going to be a problem?"

"We've got a vast knowledge of human physiology, so I'd say no."

I nodded, glad to hear that. "We've also got Fae in residence, roughly twenty who come and go. Both male and female, so you've got your pick as far as feeding's concerned."

There was a flicker of heat in the male's eyes. "I have no personal preference. Both are equally satisfying."

Well, there you go.

Apollo scanned the space once more, then turned to face me fully. "I can assure you, Penelope's care will be our utmost concern until delivery. You can trust that I understand she's mated, which means she cannot bear my touch. Amethyst will be handling things in that regard. I, however, will be on hand to assist once the baby's born. Michael impressed upon us the importance of her status."

I smiled. "I won't lie; as far as I'm concerned, Penelope's well-being should come before anyone else. But those are the words and emotions of a *reuthet*. She is my main concern, always. I take it you're not mated."

"I am not." Apollo's stare remained even. "Nor have I any desire to be so. I prefer simple if you know what I mean."

"To each his own," I told him. "And I'm glad you're both here."

"It's my understanding vampires are in residence, as well?"

I motioned back the way we'd come. "We have one residing within these walls, the daughter of the Alpha. There are five more, including the Alpha, who reside in the residence adjacent to ours. They have access via the tunnels. It goes without saying, if they need medical attention, I'll expect you'll be complicit in providing."

"We're not here to make waves," Apollo said. "We go where we're told."

Stepping forward, I maintained direct eye contact. "We all take orders," I said simply. "However, here, in my home, we're not merely soldiers in a war. This is a family, Apollo. Every member, be it angel, vampire, Fae, or human. We command the same respect for all. I hope you'll find your place within this family, as it appears it will only continue to grow from this point forward."

I noticed a shift in the male, as though he hadn't expected as much.

"We're not official within these walls," I continued, "but

we care for our own no matter where we are. Like I said, I'm glad you've joined us, and I hope you'll find your place here."

In a rare gesture, I held out my hand.

When Apollo met it, clasping my palm and squeezing firmly, I knew we had an understanding. Perhaps Michael dictated the outcome, positioning the pieces as he saw fit, but we didn't live by Michael's rules down here.

And though the archangel would be spending more time on Earth, I had no intentions of changing that now.

I retrieved my hand. "Now, come on. Let's grab something to eat."

"Yes. Let's."

ECLIPSE

"How is she?"

I managed to make it as far as the kitchen island, but I had to drop onto a stool once I was within range. "It's brutal."

Obsidian chuckled. "Never thought you'd say that, huh?"

"Never." Then again, as a highly sexual male, my pleasure receptors were tuned to flare up at even the mention of sex. However, I was beginning to wonder if friction burn was a thing and, if so, how long before I felt it.

"Maybe there's a patch or something you could wear," Reidar noted. "Curb the cravings."

I flipped him off, then hung my head. I was exhausted, and I could only imagine how Orianna was doing. We'd slept maybe a total of two hours in the past nine. The rest had been spent attempting to ease the *amnigh*.

"I think, at the very least, we need to task the healers with finding something that'll help," Reidar tacked on.

"Wouldn't matter. Orianna's opposed to drugs."

"Yeah, well, maybe they can come up with something that'll stop all that fucking energy then," the male rumbled. "Because fucking hell, man."

I grinned as I peered over at Obsidian.

"Hey," Obsidian said with a smirk, "I have to agree with him there. And I've only endured from you. They've been dealing with this since I brought Penelope back here."

"Or maybe you can just keep your *amsouelots* away until you've undergone the *lintamair*," Reidar suggested.

"Not happening," Obsidian countered. "Safer here."

"Yeah, well, tell that to my dick."

I chuckled again, thanking Phillip when he passed over a cup of coffee. "I'll need the evening meal delivered to my room."

The *heurosp* nodded, smiled widely. "It would be my pleasure, sire."

When the male walked away, and Reidar started toward the dining room, I motioned Obsidian toward the office at the back of the house.

"What's up?"

I took a deep breath, ignored the churning in my gut. "I need someone to prep the mating chamber. Preferably ... you."

Obsidian's eyes widened. "Brother, it would be my honor."

Another deep breath cruised through my lungs and back

out, a bit heavier this time, as the emotion grabbed hold of me by the throat. "I know I have to do this," I said softly, "but I'm not sure how I'll survive it."

Rather than placate me with words, Obsidian moved close, took hold of my head, and dragged our faces closer. With foreheads touching, my shoulders began to shake. I'd been holding it in since I mentioned it to Orianna. I was fairly certain it was a spur-of-the-moment thing, but in the end, I knew it was a necessity. Ensuring my female's safety was paramount, and this, no matter how hard it would be, was the only way.

"I won't sugarcoat it, it's the hardest thing you'll ever do," Obsidian said gruffly. "But know we're all here for both of you. You will survive this, as will she."

"My brain understands that," I told my brother. "My heart's the problem."

"I know."

We remained like that for a couple of minutes before I squared my shoulders and pulled away from the embrace.

"I'm going to need you in the next couple of days," I told my brother.

"I'm not going anywhere. Whatever you need."

I thanked Obsidian, then forced my feet to carry me up to the third floor. I knew our meal would be delivered any minute, and I wanted to share it with Orianna before we were pulled under once more. My cock had already hardened, growing more insistent the closer I got to our private quarters.

When I walked into the room, I saw the bathroom light was now on, the fire still going, keeping the room warm. Orianna was curled up on the bed, her blond hair fanned out over her pillow. I perched on the edge of the mattress and ran my fingers through all that silk. I watched her face, listening to the soft breaths she took as she succumbed to exhaustion. I wasn't sure how we would make it through the next three days, but at least I would be distracted.

Right now, it was imperative my brain shut down.

Orianna must've sensed my presence because she rolled to her back, eyes peeling open and a beautiful smile pulling at her mouth.

"Good evening, *sezari*." I mirrored her smile.

"Please tell me there's food."

"Phillip's having it sent up. Should be here in a few."

"I'm starving."

As was I.

Her smile slipped, her expression sobering as she reached up and ran her fingers over my cheek. "Everything okay?"

I tried to nod, just as a reassurance, but I couldn't lie. "It will be," I said instead.

And I was going to latch onto that thought and run with it.

Because what else could I do?

KAJ

"Whatever you do, I suggest you don't go near that mansion," I warned the males seated at the table in the dining room. "At least not for a couple more days."

"I've heard," Blāz replied with a smirk. "So that mating heat ... it's a real thing, huh?"

"Real and brutal," I admitted.

"What's it like?" Huracān asked.

"One minute you're going about your own damn business, and then ... fuck," I grumbled. "Out of the blue, the need overwhelms you."

"Damn good thing they've got Fae," Blāz said.

I happened to be looking at Mirakel, so I noticed the male flinch. Not the first time he'd done so in the past couple of days, ever since that female had fed him. As easy as it would've been to give the male shit about it, I had sympathy for him. After all, I knew exactly what it felt like to be bowled over by one of those females. From the very first drop of Acadia's blood that hit my tongue, I was transformed, my entire existence altered.

"How's Bijou doing over there?" Huracān asked.

"Oddly enough, she's found herself a friend," I explained.

"The human male?"

"Actually, the human female. The older one."

"Orianna's mother?" Blāz asked.

Interesting how my males knew all about what was going on over at Angel Central, despite the fact not one of them had gone over. At least not that I knew about.

"Yes," I confirmed. "They've taken to one another quite well."

I figured it had to do with the fact Bijou had lost her mother. Probably found comfort in having a motherly figure in her life. I hadn't met the human female, had actually done my best to keep my distance.

"Those angels sure like to give us shit for interacting with humans. They don't seem to have a problem with it," Blāz added. "Got them traipsing all over hither and yon."

It was true, the angels were interacting more with humans now, but they weren't casual acquaintances. The two humans currently in residence were family members of the *amsouelots*. They were obviously the exception to the rule.

"I heard they sent one back out in the human world," Huracān prompted. "Know if that's true?"

I nodded, pushing my plate away. "Yeah. Scrubbed her mind, sent her back."

For whatever reason, Blāz found that amusing, based on the chuckle he let out.

"You meet the healers yet?" Kidel asked, speaking up for the first time since we sat down.

"No. But they've arrived." Clearing my throat, I wanted to bring the conversation back to business, the intention of this gathering. "I need an update on the status of the electronics."

Blāz began spilling words that made little sense to me, but I trusted the male to know what he was talking about. Something along the lines of sensors and detectors, moving on to cameras and the official status of the steel shutters.

"No more bugs?"

"None," Blāz confirmed. "I've tested them for the past two days. All settled. The house is now safe to traverse during daylight hours."

"Good. Let's get some furnishings, and we can officially move in." I peered over at Mirakel. "Any updates on *vestrahn* coming to work here?"

Mirakel's neon blue gaze settled on me. "At this time, I'm not comfortable bringing any into the mansion, so I had a conversation with Phillip. The male informed me they would gladly loan a few of theirs to manage the place until we can hire our own."

I wasn't going to intervene in that regard. As my *adighrielin*, Mirakel would expect to have the final approval on all souls who would be within the residence of the Alpha. Considering he was my first line of defense, it only made sense he was being precautious. And for now, we were capable of cleaning up after ourselves. Not since the Seattle camp had we had *vestrahn* in residence. We'd been doing it for long enough, grown males and all that shit.

"I know it'll take time for us to settle in completely," I told my males, "however, we can't get too lax. I doubt Darko has nixed the idea of taking me down, and that's a situation I can't let fester. We can show absolutely no weakness as we get our reign established."

"Understood," Mirakel said. "And agree. Which is why I've set up meetings with the noble families within the region. Huracān and I will be meeting with them starting next week."

"Really?"

The male nodded. "The meetings are twofold. I intend to gauge their stance on the *kirlesgun*, as well as identify all males who are of fighting age."

I remembered doing the same thing for Kardobahn. Not getting input on the *kirlesgun*, because the king's regime had already been established before my birth. However, I had ventured out, seeking those who were not so much willing but rather strong enough to fortify the ranks within the Zenith.

It took years to find worthy fighters to fill those spots and decades to train them to be the most powerful among our species. The task laid out before us wasn't a simple one, but it was doable, provided we remembered this required patience.

One day at a time was sometimes easier said than done.

Unfortunately, it was not merely a suggestion but a way of life because we were officially back to square one.

45

OBSIDIAN

There was a wealth of emotion that flooded me as I stood with my brothers and the *fiestreigh* outside the mating chamber far beneath the mansion. Every member of our family—warriors, angels, and Fae—had descended below ground wearing the traditional black, weaponed up, and prepared to stand vigil over Eclipse and Orianna for the next forty-eight hours.

Even Penelope would be joining us, despite my argument. My female insisted she was fully prepared to remain with us, even if I demanded she sit comfortably in a leather armchair I had brought down. Initially, I was prepared to deny her the opportunity, but thanks to Amethyst, who assured me her pregnancy was smooth sailing and that she'd be close by, I had no leg to stand on. For perhaps the first time in my existence, I was overruled by females. I got the feeling that wouldn't be the last time.

From the moment Eclipse came to me, told me of his decision to officially mate Orianna, I had shared my brother's pain. Seemed like just yesterday I'd undergone it myself, and if I lived to be two billion years old, I would never forget what it felt like to pierce Penelope's heart, to watch the life drain out of her. There was still an echo of pain deep in my chest from the memories alone.

So, for the past couple of days, we'd done what we could to pass the time. The never-ending minutes had ticked by, and after an intense sparring session in which Eclipse took on all six of his brothers, I got the feeling he was as ready as he would ever be. Now the male was down to the final hour. Orianna had to die exactly twenty-four hours prior to the full moon, and behind me, Eclipse was already inside, awaiting his female's arrival.

Every so often, I would glance over my shoulder to ensure my brother was still holding it together. As it was, Eclipse was on his haunches, head bowed, breaths sawing in and out of his lungs, his back rising with every draw of oxygen. Once in a while, a soft sound would escape, the sort you'd expect to hear from a wounded animal. I would wince, a renewed sense of solace for my brother. I knew how Eclipse felt, and I fucking hated that they had to endure this, but death and resurrection were necessary in this ritual. More so, ultimate faith in the Father who art in Heaven. In the end, Orianna would be safe, and I figured that was what Eclipse was hanging on to as he fought the urge to run far and fast.

I remembered being in that mating chamber, looking into Penelope's eyes. She was the strong one that day. If it hadn't been for her insistence, I never would've gone through with it. From what I'd seen of Orianna over the course of these past couple of months, she was equally strong. Any female who mated us would have to be, I figured.

The door to the stairwell opened, Zeus and Aphrodite strolling in, the canines seeming to sense what was taking place. They'd become close to Orianna, and it made sense they'd want to accompany her down here.

Penelope stepped out next, Orianna behind her, and Acadia pulling up the rear. The female procession moved forward, all angels standing tall, wielding the weapons they would rely on to fight off anyone who attempted to harm them in the coming days. The same as we would every day for eternity.

As Orianna neared, I could hear the rapid thump of her heart. She appeared stoic, but there was definitely fear. I knew she was aware of what was going to happen because she'd seen the vision herself. That was more than Penelope'd had going into this, and I hoped it was enough for her to get Eclipse through it.

Penelope kept one hand linked with Orianna's as they stepped up to me.

"You are a brave female," I said softly. "My brother needs your strength right now, the same as you need his. Go forth with the knowledge the two of you are in this together. From now until eternity."

Tears were forming in Orianna's clear blue eyes, but she nodded, then took a step forward when I moved aside and allowed her entry into the room.

When Penelope released her, Orianna completed the trek, crossing the threshold into the room. I willed the door closed with my mind, then stepped back in front of it where I would remain for the entirety of the ritual. My female stood at my side, showing her support as well.

There was a flutter of sound as all wings expanded, spreading wide to shield the wall at our back, forming a solid circle around the space. I took Penelope's hand in mine, gave it a gentle squeeze.

She returned the gesture, and I knew in that moment that, despite the horror of the act, it was worth it. Orianna would be better off when it was completed. The same would be the case for Eclipse.

Thanks be to God.

ECLIPSE

I felt the shift in the air when Orianna stepped into the mating chamber. Very similar to the shift the night I sensed her at the Dungeon. Seemed so long ago and, at the same time, like just yesterday.

"Eclipse?"

It took effort, but I forced myself to my feet, my legs not nearly as strong as I'd hoped they would be. I'd long ago lost sensation in my knees as I'd remained on that hard stone floor, trying to come to terms with what I had to do. I was no closer to being okay with it than when I first learned of the ritual long ago. If it weren't for the *amnigh* and the pain Orianna was in, I would've put it off for another month or ten. Perhaps indefinitely. This was the absolute last place I wanted to be.

Soft hands curled over my cheeks, and I forced my eyes open, seeing Orianna for the first time since Penelope sent me out of our room so she could tend to my female.

My *amsouelot* looked absolutely stunning in the pale blue gown that covered her, the wide sleeves bunched up at her elbows as she kept her hands on my face. Her hair was pulled up into some fancy do on top of her head. It was the first time I'd seen her with her hair up, and I found I liked it. Then again, she could've cut it all off, and I would've been fine with that, too. Her beautiful visage was only the packaging; it was her inner strength that I had fallen in love with.

Out of the corner of my eye, I saw the small table and the two items resting atop it: the cheap alarm clock—the hands telling me we had roughly five minutes—and the Jagdkommando dagger, the sharp blades catching the light. A shudder ran through me at the thought of what I had to do with that wicked sharp blade.

"It's going to be okay," Orianna said softly. "I've seen it, Eclipse."

She'd seen herself lying on the cold floor, my body covering hers. But she hadn't seen me jamming that blade into her heart, nor had she felt the pain associated with a mortal wound.

The thought had me stumbling back, my throat closing as emotion threatened to take me to the floor. How could I possibly do this? I peered down at my hands, which were shaking so hard I wasn't sure I could hold the dagger. How could they cause her pain? It was my ultimate vow to never forsake her, to always protect her. Yet I was the one who would end her life? Fucking irony, that was.

"I can't," I muttered, eyes closing. "Orianna. I don't know how."

Those soft hands were strong when they gripped my

wrists, jerking me to attention. I forced my eyes open, met her pale blue ones.

"I love you, *sezari*," I rasped, the words barely passing through to my lips. "I don't know how to do this."

"Yes, you do." She stepped closer. "I love you, too, Eclipse. We're stronger together. I know that, you know that."

How could she be so fucking calm about this? So fucking stoic? In less than four minutes, she was going to die. I was going to plunge that silver dagger into her chest and stop her human heart. I would much rather the wound be inflicted upon me. I could handle that sort of agony. This ... thinking about it was too much.

Sacrifice.

The word sounded in my head.

The ultimate sacrifice, warrior. It's what's required.

Michael.

The archangel was in my head, and those words were oddly ... soothing.

Know I'll be here with her when you can't be. She'll be kept safe until she's returned to you. And when she does, she'll be yours forever.

I'd never known Michael as a gentlemale. No, he was more of a smart-ass, an instigator.

Trust in your faith, warrior. Trust in your love.

I forced my eyes open. The hands on the clock were a minute out from where they would forever stop for Orianna's human existence. It was now or never. With strength I didn't expect, I moved toward the dagger. I gripped it in my palm, shielding it behind my back because, fuck, no reason she should have to look at it too closely.

"Come here, *sezari*."

Orianna came to me without hesitance, as though she was

okay with this. I wasn't sure I understood how that was even possible, but I was out of time for questioning it.

"I trust you, Eclipse. And I have faith in you and Him. If this weren't where I was meant to be, I wouldn't be here."

For whatever reason, that settled me. Not enough for me to think this was okay, but enough for me to get my priorities in line. With my free arm, I turned her away from me, my left arm curling loosely around her neck. I pulled her back to my chest, her heart just off-center of mine.

"Close your eyes for me," I pleaded. I couldn't live with the thought of her seeing what I had to do.

"I love you," she whispered as she rested her head on my shoulder. "With all that I am."

Tears sprung forth, but I slammed my eyes shut. Pressing my lips to her temple, I swallowed the sob that threatened, lifting the dagger. Even with my eyes closed, I could sense exactly where she stood, the precise spot where her heart was. My training and experience had prepared me with the knowledge of how much pressure was necessary to go through flesh and bone, to penetrate that delicate organ that kept her alive.

"Close your eyes, *sezari!*" The words burst from my mouth.

My chest burned, my eyes opening as I glanced at the clock once more.

"I love you," I breathed against her temple.

My throat closed up as my arm pulled back. Thank the Lord Almighty, I would not remember the moment of impact, when I drove that blade clean through her chest and into her heart. My mind would forever block out Orianna's horrific scream, the way she reached for the forearm holding her as I lowered her to the floor. I would never relive the bloom of her blood as it drained out of her and onto the ground beneath us.

No, what I would remember for eternity was the cold that settled over me, an arctic blast that turned my blood to ice and my bones to stone. It was the punishment I deserved for what I'd done. It consumed me completely when Orianna took her last ragged breath, her eyes pleading with me as though I could save her from this.

And when those beautiful blue eyes closed once and for all, I, and everyone else in Darkness, would remember the tortured roar that screamed up from deep in the Earth and rocked the very foundation of the mansion that kept us sheltered.

46

ORIANNA

My eyes flew open, and I squinted into the soft white surrounding me. It was everywhere, from the walls to the billowy curtains that formed a canopy over the bed with its white comforter and pillows.

When I sat up, I expected to see angels, but no one was in the room with me. Not that I could tell anyway. There was no sound. No air being driven through vents, no subtle creaks of a house settling, no footsteps, no bird song out the window. Nothing.

But it was a tranquil emptiness. A serene stillness I had never encountered before.

My hand shifted to the wound over my heart, expecting to find blood gushing from the hole that had been carved into my chest, but it wasn't there. There was no evidence that evil blade ever plunged through me. It was as though it had never happened.

Forcing my legs over the edge of the bed, I pushed myself to sitting, peering around, taking it all in. I appeared to be completely alone, but there wasn't an emptiness associated with it. As though someone was still with me, watching over me.

"Hello?" I called out, my bare feet moving over the marble floor. It was surprisingly comfortable, not cold the way it was at the mansion. Even with the windows open, the breeze fluttering through, it was the perfect temperature.

Hoping something would clue me in as to where I was, I started for the open window.

"Orianna?"

That familiar voice stopped me in my tracks. My hand went to my mouth as I slowly pivoted. "Amber?"

A soft smile pulled at my sister's mouth. "In the flesh."

I frowned, tears instantly springing to my eyes. "I … but … wh—"

"It's okay," Amber said, moving closer. She reached out and took the hand I still had covering my mouth. "I'm here."

And that was the moment fear settled in. If Amber was here, and what Barin said was true, that meant...

"Where are we?"

"Heaven."

The implications of that hit me square in the chest. I'd come to terms with the fact my sister was dead, but … well, truth was, dead was merely a term. It had never meant anything. Sort of like, *Amber is smart*, or *Amber is mad*. Merely an adjective: *Amber is dead*. Easier to accept that way, or in my case, easier to pretend it didn't mean what it did. I had never thought of it in the verb tense: Amber died.

Yet here she was. In Heaven.

"But I've been looking for you," I told her.

"I know. I've been watching you for the past year."

"You've been dead a year?"

"A few days short of a year, but yeah." Amber's fingers rubbed my hand, soothing me. "I was watching you the night you met your angel."

I wasn't sure what to say to that. My eyes bounced over Amber's face, absorbing her image. She looked the same as the last time I had seen her, so long ago. Her features still soft and round, youth clinging despite the years that had passed.

"That guy thought I was you," I told her, thinking back to that night. "The one with the gun."

"Yeah, well." Amber's grin widened. "I might've nudged that encounter a bit."

"So he didn't know you?"

A soft chuckle escaped my sister. "I'd never seen him before, and I seriously doubted he knew Dad. But he was out to do harm, so he wasn't an innocent bystander, I assure you."

Well, that certainly explained the weirdness of the situation.

Amber's face sobered. "And I've been watching you these past couple of months."

"So you saw Mom?"

There was a sadness in Amber's blue eyes. "I check in on her all the time."

"She's with me. At the mansion," I said, though I realized it wasn't necessary.

"I know. And she's happy there. Don't let her fool you. She's taken to that young vampire, too. I think she needs someone to bond with since she's unable to physically take care of someone. She and Bijou are connecting."

I had noticed that, too.

"And you?" I asked my sister. "Are you happy here?"

579

"I'm not running anymore." She said it as though that was a relief.

"That doesn't answer my question."

Amber's gaze shifted over my face. "I'm finally at peace, Orianna."

"What about your … remains? I've never found your body."

"My ashes are being held at a funeral home in Harper, Kansas, of all places." Amber grinned. "It's right across from a Casey's General Store. So, when you go get them, which I know you will, could you do me a favor?"

"Anything."

"Spread them out over Darkness, where you live. That way I can be with you and Mom forever."

Tears came, and I couldn't stop them. They dripped down my cheeks, unbidden.

Amber gently squeezed my hand. "I'm happy now. Truly.." She leaned in closer. "But I don't want you to think I wasn't happy when we were younger. Before..."

I smiled. "I know we were. Then life got in the way."

"It tends to do that from time to time." Amber took my other hand, holding them both. "But it's time for you to return to that life."

"What?" I glanced around. "I thought I had twenty-four hours."

Amber smiled. "Time moves much faster here."

"But..."

"Your angel's waiting for you, Orianna. He needs you right now. He's hurting, and he needs you to ease that pain."

Thinking of Eclipse was the only thing that could possibly pull me away from this moment. I wondered if Amber knew that.

"I do," Amber said with a giggle.

Unable to help myself, I threw my arms around my sister, hugging her tightly. "I miss you, sis. I love you so much."

"Ditto," Amber replied. "Now, go back to your man and spend the rest of eternity happy."

I stepped back, smiled. I was about to say something when everything washed away, like someone had poured paint over the current picture, erasing it. I had the sense of falling, similar to taking that first hill down on a roller coaster. My stomach fluttered and I briefly prayed there was something below to catch me. There was no hard landing, though, just a gentle thud, as though I'd been returned to my corporeal form. And there was a familiarity with my new location, but I felt trapped, held captive by my own body.

His voice was the first thing I was aware of, his soft sobs surprisingly loud.

Eclipse. Words wouldn't form, but I knew he was there.

"*Sezari*? Oh, God." Eclipse sobbed.

I was trapped in my own body, but something told me I was all right. There was no need to panic because Eclipse was with me. I was safe because he would make it so.

I wasn't sure how much time passed, but each of my senses slowly came back online, and I found we were no longer in that stone room, but instead...

"Where are we?"

"We haven't gone far," he said softly.

Taking his word for it, I scanned the room once more.

"It's exactly as I imagined it," I whispered, curious as to whether my voice would work.

It did and so did my muscles as I lifted my head and glanced around the room. It was what I'd call modern farm-house. The traditional white-washed bed's large headboard was against one wall. The pile of cream and navy pillows were a bit rumpled, as was the navy-blue throw blanket across the bottom. It was exactly the bedroom I always envisioned I would one day have if and when I finally settled down.

"It suits you," Eclipse said, his hands curling around my cheeks, his eyes holding mine as though I was a lifeline he refused to let go of. "Perhaps we'll have to remodel."

I smiled. "Perhaps."

But that would have to wait. Right now— My eyes shifted to his neck, followed by a strange tingling in my upper jaw. I tested the sensation with the tip of my tongue, and felt the sharp canines growing longer. A smile pulled at my mouth as it became clear that I now sported fangs. And that meant...

"You need to feed, *sezari*."

Yes. Yes, I most definitely did. "But I want to feel you over me when I do. Naked."

Without preamble, Eclipse got to his feet, discarding the jeans he was wearing even as I worked the thin gown up and over my head, tossing it somewhere on the far side of the room. When he returned to me, his warmth covering me, I ran my hands over his forearms, his biceps, up to his shoulders. My sense of touch was heightened, but he still felt the same, only better. And though it had supposedly only been twenty-four hours, it felt like years since I'd last touched him. The only thing I wanted to do was hold him for the next ... eternity. His warmth alone soothed me.

"Feed from me," Eclipse demanded.

Those words triggered the tingling in my upper jaw, but it was the curiosity that spurred me forward. I remembered wondering what his blood would taste like, and now I was going to find out firsthand.

I dragged his head toward me, but rather than go right for the jugular, I melded my mouth to his. I felt him relax more, his hips settling into the cradle of my thighs. It wasn't long before that gnawing pain in my gut grew insistent, forcing me to release his mouth. I needed no instructions as Eclipse settled his weight on his forearms, turning his head so I had access to his vein.

My fangs had elongated more, the perfect length to pierce his flesh, spearing into him with minimal effort. Instinct took over from there, my lips sealing around the wounds as I sucked. His blood flooded my mouth, the taste so rich, not at all like what I'd expected. There was no copper tang, as was the case with human blood. This was more of a rich wine that I was addicted to within seconds.

I was vaguely aware of Eclipse's body tensing, his muscles locking up, the heat of his heavy flesh pressed against my belly.

"*Sezari* ... oh, fuck ... oh, fuck." He pressed his neck toward my mouth as his hips jerked.

He was coming, I realized, his release spraying over my stomach. There was a tremendous power in knowing I had that sort of power over him. I'd succumbed to it from that very first night we were together when I insisted he take from me. At the time, I hadn't even known what he was or why I was compelled to offer my vein, but it had felt right. And now ... it was my turn to return the favor.

When I felt his hips jerking once more, I sucked harder on his vein, wanting to feel his release once more before I let him go. It came a minute later on a strangled growl that triggered a mini explosion within me. As he settled, I retracted my fangs and sealed the punctures before finding his mouth with mine once more.

I wasn't sure what I'd done to deserve him, but I knew without a doubt I would never let him go. I would spend the rest of my immortal existence ensuring he never endured the sort of pain I could feel echoing inside him.

From now until eternity, we would take care of one another.

Exactly as it was meant to be.

47

MIRAKEL

Turned out, it was true, vampires could go an extended amount of time without feeding.

I learned this the hard way. By refraining.

Now, I was as good as fucking useless, unable to move, more than likely on the verge of death. I figured my body was attempting a shutdown, my organs seizing up, and it was my own fucking fault. Kaj had been insistent, yet I had defied the order because I couldn't fathom taking the vein of that Fae again and the thought of feeding from anyone else...

I groaned, attempting to turn to my side, but it didn't work. There wasn't an ounce of strength to be summoned.

The knock on my door went unanswered because I couldn't get my tongue to form the words or my vocal cords to relay the message. So I remained where I was, peering around the last place I would ever see. The sleeping chambers I'd been given had been simple at one time. A week ago, I figured. Back before those two *heurosp* had taken it upon themselves to spruce it up. Now I had a room full of furniture, ridiculously soft sheets, a thick, heavy comforter to keep me warm, and matching drapes covering the steel shutters on the windows.

It was actually quite lovely, though that word wasn't usually in my vocabulary. However, it suited the inviting space I had to lay my head.

Too bad I wasn't going to get to enjoy it for long. Hell, I didn't even get a chance to check out the huge Jacuzzi tub in the bathroom.

Oh, well.

Didn't matter now. I was letting down everyone I knew because I was an idiot, refusing to feed. As I thought about it, I almost couldn't remember why I thought this was a good idea. That night when I held that female in my arms and came like a fucking teenager as I took her vein … it seemed a lifetime ago, a distant, vague memory.

Another knock sounded on my door, and again, I couldn't summon the strength to answer. I listened, my hearing beginning to dim as a buzzing formed in my head. I waited to hear the sound of footsteps as they left me there to die, alone on this too-comfortable bed, in this too-big room.

The rattle of the doorknob had hope flaring in my chest, but I was too weak to do anything about it. My head wouldn't even turn to see who it was.

I grunted softly, attempting to catch their attention in case a *heurosp* was coming to tidy up if it was night or to pull down the blankets if it was day. I had no idea which it was, and I honestly didn't care.

"Sire?"

My eyes widened as that beautiful face came into view

beside my bed. She was just as lovely—there was that word again—as she'd been the first time I saw her. Purple eyes, that silky, shiny strawberry-blond hair. Perfectly set eyes, delicate nose, fucking perfect mouth.

Turned out I had *some* energy left because my fangs shot down from my jaw.

"Oh, sire," she said softly. "You've waited too long."

I tried to shake my head to tell her to leave me be, but my lack of strength rebelled against the instruction from my brain.

My eyes were about the only thing that still worked, so I settled on memorizing Briony's delicate features. Maybe I could take that image with me into the afterlife, hold on to it once I was in the vast beyond, wherever I was being sent.

When her wrist came in contact with my mouth, I moaned softly, but I lacked the strength to pierce her flesh.

"Here, let me do it."

I watched as she lifted her wrist to her mouth and punctured her own vein before returning it to my lips. The first drop was an awakening, my cells seeming to realize I would not be relocating to whatever afterlife I was allocated to.

My body greedily took what she offered, and when my arms were strong enough, my hands found her flesh, circling her forearm and holding her wrist against my lips. I closed my eyes, attempting to keep the rest of my body under control, but it wasn't working. She was just so soft, her blood the sweetest ambrosia, her scent... I could feel my dick thickening beneath the blankets. I was naked, a status I was not all that happy with considering what was going on down south.

Thankfully, the blanket remained in place as I fortified myself with the life that flowed from her vein. It wasn't until I heard her soft gasp that I opened my eyes and looked at her face. There was a gray tinge to her skin, a sickly pallor that sent panic racing through me. I immediately released her, though I wasn't nearly close to getting my fill.

"I shall leave you now, sire." Her head lowered as she sealed the wounds on her wrist.

"What ails you?" I asked, the words a gruff whisper, as though my diaphragm hadn't quite gotten with the program.

"Nothing for you to concern yourself with, sire."

To hell with that. I sat up. "Wait."

Her hand was on the doorknob, but she stopped moving.

"Come here," I insisted.

She followed my command, but I could sense it was second nature.

"What ails you?" I repeated. "When's the last time you fed?"

"I am not sure, sire."

Because I was naked, I couldn't get to my feet, so instead, I patted the mattress beside me. "Come here. Take my vein."

Her amethyst gaze, clouded by her need to feed, lifted to meet my eyes. "Sire, that is not how Fae feed."

"Then how do you do it?"

"We siphon energy."

"And how does that work?" Perhaps I sounded like an idiot, but so be it. "Can you take from me?"

"You have little to spare."

"That's not a no," I stated, motioning her toward me. "Tell me what you need me to do."

Her hesitation was dangerously close to pissing me off.

"Tell me," I demanded.

"It would be best if you turn toward me," she relayed. "I must put my hands on your chest."

Fucking hell. She was going to touch me? Great. Lovely. Fan-fucking-tastic.

Why was this a good idea again?

Clearly she must've detected something that bothered her because she pivoted to go.

"Briony, get over here," I said gruffly, resigning myself to having her hands on me.

I could do this. I could. I would simply pretend she was … someone else. Yes. Someone less … lovely.

Dropping my legs over the side of the bed, I pulled the comforter across my lap, ensuring my erection was covered.

She came to stand before me, so I spread my thighs, allowing her room to get closer, tucking that damn blanket beneath my thigh to ensure it stayed put.

"Is this going to hurt?" I asked, not that I cared. Pain was irrelevant at the moment. However, if it did hurt, perhaps I'd have something else to focus on.

"No, sire."

I took a deep breath, then squared my shoulders, broadening my chest.

Her purple eyes lowered, and I saw the approval there, which did little to help the situation.

Then again, it was nothing compared to the instant her palms pressed to my chest. My back bowed into the touch, my chest heaving as I felt the strangest sensation tear through me.

Briony inhaled deeply, her fingertips curling inward, clutching me as she took what she needed.

Of course, my cock swelled in response. I had to grind my hand down on the damn thing to keep it from lurching out from beneath the blankets. But even the pain I inflicted did nothing to halt the orgasm that tore up my shaft, the electricity slamming along every nerve ending in rapid succession. I growled low in my throat as I came. It just so happened my eyes were open, and I was watching her when I did. Briony's eyes met mine, and I saw the erotic response as it exploded within her. She moaned, slamming her eyes shut as her body shuddered.

Seeing her succumb to her orgasm triggered another within me.

Even as the exquisite sensation splintered me, I knew we had to stop this. If not...

Well, fuck, we'd be right back where I was before her arrival.

BIJOU

I had noticed a change in the mansion for the past week.

Ever since everyone disappeared for two days.

And by everyone, I meant every single soul in the place except for the humans. I wasn't sure where they went, but even with their return, there was a difference in the place.

For one, that strange sexual energy had ceased. Thank Heaven for that. Right before their disappearance, it had gotten brutally intense within the walls of the angels' residence, more so because I had absolutely no outlet for my sexual frustration.

Not since our encounter in the sauna had Oliver spoken more than two words to me. No more playing pool, no swimming, no movies. Our interactions had halted altogether, and I knew it was my fault. I'd all but insisted he take care of me, and oh, boy, had he. When Oliver's mouth had gone ... where it had gone, I thought I was having an out-of-body experience. Never had an orgasm consumed my entire being until then. Probably for the best since the only ones I'd experienced were of the self-inflicted variety, and it looked as though any in the future would be the same.

Which was the reason I was ignoring my own sexual needs. Nothing I could do for myself would come close to achieving that cataclysmic event, so why bother trying, right?

Thankfully, I had the company of Orianna's mother to keep me distracted. Since I'd stumbled upon the female in the bedroom near the back stairs, I had found myself drawn to her. And as it turned out, Elizabeth McKay seemed to be fond of me. Good thing the human didn't realize I was a vampire. I could only imagine the reception I'd receive if she had.

But for now our friendship was continuing to grow, our mutual love of *Friends* keeping us tight. We'd spent the past couple of weeks having marathon sessions in the female's room, Elizabeth settled in that moving chair while I took the spot on the upholstered chair beside her. Over the past couple of days, Orianna had begun to stop by more often. It was clear to me she had something she wanted to say to her mother, but she couldn't quite let go of whatever it was.

Speaking of Orianna...

The female appeared in the doorway, drawing our attention.

"Honey, are you all right?" Elizabeth asked by way of greeting.

"I'm..." Orianna nodded.

"Perhaps I should give you two a minute alone."

Before I could get to my feet, Orianna was at my side, gently touching my arm. "Please don't go."

There was pain in Orianna's brilliant blue eyes, the color having changed since her return from wherever they'd gone.

No longer were they a soft cornflower blue but more of a ... well, it was difficult to explain because they were technically the same color, only now they seemed lit from within.

"Mom, could we turn off the television for a minute?"

"Of course, honey." Elizabeth stabbed the button on the remote to kill the image on the screen.

"I need to talk to you about something." Orianna dragged the other upholstered chair over so it was closer to her mother.

"Is it about Amber?"

Orianna nodded. "It is, actually."

Elizabeth's eyes brightened, so much hope flooding her face. "Did you find her?"

"I... Yes, Mom. I did."

Oh, boy. I could tell this story wasn't going to have a happy ending. I knew all about Amber, Elizabeth's oldest daughter. During the time we'd spent together, I'd gotten an earful about both females. At first, the conversations were all about Amber and how much Elizabeth missed her. However, those discussions had shifted to be more about Orianna and how proud Elizabeth was of her youngest daughter. It was clear Elizabeth loved them both equally, but her heart ached for her oldest because she didn't know where she was.

"Mom." Orianna reached out and touched Elizabeth's hand.

"Are you bringing her home?" Elizabeth asked, although Orianna hadn't said anything more.

The two females stared at one another for a long moment, the air between them crackling with the pain of loss.

"I'm bringing her home," Orianna confirmed, her voice quivering, tears forming in her eyes.

"That's all I've ever wanted," Elizabeth said, her other hand covering Orianna's.

I swallowed the emotion that was suddenly clogging my

throat. Even as a bystander, I couldn't help but feel for the two of them. I still ached from the loss of my mother, a feeling I didn't wish on anyone.

"I need to make sure you understand what I'm telling you," Orianna said, the last word dying on a sob.

"I know, honey. I've suspected it for a while. Amber's no longer of this world."

Orianna sobbed. "No, Mom. She's not. She's... Amber's in Heaven."

Tears formed in Elizabeth's eyes, and it was then the older female reached for me. Of course, the sentiment was enough to have tears forming in my eyes, as well. I ached for their loss much as I did my own. I remember when my mother passed, could still feel that dull throb within my heart. I doubted it would ever go away, no matter how much time passed, but I realized that accepting it helped. Knowing that those you loved were in a better place didn't erase the pain, but it eased it somewhat.

"She's been cremated," Orianna explained. "I'm having her brought here, and we're going to spread her ashes. That way, she's with us always."

Tears continued to drip down our cheeks, all three of us, as we sat together, trying to come to grips with the facts.

"Thank you, baby," Elizabeth turned her full attention to Orianna. "I know I had no right to ask you to do this, but ... thank you."

Orianna nodded, then got to her feet.

I wasn't sure what to do, but I got the feeling Elizabeth needed some space.

"I'll be back in a few minutes," I told her.

Elizabeth nodded, the motor on her chair coming to life as she started moving toward the balcony doors that overlooked the grounds below. There was nothing we could see because of the cloak the angels kept over the mansion, but that never stopped Elizabeth from staring out into the darkness.

"Thank you for staying," Orianna said when we stepped into the hall. "I didn't mean to burden you with that, but ... well, I know my mom's close to you. She's going to need a lot of support."

"I'm here," I said. "For both of you. No matter what you need."

Another tear fell down Orianna's cheek. "Thank you." A sad smile formed. "That means a lot."

48

ECLIPSE

While Orianna took her mother up to the fourth floor via the elevator, I opted for the stairs.

Ever since my *ereswa* relayed her encounter with Amber in Heaven, I'd been waiting for this moment. Although Orianna seemed at peace after having visited with her sister, I knew the same was not the case for Elizabeth, who was now mourning the passing of her child. I couldn't imagine how difficult it must be and prayed no one had to endure it. The loss of a loved one was hard enough, add to it that of a child … I couldn't fathom it.

Now, as I stepped through the doorway on the fourth floor, which was nothing more than an attic with a couple dozen dormer windows interspersed along the various branches extending off from the center of the mansion, I watched as mother and daughter moved toward the south side so the north wind would be coming from behind us.

I had already delivered Amber's ashes to the windowsill after Echo and Naos had gone to Kansas to retrieve them. The soft sound of footfalls signaled me to those who'd come to join us. Bijou was leading the way, Penelope and Obsidian behind her. I had expected that to be all, but more came: Reidar, Miklós, Søren, Oliver, then more of the *fiestreigh* and several of the *heurosp* filling in the empty space as they formed one long line behind the two females, all there to support our family member.

I had briefly considered lowering the *dhira* so Elizabeth could see beyond the darkness but opted against it. It was in place to ensure we were concealed from the demons, and since we'd yet to have a breach on the mansion, I was hesitant to tempt fate. But it wasn't necessary because Orianna could now see clearly out into the night, and she had the ability to give her mother the same sight. A simple touch upon her temples would clear the way.

So, as we all stood silently behind the two females, I said a silent prayer to the heavens, thanking the Almighty for offering these females the closure they needed. It wasn't as they would've preferred because Amber was no longer of this Earth, but it was more than they'd had for quite some time. At least this way, there was the potential for moving forward. The wounds would never heal completely, but over time, perhaps they would ease to something bearable.

When Orianna's tears began to fall in earnest, I stepped up behind her, wrapping my arm across her chest and pulling her into me. I was there for her, would always be, no matter her need. When she stepped forward, I did so as well. Another step, and she was opening the windows wide, allowing the night to come in.

It wasn't Orianna who delicately touched Elizabeth's temples but Penelope. Obsidian's *ereswa* stepped up and placed a gentle hand on Elizabeth's frail shoulder, then touched her temple with her other hand.

Elizabeth inhaled sharply as Orianna opened the urn, then held it up to the night, allowing the perfectly timed gust of wind to swoop in and carry them off, the remains of her sister drifting up and outward. A heavy sob racked Orianna, so I took the urn, set it aside, and pulled her into my arms, wrapping her tightly. No one said anything as we remained like that for long minutes.

Time became irrelevant as still no words were spoken, but they weren't necessary. Perhaps Elizabeth didn't realize it, hadn't noticed the wings that had expanded from one end to the other as the angels surrounding her provided a protective barrier behind. We could not change fate or affect free will, but we could provide comfort and strength in one's time of need.

With a nod of my head, I dismissed the others, wanting to give mother and daughter a few moments alone.

T he dawn came and the house went into quiet mode as usual, the universe continuing to spin despite all that had gone down during the night.

I found Orianna in our private quarters, sitting on the bed, legs out in front of her, hands clasped in her lap. She was leaning back against the headboard, staring into space.

"You all right?"

Her eyes shifted to me, and a small smile formed. "I am now. I was thinking about a bath."

From where I was, moving toward the bed, I willed the water on in the bathroom.

"One of these days, I'll catch on to that," she said with a wider grin.

"Give it time, *sezari*. We've got plenty of it." I held my hand out, urging her to come to me.

There was a bit more spunk in her movements when she hopped down to the floor and sauntered toward me. I couldn't help it, just looking at her made me smile. Though she'd been the most beautiful human I'd ever glimpsed, as an angel, she was blindingly radiant. Her blue eyes were now lit from behind, proof her soul was safely ensconced in Heaven with mine. Though there was no way to predict what Lucifer would do, ultimately, she should now be off his radar. Not that I would ever lower my guard when it came to her safety, but I could breathe a bit easier now that the target was no longer on her back.

I pulled her into me, my hands sliding beneath the soft sweater she wore, one of the many the *heurosp* had purchased while the *lintamair* had been underway. Now, Orianna's side of the closet was as full as mine, our lives officially merged upon this Earth, where we would reside until our mission was over.

"I want you naked," I whispered, tugging the sweater upward.

She allowed me to undress her as we made our way to the bathroom. By the time we reached the tub, I'd discarded her clothes along with mine and easily lifted her into my arms and carried her down into the tub. I kept her in my lap as we settled into the warm water, the ends of her hair darkening as they got wet.

"I love you, *sezari*." I'd made sure to tell her as much, in exactly those words, because I hadn't realized how much she had wanted to hear them. From time to time, I spoke in my language because it felt a bit more intimate, but I continued to use her English words, as well.

Orianna pulled back and met my eyes. "*My heart belongs to you and you alone because you are my heart.*"

Those words in my native tongue ... I hadn't expected to hear her say them, so it caught me completely off guard. I jerked her toward me and sealed our lips as emotion churned in my chest. That had been the case since the night I'd taken her life, and it didn't seem to be letting up. With every passing minute, I found myself connecting with her more and more. I figured one day I'd be as much one with her as we were during our most intimate moments.

Speaking of intimate moments...

I growled softly, then dragged my lips along her jaw. "Take me inside you, *sezari.*"

Her eager moans drifted to my ears as she reached between us, taking me firmly in hand and guiding me into the warm haven of her body. More groans from both of us as exquisite pleasure blanketed our private moment.

As she took me deep within her, I cupped her head, pulling her mouth to my neck. I wanted to be inside her in all ways, to provide her sustenance while she gifted me with pleasure. I heard her soft hiss, felt the sharp tips of her fangs, then was obliterated by sheer ecstasy. There was no way to accurately describe the sensations that flooded me when she took my vein.

I slid my arm around her waist, holding her tight to me as my cock swelled deep inside her. She shifted just the slightest bit, and I went off like a rocket, a dark rumble tearing up my throat as the orgasm shattered me. That was only the beginning. For the duration of her feeding, I continued to ride that wave again and again, crashing several more times. Good thing we weren't restricted to only one orgasm.

By the time she sealed the punctures on my neck, I was desperate to move, to drive deep inside her. It would've made sense to switch, to feed from her, but I couldn't contain myself. As soon as she pulled back, I lifted her, my hands curling around her thighs as I rose out of the water. Settling her on the tiled ledge, I bent my knees and began driving into her, hard, fast. Oh, so fucking deep. Absolute heaven.

"*Sezari...*" I couldn't stop; the need to mark her was greater than anything I'd ever felt.

"Come for me," she pleaded, her legs tightening around my hips as she braced her arms on the edge of the tub. Her breasts bounced with every brutal thrust of my hips, and I'd never seen anything more beautiful.

I gritted my teeth, my fingertips digging into the soft flesh of her hips as I slammed in once, twice. On the third stroke, I exploded deep within her, a rumbling howl escaping me as I did.

And just like that, every ounce of my energy dissipated. I had enough to pull her back into the water, but that was it. When I flopped onto the contoured seat, and she giggled, I found myself laughing. I loved her sweet giggle. Then again, I loved every single thing about her.

"Find it amusing, do you?" I teased, repositioning her so I could easily slip inside her once more. "How about I return the favor."

And I did.

Quite a few times, in fact.

49

ORIANNA

We finished off December without a hitch.

In fact, things had settled enough we made it through a baby shower for Penelope on the first day of the new year. I made the suggestion, not thinking about the difficulties of shopping for baby things when Fed Ex and UPS didn't know you existed. Good thing we had the *heurosp*. The immortal humans had gone out during the day and picked up everything we requested, including the huge feast we indulged in afterward.

And yet, twenty weeks into Penelope's pregnancy, and still no baby. All was good, though, and for that, we were grateful.

Though not confined to bed rest, Penelope didn't do a lot of moving around. Most nights, after the evening meal, she would get settled in the sunroom. There was always someone with her, watching television or talking. Miklós had even set up an Xbox and was attempting to teach Penelope the benefits of first-person shooter games. Whatever that was.

I divided my time between keeping Penelope company, hanging out with Zeus and Aphrodite, and watching *Friends* with my mother. Turned out I was quite a fan of the show. For the past couple of weeks, Amethyst—or Dr. A as we'd started calling her—had started building a rapport with Elizabeth. Enough that Dr. A was able to document all of the medications she was on and was working to eliminate what she could while developing a pain management plan. It was still early in the process, but I held out hope that they'd eventually get a handle on the addiction, perhaps even give my mother some semblance of normal.

Now, as I wandered through the front hallway toward the sunroom to check on Penelope, I was expecting a quiet night since most of the males were out patrolling the streets of Telluride and Darkness, the others having returned to their searches for the other *amsouelots* while still maintaining a steady search for Asmia. No one was giving up on the female, and I prayed every day that she would come home safe and sound.

Tonight, Eclipse was out with Reidar and Kaj, Miklós and Søren manning the war room below, and there were three pints of mint chip waiting for me, Penelope, and Bijou in the freezer. Quiet, peaceful night in. Just what the doctor ordered.

"Hey, Pen!" I called out, starting toward the kitchen from the front hallway. "Ready for that ice—"

The explosion that rocked the very foundation of the mansion sent me stumbling, the blast from behind me, knocking me forward and into the stone fireplace. For a moment, I thought I'd been knocked unconscious because the entire mansion went dark.

When I realized I was, in fact, still awake, my attention splintered, going in several directions at once. I could hear shouting and screams, even got the scent of smoke, but I had no idea where it was coming from. Fear washed over me as I tried to determine which direction to go first. I hadn't gotten a handle on that whole vanishing thing, so I was helpless in that regard. But I needed to find my mother. Penelope. Miklós. Bijou. Acadia. Zeus and Aphrodite.

Oh, God.

As some smoke cleared, I realized the entire front section of the mansion was missing. From where I was kneeling, just inside the formal living room, the kitchen at my back, I could see the darkened trees in the distance, the moon's light casting their shadows over the front lawn.

My heart began to pound as I glanced around, not sure which direction to go. If anyone had been at the front of the mansion... I didn't even want to think about what that meant. My best bet was to go to those at the back, but I feared what might be coming in through the now massive hole in the front wall. After all, that explosion hadn't happened all by itself.

As I got to my feet, prepared to head toward Penelope, my eyes caught on something at the front, just beyond the drive that curled beneath the portico. My eyes skimmed the darkness, tracking every detail, pulling it together into an image that made sense. The explosion that came next was not one ignited by some sort of explosive. It was like thunder, and it roared again and again, one right after the other, the ground shaking beneath my feet. I stepped forward to see what it was, and that was when my breath hitched in my throat.

Those massive sounds were males as they landed in front of the mansion. First Obsidian, then Stygian, followed by Eclipse, Aphotic, Shadow, Piceous, and last but not least, Cimmerian. Their wings—one black, one white—expanded outward, stretching to meet the next until there was a solid wall of angels standing sentry at the front of the mansion, blocking the vulnerable section that was missing.

My heart pounded when I realized that was exactly what they were doing. The warriors had created a barrier separating whatever was coming at them from those of us trapped in the mansion behind them.

"Orianna!"

I spun around to see Oliver racing toward me. His eyes were wide, and there was a cut on his forehead, soot along his jawline.

"Come on," he urged, reaching for my arm but stopping quickly as though he had just realized the pain it would cause me. "We have to get you to safety."

"Penelope?" I asked. "Where's Penelope?"

"Kaj and Acadia came for her. They're taking her to the Lair."

"My mother?"

"Bijou's got her."

"But how?" With the power out, the elevators wouldn't work. How...?

The words died in my throat when I saw the female carrying Elizabeth in her arms as though it was no effort whatsoever. I marched toward them, paused as I waited.

"This way," Oliver said again. "We have to get out of here now."

I glanced once more at the front of the house, noticed the warriors were still there, still holding their ground, but there were more out there, the *fiestreigh* having come to fight on the front lines against whatever evil was coming for us.

"Zeus! Aphrodite!" I became frantic as I sought the dogs. "Zeus!"

There was a single bark in answer, but it wasn't from the main floor, I realized. No, had it not been for my new and improved hearing, I probably wouldn't have heard it.

"Orianna, we have—"

"I'm not leaving without them," I insisted, running for the stairs at the back of the mansion. I took them up to the third floor, then sent up another thank-you to the man upstairs when I realized the electronic scanners ran on a backup generator or battery. Once I was let through, I slammed the door inward and came to an abrupt halt. The damage there was far greater. Not only was the front of the mansion obliterated, the ceiling above had started to crumble.

I kicked through the rock and debris on the floor. "Zeus! Aphrodite!"

The bark came from the corner of the living room, where the two canines spent most of their time. It took a minute, but I managed to dig through the downed boards and stone until...

My relief was nearly too much. My head spun from the light-headedness, but I held it together as I dragged the boards away and freed both dogs. Neither appeared to be hurt, but they'd been trapped.

"Good boy," I told Zeus when he nudged Aphrodite toward me. "Come on. Let's get out of here."

With the dogs on my heels, we made it back down to the main floor, then deeper, below the mansion, to the underground tunnels. I followed, noticing the gas lamps were lit, which meant others had moved through there recently. The dogs and I circumvented the tunnels and finally ended up in the mansion the vampires had moved into.

"We need to stay together," Oliver said, his voice surprisingly calm and collected as he motioned me to join the others.

With Bijou's help, we were able to get Elizabeth settled on the sofa in the recreation room that was in the center of the main floor. Far enough from windows and doors but still too much in the open as far as I was concerned.

"Where's my father?" Bijou asked Oliver.

"He went with the Zenith out to fight," Penelope informed them, her hand protectively covering her swollen belly.

I watched as the young female nodded, her concern for her father's safety evident.

My heart clenched in my chest as I thought about Eclipse standing out there, protecting all within these walls.

I peered up at the sky. "Dear God ... *please*."

I had no idea what else to say.

ECLIPSE

I could feel the power attempting to push toward us even as we used every ounce of strength we possessed to push back.

I had no idea how long between the explosion that tore the front of the mansion clean off and the time we'd made it there, but I knew it wasn't long. The alarm systems had gone off, but not even those countermeasures were as effective as telepathy. Miklós had announced the explosion probably before the first rumble finished. Having been out with Reidar,

I made it back to the mansion within seconds, and I wasn't the first to arrive.

My first and only thought was to protect those within the mansion. Orianna, Penelope, the humans. Clearly my brothers had the same thought because that was where we landed, wing to wing, spread out to protect our loved ones while the *fiestreigh* tore ass toward the intruders who'd somehow breached the *dhira*.

As we stood there, withholding the brutal force attempting to breach the mansion, no one spoke. It would require more energy than we had. But the mental conversation was going full throttle. The most I could ascertain was that Eevuhl was making a go at the mansion. How the demon had located us, I had no idea, but it didn't matter. They'd found us, and the bastard was coming at us with all his efforts. Which, unfortunately, were vastly greater than I would've liked. There was a reason the *trielair* had lasted this long. They were far more powerful than the puny fucking demons.

What I couldn't understand was why. What the fuck did he want here?

We need more power.

I agreed with Obsidian, but I wasn't sure how we would do that. Summoning the energies of the universe would work only once, and then the mansion would be left undefended. As much as I wanted to believe the *fiestreigh* would be able to hold Eevuhl off, I knew better. Their efforts were best focused on whatever minions the male had brought with him, and based on what I could see, there were a good dozen or so. Which meant we couldn't risk it.

And then he appeared, the demon in all his disgusting glory.

Eevuhl emerged from below the horizon, his enormous body no longer contained within the shell of a human. Somewhere close to ten feet tall, the thing was more dragon than demon, absolutely grotesque as he moved toward us, one earth-rattling step at a time. Nothing was slowing him down, not even the gunfire coming from a higher vantage point behind us.

"We have to hold him," Obsidian ground out. "I will not let him get past me."

I knew that wasn't merely a statement; it was a declaration. Obsidian was willing to give his life to ensure Eevuhl did not get to Penelope. I understood clearly because that big demon bastard would have to step over my cold, dead body before he made his way to Orianna.

As I attempted to figure out what our next steps were, watching that evil asshole who was aptly named closing the gap between us, I felt true fear for the first time in my existence. Not for myself, not even for my brothers. We could hold our own and would because this was our mission. No, that steady influx of adrenaline was spurred by my concern for my *ereswa*.

For a second, I almost lost my grip on my control, but then there was a sonic boom that damn near knocked me off my feet. But it wasn't Eevuhl breaching the barrier, nor was it the *fiestreigh* taking the shithead down—unfortunately.

The male who appeared before us was what those humans might call a gift from God.

In reality, he was an archangel.

A really fucking powerful one who seemed quite pissed about the situation he'd literally landed in.

"We have one chance at this," Michael announced, facing off with Eevuhl but speaking to us.

Although I had heard his voice a million times, I'd rarely heard it in its full angelic glory, as though broadcast through a bullhorn, the tenor so deep and powerful I imagined most would retreat from the sound alone.

A round of encouraging grunts sounded.

"What does he want?" Obsidian snarled.

"The child."

Despite the *rat-tat-tat* and the various other sounds of a battle, I was pretty sure you could've heard a pin drop at that moment. At least inside my head and I could only imagine what Obsidian was hearing right about now.

The deep roar sounded from my left, which meant the meaning of those words had registered with my oldest brother.

"Unfortunately, my powers aren't nearly as beneficial here on Earth," Michael said, his words spoken so low I knew he had to be projecting them.

"Well, I fucking hope you have a plan," Stygian growled.

"I do, but Obsidian's probably not gonna like it."

"Try me," Obsidian barked.

Probably not a good thing to say to an archangel.

The sudden blinding light was enough to have me closing my eyes, and when I opened them, Michael was...

"Holy. Fuck."

I wasn't the only one who muttered the words when I realized what had actually happened.

Obsidian stepped forward, breaking the daisy chain of wings, but he had good reason. Those fucking wings of his had expanded to twice their original span. No longer was one of them black, they were both brilliant white. The only thing brighter was the blade of the sword he wielded.

The thunder continued as Obsidian broke off in a jog toward the demon gunning for us.

I was fairly certain the world stopped turning when Obsidian and Eevuhl collided. But it wasn't only Obsidian. Michael had merged with the male and that cataclysmic amalgamate was a strength not even the most powerful of demons could hold.

Obsidian wielded that sword as though it was an extension of his arm. It felt like eons as the two battled it out, while my brothers and I held our breaths, maintaining the barrier between the battle and the mansion.

The roar that sounded could've been the demon, could've been Obsidian, perhaps a combination of both, but by the time the winds settled from the displacement of air, there was only one standing.

The other was dissolving as the steel blade pierced its chest, sending it back to its maker where it belonged.

No sooner had Eevuhl headed off for his eternal damnation in Hell than Obsidian turned around and ... collapsed, falling face-first to the cold, hard ground in front of him, like a statue that had been cut off at the knees.

As it became evident there was no longer a threat, I released a breath, my brain kicking into high gear. I broke rank as I started racing toward my fallen brother. The others were right beside me, moving as though one toward the one who needed us most.

It took three of us, but we were able to carry the unconscious male into the mansion, bypassing the front door and going right through the destroyed wall.

Unable to vanish because of our burden, we carried Obsidian's limp body below ground, down the stairs, weaving through the tunnels until we reached the medical unit, which was ... completely empty.

For about a second.

A storm of people came from all directions. Fae, vampires, angels, even humans, all flooding the space, questions and comments filling the air, panic continuing to rise though the actual threat had been eliminated.

But it wasn't over. Not yet.

I was able to help ease Obsidian down to the floor, but I lost my shit after that. My mind scrambled as I pushed through bodies until I found the one I was looking for. Orianna was walking alongside Bijou, who was carrying Elizabeth back to the mansion. My *ereswa* hurried forward the instant she saw me, and only then did my heart jumpstart.

"Where is he?" Penelope cried out, her hand covering her belly, tears streaming down her face as she hurried, the female healer at her side, assisting her.

A sharp whistle sounded, and then everyone parted, giving Penelope space.

Amethyst hurried toward her brother, the two healers flanking Obsidian, likely doing an initial assessment. Based on their expressions, neither knew what the hell to do. Stygian was dutifully relaying to them what happened: the merge of the warrior and the archangel, the battle with Eevuhl, the demon's demise, and Obsidian's collapse.

"Obsidian!" Penelope's tormented cry ripped through the space.

Everyone watched helplessly as she dropped to her knees, cradling his head on her thighs as she openly wept.

The instant Orianna saw Obsidian, she gasped, and that was when I noticed what she did.

It was her vision: Penelope kneeling beside Obsidian, tears running down her cheeks, the male unmoving, eyes closed.

"Get back," Stygian commanded, forcing everyone except for Penelope back a few feet.

For the second time that night, time stood still as we stared at our fallen brother.

"Obsidian," Penelope cried softly, her hand sliding into his. "Come back to me. Oh, God. Please come back to me."

The healers seemed both confused and eager to do something to help, but they were now being held back by Stygian, as though the male knew something the rest of us didn't. Perhaps he did because a few painfully long minutes later, Obsidian's chest lurched as though someone had shocked him with a defibrillator. There was a rustle of sound, like wings, but it faded quickly.

Obsidian groaned, then turned his head, his eyes opening on Penelope's face.

"*Ayreme*," he rasped, his trembling hand lifting to cup her face.

Penelope bowed her head, rested it against his forehead, and sobbed.

Grateful they were okay, I turned away from the sight and wrapped Orianna in my arms, holding her tightly. I took a moment to swipe my hands over her, assuring myself she was in one piece. Orianna's arms curled around me, holding on to me as she softly cried.

I hated to hear her anguish, but at the same time, it was the most precious sound in the world.

Because it meant she was still with me.

50

Three days later...

KAJ

Chaos.

That was the only way I knew to describe the aftermath of the demons' attack on the mansion.

It lasted for three solid days before we began to see a sense of normalcy return.

First came tending to the wounded.

Aside from the shock of having an archangel take over his body, Obsidian had been mostly unharmed. A few scratches, couple of bruises. Nothing major. Rest had been the prescribed treatment, and true to form, Obsidian had ignored the healers' suggestions, claiming to have far too much to deal with.

The rest of the warriors were unharmed, though drained from their efforts, too. Same as their oldest brother, they had refused to stay down. Most of their soldiers had required no treatment, their wounds healing before the dust had even settled, but there were two *ladeares*—Magnar and Mordecai— who'd required some time in the infirmary. Both had been watched for the first twenty-four hours but were now back to their regular routine.

The worst of the injuries had been to two of the *heurosp*, who'd been dutifully working at the front of the mansion when the explosion occurred. Both had sustained minor burns and serious abrasions, but by the grace of God, they hadn't been directly in the blast zone. One of the two, a younger female I had never met, was still in the infirmary, undergoing treatment for the burns, while she sported a cast on her broken wrist.

I still wasn't sure how we hadn't lost anyone during the ambush. After Mirakel had demanded I stay put, I had gone in search of my daughter and Acadia. The instant I'd seen with his own eyes that both females were unharmed, Acadia and I had moved Penelope to safety. At that point, I had shucked Mirakel's orders and joined the fray. While the angels had held that big fucking bastard off, I'd gotten in a good hand-to-hand session with three demons.

The instant Obsidian/Michael lodged that blade in Eevuhl, the rest had turned to ash, drifting off into the breeze. Neat little trick, that one. And thank fuck for it. It didn't take long to realize those little fuckers had been doubling upon our arrival. It'd been touch-and-go for a bit, and I had feared we would be overtaken by the damn things, but then ... *poof!* Vanished.

And though I would survive, I suffered a fan-fucking-tastic knife wound to my left thigh. I managed to sneak it by the healers because the last fucking thing I wanted was to have someone getting all handsy. Problem was, it should've healed by now, but it continued to fester, and I was beginning to get concerned.

Of course, I knew what the problem was. I'd yet to feed, and it didn't help that my female was acting as a sieve for all the males in the mansion. Every single time she offered her vein, the pain grew more intense, as though pieces of my soul were being chipped away and that damn wound was relaying the information to my brain.

As much as I wanted to put it off, I couldn't. Feeding was inevitable, and if I wished to get back to one hundred percent, I had to give in. Problem was, Acadia was in no position to provide for me, and because of the way things stood between us, I couldn't muster the courage to ask.

Which meant I was forced to take the vein of another.

I'd considered taking from a male but found the few we had were currently being put to work helping to rebuild the mansion. Now, as I sat in my private chambers in the Lair, I waited for who would come for me. I'd asked Mirakel to find someone, anyone. Just not Acadia.

A soft knock sounded on my door, and I urged them in with an abrupt bark. My stomach churned from the need for blood but more so from the ache of knowing my female would not be the one providing for me. I only hoped I could keep the blood down; otherwise, it would be a wasted fucking effort.

"Sit," I commanded the female who stepped into the space.

Though she was beautiful in her own right, the female was the opposite of Acadia. Where my female had delicate ivory skin, this one's was a soft, creamy brown. Where Acadia had long, dark locks, this female's hair was short and tight to her head. Because I knew their eye color was the same, I refused to look directly at this female as I joined her. In an effort to show

623

her I wasn't a threat, I had her sit in the chair positioned by the fireplace while I went to my knees before her.

"I'll take your wrist," I said, my words rough as I accepted my fate.

She didn't speak, but I didn't want her to. This was difficult enough without chitchat.

The sleeve of her robe was pulled back, revealing the thin wrist. Biology had my fangs dropping into my mouth, blood rushing in my ears as I succumbed to my hunger. It took two tries before I could touch her, lifting her arm to my mouth. Two more attempts and I finally pierced her vein. At that point, I closed my eyes and thought of Acadia. This female's blood didn't taste the same, but it was powerful enough to sate me, so I took as much as she could part with. And when I finished, I remained on my knees after dismissing her from the room.

For a few minutes, I worried I was going to expel all I'd taken in. Breathing in through my nose and out through my mouth helped to settle matters. At least where my stomach was concerned. As for my heart ... yeah, I seriously doubted that thing was going to find peace for a while. If ever. I felt as though I'd betrayed the female I loved, but I knew it couldn't be helped. Vampires had to feed. It was a biological necessity. The longer we went without it, the worse we would get until, eventually, we would die.

My body hadn't responded the same to that female as it did to Acadia, so at least there was that.

I wasn't sure how much time passed between the time she left and when I finally got to my feet. But when I did, I shored up my nerves and headed out of my room, down the grand sweeping staircase, and to the main floor below. I didn't stop, ignoring those who were still hanging around. We'd moved a few people into the Lair until the mansion was back to its former glory, and the additional souls were adding to the chaos.

Hoping to help Obsidian and his brothers, I headed for the mansion, traversing the tunnels, making my way past the infirmary, beyond the war room, which was a hub of activity, through the bar that was, not surprisingly, vacant. Despite the energy I now had, there was still an emptiness within me. But it wasn't until I made it up the stairs to the mansion's kitchen that I fully understood why. There, sitting in the sunroom, was Acadia. Her eyes appeared vacant when they met mine.

I stopped, swallowing past the lump in my throat.

She knew. My female knew I'd fed from another. It was the first time I'd done so since my return nearly three months ago. For the past eighty-four days, I'd relied on her blood to sustain me, and now I'd sought another. I briefly wondered if she felt the same pain I did when it happened. Fuck, I hoped not. Regardless of how things stood between us, the last thing I wanted was to cause her pain.

I'm sorry, I relayed directly into her mind.

Acadia didn't respond, her vacant gaze still on mine, and I knew I'd hurt her. Perhaps in a manner she would never be able to recover from.

Truth was, I didn't necessarily blame her.

But more importantly, I had to wonder if, on some level, I hadn't done it on purpose. As a way of protecting her from me. Didn't matter that I'd bonded with her, that I wanted to spend eternity with her; deep in my dark soul, I knew that she was better off without me.

It well and truly sucked, but it didn't make it any less true.

ECLIPSE

"How're you feeling, brother?" I asked Obsidian when I joined the male in the underground bedroom he and Penelope had temporarily moved into.

"I'll live," Obsidian grumbled, offering a smile. "And I thought lightning bolts were a bitch."

"Yeah?" I chuckled. "I suppose sharing a body with an archangel does make electricity look like kid's play. Have you heard from him? Michael? Since, you know..."

Obsidian shook his head and propped himself up on the pillows of the enormous bed. "No. And I've reached out. Nothing."

I had worried that would be the case. I wasn't sure whether anyone considered that Michael's hands were supposed to be tied here on Earth. For him to have used his powers against Eevuhl, even through Obsidian's physical form, that didn't change the fact he intervened, which violated the Almighty's rules. Heaven only knew what punishment for such an egregious act of defiance might be.

"How's Penelope?" I asked, nodding toward the female currently perched on a small settee in the corner, her feet propped up on an ottoman, eyes closed, a pair of headphones covering her ears.

"Surprisingly, she's content."

That *was* surprising, considering she'd already passed her due date. Not by much, mind you, but according to the good healers, she was now twenty-one weeks along. Granted, none of us knew exactly how an angel birth on Earth would play out. Perhaps she could carry that baby for a full forty weeks like humans, but if she did... I seriously doubted she'd be able to hold that thing in there. As it was, her belly appeared stretched to maximum capacity.

Obsidian glanced over at her, his eyes softening the same way they always did when he looked at the female.

"You two need anything?" I offered.

My brother's attention returned to me. "Yeah. An update. How's it going with the construction?"

"Almost complete. What takes humans six months takes us only a few days."

"Damn good thing, too. I intend to have my *ereswa* back in her own bed when the baby's born."

I knew that. It was the very reason we were busting ass to make it happen. Thankfully, on the third floor, all of our rooms faced the rear of the mansion, with the hallway as well as the additional spaces, including our private recreation area and the room Penelope had been working on as the female getaway along the front. Those had been obliterated, as had many of the bedrooms on the second floor. Thankfully, we still had overflow below ground, plus space in the vampire lair. For now, we were scattered, but if all went well, we'd be back to normal by the time the calendar flipped to February.

"We have to have more protection," Obsidian said softly. "This can't happen again."

My brother didn't have to tell me that. I felt the same, and with the help of the *fiestreigh*, we were designing some additional security measures, including a wall that would surround the entire grounds, something we could defend in the event— God forbid—something like this happened again. As it was, we had no idea who knew of our location. Though we'd considered vacating Darkness entirely, we concluded that if they had found us once, they would find us again, so the best thing we could do was simply be better prepared.

"We're working on it," I assured my brother. "But you let us handle that. Right now, you need to work on recovering. Before you know it, you'll have something else to focus on."

Once more, Obsidian's gaze swung to Penelope, and he smiled. "That I will."

"If you need anything, holler. Everyone's here right now, and they'll remain in residence until we decide it's safe to venture out. Won't be for a few weeks, at best."

Everyone had agreed to remain in Darkness for the time being, especially with the baby coming any day now.

"Thanks."

I turned toward the door. "And if you hear from Michael ... tell him I said thanks."

"Trust me," Obsidian's voice was stronger than before, "I have every intention of letting him know how I feel about what he did." The male's smile flashed fangs. "But I'll mention you're appreciative, too."

I smirked. Though Obsidian clearly hadn't appreciated being violated by an archangel, we all knew Michael had been our saving grace. Had it not been for him ... well, I didn't want to think about where we might be now.

After closing the door behind me, I remained in the hall, listening to the familiar sounds. The war room had been overflowing since the incident, the *fiestreigh* insistent on using this as a lesson and fortifying the mansion against an attack of this nature in the future. The bar, which was currently empty, would be full by the time the sun was coming over the horizon. We'd all taken to hanging out a bit more than usual. That was what happened when you were grateful to have those you cared about in one piece after a tragedy. We were damn lucky. So fucking lucky. We lost no one during the attack, although we were caught completely off guard.

Something we had no plans of letting happen again.

Rather than walk through the mansion, I disappeared myself, resuming form in the main-floor kitchen. I peered up into the sunroom to see Orianna sitting on one of the far sofas with Zeus and Aphrodite. She'd been attached at the hip to those two since the incident. When I heard how she'd gone upstairs and dug them out of the rubble, my heart had squeezed in my chest. Despite the danger she'd been in, her first instinct was to get the family to safety, and Zeus and Aphrodite certainly qualified.

"Sire?"

I pulled my attention to the here and now, turning toward Phillip. "S'up?"

The male smiled. "It's imperative we make a grocery run." His eyes lowered. "And I apologize for having to bother you with the specifics, but I felt it necessary to seek approval before I allow them to head out."

While it would've been great if we could've locked down the mansion indefinitely, I knew that wasn't possible. The rest of us took for granted all that went on behind the scenes, such as grocery shopping and laundry, because we weren't burdened with the chores. However, I was well aware of all the effort that went into maintaining the residence, as well as taking care of the lot of us.

"For the time being," I told Phillip, "the only request I have is that they take someone with them. I'll let Reidar know you've got errands to run, and he can assign someone. Just pretend they're invisible."

Phillip grinned. "As much as is possible, sire." His shoulders squared. "Is there any news on the expected arrival?"

"Not yet, but I'll make sure you're one of the first to know."

The male put his hands together. "That would be wonderful, sire. As you might expect, we're quite delighted to welcome a babe into the world."

Having something to look forward to certainly wasn't a bad thing. Especially a blessed event such as this.

And it seemed we were all counting down.

51

OLIVER

I was exhausted.

Not that I was complaining. I figured I had no right to bitch and moan, considering all that had gone down. A week ago, we'd been looking forward to chilling with beers and watching a couple of angels give a go at the dueling pianos. Now, we were grateful we were all alive to do that.

It was hard to believe we'd been attacked. In this fortress of all places.

And fine. Maybe I'd gotten used to feeling safe within the mansion. I'd been whisked out of my everyday life, saved from what would've probably been a horrific death at the hands of a demon who'd been wearing the suit of a human stripper. Since then, the most drama I had endured was the arguing between Winnie and Reidar before she went back to the human world.

Now...

Well, fuck. Where did I begin?

We were putting the final touches on the exterior and would soon be moving on to making the repairs to the interior of the residence. As for the bedroom I'd been sleeping in... that fucker was decimated by whatever that demon did to the house. Had I been in that room, I would've been incinerated. Damn good thing those demons couldn't come out during the day. Had they, I figured I would've been having these thoughts from somewhere else, and I didn't really want to dwell on which direction I would've gone if I'd officially checked out.

New lease on life? Yeah. Perhaps that was what this was.

I'd spent the past week feeling a blush heat my face every time one of the angels thanked me for assisting in getting everyone to safety after the explosion. Back in my office job, I'd craved the praise. Then again, I would've been the first guy out, running for my life, and to hell with everyone else.

Here ... I'd done what I felt I needed to do, and well, I didn't want the pats on the back. I felt it was as much my duty to pitch in as everyone else. And I was putting forth the effort as much as I could with the rebuild. No way to ignore the fact I was human and couldn't perform the same as the angels or even the vampires. I still remembered how Bijou had hefted Elizabeth into her arms and carried the woman down two flights of stairs, then through the tunnels below the mansion to get her to the Lair. She'd never even broken a sweat.

So, yeah. She was stronger than I was. The old me would've felt inferior. The new me found it hot as hell. Don't ask me why because I honestly didn't know.

What I did know was that I was ready to sit down and have a convo with Bijou. Something about having the place blow up around you put things in perspective. So putting off telling her how I felt... Well, I didn't want to wait any longer. Ever since our encounter in the sauna, I'd avoided her, scared that if I were around her too long, we'd end up naked and doing a hell of a lot more than a bit of oral exploration.

I figured if that happened, then so be it. Perhaps it was meant to be.

As I strolled beyond the rooms sealed off with thick plastic sheets, I found myself smiling. I'd been looking forward to dawn all night, eager to get a few moments with Bijou and perhaps get our friendship back on track.

That smile faltered when I stepped up to Bijou's bedroom door and lifted my hand to knock. It wasn't closed all the way, and I realized she wasn't alone. Madok, the Fae she generally fed from based on what I'd heard, was facing away from the door. Bijou's hand was curled around his head as she held him in place, her fangs fixed deep in his neck. Her eyes were closed, and from my perspective, the two of them looked rather intimate despite the fact they were both fully dressed.

From a logical standpoint, I knew the angels and vampires required blood. I understood they took the blood of the Fae because that was how it was designed. From an emotional standpoint, I knew it wasn't so much intimate as necessary.

All good and fine. Made perfect sense.

This ... seeing it with my own two eyes... Fuck, I was at a loss for words. The scene before me should not have been erotic in any manner, yet it was. To a degree. If I superimposed myself over Madok, it was the hottest fucking thing I'd ever witnessed.

But that was not me inside that room. That wasn't my neck those fangs were buried in.

That was someone else.

I had never felt the sort of pain that ripped through my sternum as I watched her feeding from him. It wasn't until that moment that I realized I'd been banking on Bijou forgiving me and us finding our way back to one another. Or rather, *to* one another since back wasn't really a direction we could've gone. Before that one intimate moment in the sauna, there'd been only friendship between us.

But I wanted more.

I wasn't sure if I made a sound or if Bijou simply sensed I was there, but those eyes opened, and I was hit square in the face with that lovely green.

Rather than pull away, Bijou remained where she was, clutching Madok's head as she sucked at his neck. Those beautiful irises seemed to glow from within, as though daring me to say something.

Even if I had known what to say, the words never would've made it past the lump in my throat.

Bolting would've been a brilliant idea, but my brain was mush as I watched, helpless. It wasn't like I could barge in and insist she not feed from the Fae. Sure, I could offer up my vein, but we both knew that would be pointless. I'd already learned that vampires and angels could not survive on human blood.

Being that I was a mere human ... well, I was just shit out of luck.

Truth was, I wanted to fucking throw something. To get angry because she was supposed to belong to me.

Not that she knew that, but hell.

My shoulders slumped as defeat reared its ugly head. I held Bijou's stare for a few more painful seconds, and when she didn't release the Fae, I managed to duck my head and stroll off down the hall.

Heart right in my damn throat.

ORIANNA

aving spent the past week helping out with the house, attempting to keep some sort of order amongst all the chaos, I had tumbled into bed every morning and fallen asleep within seconds. It didn't bode well for what had been a dynamic sex life. On those mornings I could've summoned the energy to crawl all over Eclipse, he'd been the one falling asleep before he hit the pillow.

Quite the pair we were. Mated for one day shy of a month, and we were hitting the sack like an old, married couple: comfortable to be in the same room, but anything more required effort.

That so was not going to be us. Nope. No way was I allowing this heat between us to even simmer. We no longer had to battle that *amnigh*, which was a true blessing, but that didn't mean I wasn't aching for him. Just the slightest glimpse of Eclipse warmed me from the inside out.

Which was why this morning I was vowing to get us back on track.

Though I'd managed a full night, I had purposely not worked to the point of exhaustion. Now that the morning meal was finished, I was in our private suite, awaiting Eclipse's return. He mentioned wanting to check on Obsidian and Penelope, so I took the opportunity to sneak in and set the mood. A couple of candles, the fire burning in the fireplace, and I was good to go. The *heurosp* had already come in and turned down the bed, so there was nothing for me to do there.

Figuring I had a few minutes, I made a beeline for the bathroom and washed my face. I followed it by brushing my teeth, then slipping into the closet to change. I had just pulled on one of Eclipse's long-sleeve button-downs and had managed to push one button through the little hole when he appeared in the doorway looking like sin on legs.

Because he was inspecting me like I was dessert and he didn't know where to start first, I slipped another button into place, then another, efficiently concealing me nakedness behind the dark fabric.

"Not sure why you're bothering." That gruff rasp in his voice told me he was as eager for my plans as I was.

"Did the candles tip you off?" I teased, hooking another button as I stepped toward him.

Eclipse shook his head. "I can smell you."

A shiver ran down my spine.

I was about to tease him with something else, but the words died on my tongue when he surged forward, pinning me against the four-sided, waist-high dresser in the center of the closet. I had enough breath to giggle, but then that disappeared when he lifted me and set me on the smooth marble top. No romance was associated with his actions—he was far too intent for that—but I was absolutely fine with the whole caveman thing. Based on the hungry expression on his face, foreplay was about to ensue, and there was no reason to hold him back.

I shrieked when he gripped my calves and lifted my legs, spreading them wide. I was forced to put my hands behind me to keep from sliding on the smooth surface, and when I did, Eclipse took full advantage, his mouth finding my hot, aching sex.

"Oh, God," I moaned, easing onto my back and offering myself up to that exquisite tongue of his.

It was then I realized there was a mirror on the ceiling. A freaking mirror.

Holy shit. The scene that appeared there—me on my back, Eclipse's dark head between my legs—that was erotic and mind-blowing.

The racy image disappeared when I closed my eyes, pleasure licking at every nerve ending, building deep within me.

Eclipse feasted on me like a starving man, licking, sucking, driving me right to the edge and over within minutes. But he didn't stop there. No, my male made up for lost time, making my head spin with one orgasm after another until I was too sensitive for more. Only when I pleaded did he lift his head and meet my gaze. I half expected him to carry me out of the closet and into our bedroom, but he clearly had other plans.

The partially buttoned shirt that covered me was no match for him. Eclipse gripped both sides and ripped it wide, the little buttons pinging off the glass doors that protected our clothes. Then the warm suction of his mouth was on my breast, my hand speared in his mohawk so I could ensure he didn't get away. I could tell he was working his jeans off, and I wished I was in a position to help because it was taking too damn long.

When he dragged me to my feet, I squealed again, giggling as he spun me to face away from him. Before my hands caught purchase on the dresser, the shirt was tugged down my arms and left somewhere on the floor.

The floor-length mirror was directly in front of us, offering quite the view even with the dresser blocking part of the scene playing out.

"Brace yourself, *sezari*."

I did, and just in time. Eclipse held nothing back when he pushed deep inside me, filling me, stretching me. It was absolute perfection, and I wondered how the heck we'd managed to go nearly a week without it.

The two figures in the mirror were hotter than I expected, but mostly, I loved watching Eclipse as he drove in deep, the sheer pleasure etched in the handsome lines of his face.

His silver stare met mine in the mirror and held for long moments while he drove us both toward that inevitable peak.

As his hips thrust against me, his hand appeared, sliding my hair back from my neck. I tilted my head, never looking away as his fangs descended. He held my gaze as he leaned in, but then his eyes closed as he sank into my flesh. The orgasm was instant. It rocketed through me, making my legs weak. Thank goodness we had the furniture in the closet.

For long minutes, Eclipse took by way of feeding and gave by way of screwing deep inside me. I lost track of my orgasms as they all blended into one glorious release. When his fangs retracted from my neck and his eyes met mine once more in the mirror, my pussy clenched around him.

Eclipse growled low in his throat, a warning he was close.

"Let me feel you," I said, holding his gaze in the mirror. "Come deep inside me."

The roar that split the air had the hair on the back of my neck standing on end as another lightning bolt struck. I watched his face, saw the moment he let himself go. He was the sexiest male I'd ever laid eyes on. More so now than even those four short months ago when we met. Funny because, at the time of our introduction, I thought no male could possibly be hotter. At some point along the way, he'd outdone himself. Probably because I was seeing more than the attractive exterior. Beneath was just as alluring, maybe even more so.

"I love you," I whispered.

His eyes lifted, the silver glowing brightly as they did when his emotions came to the surface. "*My heart belongs to you and you alone because you are my heart.*"

I smiled. It was what I'd first learned to say in his language.

I leaned my head against his cheek. "And you, my sexy *reuthet*, are my salvation."

52

OBSIDIAN

"Obsidian?"

I came awake in the darkened room, my ears tuning in to see if I'd imagined someone calling my name.

"Obsidian?"

A soft hand landed firmly on my forearm.

"*Ayreme?*"

"It's time, Obsidian."

Time? Time for—

"Oh, fuck!" I was out of bed and on my feet before my eyes were completely focused. A toe met the edge of the bed. A snarl ensued as pain bloomed hot and bright in my foot. I stumbled, damn near going to a knee but managed to hold myself upright as I tumbled forward onto the mattress, catching myself with my arms.

I was so damn ready to be back in our bedroom.

Penelope chuckled and a lamp turned on, then another.

As I stood buck naked at the foot of the bed, I stared at my *ereswa*, wondering if she'd just played a prank on me. I scanned her face and realized the sweat dotting her forehead wasn't likely the result of her amusement with my unfamiliar-room acrobatics.

When she went to sit up, I stumbled around to her side of the bed. "Here. Let me help you."

"You, my dear *reuthet*, should probably put some pants on."

Right. Pants.

As she dangled her legs over the side of the bed, I snagged my jeans from the floor. I'd discarded them when I'd crashed for the day, so they'd work for now. I didn't bother with a shirt or shoes. No time.

"We don't have far to go," she told me when I damn near tangled my cock in my zipper. "No need to rush."

"You're having a baby," I countered. "I'd say that's a damn good reason to rush."

"Are you sure you're going to be able to do this?"

"What?" I frowned. "You're the one who's got the hard job. Why are you asking me shit like that?"

I held out my hand to help her to her feet. Her small hand went to her belly, her breaths a bit more labored than I'd realized.

"Oh, fuck it." I lifted her into my arms. "I'm carrying you."

Another soft giggle. "I really can walk, you know."

"You shouldn't have to." In fact, I didn't want her to have to do anything more than ... whatever was necessary to get that baby out.

Penelope's arms wrapped around my neck, and though I

could tell she was uncomfortable, she did her best to soothe me. "Breathe, honey."

Yeah. There'd be time for breathing later. Right now, I needed to get my female to the birthing room we'd set up for this very purpose.

"Did you call Dr. A?" I asked.

"Yep. Before I woke you up."

I paused and stared down at her. "What? You told her before you told me?"

Penelope's smile was radiant. "I've been timing the contractions for the past two and a half hours, Obsidian. I wasn't about to wake you so you could do *this*"—she motioned to me carrying her—"before it was really time."

I grunted but started walking again.

The trip from our bedroom to the infirmary was less than a minute, and when I arrived, I was surprised to see Amethyst and Apollo both there, getting everything set up. The entire space was brightly lit by the LEDs in the ceiling, intensified by all the white—floors, walls, trim. The only color was the dark blue of the scrubs both healers wore. The scent of Lysol drifted in the space, like it had recently been wiped down.

Both healers looked up when I appeared, their eyes scanning the scene before them. Apollo offered an amused smirk, and Amethyst's smile was a bit more subtle.

She motioned me toward the room to the right of the small station that held a computer and a printer. "You can get her comfortable."

I managed a nod, strolled past the healers and into the twenty-by-twenty room. It was about twice the size of the rooms they used to treat injuries, but I figured it was necessary since they had quite a bit more equipment set up, including what appeared to be a box to hold the baby. It wasn't a box, of course, but to my overtaxed brain, it might as well have been.

Realizing I wasn't moving, I got with the program. I strolled to the bed and set Penelope down as though she was made of blown glass. I waited until she confirmed she was situated before releasing her and standing to my full height. Unable to help myself, I fluffed a pillow and propped it behind her head, removing the flat one. I then fluffed that pillow, too, and set it under her left arm so she could prop up a bit. On to finding the controls for the bed. I passed that over to Penelope, not wanting to hit something that might launch her across the room.

Fuck, why was it so hot in here?

I wiped my brow with the back of my hand and forced a smile. "Are you okay? Can I get you anything?"

Penelope looked up at me, those golden eyes glowing, her face radiant even with perspiration on her upper lip. "I'm perfect."

Yes, she was, but that was beside the point.

When Apollo stepped into the room, I growled low in my throat, reaching down and dragging the thin cotton sheet up over Penelope, covering her from the waist down. She was appropriately dressed, wearing one of my dark T-shirts, in fact, but the beast within didn't appreciate another male in the same room as her.

"Don't worry, big guy," the healer said. "I've done this a million times, but I'm going to excuse myself from the room during her exams as well as the birth. Wouldn't want you getting all territorial on me when they need you focused."

The male stepped forward, turning his full attention to Penelope. "How's it going?"

"Good. I'm good."

"Won't be long now." Apollo tapped the side rail of her bed before turning away.

Another growl rumbled up my throat. I didn't mean to go

all He-man on the healer, but there was no denying I didn't like the idea of any male looking at my female in any capacity, much less while she was only partially dressed. Healer or not.

Apollo put a hand on Amethyst's shoulder, leaned in. "I'll be monitoring her vitals outside the room. I'll be on standby if you need me."

Amethyst turned to look at me. "I will need him to come in once the baby's born. It'll be easier with two of us. That way, I can continue to take care of her."

"Is there a problem?" I asked, suddenly feeling as though there wasn't enough air in the ridiculously hot room.

"Not at all. And we don't anticipate there will be. Everything shows to be perfectly normal. Her vitals are good."

"Take a breath, big guy," Apollo said before stepping out into the hall.

Breath. Yes. That would probably be a good idea.

Maybe more than one.

Okay, maybe not that many or that fast.

I was light-headed.

"Have a seat," Amethyst urged, dragging a chair toward me. "Now."

With my eyes on Penelope, I eased into the chair. My *ereswa* was smiling. Smiling. She held out her hand, and after a second, my brain got with the program. I reached for her, linking our fingers.

She relaxed back on the bed and stared over at me, another beautiful smile forming. "You'll be fine, Obsidian. I promise."

For fuck's sake.

And here I'd thought I would be the one taking care of her.

MICHAEL

lthough I'd been trying to keep watch over Obsidian and Penelope, I heard the news of the birth via a message from the child's guardian angel.

A fucking message.

No sooner had it come in than I disappeared myself.

It took a mere breath for me to vanish to Earth and take form in the infirmary. Easy peasy.

Or not.

Evidently, I overshot my trajectory, and rather than end up in the main waiting area, I found myself in a storage closet, my wings pinned up against a boatload of little rolls of white paper. When I turned, I knocked a few to the floor. In my attempt to pick them up, I knocked over a few more. That was when I said fuck it, as Shadow liked to say.

I frowned, pushed my way out of the closet, and stumbled into another anteroom before finally making it to the waiting room proper.

It was empty.

Where was everyone?

Surely they hadn't decided to do this in a bedchamber. That seemed ... awkward.

I strolled across the gleaming white tile that reminded me far too much of Heaven. I leaned forward, glanced down the wide hallway that led back to the bar—nothing and no one—then the opposite direction, leading to the winding tunnels that ended at the vampire lair.

Not a soul.

Hmm.

What the hell?

The gentle click of a door came from behind me. I spun around in time to see Obsidian's broad back as he pulled a door closed behind him. When he turned around...

My heart stopped beating. My lungs ceased to inflate. I was pretty sure my molecules dissolved into nothingness and I wouldn't have been surprised if I simply drifted on the warm air pushed through those metal squares in the ceiling.

Obsidian smiled. "We've been waiting for you."

Speaking required breath, so it took a moment to get my shit together, but I managed to squeak out a response. "Me?"

"Yes, you."

My gaze darted between Obsidian's face and the tiny bundle he held in his enormous arms.

A thick hand reached up and landed on my shoulder. I felt it even through the armor plating that protected me.

It took effort, but I tore my gaze from the babe, meeting Obsidian's eyes. "Healthy? Strong? How about Penelope? She okay?"

"Everyone's perfect."

I believed Obsidian's tone more so than words, and based on the relief I detected, they were all well. Thanks be to God.

"I'd like you to meet our daughter."

A daughter. A precious baby girl. The pink blanket and cap should've given that away, but ... yeah.

"She's beautiful," I heard myself say.

"Ari'el."

My gaze shot up to Obsidian's face as every cell in my body

stopped firing at once and there was a weird buzzing in my head and a strange sensation in my chest. Pressure. So much pressure.

The firm hand on my shoulder tightened ever so slightly, pulling me back together.

"Ari'el," I whispered, eyes lowering to the babe as a tear formed. I hadn't shed any since ... not since my sweet *ereswa* had been taken from me. Her name: Ari'el.

"Without you, she wouldn't be here," Obsidian said, his voice low and reflecting the same emotion filling my chest.

Memories of that day on the front lawn of the mansion, Eevuhl coming at us, coming for the baby... "That was as much you as—"

Obsidian canted his head to the side, waiting until I looked at him again. When I did, he said, "I'm not talking about that."

I stared at the male I'd created, the one I considered my only child. Was he saying...?

"Fuck me running," I mumbled, using that weird turn of phrase Eclipse had always been so fond of. I'd never understood what it meant, still didn't, but it seemed fitting somehow.

Obsidian chuckled. "You want to hold her?"

I felt as though I should bow before her for some reason. I refrained and managed a nod instead.

When she was placed in my arms, I stared down at the most precious thing to have ever touched me. Perhaps she was not of my blood, but she was as much mine as Obsidian was, and that ... for me that was everything. They were all I had of my very own, and I'd take it.

My eyes remained on her, scanning the tiny face, her little pink nose, the wisps of black hair peeking out from beneath that pink cap. I wondered what her fingers and toes looked like. Were they equally small?

There was a sound behind me—a door opening, footsteps, a lot of them, actually. Instinct had my wings closing around me, shielding the baby in my arms to ensure no one harmed her.

Obsidian chuckled. "They've been waiting their turn," he said, his voice muffled from outside my feathered cocoon.

"Perhaps they could wait a few more minutes?" I asked, letting my wings pull back so I could look into the male's face. "I'm not ready to leave her just yet."

"If you'd still like to stay," Obsidian said softly, "we'd be glad to have you."

My eyes flipped up to Obsidian. "Truly?"

The male nodded. "Keep in mind, it might not be easy. But as far as I'm concerned, you're welcome here."

I swallowed past the knot forming in my throat, my attention returning to the tiny, warm bundle in my arms. Oh, how I wanted to stay. It would mean everything to me. Of course, I understood Shadow and Piceous would likely get up in arms about it, but ... well, I would deal with them when the time was right.

Unfortunately...

I glanced up at Obsidian. "I'd appreciate if you'd keep the offer open. I've got penance to pay after ... recent events. But I'll return as soon as I'm able."

Obsidian's dark brows lowered, and there was concern there. "Is everything all right?"

I looked at Ari'el once more. I smiled because how could I not? "It will be."

It definitely will be.

EPILOGUE

KAJ

When an archangel asked for a face-to-face, it wasn't exactly appropriate to tell him to get fucked.

I had learned that the hard way.

And now, here I was, completely incapacitated while that fucking archangel stared at me with iridescent eyes that appeared to be transforming from their original dark brown to that familiar silver and a mischievous smirk on his oddly handsome face.

"Let me go," I grumbled. "For fuck's sake."

"Will you be good if I do?"

Like I was a recalcitrant five-year-old. Whatever.

Since I could move my eyeballs, I rolled them. "Of course."

The release on my muscles was instantaneous, causing me to stumble forward. I righted myself, squared my shoulders, and turned to face the male who'd not so much *asked* to have a sit-down but rather *declared* it to happen.

Apparently, that meant it was happening.

"What's up, Michael?" My tone was reflective of more resignation than curiosity.

"I am here on a mission," the archangel said, his voice deeper than usual, reflecting the sincerity of his visit.

"What's new? That's your only setting, is it not?"

Couldn't the male simply pop in for a beer, not pay me a visit to launch his latest efforts to thwart his asshole brother?

Because I knew exactly why the male was there. In fact, I'd been expecting the visit since the attack on Angel Central a month and a half ago. For a brief time, I had thought I'd gotten a reprieve when the male disappeared for a solid month after visiting his granddaughter for the first time.

"Drink?" I offered, strolling toward the decanter of whiskey set up on the sideboard of our formal living room in what was now officially referred to as the Lair.

"A bit early, is it not?"

"It didn't require a question," I grumbled, pouring two fingers into a squat glass. "But I'll take that as a no."

"I assume you recall Eevuhl's visit and his ultimate demise?"

I smirked, tossed back my drink, poured another. All while I ignored the throbbing in my thigh from the knife wound I'd endured during the attack Michael was referring to. I had healed just fine, but there was still the ghost of an ache now and then, usually brought on by thoughts of Acadia. I hadn't seen the female since that day when I'd first taken the vein of another Fae rather than go to her. Since then, I'd continued to feed from the various females, doing my level best not to think too hard on it before, during, or after.

"I recall," I told the archangel, remembering I had an audience.

"Then you shall understand the necessity of this meeting."

"I might," I told him, carrying my glass with me as I strolled back in Michael's direction. "Should you be so inclined to enlighten me."

"Perhaps you also recall the mission my warriors are on, their search for the *amsouelots*."

Oh, yeah, I was well aware. "I'm all caught up on their drama, yes."

"Then you're aware Lucifer has altered his course?"

That got my attention. "He's not continuing his efforts to lay waste to humankind?"

"He's still moving forward with that plan," Michael stated, clearly missing the levity of the statement. "However, his endeavor to claim the *amsouelots* to obtain control of my warriors is no longer his top priority."

"I've never thought of him as one to give up so easily."

Michael's head lowered as he began to pace. "He's not giving up, of that I'm certain. His attempt to acquire the child is proof he's realized there's a far greater power to be wielded."

"Ari'el?"

There was a soft growl that escaped the archangel, a sound usually reserved for the warriors. It was odd to hear it from the almighty male, but not necessarily unexpected.

"I have it on good authority he's shifted his objective," Michael explained.

"Which means?"

Michael stopped pacing to meet my confused stare. "Rather than merely possessing the souls of their *amsouelots*, my brother endeavors to possess the souls of their offspring."

Figured. Bastard was underhanded like that. "Then eliminate their ability to breed. Seems fairly simple to me."

Michael sighed. "If only it were that simple."

I stared, waiting for all the pieces of the puzzle to come together. It didn't take long.

"You can't intervene," I mused. "You've granted them permission to seek their *amsouelots*, and now you have to let it play out."

Michael nodded, seemingly surprised by how quickly I had come to that realization.

"What is it you want from me?" I asked, knowing somehow this was going to affect me in a major way.

"I'd like the vampires to pledge their loyalties to me and my warriors."

I frowned. "Not sure I understand. We've fought alongside them. What more do you want? An official declaration? Fine, we'll help out when we can."

Michael shook his head. "I want you to fortify the ranks of the Zenith with the future warriors who'll be undergoing training in the near future. Not only will this benefit the warriors and provide additional protection for their offspring, it will also provide the strength necessary to ensure the survival of your race."

Was the male speaking in tongues? I had absolutely no idea what that meant.

Clearly Michael noticed my confusion because he continued. "Seven hundred years ago, your father and I had a conversation. We came to an understanding, one that I"—Michael held up a hand—"*we* believed, because your father was in complete agreement, was most beneficial to the survival of the vampire race."

The male had my full attention.

"It was at that time we declared your father Alpha of your species, the most powerful vampire in existence."

"I've heard the stories," I told him. Though I'd never heard mention of Michael.

"Though your birth would come nearly two hundred years later, it was predestined. As was the birth of your daughter, Bijou."

I could hear the rapid thump of my own heart, so loud in my ears, but I wasn't sure what caused it.

"Her destiny was defined long ago," Michael said.

A snarl escaped me as I stared at the male. I had no fucking clue where this was going, but the mere mention of my daughter brought out my inner beast's protective instincts.

Michael's color-shifting eyes locked on my face. "Kaj Courtenay, you are not only the Alpha of your species, you are the father of the female who shall mate the original vampire."

"Wait. Huh?" I stared at the archangel. "My daughter is to mate the *original* vampire. Not to sound all Adam-and-Eve oddity or anything, but exactly how does one mate one she's related to?"

"There are no direct descendants of the original vampire," Michael stated, as though that made all the sense in the world.

"No?" I motioned to myself. "Exactly how did I come to be without the original vampire breeding?"

Those strangely colored eyes remained on my face. "The original vampire did not mate, nor did he breed."

Okay, so clearly we were getting nowhere fast. "You lost me." I waved a hand. "But it's all moot anyway. The original vampire is *dead*."

"Quite the opposite. He is very much alive, merely ... preoc-cupied at the moment."

"Meaning...?"

"I've kept him hidden for his own protection."

"You?"

"Yes."

"For seven hundred years?" I got the feeling that didn't mean he was locked in a cage somewhere. For one, Khari was far too powerful. He would've easily broken free. "Where is he?"

Michael took a deep breath. "Khari is currently in a human vessel."

Unable to help myself, I laughed. "A human vessel? The original vampire is sporting a human meat suit? Tell me, what poor sap is giving the male a ride?"

"You know him as Oliver Calazans."

My smile fell instantly. I stared at the archangel, slack-jawed and dumbfounded. "What did you say?"

"Do you really need me to repeat?"

I shook my head. "Fuck. Me. Running."

"Still not sure how that's a thing, but..." Michael waved it off with a hand. "It's time we resurrected the original vampire, Kaj. And I need you to do it."

"What happens to Oliver?"

"The human will be fine. Once they've split, he'll go on about his life in a normal fashion."

"Normal?" I huffed. The human lived with angels, Fae, and vampires. What exactly about that was normal? And to find out he'd been sharing a vessel with... This was too fucking crazy.

I wasn't sure I even wanted to know what that entailed, but before I got that far, I figured I'd ask the more important question. "Say I agree. What's in it for me?"

Michael's head tilted in a haughty manner, nose lifting toward the ceiling, his eyes locking directly on mine. "I shall free the Fae from their debt, returning their rule to their rightful queen."

The male looked at me as though I would possibly know who that was. "I don't follow."

This time Michael appeared confused, his dark brows lowering. "You mean to tell me you don't know who the queen of the Fae is?"

"Not a clue."

Those dark eyes remained level on my face. "Kaj, the queen of the Fae is Acadia."

What the... Holy. Fuck.

"So will you do it?" Michael prompted. "Will you assist me?"

"Do I have a choice?"

Michael smiled, a full-fledged grin. "No. Not really. But I've heard it's polite to ask."

Yeah.

Polite.

Because *that* fucking mattered anymore.

STAY TUNED

I knew from the beginning that Eclipse was going to be one of my favorites. Probably because I got to know him. As of now, I haven't gotten to know the others well, but I'm looking forward to that introduction and I hope you are, too.

If you enjoyed *Salvation in Darkness*, please consider leaving a review.

ACKNOWLEDGMENTS

While writing is a solitary task, it's not a completely solo project. Because of that, I'd like to thank those who've assisted in one way or another. As a side note, I received no compensation for these acknowledgments, so they are in no particular order.

Steven: I have to say thank you. This past year has been especially difficult (for everyone, not just us). Being confined to the house because of the pandemic and adjusting our regularly scheduled lives hasn't been easy. But it's better with you there. Plus, I appreciate you emptying the dishwasher. I'm not a big fan of that chore.

You, the reader: Your support is what keeps me going. The emails and DMs especially brighten my day. Thank you for reading, thank you for writing a review, and thank you for hopping on social media and telling your friends about the book. You're badass like that.

TERMS FROM THE ANCIENT LANGUAGE OF ANGELS

Amnigh: intense desire, or mating heat, experienced between amsouelots.

Amsouelot: the soul destined for another.

Archsire and **Archdam**: angels who procreate specifically for angel warriors.

Ayreme: Term of endearment meaning my greatest love.

Dhira: the cloak of darkness initiated by warrior angels. Only angels and Fae can see through, disorients those who attempt to locate them.

Ereswa: loosely translates to the human term *wife.*

Gathenya: the sexual energy produced when angels mate.

Heurosp: an immortal human who works for the angels, managing the mansion.

Lintamair: ancient mating ceremony of immortals.

Neilloh: demon sent back to Earth from Hell.

Reuthet: loosely translates to the human term *husband.*

Sezari: term of endearment meaning sweetheart, baby.

TERMS FROM THE ANCIENT LANGUAGE OF VAMPIRES

Adighrielin: The Alpha's advisor, his right hand. The most honorable position within the Zenith, that which is the first line of defense to the Alpha.

Asyra: term of endearment, translates to *my heart.*

Balisra: term of endearment, translates to *my love.*

Cosrobol: blood whore; vampires used solely for feeding.

Dyrlom: honorific title for a male of same status

Kirlesgun: The current alpha's regime

Leaqua: Queen

Mielix zan: the process of identifying/imprinting on one's sexual mate.

Nehadon: vampire mate.

Phaal: king/alpha

Sonavex: the secretion injected into a mate by a male vampire upon claiming.

Tresmar: Honorific title meaning master, someone higher than.

Vestrahn: housekeeper, groundskeeper, those in service to others.

Angels of Darkness Hierarchy:

Lieterra: the right-hand of a warrior angel, tasked with tracking, doling out responsibilities, as well as performing as the warrior's assistant.

Ladeare: highest rank within the fiestreigh, responsible for soldiers under him.

Fiestreigh: the legion of angels assigned to the Angels of Darkness.

Ritarro: a position held by a Fae. It's the equivalent of a handmaiden and a coveted role.

Demon Hierarchy:

Trielair: the three demons who oversee the demon factions: Eevuhl, Mizuhree, and Aguhnee.

Mesonneir: the level of demons beneath the trielair. Equivalent to lieutenants.

Impietan: a human turned demon by a mesonneir.

ABOUT THE AUTHOR

New York Times and *USA Today* bestselling author Nicole Edwards lives in the suburbs of Austin, Texas, with her husband, their two fur babies, and the youngest of their three children, who has threatened never to leave home. When Nicole is not writing about sexy alpha males and sassy, independent women, she can often be found with a book in hand or attempting to keep the dogs happy. You can find her hanging out on social media and interacting with her readers - even when she's supposed to be writing.

NicoleEdwards.me

facebook.com/Author.Nicole.Edwards

instagram.com/nicoleedwardsauthor

tiktok.com/@nicoleedwardsauthor

bookbub.com/authors/nicole-edwards

threads.com/@nicoleedwardsauthor

CONNECT WITH NICOLE

I hope you're as eager to get the information as I am to give it. Any of these things is worth signing up for, or feel free to sign up for all. I do my best to keep each one unique and interesting.

NIC NEWS - If you haven't signed up for my newsletter and want notifications regarding preorders, new releases, give-aways, sales, etc., then you'll want to sign up. I promise not to spam your email; you get to pick exactly what you want to receive.

RAMBLINGS OF A WRITER BLOG - My blog is used for writer ramblings, which I am known to do from time to time.

NICOLE NATION - Visit my website to find exclusive content you won't find anywhere else, including Sneak Peeks, A Day in the Life character stories, exclusive giveaways, cards from Nicole, and join Nicole's review team.

NICOLE NATION ON FACEBOOK - Join my Facebook reader group to interact with other readers, ask me questions, play fun weekly games, celebrate during release week, and enter exclusive giveaways!

NAUGHTY & NICE SHOP - Not only does the shop have signed books, but there's fun merchandise, too—plenty of naughty and nice options to go around.

BY NICOLE EDWARDS

AUSTIN ARROWS
Rush
Kaufman

BRANTLEY WALKER: OFF THE BOOKS
All In
Without a Trace
Hide & Seek
Deadly Coincidence
Alibi
Secrets
Confessions
Bounty
Off Course
Chain Reaction
To Have and To Hold
Missing Pieces
Smoke and Mirrors

CLUB DESTINY

Conviction

Temptation

Addicted

Seduction

Infatuation

Captivated

Devotion

Perception

Entrusted

Adored

Distraction

Forevermore

DEAD HEAT RANCH

Boots Optional

Betting on Grace

Overnight Love

Jared (a crossover novel)

DEVIL'S BEND

Chasing Dreams

Vanishing Dreams

HEREOS & HAVOC

Wait for Morning

Beautifully Brutal

Without Regret

Never Say Never

Beautifully Loyal

Without Restraint

Tomorrow's Too Late

MISPLACED HALOS
Protected in Darkness
Salvation in Darkness
Bound in Darkness

OFFICE INTRIGUE
Office Intrigue
Intrigued Out of the Office
Their Rebellious Submissive
Their Famous Dominant
Their Ruthless Sadist
Their Naughty Student
Their Fairy Princess
Owned

PIER 70
Reckless
Fearless
Speechless
Harmless
Clueless

PRIMAL INSTINCTS
Chase (Volume 1-3)
Capture (Volume 4-6)
Claim (Volume 7-9)

THE JAMESONS OF COYOTE RIDGE
Hot Chocolate Wishes
Rough & Dirty

THE WALKERS OF COYOTE RIDGE

Kaleb

Zane

Travis

Holidays with the Walker Brothers

Ethan

Braydon

Sawyer

Brendon

Curtis

Jared

Hard to Hold

Hard to Handle

Beau

Rex

A Coyote Ridge Christmas

Mack

Kaden & Keegan

Trey

Rafe

Violet

STANDALONE NOVELS

Unhinged Trilogy

A Million Tiny Pieces

Inked on Paper

Bad Reputation

Bad Business

Filthy Hot Billionaire

RULE

NAUGHTY HOLIDAY EDITIONS

2015

2016

2021